Justice
In The
Capital

Justice
In The
Capital

Rob Shumaker

Copyright © 2022 by Rob Shumaker

This is a work of fiction. Names, characters, places, and incidents either are the products of the author's imagination or are used fictitiously. Any resemblance to actual persons, living or dead, events, or locales is entirely coincidental.

All rights reserved, including the right to reproduce this book or portion thereof in any form whatsoever.

Cover design by Cormar Covers

Also by Rob Shumaker

Thunder in the Capital

Showdown in the Capital

Chaos in the Capital

D-Day in the Capital

Manhunt in the Capital

Fallout in the Capital

Phantom in the Capital

Blackout in the Capital

The Way Out

Acknowledgments

A special thanks to Mom and Dad for offering their editorial assistance. Thanks also to Special Agent Dave for his law-enforcement insight and willingness to answer my questions.

Fiat Justitia

Let justice be done.

CHAPTER 1

Chicago, Illinois

"I can light the fire if you want."

With a phone to his ear waiting for a response, Viktor Kozlov slowly surveyed the landscape to the north and then the south. A warm front had descended on the Windy City, bringing with it muggy and hot temperatures to the late spring evening. Perfect conditions, he thought.

Perfect for a night of rioting and looting.

He saw a handful of pedestrians on both sides of Michigan Avenue. The Magnificent Mile—high-end shopping, swanky hotels, upscale restaurants. The Chicago version of Fifth Avenue and Rodeo Drive. Some of those on the sidewalks carried bags from Neiman Marcus, Saks, and Bloomingdales. He thought he saw some from the Nike and Disney stores, too. He imagined the amount of money on both sides of the street—Tiffany & Co., Cartier, Burberry, Rolex, Ferragamo.

It'll be a shame to see what I have in store for all this in the next several hours. You people wearing your Jimmy Choos and carrying your Louis Vuittons had best clear out because things are going to get nasty real quick.

Kozlov saw a handful of his men—all of them strategically placed, all of them waiting to get the word, all of them itching to start the mayhem. And those were just the ones he could see. He had others, and those men had more waiting with them. They were staged on the grounds of Northwestern University to the north and Grant Park to the south. Not enough to draw attention, but enough to get the job done. It was plenty nice outside to be out and about. There were still more at Navy Pier to the east and scattered in various places to the west. And once the rioting and looting began, people watching on TV and the internet would want to get in on the fun. They would hurry down and act as free riotous labor to Kozlov and the man on the other end of the phone line.

The former Russian operative wiped the sweat running down his bald head. Being in charge of the operation, the man on the ground, Kozlov just needed to get the go-ahead from the man paying the bills.

"Is everything ready?"

"Yes."

"How big is it going to be?"

Kozlov spat on the ground and looked at the businesses on both sides of the street. "This is one of the most famous stretches of road in all of America, so probably bigger and better than the one in L.A. Maybe not as big as N.Y.C., but that was a big job."

"You did well in the Big Apple, Viktor. You deserve an extra reward for that one."

"Thank you, sir."

"So you think Chicago will be on the news tonight?"

"Yes, without a doubt. I bet within the hour you'll be able to see it on CNN."

"I want to see it on every channel," the man growled.

Kozlov paused to hear if his boss would say anything else. "Well . . . how big do you want it?"

There was a moment of silence before the man on the other end said, "Burn it to the ground."

"Yes, sir."

Kozlov smiled and tapped the screen to end the call. He tapped out a message with his thumbs and sent it to a dozen individuals. Then he waited. Waited for the people to come like molten lava running down the side of a volcano and destroying everything in its path. He didn't have to wait long.

The moving vans rolled into position and the rear doors went up. A handful of men jumped out and readied the contents. Two flatbed trucks rumbled by, their trailers full of bricks, rocks, and frozen water bottles. It brought another smile to Kozlov's face.

Let the destruction begin.

The first wave of marchers came from the north. There were men and women or whatever they identified themselves as that particular night. They came in all colors, too, most of them in their twenties and thirties. Socialists, progressives, anarchists, Marxists, communists, some hippies looking to relive the glory days, and maybe even a few who simply enjoyed being professional rioters. They all did what they were paid to do.

About the only thing Kozlov didn't like about his street soldiers was the smell. Given their body odor, he wondered if they ever bathed. He wondered if they did it to keep the cops from getting too close. For his part, he chose to direct the forces from a safe distance, not wanting to contract lice, or fleas, or maggots, or whatever third-world disease they might be carrying.

The signs being handed out of the moving vans had been used before, but they preached the old standbys—demanding social justice or reparations, the end of capitalism, or free healthcare.

Kozlov tapped out another message. *Go.*

He could hear the pinging of the phones of the rioters, apparently the anti-capitalists weren't against using cell phones. The people left the sidewalks and flooded the streets. The chanting began, somewhat coherent but rehearsed. Something about *Justice!* and *Now!*

The car horns from the early evening traffic added to the noise, and it only served to tick off those now commanding the streets. Kozlov didn't see the first brick to go flying through the air, but the shattering glass caught his attention. The looters then made their way in and started relieving a clothing boutique of its inventory.

Hearing glass breaking on the west side, Kozlov turned his head and caught the latest action. "Ooh, there goes Levi's." Another burst of window shattering. "Sorry, Ann Taylor."

The throng of rioters from the south found their way to Michigan Avenue and felt the need to make up for lost time. Abandoned cars were rocked back and forth before being overturned. The first car to go up in flames was a Subaru in the wrong place at the wrong time. The darkness of the evening was brightened by one of the trees set on fire in a planter on the sidewalk.

The looters were scurrying like cockroaches in the light, their arms full of whatever they could carry—purses, shoes, jackets. Someone dropped a pilfered Rolex on the ground near Kozlov, the man apparently having enough booty to leave it where it lay. Kozlov walked over, picked it up, and slipped it on his wrist. The spoils of war, he thought.

Kozlov smiled when he saw a crowd of gangbangers hustling into the area looking to settle some scores. He wasn't against a little bloodshed; it always made a splash on the nightly news. So if they found a few of their rivals and let the bullets fly, all the better.

The sirens in the distance caught his attention. The plan needed more time to get maximum destruction for his boss—the man wanted it to be big. There might be another bonus in it for Kozlov if he could deliver a crushing blow—full-scale destruction. He hit the speed dial for his contact.

"It's me," Kozlov barked. "I thought we had a deal. No cops." He turned his head to the north. He could see the red-and-blue lights reflecting off the windows of the skyscrapers. A curse escaped his lips at the answer from his contact. "You tell that mayor you work for to order her police to stand down! This is a political protest and she'd better do what I say if she knows what's good for her."

Kozlov moved back into the shadows of a building that had its interior gutted. He put a finger to one ear, trying to hear the response.

"I don't care what the State's Attorney says. We bought him off, too. Now, if you don't call off your cops, your boss will soon be out of a job. And don't even think about raising those bridges either."

The threat conveyed; he tapped the phone to end the call. He estimated a thousand people in the streets, filling six lanes of roadway for as far as the eye could see. His chest rose and fell faster now. He spat on the ground. He was thinking about finding his contact that night if the man didn't come through. Knowing it would take a couple calls and a few minutes, he tried to be patient.

The rioters were marching and chanting, the looters grabbing anything they could carry. Windows were smashed. Another car was torched–an Audi this time. The flower beds on the sidewalks were trampled. There were still more bricks on the flatbed trailer. There was more mayhem to inflict. They just needed a little more time.

Kozlov took a step forward to look to the north. He still saw the red-and-blue lights reflecting off the skyscrapers in the distance. If they moved toward him, he'd have to cut his part in the rioting short. His boss had other cities he wanted burned to the ground, and Kozlov wouldn't be much good if he was hauled off by the cops. His boss could probably buy his freedom from the city jail, but not from the feds. The feds were the only ones Kozlov feared.

He looked at his phone again. He thought about calling his contact in the Mayor's office and chewing him out, maybe telling the man that he might end up face down in the Chicago River if he didn't do as he was told. His eyes focused on the north, and when the red-and-blue lights went dark, a devilish grin crossed his face. His man had come through with the Mayor. And now it was Kozlov's city.

He strode forward and grabbed a brick laying on the sidewalk. He looked at the rabid, smelly hooligans around him. He chucked the brick into the passenger side window of a Porsche.

"Let's burn this city down!"

CHAPTER 2

Hart Senate Office Building – Washington, D.C.

Senator Gregory Lamont, the junior senator from Connecticut, sat at his desk with three newspapers in front of him. He preferred the print version—the feel of the paper, the ink on his hands—all of them giving him a chance to compare the stories and the political slant the reporters gave each one. The big smile on his face indicated he was happy with all of them. The TV off to the left of his desk was on but muted. He had been in a good mood ever since he turned on CNN that morning. It was wonderful.

Violence, chaos, destruction. Chicago hadn't seen such a conflagration since the riots of '68, or maybe even since Mrs. O'Leary's cow set fire to the place. It was all glorious. Utterly glorious. Being from Connecticut, Lamont didn't have to worry much about the violent mobs. Nobody cared about Connecticut. Half the rioters probably couldn't even find it on a map. All the destruction was someone else's problem—the President's problem.

That's why Lamont didn't see the violence as a concern. He saw it as an opportunity. He smelled blood in the water and wanted to strike.

He gazed out the windows that offered a view of a parking lot on the north side of the building. He was the junior senator, one of the newest senators, and that meant in terms of offices, he drew the short straw when it came to scenic views. If he stayed in office long enough, he could get something better—maybe something with a view of the National Mall or the Washington Monument. But he wasn't planning on being in the Senate long, and where he was going, the views were much better.

He had bought the seat in the Senate with the small fortune he earned as a Wall Street wizard. There were websites out there that said he was one of the wealthiest senators with his net worth just below a hundred million. Being below the century mark grated on him, but he had to blow twenty million on winning his election. He knew he could make more if he played his cards right, and he was about to lay his cards out on the table for all the world to see.

His thoughts were broken when Shannon Swisher, his political consultant, walked in the room for their morning meeting. As she approached, his eyes went up and down, admiring the way her body filled out the black skirt and beige top. Professional and sexy at the same time.

"Have you seen the news?"

Swisher's cheeks rose. "Yes. It's a beautiful thing, isn't it?"

"It just keeps getting better and better. First San Francisco, then New York, now Chicago. It's like a wildfire, and it is indeed a beautiful thing."

Swisher set her briefcase on one of the empty chairs next to Lamont's desk. Her perfume tickled his nose and made him want to strip her down and take her right then and there. He didn't care if it was nine in the morning.

There had been an attraction between the two—mutual but illicit—since they first met. At the time, she had been married, although not happily. Lamont had returned to bachelorhood, having once been forced into marriage in college after he had gotten some random chick pregnant during a raucous fraternity party. When it became clear that he was going to make millions, maybe hundreds of millions, in his career, he quickly got his mind right and dumped the wife and the kid with a decent payoff and a nondisclosure agreement. He could do better, and with his money, he could have his pick.

He had first laid eyes on Swisher when she was working as an intern at Lamont's Wall Street hedge fund. Her late father had started the political consulting firm of Swisher & Swisher in New York City and, before he died, he released her out into the wild to learn all about spending other people's money to buy the seats of power. What better way to do that than to convince insanely rich egomaniacs to run for political office?

At the hedge fund, Lamont was raking in millions at the time she was off fetching coffee. It wasn't long before they were sweating in the sheets. That she was married meant nothing to either of them. He wanted sex, and she wanted power. They satisfied each other's needs with a few rolls in the hay before he decided he needed to get serious by focusing on his work. She thought the same thing and divorced her husband. Then, she convinced Lamont to run for the open Senate seat in Connecticut—with her running the campaign.

Neither of them felt the need to get hitched. They both slept around, each of them finding it the best way to learn the juiciest secrets in Washington. The nation's capital was a cesspool of money, sex, and power. Those with the inside scoop couldn't help but spill the beans when they're naked in bed together. And, just like Hollywood, there were thousands of people in D.C. who got to where they were by hopping into bed with the right people.

"Have you given more thought to what we discussed?" Swisher asked, taking a seat in front of his desk.

Lamont nodded and smiled. "I'm going to do it."

Swisher shot out of her chair and leaned over the desk. A quick glance from Lamont revealed her bra was pink. "Are you serious?"

"I am. I've thought about it enough. We can't waste any more time."

"Wait, wait, wait," Swisher said. She stood tall and clasped her hands in front of her. "I want to remember where I was when you told me." She took a breath and let it out. "Okay, go."

Lamont stood and buttoned his suit coat. He wanted to remember it, too, when the words actually came out of his mouth. "I am going to run for President of the United States!"

Swisher gasped and then clapped her hands. She hurried around and threw her arms around him. "Yes, yes, yes."

Lamont pulled her tight and ran his hands up and down her back until he found her rear. He gave her buttocks a tight squeeze and then growled. The sex could wait. They only had power and money on their mind.

Once the embrace was done, Swisher straightened her clothes and pulled a chair close so they could talk. They both sat. "What made you decide today?"

He pointed at the TV. "The riots in Chicago. The President's losing control of the country. There's a poll out this morning that says his approval rating is dropping like a stone. People think he doesn't care, that he's out of touch with mainstream America."

"And you want to strike while the iron's hot," Swisher said.

Lamont snapped his fingers and pointed at her. "Exactly." He motioned for her to come closer like he had a secret to tell her. "I've heard some rumors that the President might not run again." He raised his eyebrows like it was big news.

"Where did you hear that?"

Lamont shrugged. "I've heard it more than once. There's a lot of gossip being spread around in the restroom off the Senate floor."

Swisher sat back in her seat. "It was once a forgone conclusion that President Schumacher would win reelection in a landslide."

Lamont pointed at the TV again. "Yeah, well . . . things change."

"He can still win. He's very popular in his party."

"Yes, but the country is in the mood for change. Big change. Social justice and all that socialist crap. All we have to do is ride the wave of discontent all the way to the White House."

Swisher rose from her seat and started pacing in front of the Senator's desk. "You said the President might not seek reelection. But that means the Vice President would run. He's popular, too. And he's black. He'll get some votes from the African-American community. Even a few extra percentage points from the black voters would doom your chances."

Lamont shook his head like he was an expert in reading the political tea leaves. "Not enough to make a difference. Any votes we lose in the black community can be replaced with illegal immigrants if we get them on the voter rolls."

A wince crossed Swisher's face. She was the one with the political savvy. She had become widely popular in election circles with her scorched-earth tactics. She wasn't above lying, cheating, or stealing—or sleeping with the enemy.

"I don't know, Senator," she said, shaking her head. "Stubblefield would be tough to beat."

Lamont held up a hand. "That's even if he wants to run. I heard some rumblings that he's not happy as Veep. He doesn't like politics. He misses the FBI."

"You hear a lot of things."

"There's so much gossip out there, Shannon. Everybody's trying to maneuver themselves in the right position. We need to get out ahead of it. Be the first one to announce before anybody else gets some crazy idea to run."

"The summer recess is coming up fast, and the election is still a year and half away. Should you wait?"

Lamont stood and looked out the window again, his mind deep in thought. It was approaching late May, and he and the rest of his colleagues would be hightailing it out of D.C. to beat the stifling summer heat and humidity.

"I think it would be good for me to announce soon. Make a big splash before anyone else can and then bury them before the race even starts. Who's my biggest competition?"

"The Governor of California?"

Shaking his head, Lamont said, "He's damaged goods. He barely survived a recall—in California!"

"What about the Governor of Illinois?"

"No, he's a terrible campaigner. He barely won in a blue state. Should have been landslide."

"Senator Crawford."

Lamont rolled his eyes. "Oh, Shannon, please. He's a pompous fool. Gotta be the dumbest man to ever set foot on the Senate floor, and if his nose gets any higher in the air, he'll tip over backwards."

"They'll all think they can run and hope to get lucky."

"That's why I need to get out there. If these riots continue, I'll be out there every day telling the country that the President is out of touch and has to go. I'll be the only candidate out there. Think of the free advertising."

Swisher grabbed a pen and notepad from the desk. "Free airtime on CNN won't be enough. We're going to need big money. More money than you have."

Lamont grimaced. Swisher could definitely turn the screws when she wanted to. He thumped the desk with his fist, knowing she was right. He had left Wall Street at the wrong time, after the bubble burst when people were taking their losses and licking their wounds. Had he stayed in and weathered the downturn, he'd probably be worth half a billion by then. Now, given the cost of a presidential campaign, he was going to be forced to grovel like the rest of the political peasants begging for cash.

"I've got some ideas for raising money."

"There will be donation limits."

The laugh from Lamont echoed off the walls. "Those limits don't mean anything. There are ways to get around them. You know that. Come on, Shannon, I'm not paying you twenty-five grand a month to play small ball. You win this campaign, and you can name your price from now until the end of time. And, anyway, I'm talking about some ideas outside the country. I've got friends around the world who would like nothing more than to see President Schumacher and Vice President Stubblefield shown the door."

"What do you want me to do before the announcement?"

"Do what you do best. Get some inside information, by any means possible. And dig up dirt on the Vice President. Anything you can find. Make it up if you have to, start some rumors, just make it all believable. If he's the nominee, we want to force him back on his heels right out of the gate."

Swisher jotted down notes as fast as she could. "What else?"

"Start some focus groups. Find out what the people want to hear from me. If they want me to spout off something about social justice or defund the police, I'll do it. Whatever it takes."

"You'll have to have an answer to the press questioning why a first-term senator from Connecticut should be the next President of the United States."

"Come up with something for me to say. Something about serving my fellow man or fundamentally transforming the country. Making things better. Something the people will fall for. Get some polling data together and see what works best."

Swisher stepped around the desk and got close enough that a wave of her perfume hit him again. She dropped the pen and notepad on the desk. "It's too early to be thinking about running mates, Senator." She ran a finger down his arm that sent a thrill up his leg. Her touch could always do it. "But there will be talk of you not having someone to be First Lady."

Lamont grunted. He hadn't thought of that. The voters would probably want the President to be married. She didn't even have to be attractive, although Lamont wouldn't have it any other way. He eyed Swisher, who had stepped closer. Both of them were breathing heavy, intoxicated by the scent of a presidential victory in their grasp.

He reached out and swept the blonde hair over her shoulder. "You could be a supermodel, you know that, don't you?"

She rubbed her nose against his chin. "I don't want to be a supermodel."

His finger caressed her cheek. "If it comes down to it, you could be First Lady."

Swisher shook her head. "I don't want to be First Lady, either." She reached down and grabbed his crotch. Then she whispered in his ear, "I'd rather have the power."

CHAPTER 3

The White House – Washington, D.C.

President Anthony Schumacher sat shaking his head as he watched the TV in his study just off the Oval Office. The fruit plate that the Navy steward had brought in ten minutes earlier sat untouched, pushed off to the side so he could make room for his notepad. The TV was tuned to one of the morning's cable news shows, the three hosts babbling on about the videos showing burning police cars and looted stores that seemed to run on an endless loop.

The President's pen drummed the paper, only stopping when he jotted down another note. He had written plenty that morning. San Francisco, New York City, Chicago. All of them had seen rioting and looting in the past week. Whether it was destruction of property or petty theft, it all grated on the former lawman. The mayhem was like a cancer, spreading all across the country and scaring law-abiding citizens.

And the President wanted something done about it.

The door to the corridor opened, and Vice President Ty Stubblefield walked in.

"Morning, Mr. President."

The President dispensed with the pleasantries and pointed at the TV. "Can you believe this? Another city up in flames. Stores looted, cars torched. A total mess."

Stubblefield took a seat at the table and looked at the screen. The clenched jaw said it all. Like the President, he had been a Special Agent with the FBI. They had become close friends and confidantes ever since they were partners together at the Bureau. Stubblefield went on to become the Deputy Director and then the Director before the President said America needed him as Vice President. Neither of them had any stomach for lawbreakers.

"There are reports out there that say the Mayor of Chicago told the police to stand down while it was all going on. What the hell is wrong these people?"

"Where do you want me to begin?"

The steward walked in. "Mr. Vice President, would you like some coffee?"

"Yes, please."

Once the steward poured a cup of coffee for Stubblefield and left, the President continued venting. "This is the third time this week. San Francisco,

New York City, and now Chicago. All of them well coordinated and nothing seems to be done about it. Do you ever hear about these people being brought to justice?"

Stubblefield shook his head and then told the President what they both already knew. "That's because those in charge want it to happen. This is their chance to implement their policies while no one is looking. If they can collapse the system, they can rebuild it the way they want it. And they can blame you for everything while it's happening."

The President sighed, not understanding how any Americans could think that way. He picked up the remote and muted the TV in disgust.

"We have to do something about this. I'm not going to put up with it much longer."

Stubblefield took a sip of coffee and returned the cup to the saucer. "What do you want me to do about it?"

"We need to stop these riots before they start. There's obviously coordination going on and there's money being spent. I heard a report that those idiots that are arrested are bailed out within an hour. That money's coming from somewhere. And if it's behind the damage that's being caused, I want it stopped. Cut off the head and end it before it can start."

"I can talk to the FBI Director," Stubblefield said.

"Where is Kurt by the way? I haven't seen him all week."

"He's at a law enforcement conference in London."

The President shook his head and snapped, "Well, that's not doing us any good here in the States."

"I'll talk to him. Maybe you can put me in charge of a task force to get to the bottom of all this. I'll get the FBI, the Attorney General, and the U.S. Attorneys together and we'll see what can be done. We can look at the domestic terrorism statutes and see if there's anything there that can be used to start charging these people. If we get convictions, we'll put 'em away for a long time."

The President tapped his index finger on the table. The idea was something, a positive step to cracking down on the hoodlums who were causing trouble. After some thought, the President nodded. "Yeah, let's do that. I'll get the press secretary to announce it once we have all the players on board."

The President saw the videos of the fires on Michigan Avenue and had enough. He pointed the remote at the TV and shut it off. Sitting back in his chair, he let out a sigh, closed his eyes, and then rolled his neck.

The two friends sat in silence before Stubblefield asked, "You all right?"

The President opened his eyes and then rubbed his face with his right hand. He acted like his head hurt, but it was something more than that weighing on his mind. "I don't know, Ty. Maybe I'm not as effective as I once was," he said softly.

Stubblefield turned slightly in his chair, like he was ready to listen. "What are you talking about?"

The President looked down at the table, trying to come up with the right words. "I think I've lost my effectiveness, Ty. Used to be I could get violence like this tamped down with a couple phone calls." He shook his head, as if he didn't know what happened. "That doesn't appear to be the case anymore."

"It's not your fault. You have to rely on the local leaders and obviously some don't feel the same way you do. Besides, we've just had a couple bad nights."

"It's been more than a couple."

"Well, that's true, but we'll get it under control."

The President exhaled, looking like the air had been let out of a balloon. "I've been thinking about not running for re-election."

Stubblefield sat stunned as that bombshell echoed off the walls. There were so many ramifications if that decision were true—for the President, the Vice President, and the country. Stubblefield leaned forward. "Not running? Why wouldn't you want to run? You'd win in another landslide."

"I'm not so sure about that."

"I think you know deep down you would. And you were made for this job. The country needs you."

"I'm not doing a very good job of it lately."

"Is your health okay? I thought your knee surgery went well."

The President waved away any thoughts of his health being in decline. "I'm fine physically. The knee's getting better, and the doctor said I can start extending my long runs a bit more." He ran his hand over the top of his head and looked at the notepad in front of him. "But I'd be lying if I said I wasn't feeling the effects of the job. It can wear you down real quick."

"Why don't you take some time off. You're going back home to Indiana for the race, aren't you?"

"Yes, and I'm looking forward to it, but just because I go back home to Silver Creek or to the Speedway doesn't mean my problems go away. I wake up in the middle of the night wherever I am and wonder where the next hotspot needing my attention is going to be. Last week it was San Francisco, then the Big Apple, and yesterday Chicago. There will be more. To make it worse, I haven't been able to do anything to stop it."

Stubblefield sat back in his chair, his arm resting on the table, his thumb and index finger on his right hand rubbing together. He looked like he was trying to decipher a hidden message.

"I finished off nearly two years of the prior administration and then got elected to a four-year term. Maybe six years is enough. It might be good to get some new blood in the White House and shake things up, provide a new perspective on how to run the country."

Stubblefield sat in silence, like he didn't want to hear what was coming next.

"I think you need to get ready to run, Ty."

Stubblefield chuckled. "You just spent the last five minutes telling me how the job has worn you down, and now you're telling me that I should run."

"You're the best man for this job."

Stubblefield pointed his finger at the President and shot back, "No, Mr. President, you are the best man for this job. There is no doubt in my mind, and the people of this country agree with me. And, come on, you don't want these no-good pricks to think they were able to run you out of office."

"You can do just as good a job as me, if not better."

Stubblefield pointed the finger back at himself. "And you don't think that they'll come after me the same way they come after you?"

"Oh, they'll do the same. And you know as well as I do that it's going to be a rough road for you. The last thing they want is a conservative black man in the Oval Office. That possibility scares them to death. But I know you can do it, and you're going to be the best President this country has ever seen."

Stubblefield sat back in his chair. "Well, it's not going to be any time soon because you and I are going to start kicking some ass and clean up these streets. Put some of the load on me and I'll do what needs to be done. That's what I'm here for."

There was a knock on the door, and the President's Deputy Chief of Staff stuck his head in the room. "Excuse me, sir, the CIA Director is in the Oval."

The President nodded. "We'll be right there." Once the door closed, both men stood and the President said, "I'll take you up on upping your responsibilities, but I want you to be ready to run just in case."

"I'll keep that in mind," Stubblefield said, gesturing for the President to take the lead.

"Let's go see if Bill has some good news for us," the President said. They walked through the hall past the President's study and entered the Oval Office. "Morning, Bill."

"Morning, Mr. President," William Parker said. He nodded at Ty. "Morning, Mr. Vice President."

"Ty and I were just talking about the mayhem in Chicago."

"Yes, I saw it. What a mess."

"We were hoping you might have some good news for us."

Director Parker gave them a smile and then patted the thick briefing book under his arm. "Actually, I think I might."

The President motioned for him to take a seat on the couch. "Well, let's hear it then."

The President and Vice President moved their chairs closer to the coffee table in front of the couch as Director Parker opened his briefing materials. Parker had started with the CIA as an intel analyst before spending two decades in Congress. President Schumacher nominated him to become CIA Director in his first year in office, and he never regretted it.

"Okay, Mr. President, I know you both have been concerned with the unrest that has been occurring, and I took it upon myself to do some digging to see if there was a foreign influence at play."

The President leaned forward, his hands folded in front of him, his eyes focused on Parker. This is the initiative he wanted people to take in his administration. "And?"

"Two things. First, intelligence has uncovered hundreds of fake social media accounts that have worked to stir up angst and even coordinated the riots in San Francisco and New York City. We're still looking at Chicago. The accounts and the websites they link to are completely fake and spew Marxist propaganda to their followers. It mushrooms from there. People pass on the information to their friends and their friends do the same and, before you know it, you have three thousand people ready to throw bricks through windows and burn police cars. We've seen it before. Their goal is to cause unrest and chaos."

"They're doing a pretty good job so far," the President said. "Who's behind it?"

Parker looked the President in the eye. "Russian trolls."

"Oh for goodness sakes," the President spat out, throwing his arms in the air and sitting back in his chair. "The Russians again?" He cursed then restrained himself from letting loose. He gazed out the windows toward the Rose Garden and said, "It's too bad Reagan was joking when he said the bombing of Russia starts in five minutes. It might have solved some of my problems."

Director Parker held up a finger. "I agree, sir, but it's not just the Russians."

"It's not?"

"No, at least I don't think so." Parker flipped to the next page in his briefing book. "We believe there is foreign money funding the attacks. The Russians take the money and coordinate the attacks, whether it be online or on the ground."

"But it's not Russian money?"

Parker paused to find the right words. "I don't think so. The Russians like to take other people's money. They're worried, and rightfully so, that if we find out they are funding the attacks, we will find ways to relieve them of their money. The Russians are good at what they do, but they'd rather let someone else pay the bills."

"Well, who's providing the money?"

Parker grimaced. "We don't know yet. We think we're getting close. Whoever is behind it has a lot of money and appears to spend a great deal of it hiding any transactions. It's always hard to get to the source of payments because the shell companies have shell companies, and they have banks that don't like to divulge client information." Parker held out his hand, like he was trying to tell the President to be patient. "We're working on it. Night and day. And as soon as I can give you a name of a country, a group, or a person, I'll give it to you."

The President sat back in his chair, clearly perturbed at the slow pace. He knew there was nothing else he could do until they got a name. "Good work, Bill. I appreciate your efforts. I want you to keep on it, though. This is the highest priority. I want a two-pronged approach to combat this violence. Ty's going to focus on the domestic angle, which might include hunting some Russians. And I want you on the foreign side looking under every bush, every rock, every darkened corner in the world for whoever is funding this crap. You understand?"

"Loud and clear, Mr. President." Director Parker stood, put the briefing book under his left arm, and extended his right hand. "I'll keep on it and get back to you as soon as I can."

Stubblefield waited until Director Parker left before saying, "Well, that was some good news at least."

"I guess. We'll take the good news when we can, but there's a lot of work to do. Information is no good unless it can be acted upon and results can be obtained. Let's get on it."

"I'll talk to the FBI Director today. Maybe I can light a fire underneath him and kick him into gear."

"Well, feel free to tell him I'm not happy."

"Yes, sir."

Stubblefield reached for the door to head back to his West Wing office. The President stopped him and said, "Do whatever it takes, Ty."

The Vice President gave the nod that came with decades of friendship. "You got it."

CHAPTER 4

St. Louis, Missouri

Viktor Kozlov stood on the west side of the Old Courthouse in downtown St. Louis on that clear May evening. The wind was from the south, bringing with it warm temperatures and the unmistakable scent of beer being made at the brewery in south St. Louis. Good conditions for what he had in store.

He looked east toward the towering Gateway Arch, its stainless steel bathed in the reflection of the setting sun. There had been dreams. Ever since he received his orders to leave the successful operation in Chicago and move south down Interstate 55 to St. Louis, there had been dreams. Grand dreams of destruction so momentous that it would rival even the best special effects Hollywood could make.

He closed his eyes, imagining what it would be like to see the Arch crashing to the ground, shaking the earth and crushing anything beneath its nearly 40,000 tons of concrete and steel. What a wonderful sight it would be.

The phone buzzing in his phone shook him from his reverie. "Yes?"

"You did good work in Chicago, Viktor."

Kozlov spit the remnants of a toothpick to the ground. "I thought you would approve." He glanced at his watch. "Is it late where you are?"

"Yes, but I wanted to watch your latest handiwork. I presume what you have in store will make the nightly news."

Kozlov looked around. There were thousands of people in the area. The Cardinals were in town and the team's rabid baseball fans were starting to gather for an evening of fun at the ballpark two blocks from where he was standing. It all brought a smile to his face. They had no idea what was in store for them.

"Oh, it'll be on the news. I guarantee that."

"I don't want it just on the local news," the man snapped through the phone. "I want it on the national news, the international news, and on every airport TV. I want it on the news in the freaking space station. I want every TV in the world to see the beginning of the end of the United States right before our eyes."

Kozlov spat again. He glanced up at the Arch with the same look in his eyes. The dream hit him again and he wanted it to come true. It was such an enticing target. So enticing. His boss would consider it a masterpiece. Its fall would be such a blow to the people of America and its worthless President. But even Kozlov knew it would take fighter jets to take it down, and he didn't have that. Yet anyway. But the man on the other end had enough money to buy a whole fleet.

"It will be big. There is a baseball game tonight. The Cubs are in town so the ballpark will be packed. And there are a lot of civilians milling about right now. Most of these idiots are already drunk. Once it starts, it will be chaos."

"And the drunks will be part of it?"

"Oh, yes. I bet they'll be looking to fight anything that moves." Kozlov could almost see the smile on the man's face through the phone.

"That's good to hear. Maybe I'll have to find the game on the satellite and watch it all unfold."

"You do that." After another check of his watch, Kozlov said, "I should go. I need to make sure everything is ready."

"Good luck," the man said. "Make me a happy man tonight."

Kozlov walked south, crossed the street, and continued on past the Hilton Hotel. From there, he got a good view of the ballpark. The stadium lights were on, but they hadn't taken full effect. The red seats were nearly filled with red and white clad fans, with a smattering of Cubbie blue throughout. He made two calls and then headed back north to Kiener Plaza across from the Old Courthouse.

One last check of the watch, and Kozlov sent out the call to action on social media. It wouldn't take long. It never did. The participants had been waiting all day for it. The moving truck pulled into a parking spot. The rear door opened, and the signs painted with demands for *Justice!* and *Fight the System!* were readied. Kozlov saw another van to the west, the opened rear door revealing a load of bricks, frozen water bottles, and Molotov cocktails.

The horde of rioters and looters came from every direction. Hundreds that had gathered on the Arch grounds were marching up the street—not the sidewalks, the street. Car horns could be heard blaring over the shouts for *Progress!* More came from the west and found their way to the vans near Kiener Plaza.

"Go!" Kozlov yelled to the protesters and pointing to the south. "Go to the ballpark!"

The streets were flooded with people. The first pitch at the ballgame was thrown at the same time the first car parked on the street was overturned. It soon caught fire.

"What do we want!?" the protest leader yelled

"Justice!" came the response.

"When do we want it!?"

"Now!"

"No justice!"

The response followed, "No peace!"

The two main thoroughfares to the ballpark became a sea of humanity. Car windows were shattered, and frightened owners left their vehicles in the middle of the street and fled in fear. The drunks at the outdoor patio saw what was happening and started yelling. The rioters yelled back, and it didn't take long before a full-blown free-for-all was underway—fists flying and profanities shouted.

"Keep going!" Kozlov yelled from the sidewalks. "Keep going!"

Heavy black smoke started billowing out of the parking garages near the ballpark after several cars and some strategically placed piles of tires were torched.

The police arrived on the scene, but they were sorely outnumbered. They left their squad cars to find a safe place to call for backup. The crowd surged forward, the late stragglers to the game running for their lives.

With the lack of stores near the ballpark, those intent on looting had to be content with destruction. Decorative trees were torched, planters overturned. The shattering of glass echoed off the buildings. The rioters had no fear of arrest. They had seen the authorities in the other cities look the other way, and they knew it would be the same in St. Louis.

Two police helicopters roared overhead, their spotlights shining and their loudspeakers threatening arrest. The unruly swarm was oblivious to the demands.

Kozlov took notice of the choppers. He hit the speed dial and called his contact at City Hall. "Tell your police to stand down!" He plugged his left ear with his finger to hear the response. "There is nobody being hurt here! This is free speech! This is what social justice looks like! The people have the right to have their voices heard!" After another response, Kozlov yelled, "You call off your dogs or it'll be the end of you and your boss's job!"

Kozlov hung up and then shouted to the troops. "Force your way in! Force your way in! They can't stop you! Go! Go! Go!"

The unruly horde of anarchists, protesters, and assorted hooligans followed his call and headed for the gates to the ballpark. Stadium security guards were no match, and the mob was soon jumping over turnstiles.

Kozlov encouraged them all, even helping some long-haired loser over the barricades. Fans in the upper deck had a front row seat of the growing chaos coming from the direction of centerfield and decided it best to flee to the exits. The players on the field did the same. The rioters made their way onto the field and started ripping up the grass. One man planted a black flag espousing some socialist cause right behind second base.

Kozlov watched it all from the centerfield concourse. He looked around, black smoke filling the air, sirens all around. It was glorious. He soaked it all in. He knew it wouldn't last forever. Some semblance of order would be restored. Even the rioters needed to go home to smoke their weed and cash their welfare checks.

He called it a success. He knew his boss probably had a smile on his face—wherever in the world he happened to be.

It was time to go. The rioters were moving like locusts to the south, and the fans fleeing in terror sought safety to the north.

Kozlov joined them. "It's going to be okay!" he yelled to a family, a mom and father with two crying kids. "Just keep walking north. It's safe there."

He did the same. There was no second wave, although he couldn't be totally sure if some troublemakers doubled back to continue the fight with the drunks. A few blocks to the north, he turned toward the east and blended in with the crowd. He caught sight of the Arch, the setting sun had given it a red hue, almost bloody. Or maybe it was from the car fires. Whatever the cause, he smiled and dreamed. So enticing.

Maybe someday.

Number One Observatory Circle – Washington, D.C.

Vice President Stubblefield sat in his office at his official residence. It was early the next morning, and he didn't see his mood brightening anytime soon. His chief of staff had notified him shortly after 8 p.m. Eastern time that a riot had broken out in St. Louis. Preliminary reports indicated the property damage would be in the millions.

Stubblefield called the President, who said he was made aware of the unrest while at his home in Silver Creek, Indiana. Being a Cardinals fan and a frequent visitor to St. Louis, the President took the riot personally, calling it an "act of domestic terror" and an "attack on the fabric of our lives." He had called the Missouri Governor and offered immediate help. The Governor thanked him but said, after a couple hours, the situation was under control. Sadly, one law enforcement officer was killed. The President told the Vice President that he would call the officer's family later that afternoon.

Shortly after dawn, Stubblefield called FBI Director Duncan. A career FBI man like Stubblefield had been, Duncan had worked his way up the hierarchy with stops in New York City and Atlanta before being summoned to D.C. and a Headquarters position. He and Stubblefield had known each other at HQ for over a decade, and Stubblefield eventually recommended Duncan take over when the President asked him to be Vice President.

Now Stubblefield was wondering if he made a mistake. When Duncan answered, Stubblefield asked, "Where are you?"

"Well, good morning to you, too, Mr. Vice President."

"I asked you a question, Kurt."

"Jeez, Ty, no need to bite my head off. I'm in London at the Conference of International Law Enforcement. You know that."

"Did you see the news?"

"What news?"

Stubblefield could hear the Director grasping for a TV remote. "The news out of St. Louis, Kurt."

"Yeah, I saw that. I was notified last night. It looked like another riot, so I didn't make much of it. Just people blowing off steam."

"Blowing off steam!" Stubblefield pounded the desk with his fist. "They caused a full-blown panic, Kurt, not to mention a million dollars in damages. Oh, and did I mention that another cop was killed last night? That's the third officer in as many weeks."

"Man, I hadn't heard that," Director Duncan said softly, sounding honestly upset at the news he hadn't heard. "That's too bad."

"I got to tell you, Kurt. The President is not happy with you right now. I'm not either. Neither one of us like the way you're running the Bureau. I—"

"Ty, it's not your Bureau anymore," Duncan shot back, like the thought had been festering in his mind for a while now. "I'm in charge. I've got people working on it. It's mainly just a bunch of punks causing trouble. And it's for local law enforcement to handle. The Bureau doesn't sully itself with pickpockets and looters."

"Kurt, this is the fourth city to go up in flames in the last two weeks. And where are you? You're off sipping cocktails across the pond!"

"I'm making contacts, Ty. It's called making friends so they can help us when we need it."

"That's not going to do us any good here, Kurt. I want you back in D.C. by the end of the day."

"Ty, there are still two more days in the conference."

"By the end of the day!" Stubblefield barked.

"On whose orders?"

"The President's," Stubblefield said before hanging up.

Stubblefield sat back in his high-backed leather chair and cursed. His chest rose and fell. He tried to tamp down the rage that had bubbled up inside him. He knew this was what the President was talking about when he mentioned the pressure of the job. People's lives were on the line. The future of the country as Americans knew it was at stake.

And the Vice President felt like he was the only one who could save it.

His eyes were drawn to the envelope that the CIA Director had sent over that morning. It was good intelligence, actionable intel, and Stubblefield knew it was time to act. The American people couldn't wait any longer. He yanked the phone out of the cradle and punched a button. "Have Mark and John come in here."

Mark Simpson, the head of the Vice President's Secret Service detail, hurried in followed by Special Agent John Stewart.

"Yes, Mr. Vice President," Agent Simpson said, looking at the Veep and the entry points to the office. "Is everything okay?"

"Yes, everything's fine." Stubblefield motioned them forward. "I need you to do a favor for me."

CHAPTER 5

Near Mineral, Virginia
How many times have I cheated death?

Duke Schiffer wiped the river of sweat off his forehead before it could run down his tinted sunglasses. He ran alone today, as he did most days. He preferred it that way. Running was not a time for idle chit-chat or talk about the weather. It had a purpose. Well, actually, it had multiple purposes. One, it kept him fit. Two, it cleared his mind. And in his line of work, fitness and mental clarity were essential.

The morning sunshine had warmed him, loosening his tight muscles, and he kept on the asphalt path as it slithered into the shade of the Virginia forest. He checked his watch to make sure he was on his optimal pace.

The run gave him time to think, to make sense of things. If he could make sense of things. He had been the guy Vice President Stubblefield had called on ever since their days together at the FBI. When the going got tough, Stubblefield called Duke Schiffer.

And Schiffer had never let the big man down.

Hidden beneath the tall canopy of hickory and maple trees, Schiffer saw no one. He rarely did, especially on a weekday. That's why he chose this route to get his eight miles in. But the solitude never kept him from staying alert. Trees provided cover for an assassin trying to pick him off and score points with whoever he ticked off over the years. And there were plenty of them out there—terrorists, thugs, reprobates, other assorted human debris. His eyes scanned from left to right and then back again. He went without earphones, preferring the sound of his footfalls rather than Springsteen. Plus, the music proved to be a distraction rather than a motivator.

And it kept him from hearing anyone on the hunt to kill him.

How many times have I been on the verge of dying for my country?
Too many to count.

That was the answer he came up with. He really thought he was a goner in Philly a few years back. His would-be killer made the mistake of taking too long to do the deed. Those idiots always thought it was like the movies—where you had to make some profound comment into the camera to show how big of a hotshot you were. Schiffer used the time to figure out a way to kill the man.

There was that time on the lake behind his house that could have ended badly. When he closed his eyes at night, he could still feel the bullets whizzing by him as he dove deeper into the water. Churchill once said, "There's nothing more exhilarating than being shot at without result." Schiffer knew what he meant, but he had enough exhilaration to last a lifetime.

Egypt was close, too close. It wasn't just one or two bad guys with guns. It was a whole army of crazed terrorists thirsty for blood. There was a lot of luck in that operation. Luck, a few Israelis, and the United States military. Jumping off an exploding container ship in the middle of the Atlantic probably cost him another one of his nine lives. And the bomb in New York City should have done him in. That he didn't meet his maker that day told him God wasn't ready for him.

But those days were behind him.

Schiffer tapped his watch to stop the clock. He was halfway into his run and at his turnaround point. It gave him a chance to take a breath and scan his surroundings. Everything looked so different when coming from the other direction. The trees were different, the foliage different, the shadows different. He looked for something out of the ordinary. Something that didn't belong off the path in the forest. Someone looking to kill him. A trained assassin in a serviceable ghillie suit would have fighting odds.

Schiffer would never stop looking. He couldn't stop looking. Otherwise, he might end up dead.

He grabbed the water bottle off his right hip. He had another one on his left. He balanced the belt with a Glock 43X at the small of his back. He didn't like to run with the gun, the less weight the better. But, to him, it was like his American Express card. He never left home without it. Not in this day and age. And not after what he had been through.

But those days were over. It was time to pass the reins to the younger generation. At forty-four years of age, he wasn't as spry as he used to be. Although no one would ever think it. He could still outrun, outgun, and outsmart every one of those young whippersnappers who thought they were Uncle Sam's gift to covert operatives. He put the bottle back in its holster, tapped his watch, and headed back toward home.

With three miles to go, he picked up the pace. His thoughts centered on his soon-to-be bride, Alexandra Julian, the former U.S. Ambassador to Egypt. She was back at the house, no doubt spending her day off flipping through bridal catalogues. The wedding was right around the corner, but that didn't keep her from looking at all the magazines to see if there was something she had to have for their special day. The thought of her brought a smile to his face and an uptick in his heart rate. She would be the focus of his life from now on. Sure he would occupy his time training new recruits for the CIA and the FBI and any other government entity feeling the need to load their human arsenals with the best America had to offer. But it was time. Time to move on. Time to focus on Alexandra and their life together.

They had first met when he was sent to Egypt to rescue her from the clutches of terrorists hell bent on starting World War III. How he got her out of the devil's den in one piece still amazed those who knew about it. It amazed him, too.

He still remembered the first time he held on to her. It was in the morgue of a Cairo hospital. There were bad men after them and, if they had found them, instant death would have been better than the torture they would have had to endure. All they could do at the time was hold onto each other. They never stopped holding onto each other ever since.

During her time as Ambassador in Egypt, she had been known as the American Jewel of the Nile. She hadn't lost any of her beauty having turned forty, and Schiffer spent half of the previous afternoon watching her tan her gorgeous hot body under the Virginia sun. He gave thanks every day knowing he was going to come home to her for the rest of his life.

Schiffer exited the canopy of trees and the heat from the sun's rays warmed him. His shirt was nearly drenched. He was only a mile from home now. While they had a place near D.C., rural Virginia would be their home. A place where they could drink iced tea on the back deck, spend some time splashing around in the lake, and chase the kids across the lawn. He could get used to that—a husband, a father, a retiree enjoying the fruits of his hard-fought labors. He almost let a smile creep out of the corner of his mouth. Yeah, he could get used to that.

Alexandra had said something to him before he left on the morning run. Something about flowers. He thought she mentioned white lilies and yellow roses. He remembered she liked them both. But he thought she said something about having them at their wedding. They needed to make a decision soon to make sure they got what they wanted. He told her he'd think about it while he ran. He looked at his watch. He was making good time with only a mile to go.

He was fine with the flowers. That's what he would tell her. *Whatever you want, babe.* He wasn't sure why she asked or why he didn't just tell her to go ahead with the lilies and roses. Maybe he was supposed to act like he was fully involved in the planning of the wedding. That must have been why he told her he'd think about it.

He came to the intersection and turned left. He smiled after passing the *Dead End* sign. It always made him chuckle for some reason, like it offered a warning to anyone looking to do him harm. He could see the white house on the lake in the distance. He was almost home, almost back to his soon-to-be wife Alexandra.

The only thing in his way was the car coming down the road toward him.

The thoughts of flowers vanished from his mind. He squinted slightly, trying to keep the sunlight from hindering his view from behind his sunglasses. He slowed his pace as the car picked up speed. Thinking the car could be a diversion, his eyes quickly scanned the trees in the distance to the west and the lake to the east. He was wide open. A sitting duck in rural Virginia.

What if they had Alexandra? What if they already killed her?

The car kept coming, and Schiffer kept running. He could make a run for the lake or the trees. His mind worked in overdrive. The trees would allow him to stay afoot. The lake would put distance between him and the car. But Alexandra was up at the house. He had to get there. He used his right hand to pull up the back of his sweaty shirt.

His left hand reached around to grab his pistol. He had ten rounds in the magazine and one in the chamber. He could see the driver round the bend, the car heading straight for him. The man had both hands on the wheel. One hundred yards now. Schiffer readied to pull out his Glock. He'd shoot the passenger first, the man whose hands he couldn't see. The driver would be next. If there was anyone in the back seat, he'd kill them too. Then he'd sprint to the house to check on Alexandra.

Fifty yards now.

Schiffer slowed, pulled the pistol from its holster, and then planted his feet. Aiming the gun at the man in the passenger seat caused the man behind the wheel to slam on the brakes. The car skidded to a stop, and the hands of those inside went up. Schiffer inched forward, his eyes darting to his left and right to make sure no one was coming from the sides. He'd shoot the driver first now, disabling the vehicle at the same time.

Schiffer crept closer. He thought this was the life he was running away from for good. He thought his days of defying death were over. But those looking to kill him never asked if he was retired. They just kept coming.

He gripped his gun tighter, the index finger on his left hand a split second from pulling the trigger. He took another step forward and then stopped when he could read the license plate—U.S. Government. It could easily be faked, he thought. He eyed the driver and passenger again, closer this time.

They looked familiar. He realized he had met them before. He cursed and shook his head, his heart rate slowing but his shoulders feeling heavier by the second.

Retirement was going to be put on the back burner.

The passenger held his badge out the window indicating they came in peace. Schiffer lowered the gun but kept it by his side. The driver let off the gas and the car started rolling toward him. Both occupants were smart enough to keep their hands where Schiffer could see them. He stepped to the side of the road as the car approached.

He bent at the waist to look at the two Secret Service agents inside. The

passenger did the talking.
"Get in. The Vice President wants to talk to you."

CHAPTER 6

Near Mineral, Virginia

Duke Schiffer told Stubblefield's security men to head on back to D.C. He didn't need a ride. He knew the way and could drive himself. Plus, he needed a shower. He walked into the kitchen and found Alexandra at the table, looking beautiful as always and scrolling through bridal websites. A handful of brochures and magazines were strewn across the countertop.

"Shouldn't you be done with the planning? The wedding is less than three weeks away."

Her eyes still focused on the computer screen, she said, "I'm just looking for any last-minute additions."

Schiffer decided not to ask how much her "last-minute additions" would cost.

Seated on a barstool still wearing her plaid pajama pants and white T-shirt, Alexandra didn't look up from the screen when she said, "Two agents from the Vice President's detail were here to see you."

Schiffer unholstered his water bottles and went about refilling them. "Yeah, I ran into them on their way out."

Her eyes left the screen, and she rested her chin on the palm of her hand. She gave him a look that reminded him how sexy she could be. She was a stunner when she was all dressed up, but even in pajama pants, a T-shirt, and her morning hair up she was adorable. The morning sunshine filtering through the east windows highlighted every inch of her beauty.

"Are you going to tell me what they wanted, honey?"

Schiffer turned his back and put the water bottles in the fridge, taking time to gather his thoughts. He was still getting used to being referred to as "honey." He had never gotten that far in a relationship to receive that term of endearment. "They said the Vice President wants to talk to me."

"Can't he call you on the phone?"

"Apparently not."

"Seems kind of strange, don't you think?"

"It could be nothing."

She sat up on the barstool and crossed her arms. "So you're going?"

Schiffer shrugged. "It's not like I have much of a choice. The big man wants to talk."

"I thought we were going to decide on flowers today. We need to make a decision."

"Well something came up. I can't imagine it will take long. Besides, I decided on the white lilies and yellow roses."

"You're just saying that because those are the ones I like."

He walked over and grabbed her in his arms. "Anything to make you happy, babe."

"Anything?"

He noticed the look in her eyes, but reading women wasn't his specialty. He wasn't sure if she might be referring to the wedding or something else. "Of course."

"Good . . . because I want to come with you."

Damn. He was hoping it was about the wedding. Then he could tell her whatever she wanted was fine with him and be on his way. "I think it might be best if I go alone since I don't know what it's about."

Alexandra stiffened. "Is this what it's going to be like being married to you? You get summoned on a random day and off you go without giving me a hint of what you're doing."

"Well, I don't know what I'm doing." When she didn't respond, he said. "You do know that this is my life. This is what I do."

She hopped off the stool and walked over to confront him. "Correction. This *was* what you do. You told me you were ready to put that part of your life behind you."

Schiffer took a breath. He thought about counting to ten but only got to three. "The Vice President of the United States needs to talk to me. I think I should at least be able to go up there and hear what he has to say."

"But without me?"

He cocked his head. "Maybe it's about you."

Alexandra rolled her eyes and then got closer. "I doubt that. I already told the President I'm not interested in being Secretary of State."

Maybe not then, but there had been interest in the past. Foreign service was in her pedigree. Her father was once U.S. Ambassador to Egypt, and her mother taught at American University in Cairo. They raised their daughter to take an interest in the world around them—wherever in the world they were at that time. But their lives were cut short in a terrorist attack in Sharm el-Sheikh. Alexandra had also been the victim of a terrorist attack in Egypt, a stark reminder that violence knows no borders.

But there was something good that came out of it. Captivity had brought Duke Schiffer into her life. So for now, she was content to stay out of the limelight and focus on the man she would marry.

She reached up and stroked his cheek. "I've got more important things to worry about right now than my next career. And that is you, my love."

Schiffer tightened his squeeze on her, pulling her body against his. He liked what he was hearing.

"Maybe you and I can do things together," she said.

He pulled his head back. *Together? What does she mean? Shopping? Wedding planning? A little romance?* He hurried to think of something. With a wink, he said, "I'll keep that in mind." He kissed her cherry red lips, something he was definitely getting used to. "I should get going. I need a shower."

She wrapped her arms around him, sweaty shirt and all, and said, "You'll let me know what he wants, won't you?"

Without hesitating, he lied and said, "Absolutely." He kissed her again to stop any further questions. After a tap on her rear, he stopped at the kitchen counter and noticed the floral centerpiece arrangement Alexandra had been looking at. He pointed at it and asked, "Is that the one you like?"

"Yes, I thought it was simple yet elegant."

Schiffer snapped his fingers. "I like it, too. Let's go with that one." He turned to walk away before looking over his shoulder and saying, "honey."

The ninety-mile trip through the back roads of Virginia and Interstate 95 took almost two hours with the traffic. Schiffer had just gotten his jet-black Jeep Wrangler Unlimited Sport back from the body shop the day before and he was happy with the work. Along with an aggressive outside suspension lift, he had requested some "modifications," which included magnetic mounts for pistols on both the driver and passenger sides—"his and hers," Schiffer told Alexandra. He had been teaching her how to shoot with different guns—pistol, shotgun, and rifle—telling her he couldn't be around all the time and she needed to know how to protect herself when she's home alone. The Jeep also had built-in holsters near the center console, ammunition drawers under the rear seat, and a lockbox in the back for his assault rifles. The only other additions still to be completed were the installation of the flashing red-and-blue lights for the front and rear and some darker window tinting.

Schiffer took the back way to the Vice President's residence, going on the west side of Arlington National Cemetery and Fort Myer and hoping to bypass the congestion of Foggy Bottom. He crossed the Potomac using the Francis Scott Key Memorial Bridge and headed north through Georgetown.

He slowed on Wisconsin Avenue as he passed a handful of foreign embassies. He didn't mind those of Norway, Finland, or Switzerland. Although every country spies on everyone else, friends and enemies alike, he didn't have much concern with some countries. Who cares what Denmark does?

But the presence of the Chinese Embassy never ceased to worry him. Some naïve people might say that the official Chinese Embassy is located two miles north of the Naval Observatory and there's nothing to fear, but Schiffer would remind them that the Chinese Embassy's visa and passport office was on the other side of the gates from the Observatory. There had to be a reason, and Schiffer knew better than to trust communists.

He drove around to the Massachusetts Avenue entrance and checked the time on his watch with the Naval Observatory's Master Clock digital display at the corner. Exact. He continued to the checkpoint.

He lowered the window and told the guard, "I'm here to see the Vice President."

The man didn't ask for a name or identification. He looked back to the guardhouse, got the go-ahead, and then nodded at Schiffer. "Thank you, sir. You know where you're going?"

"Yes, sir, I do," Schiffer said, raising the window.

Number One Observatory Circle – Washington, D.C.
Situated on the 80-acre grounds of the United States Naval Observatory, the Vice President's official residence had been built in the Queen Anne style, complete with turret rooms and an inviting wraparound porch on the front side. The 9,000-square foot house had plenty of bedrooms, a formal dining room, and a handful of other rooms that took in the natural light from the numerous windows. Those windows looked out toward the Observatory grounds, which were wrapped with dense trees, high fencing, and other hidden security measures.

Vice President Stubblefield hardly saw any of it.

He did most of his work from his office in the West Wing of the White House. He had another ceremonial office in the Eisenhower Executive Office Building just to the west of the White House. The residence also had an office, but he mostly used the house to eat and sleep. Although the Second Lady, Tina Stubblefield, suggested they entertain more, the Vice President begged off saying he was there to work, not to party.

And today's work included matters best left to the relative anonymity of the residence, not to the prying eyes of the press doing their live shots on the North Lawn of the White House or else stalking out the Vice President's motorcade. The list of visitors would not mention that Duke Schiffer, the Vice President's go-to man when the country needed it, entered that late morning.

The Vice President's secretary knocked on the door and entered. "Sir, he's here."

"Send him in."

The six-foot-four Stubblefield met Schiffer at the door and extended a hand. "Duke, good to see you."

"Always a pleasure, Mr. Vice President."

"Come on in." After closing the door, Stubblefield motioned for Schiffer to take a seat in one of the chairs in front of the desk. The Vice President took the other.

"You know, I sent a car down for you."

Schiffer nodded, like he somewhat appreciated the offer. "I prefer to drive myself." He smiled. "You could have called. I almost shot two of your men."

Stubblefield chuckled. "So I heard. Sorry about that. Would you have come if I called?"

Schiffer smiled. "Depends on what you wanted."

"That's why I sent the guys. Let you know it's important."

"Still, you could have told me over the phone."

Stubblefield shook his head, his face stern. "No . . . no phones on this one."

"Huh . . . must be serious then."

Stubblefield glanced out one of the windows and the green leafy trees in the distance. He wasn't ready to talk specifics yet. He felt the need to feel Schiffer out. "How's the wedding planning coming along?"

"I wouldn't know."

"It's still on, isn't it?"

"Of course, I've just been ordered to stay out of the planning."

"That's probably a good idea. When is it again?"

"Couple weeks." When the Vice President smiled, Schiffer said, "She's getting everything ready for the National Cathedral. She wants it to be 'spectacular'." He used air quotes around "spectacular."

Stubblefield nodded. "That'll be a nice place for a wedding. Everybody will remember it. I know Tina is looking forward to it." He paused to choose his next words carefully. "But I'm still not sure which side I'll be sitting on, though. Since Alexandra's brother is your best man, she asked me to walk her down the aisle. I hope you don't mind."

"No, not at all. I'm glad you're going to do it. Not too many women get the honor of having the Vice President of the United States walk them down the aisle." Schiffer shifted gears, ready to move on. "She might be having second thoughts, though, because she wasn't too happy that I came up here today."

"She not happy with you meeting with me?"

"She wanted to come."

Stubblefield paused in thought before saying, "The President would still consider her for a position in the administration if she's interested. She has a lot to offer this country."

"I'll let her know you said that."

With the talk about their personal lives done, Stubblefield leaned forward. "You watch the news?"

"I try to avoid it if I can."

Stubblefield chuckled and sat back. He shook his head and looked out the window and said, "I wish I could do that." He returned his focus to Schiffer.

"I have some things to discuss. Obviously, it's strictly between you and me."

"Of course."

The Vice President took a deep breath and let it out. "First thing is the President is thinking about not running for re-election."

Schiffer's eyebrows rose and scrunched. "Is he okay?"

Stubblefield held out a hand. "He says he's fine physically. It's just that . . . um . . . the job can really wear a person down, Duke."

"I can imagine." Schiffer cocked his head to get a good look. "So does that mean you're going to run?"

Stubblefield drummed the armrest with his fingers. "I've never wanted to be President, Duke. Never in my wildest dreams did I ever want it. And I never wanted this job either. I had my dream job as Director of the FBI."

"So what would it take for you to run?"

"I love my country, I love the flag, I love the men and women in uniform. And I don't want the socialist thumb suckers to run and ruin this country with their pie-in-the-sky dream of utopia."

Schiffer smiled. "If that's your slogan, I'll donate to your campaign."

"I'll keep that in mind." Stubblefield stopped to reflect on what he wanted to say. "I'm a dangerous man, Duke. I'm a black American who doesn't toe the leftist line. That makes me a huge target. They can't let me win. If I win, it could be the end of their movement."

Schiffer shifted in his seat and thought of what he wanted to say. "You probably didn't bring me here so I could give you political advice."

The Vice President shook his head and cracked a smile. He reached for a large manilla envelope on his desk. "No, whether the President is running or not is not the main reason I asked you to come up here. What I'm about to tell you might lead the President to make a decision, but it's a problem he wants addressed as soon as possible."

"Okay."

"You've probably heard about the riots last night in St. Louis."

Schiffer nodded. "Fourth city in two weeks."

"Yeah, and I can tell you that the President is not happy. I'm not either. I chewed out the FBI Director this morning on the phone because he's over their hobnobbing with the elites in London." Stubblefield raised a hand that said he was deviating from his train of thought. "I think Kurt's gone Hollywood on us."

"Hollywood?"

"Only cares about his image, not that of the Bureau or the safety and security of the American people. I think he wants to get in nice with those in the establishment to make sure he's on the invite list for all the cocktail parties and fancy dinners. All things you, me, and the President don't give a crap about. The President is trying to get him to see the light and be more proactive, and I told him to get his ass back here so we can stop another riot before it starts."

Stubblefield took out the contents of the envelope. "And that's where you come in."

"You want me to do something with the rioters?"

Stubblefield shook his head. He scooted his chair closer as Schiffer did the same. He spread out the contents of the envelope on the coffee table. He picked up a color picture of a man with curly gray hair wearing tinted blue sunglasses.

"The CIA sent this material over this morning. In contrast to the FBI Director, the CIA has been hard at work looking to find out the source of the funding that these coordinated riots are receiving. Of course, it's bigger than that, too. The money is funding the election bids of socialist political candidates across the country, including prosecutors who look the other way when it comes to all sorts of crime. The DA in New York City says he's no longer going to prosecute certain offenses—prostitution, trespassing, resisting arrest. The goal is to collapse the system and rebuild it. The CIA has discovered the Russians are up to no good again, using fake social media sites to stir up trouble, create division, and then coordinate the rioting and looting. They appear to be the muscle behind the operation, the ones with the tech savviness to create the online accounts and social media bots. But the money comes from someone else. We're still looking to find the people on the ground who are the leaders of the violence."

He stopped to catch his breath.

"But the money comes from someone else."

"Someone?"

"Yeah, and we think we might have found the guy behind the funding." Stubblefield handed over the picture and gave Schiffer time to study the man behind the glasses.

"What's his name?"

"Karl Bonhoff."

"He doesn't look Russian."

"He's not. He was born in Germany where he became a billionaire financier. A lot from hedge funds, some derivatives. Some of it he stole and swindled from former partners. The CIA says he'd sell his mother if he could make a quick buck. His kids, too, if he had any. He bought the software rights to facial recognition technology and has made billions selling it to any government that will fork over the money. The German government disowned him after he made an absolute fortune devaluing its currency. He made a killing on that play—at least ten billion. The guy loves money more than life, and he wants to be the richest man in the history of the world."

"Sounds like trouble."

"He's got his hands in energy and high tech and he's not afraid of manipulating things to make more money. He also not afraid to get into bed with the likes of China, Russia, Iran, and North Korea."

"All our enemies."

"That's right. And if he can undermine the United States, he'll ride it all the way to the bank." Stubblefield handed over another picture. Same man without the blue sunglasses. "It appears he's a bit of a playboy, likes his women and big houses. He's also a bit of a nomad, no country to call home apparently, but he spends time in Switzerland, Monaco, London, Paris, Spain. He has eight homes, all of them in the hundred-million range. He makes Saudi sheiks look like down-on-their-luck hobos."

"Must be nice."

Stubblefield continued. "But he's very good at hiding in the shadows. He rarely makes public appearances. He'd much rather push and pull the levers of power from his bunkers. Plus, he's good at hiding his money and how he spends it. His shell companies have shell companies."

"How did the CIA find him?"

"The guy thinks he's untouchable. But he got cocky, and when you get cocky, you cut corners and get careless. The CIA and NSA were able to unearth some evidence and piece it together."

Schiffer studied the pictures again. "So you think he's trying to destroy the U.S. from within by buying friendly candidates that will do his bidding for him—whether wittingly or unwittingly?"

"Yes," Stubblefield said. "It's insidious. According to recent intel that the CIA has unearthed, he's been secretly funding political candidates for years, from presidential candidates, members of Congress, all the way down to local races. He's paying Americans to do his dirty work. And unfortunately there are a lot out there who are willing to take his money."

"And the riots are part of his plan?"

"Yes. How many rioters and looters have you seen charged? Thieves run wild in San Francisco because the prosecutors won't charge them. Law and order are out the window. It's criminality bordering on anarchy. It's all part of a plan to get more government control—the more violence there is, the more peaceful people are willing to hand over their freedom to the government to stop it."

Schiffer dropped the pictures on the table and sat back in his chair. He looked at the Vice President. "So what do you want me to do about it?"

Stubblefield leaned forward. "I want you to find him."

Whether he knew it or not, Schiffer was tapping the armrest with his finger. He massaged his forehead with his other hand. "I thought I was retired."

"We've been through a lot together, Duke. I wouldn't ask if it wasn't important."

"Why not use the CIA? They obviously have some intelligence on him," he said, pointing at the pictures and dossier on the table. "Tell them to pick him up. Isn't that their job?"

Stubblefield shook his head. "It's the money, Duke. Powerful people in this country have taken money from Bonhoff's political action committees and they aren't going to want to take their hand out of the cookie jar. If the CIA takes him, he'll lawyer up and say he has no idea who is funding the candidates. He'll claim ignorance of having any shell companies. Once he goes free, he'll find new ways to bankroll his agenda. This has to be an operation that is kept under the strictest secrecy."

"Why not just steal his money?"

"I've thought about that, but he's bought off a lot of people, Duke. Banks included. We need to send a message."

Schiffer rose from his chair and walked toward a window. Stubblefield gave him a few seconds and then joined him. The silence that followed caused Stubblefield a great deal of concern. An operation like this, with its importance, should have been right up Schiffer's alley. The man normally would have jumped at the chance. No questions asked. But there was hesitation with this one.

And the Vice President couldn't afford to let Schiffer turn him down. Not this time. Not with this much at stake. He said softly, "America needs you, Duke."

Schiffer turned to his left to meet the Vice President's eyes. He sighed and asked, "What would you want me to do if I found him?"

Stubblefield broke eye contact and looked out the window. The silence said it all because no words needed to be spoken between the two, but Stubblefield decided to add, "Whatever you think is best."

Schiffer didn't respond. The hesitation was still there.

Hoping to seal the deal, Stubblefield turned and pointed a finger at his man. "Ten police officers aren't going home to their families because of this man. And that's just the ten we can be sure of. His money has helped fuel the attacks on our cities and our police. There's also evidence that he has helped fund terrorists who took out three soldiers in Afghanistan. He needs to be brought to justice."

"Does the President approve of this?"

Stubblefield returned his gaze to the trees swaying in the wind. He wanted to choose his word carefully. "The President told me to do whatever it takes."

The silence returned, and Stubblefield could almost see Schiffer playing the operation out in his mind. He could tell he wanted it. He could tell the operation had merit. But something was holding him back. Age? Fitness? Fear?

Schiffer let out an audible sigh. He ran his hand over the top of his closely cropped hair.

"I need to talk to Alexandra."

"I can talk to her if you need me to. And I can get the President to talk with her if you think it would help."

"No," Schiffer said, shaking his head. "I need to do it."

CHAPTER 7

Monaco

"Damn you, Ferraris! Damn you!"

With the Monaco Grand Prix airing on three eighty-inch TV screens, Karl Bonhoff could hear the Formula 1 race cars speeding through the streets of the principality, the famous racecourse only a stone's throw from his palatial penthouse on the top five floors of the forty-nine floor Odéon Tower. He proceeded to unleash a torrent of colorful expletives in multiple languages, all of them wishing ill on the two Italian Ferraris in the race. Ever since Italian authorities raided his apartment in Venice searching for evidence of tax evasion a decade before, Bonhoff held a passionate hatred for Italy that rivaled the disgust he had for his home country of Germany. Although, given his ancestry, he was still partial to the Silver Arrows of Germany's Mercedes-Benz, who were at that moment more than three seconds behind the two red Ferraris out front.

"May you rot in hell, you filthy rotten Dagos!"

When throngs of cheering Ferrari fans at the track were shown on TV wearing their red and waving their flags emblazoned with the Prancing Horse, he flipped the middle fingers of both hands to the TV.

"Screw you, *tifosi*! You're nothing but cheaters and crooks!"

The shirtless Karl Bonhoff, clad in his white shorts and sandals, his hairy chest not hiding his decent-sized paunch, felt free to curse any government, any person, anything. He was safe in Monaco, and so were his billions. Only ten miles from the Italian border, no one could come in and take a dime of his money. Monaco is the second smallest sovereign state in the world, behind only the Vatican. But where he was, Bonhoff didn't have to worry about staying in the good graces of His Holiness the Pope. He could do as he pleased. When he wanted, and how he wanted. And he could do it in the most famous tax haven in the world.

A leggy blonde walked by, her bikini top was nowhere to be found and her voluptuous breasts large enough that they could probably be seen from space. She made eye contact with him, silently offering her services, but he dismissed her with a wave of the hand, apparently still too ticked off with the Ferraris to partake in whatever she was willing to do. The woman continued to the infinity pool on the rooftop deck so she could let the astronauts see her sun herself in the nude. She was one of many women around, all stunning, all topless, and all of them ready to fawn over, at the time, the fourth richest man in the world.

Bonhoff had been married once, but it only lasted a year. After accusing him of adultery, she took him to divorce court and threatened to take half his money. He bought off the judge and told her to go to hell. She didn't get a penny. He vowed never to make that same mistake again. His money meant too much to him, and no woman would ever take it. There were no children either. The women around him now, and those like them around the world, were paid generously—written off as business expenses—and they would satisfy his needs and keep their mouths shut.

With an estimated net worth of $137 billion, he had purchased the world's most expensive penthouse for a measly $300 million two years prior. The pool was a nice addition, and it came complete with its own water slide from the dance floor above and a rope swing that let the adventurous fly wide near the edge of the building. At 31,000 square feet of space, he could live, work, and entertain like royalty.

And, more importantly, he could plot his next move.

One of his cell phones buzzed in his pocket. He looked at the screen, and the frown turned upside down. He tapped the screen and put the phone to his ear. "Viktor, I was wondering when you were going to call."

"It took me a few days to make sure the coast was clear."

"St. Louis was a great success." Bonhoff forgot his Italian hatred and exhorted, "*Bellissimo.*"

"Thank you, sir. We caused a great deal of damage. Even the ballgame was cancelled."

Bonhoff smiled. America's Pastime cancelled because of him, at least for one game. It was indeed beautiful. "It pleases me greatly, Viktor."

Kozlov paused before clearing his throat. "There was a cop killed."

"Good! The less cops there are, the more anarchy there will be. I want more of that." There would be no sympathy from him. Lives meant nothing to Bonhoff if they didn't advance his agenda. "You make sure that prosecutor looks the other way. I contributed plenty to her campaign and if she wants to continue in politics, she had better do what I say."

"She knows. She's already calling it an unfortunate accident."

"Excellent." Bonhoff paced the floor and looked out toward the panoramic views of the Mediterranean Sea. "You do good work, Viktor. You Russians are mean pricks, you know that?"

"Yes, we are, sir."

"I want every American to feel like their country is falling apart right before their eyes."

"I'll be sure to ratchet up the angst, sir."

"Where are you going next? Where should I be looking?"

"Seattle."

Bonhoff nodded. He liked the idea. The city ablaze with the Space Needle as a backdrop. That would be nice. "Good. How long until you get it together?"

"Soon. I'll let you know when I arrive and see how many people we can work with."

"I will forward the money to your account."

"Thank you."

"You sure the account is safe?"

"Absolutely. Russia specializes in hiding transactions. It will never be traced back to you."

"That's good. I want this next operation to be big. Bigger than St. Louis."

"You got it."

"You can do it?"

"No problem," Kozlov said. "Seattle is fertile ground for this type of plan. Plenty of likeminded people ready to take over the country."

"That's what I wanted to hear. Call me when you're ready."

Bonhoff tapped the screen to end the call. His mood had brightened, although that joy brought about by Kozlov's successes was tamped down by the two Ferrari drivers spraying champagne on the victory podium after finishing first and second. He didn't have time to curse before he got another call on a different cell phone. He didn't recognize the number, but it came from the United States.

"Yes?"

"Is this Karl Bonhoff?"

Bonhoff took a second to think if he could place the voice. He thought the man on the other end of the phone sounded vaguely familiar. Bonhoff was good with names and faces, but voices could be difficult. He had businesses all over the world, and it was not unusual for CEOs and other bigwigs speaking all sorts of languages with varying accents to call him at this number.

"Yes."

"Karl, it's Greg Lamont."

Bonhoff searched his brain. The name sounded familiar. He silently cursed when he couldn't remember. "I'm sorry?"

"Greg Lamont. From Wall Street a few years back. We made a heck of a lot of money together on that Germany deal."

"Gregory!" Bonhoff said. When people make him hundreds of millions of dollars in one deal, Bonhoff remembers. "Or I guess I should say Senator Lamont. I'm sorry, my ears must have been betraying me. I didn't make the connection. It's good to hear from you."

"I hope I'm not catching you at a bad time."

"No, not at all."

"Are you in Switzerland?"

"No, Monaco. For the race."

"Did your team win?"

"No." He held his tongue. The race was over and done with, and there was nothing he could do about it now. And there were more important things to think about. As with every call, he wondered how it could make him money. Everything was about money. Every call, every favor, every demand. He knew Lamont had some money, pocket change in Bonhoff's world, but he did have something Bonhoff didn't have. A Senate seat in the American political system. Money could be made. Power could be had.

"What can I do for you, Senator?"

"I don't know if you've been paying attention, but the United States has been seeing a great deal of unrest lately."

Bonhoff's cheeks rose slightly. *You don't say.* "Yes, I've seen something about riots and looting in your cities. It's a shame what's going on."

"I don't see it that way, Karl. I see it as an opportunity. I have some ideas I'd like to run by you."

Bonhoff took a seat, still facing the blue waters of the Mediterranean, and settled in for the long haul. "I'm listening."

"The President's poll numbers are down. The American people are not happy with his leadership. They think he's been in the White House too long and he's out of touch."

Bonhoff was dubious with the assessment, but he let Lamont continue.

"There's even talk the President might not run again. It's just a rumor, but I'm working on confirming it."

"That's interesting," Bonhoff said, his mind calculating the ramifications. "What about your Vice President?"

"Stubblefield? No, I don't think so. He doesn't like politics. I don't think he has the fire in the belly to run a national campaign. And even if the President doesn't run and Stubblefield jumps into the race, I think the American people are tired of the status quo. They're ready for a change at the top."

"And who would be the candidate of change?"

"Well . . . me."

"You're going to run for President of the United States?"

"I haven't announced anything yet, but I'm almost ninety-nine percent sure I'm going to run."

Bonhoff stood and walked closer to the window. He hated President Schumacher, his war on terror, and his crackdown on communist/socialist regimes. He could only guess how many billions the Schumacher Administration had deprived him of—at least $300 million from increased oil production in the United States. That he was sure of. Bonhoff practically controlled the Russian pipeline, and it wasn't making half of what it used to haul in because its customers were now buying large quantities of American oil.

"Are you still there, Karl?"

"Yes, I'm here." Although he already knew the answer, he asked the question anyway. He liked to hear people beg. "What do you need from me?"

Lamont cleared his throat. "I was hoping you could help fund my campaign. It's going to take huge amounts of cash to win. It'll be less if I can get out in front of the competition and scare off a primary challenge. Then I can focus the bulk of the money on defeating the President in the general election."

Bonhoff looked down at his thousand-dollar sandals. He thought he'd toy with the man for a bit, see if he could get the junior senator from Connecticut to grovel like one of those topless babes begging for sex. "If I remember right, Senator, you did pretty well for yourself on Wall Street. Your own money could go a long way to securing the nomination."

Lamont hurried with a response. "I did well, but not that well. I spent a boatload of money on this stupid Senate seat so I could use it as a stepping stone to get to the White House. I'm afraid it's not nearly enough. Not even close. It's going to take a lot of fundraising and *a lot* of dark money."

Bonhoff thought the man sounded small, like he knew his net worth was so puny the women out on the pool deck would laugh at him.

"I don't know, Senator. I contributed to Schumacher's last opponent and she got her ass kicked along with that idiot running mate of hers. What was his name again?"

"T.D. Graham."

"Yeah, what a colossal fool that guy was. He was so stupid he got himself kidnapped down in Mexico."

"Don't remind me. It was not my party's finest hour."

Thinking he'd jerk Lamont's chain so he'd have to beg some more, Bonhoff was about ready to tell Lamont to call him some other time.

But Lamont beat him to it. "I think it will make you a heck of a lot of money, Karl." Silence followed and, apparently having the man's attention, Lamont said, "If I'm President, you've got a seat at the table. And that seat gets you a voice in the world's largest economy."

Bonhoff admired the Senator's quick pivot. Lamont definitely knew how to scratch a rich man's greedy itch.

"I know you want to be the richest man in the world, Karl. I read it in the last issue of *Forbes*. You're not that far away. If I'm in the White House, I can get you a fighting chance at the top spot."

Bonhoff smiled. He did like the man's style. "So, it's a case of you scratch my back, and I scratch yours."

"That's right. We both win."

Bonhoff had much to say. Too much to be discussed over the phone. He needed to think, to come up with a plan. He had a hand in causing the havoc that was plaguing the U.S. and getting into bed with Lamont could finish it off. If Bonhoff's dark money won the election, the press would claim that President Lamont is the most powerful man in the world. But Bonhoff would know better. Not only would he be the richest, he would also be the most powerful.

And he liked the sound of that.

"Senator . . . perhaps we should meet."

CHAPTER 8

Washington, D.C.

With the turn of the calendar, June saw many in Washington flee from the city in hopes of beating the oncoming summer blast of heat and humidity. Members of Congress scurried home to escape the onslaught of tourists and to begin the annual rite of begging for money for the next campaign. The Justices of the Supreme Court left, too, looking forward to traveling and giving speeches in relative anonymity outside the glare of the nation's capital.

But one branch of government stayed behind. Those in the Executive Branch had to make sure the country was safe and secure, so leaving was not an option. They sidestepped the tourists, took refuge in the air conditioning, and longed for the days when all the movers and shakers returned to fight the next battles in the political arena.

Nate Russo was one of those who stayed behind. As the Vice President's Chief of Staff, he was on call twenty-four hours a day, seven days a week. If the Vice President was up, Russo was up. If the Vice President was asleep and something happened in the middle of the night, Russo had better be ready to brief his boss at a moment's notice.

But that Tuesday night was slow, and Vice President Stubblefield had no assignments or work for Russo. He rarely did, and it gnawed on Russo every single boring day at the office. Having graduated at the top of his class at Harvard with a degree in political science and public administration, Russo packed his bags and set out for the nation's capital with the dream of working his way to the upper reaches of political power.

During the Clinton Administration, he started out at the bottom by working for Congressman Butch Fengler from Tennessee, "a real rube," as Russo described the man. He oftentimes wondered if the Congressman had been educated in a one-room schoolhouse or maybe even a log cabin. The man might have been a world-class charmer, one who could fool people to vote for him, but Russo knew he was ten times smarter than "the hick from the sticks."

Russo, however, obediently kissed the man's ring like a low-level staffer should and did good work. That work caught the attention of Senator Holden Edison from New Hampshire, a fellow Harvard grad, and Russo took the next step up the political ladder as the man's director of communications.

After a decade with Senator Edison, Russo saw his next opportunity. Then Vice President Brenda Jackson was in need of a chief of staff, and Russo jumped at the chance. He had worked with her staff on immigration legislation when she was Governor of Arizona, and he dutifully pointed that out when he interviewed with her. He received glowing reviews from Representative Fengler and Senator Edison, and Vice President Jackson welcomed Russo aboard.

From then on, Russo was a workaholic. Taking every assignment, reading every briefing book, talking with every staffer on Capitol Hill, he did it all. Whatever Vice President Jackson needed. He knew he was only one election away from becoming the Chief of Staff to the President of the United States—the gatekeeper to the Oval Office and to the most powerful person in the world. He started dreaming of how he would decorate the Chief of Staff's office in the corner of the West Wing opposite the Oval Office. His office would be closer to the President than that of the Vice President. And, in all reality, he would have the power.

It all came crashing down when Vice President Jackson resigned to take care of her ailing husband. The current Vice President, Ty Stubblefield, took her place and kept Russo on, wanting the experience and continuity as he got up to speed. But Russo's office was moved across West Executive Drive from the West Wing into the Eisenhower Executive Office Building, and he was rarely summoned in the year he spent with Stubblefield.

Russo was not impressed. He lamented to friends that the Vice President knew little about politics or the way the sausage of legislation is crafted. Stubblefield acted like he didn't even care about it, his focus being on law enforcement and national security. How could he not care about legislation and the bureaucracy making the country work? Russo didn't know. What's worse, he once overheard Stubblefield say he didn't trust people from Harvard. It was like a slap in the face to that Ivy Leaguer.

Lately, Russo took to spending his evenings wondering whether he should quit and move on with his career. He discussed most of his ideas with his friend Jack Daniels, other times with Captain Morgan or Johnnie Walker, at the Round Robin Bar inside the Willard InterContinental Hotel two blocks east of the White House.

"Evening, Nate," the bartender said. The two were on a first-name basis.

Russo gave the man an upward nod. "Jake."

"What are you having tonight?"

"Jack Daniels."

"Ah, going back to your roots with some Tennessee whiskey, huh?"

Russo kept his eye-roll to a minimum. He had no roots in Tennessee, but Jake the bartender knew everyone's resume like it was his own. He even pointed out once that Congressman Fengler came in a few years back and ordered a mint julep. Russo made sure to never order one.

Russo took the whiskey and a seat at the circular bar. The place was eighty-percent full, half of those being tourists wondering if they could afford anything off the drink menu or hoping to see someone they knew from TV. He took a sip and let the liquid wash down his troubles. It was the best part of the day in his mind.

He drank the first whiskey slowly, but he soon lost the desire to savor the second and was on his third within a half hour. With a good buzz going, he closed his eyes and thought about his future. They shot open when he heard a woman's voice next to him.

"Hey, stranger," Shannon Swisher said, running a hand down his back. "I haven't seen you in a while."

Perhaps it was the whiskey, but Russo thought the back rub felt good. It had definitely been a while since he felt that kind of touch. He knew Swisher from their days together at Harvard, and Swisher's consulting firm had helped put Senator Edison over the top in a tight election. They kept in and out of touch over the years—which is the way of the world in Washington. You try to know everybody, but there are only so many people you can latch onto at once.

"Yes, it has, Shannon. Good to see you."

Swisher sidled up next to him and pointed at his near empty glass. "What are you drinking?"

"Jack."

She caught the bartender's attention. "Two Jacks," she said, pointing at Russo's glass and the empty spot in front of her.

After the bartender set them up, Russo raised his glass. "Thanks."

Swisher clinked her glass with his. "Sure thing." She took a sip. "How are things going with the Veep?"

Russo shrugged and frowned. "It's a paycheck."

"That bad, huh?"

"There's not a lot going on."

"Really? There's always something going on, especially with this administration."

Russo shook his head and sulked like a kid who hadn't received an invitation to the party. "Wish I knew what it was."

Swisher leaned forward and set her elbow on the bar, her chin resting in her hand. "You want to talk about it?"

Russo gave a quick shake of the head, but he wasn't very convincing. He gave off a vibe that said he needed to unload some baggage on anyone who cared to listen.

"Come on, let's grab a table so we can talk. We Harvard alums need to stick together so we can save the world from the rubes and the hicks from the sticks."

Russo chuckled. The first time he laughed in a good long while.

She motioned toward the tables in front of the oak-paneled walls decorated with portraits of the famous and powerful who had once sipped their liquor and swapped their stories in the place. There was a leather-backed bench seat lining the walls with small tables and a chair opposite. The spot under the portrait of Thomas Edison was taken so they headed for the open table under the watchful eye of Woodrow Wilson.

Swisher took the bench seat that faced the bar so she could see if any other movers and shakers came in. When Russo started to take a seat across the table, she waved him off. "No, no. Sit over here," she said, patting the leather next to her. "That way I don't have to yell across the table."

Russo hesitated for a second, but when she patted the seat again, he decided it couldn't hurt. They were old buddies after all—and she was a beautiful woman. He took a seat on the bench behind the small table. Once he was situated, Swisher took a sip and then scooted closer.

Trying to be discreet, she turned slightly to front him and said, "So, you want to tell me what's going on with you?"

Russo gritted his teeth. He had kept his problems inside for the better part of a year now. He didn't dare vent his frustrations to anyone in the Vice President's office because they would tell him to suck it up or hit the bricks if he wasn't happy. He knew he could be replaced with someone else at the drop of a hat. He usually confided in Jack Daniels and friends, but now he had someone who would understand, someone who knew the way Washington, D.C. really worked.

And she smelled good, too.

"I guess I'm feeling underappreciated. I think I have a lot to offer, but it seems like I'm kept out of the loop more often than not." He looked at her with wide eyes. "I mean, I graduated first in my class at Harvard! I should be doing more than fetching coffee and pushing papers around."

Swisher set her elbow on the table and rested her cheek against her fist, her full attention on the man next to her.

"It's been like this since the start. The Vice President doesn't trust outsiders."

"And you're an outsider?"

Russo shrugged. "I guess that's the way he sees me. I don't know why. I told him I'd do whatever he wanted, be the gatekeeper to his office, but that's not his management style. He's very hands-on." He let out a depressing sigh. "It was my dream to become the President's Chief of Staff. That's where the real power behind the scenes is. I thought I had it in the bag with Vice President Jackson. We got along great, and I was only one election away from having it all."

Swisher reached over and patted Russo's hand. He flinched at the touch but didn't take his hand away. They were old friends, and she was consoling him in his time of need. Nothing wrong with that, he thought.

She broke eye contact with him and looked toward the bar. "Jake!" Swisher shouted over the din of the crowd. Once she got the bartender's attention and held up two fingers. "Two more!"

Once the drinks were in front of them, Swisher said, "I think you need to look for something better, Nate. You're too good for the Veep. You need to start laying the groundwork for the next administration."

"The Veep might be the next administration," Russo lamented.

Swisher took a sip of whiskey. "I heard the President might not run again."

"That's what I heard."

"So, it's true? He's not running?"

"It's not for certain yet, but I know there has been talk. I've overheard bits and pieces in the last week."

Swisher nodded like she had heard the same. She tapped him on the hand. "But there's no guarantee that the Vice President will win. He's not a politician. You said it yourself, he doesn't know the ways of Washington. People want someone who can reach across the aisle, build a consensus, implement their vision, and that takes political know-how."

Russo raised a glass. "You're preaching to the choir, Shannon."

She leaned in closer, her perfume hitting his nose and her blonde twirls catching his eyes. *Dang, she's hot.*

"I have someone who can win, Nate."

Russo looked at her, her moist red lips distracting him for a second. "Who?"

"It's not official yet, but it will be soon. If he's going to win, he needs money and insider information. He's working on the money angle as we speak."

Russo gulped. "And I'm the insider information part?"

Swisher quickly shook her head. "I'm not asking you to divulge state secrets, Nate. I would never do that, and I know you would never think of doing such a thing. I'm just asking for information, maybe a few days in advance so I can make use of it in the campaign."

"The President and Vice President hate leaks to the press."

Swisher rubbed the back of his hand. "I'm not the press, Nate. I'm an old friend from Harvard who wants to run a winning presidential campaign and make you the next Chief of Staff to the President of the United States."

Russo felt a jolt shoot up from his toes. The President's Chief of Staff. Could his dream job still be a possibility? It didn't sound possible to him. "I don't know, Shannon. I'm not sure I can give you much."

"Nonsense. You can give me a lot." With her left hand on top of his, her right hand made its way under the table to his thigh. His muscles tensed. Higher and higher her hand went until he flinched at the happy intrusion to his crotch. The woman sure knew how to grab a man's attention. "I want to win, Nate. You want to win. We want the country to win. And that's why we have to work together."

Russo felt a trickle of sweat slide down his cheek. He noticed the bra strap peeking out of Swisher's blouse.

"Should we be doing this, Shannon?" blurted Nate.

"It's just two old friends having a good time." She rubbed the back of his calf with the top of her left heel.

Nate blinked his eyes trying to focus. A closer look revealed the bra was candy apple red, and with the booze in his system and the delusions of grandeur filling multiple parts of his body, Russo felt like a bull ready to charge.

"I've got a suite upstairs, Nate. I'd like to talk some more." Her right hand squeezed harder and his back straightened. "I've got a great view of the Washington Monument."

Russo smiled. He was too drunk to say he'd be happy to show her his own Washington Monument. But he was indeed happy. He had come into the bar lamenting his current state of affairs, feeling underappreciated by the people who thought they were better than him.

And now? The clouds of despair had parted and the bright light of hope was shining through. This woman had connections and plans to make his dreams come true. She had stroked his ego, and beyond, and he was going to make it happen. He was going to make his boss regret pushing him away and for treating him like a nobody. He was going to show him what he was born to do. He gulped down the rest of his whiskey and pounded the empty glass on the table. He was going to be the next Chief of Staff to the President of the United States.

But first things first . . .

He was about to get naked.

CHAPTER 9

Seattle, Washington

Viktor Kozlov had flown from Chicago to Portland, Oregon, under a fake Washington driver's license. The license was real—in the sense that it had been procured from the Washington State Department of Licensing. It hadn't been doctored, although the identifying information was all fake. Kozlov was not Peter Cristoff and his date of birth was not in January. But the picture with the man in the glasses looked exactly like the real man with the fake glasses that slid the ID across the ticket counter at O'Hare. He landed without a second look, and the lady at the car rental counter in Portland thanked Mr. Cristoff for his patronage and wished him a good trip.

The three-hour drive north on Interstate 5 gave Kozlov plenty of time to think. Of course, being Seattle, he dreamed of causing mayhem at the Space Needle. Just as he had done when thinking about the Gateway Arch, he envisioned seeing the 605-foot Space Needle crashing to the ground. He'd bet he'd get bonus points from Bonhoff if people on the observation deck were seen falling to their deaths.

But he would have to save that dream for another day. He arrived in Seattle in the late afternoon, and he was pleased with what he saw. The local politicians had done much of the work for him. The homeless were everywhere. The sidewalks were filled with an assortment of tarps and tents, the gutters strewn with feces and needles. Grocery carts full of dirty possessions and aluminum cans outnumbered the cars. The area smelled like urine and stale booze. Kozlov almost chuckled to himself. The place was already a dump, and he had been sent there to make more of a mess. He was thankful for the head start. This operation would be easy.

The Russian social media bots were beginning to churn and, once the calls went out, there would be no shortage of those looking to spend an evening destroying their city. The place was crawling with green freaks, anarchists, Marxists, black separatists, drug addicts, aging hippies, punk hippies, grunge hippies, not to mention the jealous tech geeks who were ticked off that they had made billionaires out of their bosses who had no desire to spread the wealth around. Angst and rage were in good supply. Perfect fuel for what Kozlov had in store.

At 10 p.m. Pacific time, Kozlov made the call to Bonhoff. It was 7 a.m. in

Monaco and, given that Bonhoff only slept four hours a day, Kozlov knew his boss would be wide awake.

"Is it all ready to go?" Bonhoff asked.

Kozlov spat on the ground. "Yes. You should turn on CNN. It won't be too much longer."

"How's it looking?"

Kozlov looked up to the darkened sky. He had been worried about the usual rains of the Pacific Northwest, but the skies were clear. A perfect night for violence. "Excellent conditions."

"Are you worried about the police?"

"No. They have defunded their police to only a skeleton force. It's almost comical. Perhaps they will send their social workers to stop us."

Bonhoff laughed. He had paid for those politicians to defund the police and it was his idea for the social workers. It was all a joke. "I want it to be like Portland. Something that lasts throughout the summer. Maybe have one of those autonomous zones where police aren't allowed to enter."

"I can do that. We've got the plywood and the barricades ready." He spat again. "If you really want it to last, they'll need money for food and water. Toilets, too, although from what I can tell, most of them just use the sidewalks. It's about as bad as San Francisco."

Bonhoff interjected with another demand. "I want them to make sure to pin all their troubles on President Schumacher. I might have an angle that I can exploit so do what you have to do to make Schumacher the villain."

"You got it."

"And there's a bonus if you pick off another cop. I want it to look like open season."

"Consider it done. Anything else?"

"No. I'm about ready to sit down for breakfast. Hurry up so I can watch it on TV."

Once Bonhoff ended the call, Kozlov texted three of his associates. They were right on schedule. The rabblerousers would soon be at their staging grounds. He chose the end point as the Space Needle, since it was readily identifiable to those too stoned to know where they were.

Someone set fire to a homeless encampment, and the mayhem started. The marchers came from all directions—some from the ferry on Elliott Bay, some from the light rail station east of the Needle, and from all places in between. A homeless man whose tent was set on fire threw the first punch and then the brawl was on. Two cars were torched, and gasoline was poured down the gutters and set ablaze. Windows of coffee shops and restaurants were next, and the looting began.

The mob moved west, chanting and demanding the old standbys—Hey, Hey . . . Ho, Ho . . . blah blah blah. Signs blaring *Reparations!* and *Justice!*

were recycled.

"Keep going!" Kozlov ordered, pointing to the Needle. "There are more that way."

Once the mob mentality took over, nothing was safe. Vagrants mad at the world took out their frustrations on anything of value and each other. A homeless man was dragged into the street and pummeled by no less than ten thugs looking to get their kicks. The police arrived but were quickly outnumbered. A shot was fired, and then another. Two homeless men went down, and the cops would be branded as murderers and pigs with no evidence to support it.

Kozlov noticed the reporters arriving on scene and the cameras getting everything on video.

"Keep going!" Kozlov ordered the marchers. "Louder! Louder!"

A pole was procured, and an effigy of President Schumacher was set alight and raised high above the marchers, much to their bloodthirsty delight. The American flags were next, and a cheer went up when the flames engulfed the red, white, and blue. When a tear gas canister from the cops in riot gear hit in front of the marchers, most of them laughed. One brave soul picked up the canister and threw it back from where it came.

The news cameraman found a black man willing to shout expletives at high volume. "This is the end of the United States! This is our land now! We are in control!"

"Schumacher must go!" another yelled. "We won't leave until he's gone!"

One ranted and raved about the wonders of socialism. "It is all for one now! We have broken the system and it is ours! We are the future of this country!"

Once the throng of people got near the Space Needle, the barricades and plywood started going up. Spray paint warned people that they were no longer in the United States. Instead, they were entering something called the "Community of Peace." Kozlov didn't know where that came from, but he didn't care. Two men guarding the entrance to the Community of Peace were then engaged in a fistfight.

Kozlov could smell the smoke from the fires, the night taking on a hazy gray. The stench of weed told anyone within ten miles that the rioters had come prepared and were settling in for the long haul. What else did they have to do with their pathetic lives?

Off to the west, he caught sight of a flaming ferry drifting aimlessly in Elliott Bay. He thought it was a nice touch, and it would earn some news photographer a handful of awards for capturing the spirit of the riot before the ferry sunk to the bottom.

By the break of day Pacific time, news around the world would show the unrest and marvel that the rioters had taken over a major American city. Many would say that President Schumacher was no longer in control of the country and that anarchy ruled the streets. The giant flag of a group of separatists hanging from the Space Needle would be evidence of those claims.

It was said the people were rising up and demanding change. Kozlov surveyed the scene one final time. Before they were all done, it would look like an invasion of locusts had come through, destroying everything of value, and leaving it in ruins. Then they would move on.

And he couldn't wait.

CHAPTER 10

Near Mineral, Virginia

The next morning, Duke Schiffer turned on the TV in the kitchen and watched in disgust. Seattle had been overrun by a violent horde of reprobates and thugs and no one in charge of the city seemed to know what to do about it. Or, worse yet, no one in charge wanted to do anything about it. Instead of arresting the troublemakers, the politicians claimed the rioters were simply expressing their First Amendment rights and airing their grievances, some of which were alleged to have had origins all the way back to Columbus. To Schiffer, the inmates were running the asylum and the politicians were fine with it—anything to undermine the system as it has been known for two hundred plus years so they could reform it in their own warped image. He felt the rage inside him, and the only thing that gave him hope was the knowledge that he had the power to do something about it.

He called the Vice President and said, "I'll do it." He was smart enough not to say any more, and Stubblefield told him to get up to Washington as soon as possible so he could get further briefed on the plan.

Now the only thing he had to worry about was telling Alexandra that he was leaving—to an undisclosed location for an undetermined amount of time at an unknown level of danger. *Oh, and that wedding that's right around the corner, honey, you might want to think of another date to choose from in case I can't make it back on time.* He had a thought that going one-on-one with the rioters might be easier.

"You were up early today," Alexandra said.

She was wearing a pair of plaid boxers and one of his white dress shirts with the top two buttons unused. *Man, oh man.* Schiffer knew telling her was going to be harder than he thought. She held up the carton of orange juice to see if he wanted any.

He nodded and handed her an empty glass. "It's a nice day so I went for a run."

She filled the glass and put the carton back in the fridge. The TV in the corner was muted, but the pictures were replaying the destructive events of the previous evening. She took a seat on the stool at the kitchen counter to eat her breakfast. "Did you see the news?"

"Yeah."

She bit into a blueberry muffin and looked at the TV. "What is wrong with those people?"

Schiffer took his glass of orange juice over to the window and looked out toward the lake, a speedboat off in the distance catching his eye. It looked so peaceful and inviting out there. It hadn't always been like that. There had been violence on the lake, and he just happened to be the intended target. Two terrorists had been sent to hunt him down a few years back. That was the last mistake they ever made, and Schiffer and his neighbor had to fish a couple of dead bodies out of the water.

He thought those days were behind him. Instead, he dreamed his days would be filled with swimming, boating, and fishing. Lots of running, some biking. He'd enter a triathlon or two to stay in shape. That had been his plan. He'd do a little work on the side for the government, but he would spend most of his days sitting on the back deck enjoying the view and having fun on the water with Alexandra and however many kids the future had in store for them. Whatever dreams he had, she was always by his side. That was what he wanted.

But now he was looking at getting back into the thick of things, and the people he would be looking for had the money and the power to make his job very difficult. There was a good chance he wouldn't be coming back. He thought those days were over. If he had nine lives, he was sure the number of lives left were getter fewer and fewer. He took another sip.

"Did you hear me?"

He returned his focus to Alexandra. "I'm sorry, what?"

"I said, what is wrong with those people?"

He looked her in the eye and shrugged. "I don't know if I have a good answer."

Alexandra shook her head and frowned. The TV screen showed a man taking a baseball bat to a Seattle police vehicle. His thug friends were cheering him on. "I wish the President would do something about it."

Schiffer returned his gaze back to the water and finished the last of the orange juice. The speedboat was making a return run. He thought it looked like fun. A lot more fun than what was in store for him. He could feel his stomach tightening. *Better get it over with.*

"About that," he said, putting the empty glass on the counter. "I've been wanting to talk to you about something. The Vice President has some ideas on how we might put a stop to the unrest." He thought about what he said and then added, "By 'we' I mean me."

Alexandra stared at him, as if she didn't understand. He had obviously caught her off guard. After a couple seconds, she asked, "So he has an operation for you?"

"Yes."

"When would you be leaving?"

"Today."

Her eyes widened. "Today? . . . And you're just telling me now?"

"I didn't make the decision until this morning."

"Without even discussing it with me."

"I'm sorry. It's just something I have to do."

"Well, did you forget our wedding is like two weeks away?"

"No, I didn't forget, honey."

She gave him a look that said "honey" might be off the table for the foreseeable future. He expected the blowback, but it was the first time he had to deal with a prospective bride when making those types of decisions. He pointed at the TV as if the pictures sealed the deal for him. "I don't think there's much to discuss. This has to be stopped. You wanted to know why the President wasn't doing anything. Well . . . now he's doing something."

She stood and walked closer to him. "Well, where are you going?"

"I'm not sure yet."

"How long will you be gone?"

"I don't know."

"Who are you going after?"

"I can't say."

"You don't know or you won't tell me?"

"The latter."

She let out a heavy sigh, the sigh of a wounded, out-of-the-loop fiancée, and put her hands on her hips. "Is this how it's going to be our entire marriage?"

He looked at her and remembered his dreams for them. "I hope not."

"Well, why don't you tell the Vice President to send someone else?"

"There is nobody else. Besides, it's too important."

"Isn't getting married important to you?"

His voice rose. "He only trusts me, Alexandra."

She sighed again and then folded her arms across her chest. "I can't believe you didn't tell me."

"I'm sorry. I thought I was done with operations, but . . ."

"But what?"

"Like I said, it's too important. America is the greatest country on the face of the earth, and there are people out there who want to transform it to their liking—and their liking does not include the unalienable rights life, liberty, and the pursuit of happiness."

With her eyes growing moist, he thought he was winning her over. He reached out and brought her into his arms, hoping to convince her once and for all.

"There's nothing I want more than to get married to you and spend the rest of our days together. That's what would make me happy. But if we're going to raise our children in a country that values freedom over tyranny, I need to do this. And I need to do it now before it's irreversible."

He went in for a kiss, but she put her hands on his chest stopping him.

"I want to go with you."

He chuckled, thinking it was funny that she sounded so serious. He shook his head. "You can't go with me."

She backed out of his embrace. "And why not?"

"Because I don't know where I'm going and I don't know how long I'll be gone."

"Maybe I can help you."

"How do you think you can help me, Alexandra?"

"I'm not naïve, Duke. I was involved in the current administration, in case you've forgotten. I've lived all over the world and have contacts with multiple foreign governments. Plus, I can speak fluent Arabic and Hebrew. Some French and Italian, too."

Schiffer nodded his head like she was making good points. His future bride was highly intelligent, educated at Yale, and had proven herself as a foreign service officer while Ambassador to Egypt. But he wasn't going to be making a speech on Egyptian history or giving tours of the Pyramids. He was going to hunt down the man who wanted to wreak havoc on the American way of life. "You have an impressive resume, Alexandra. You really do, and I have the utmost respect for your abilities. But I'm not sure it's what we need for this operation."

Her response was quick. "Well, I have something you don't."

Schiffer restrained himself from laughing. Instead, he lowered his head, his eyebrows raised. "And what is that exactly?"

She closed the gap between them, letting her strawberry scented shampoo tickle his nose. Then she caressed his right biceps and wrapped a tanned right leg around the back of his thigh bringing them closer. With her breasts smashed up against his chest, she started rubbing his bare back underneath his shirt. Then she licked his ear and whispered lustfully, "Feminine wiles."

"Damn," he muttered, inhaling her scent and not wanting her to let go. "You got me there."

Number One Observatory Circle – Washington, D.C.

Schiffer pulled up to the gate outside the Vice President's residence in his Jeep. He came alone, but it didn't mean Alexandra wasn't with him in his thoughts. He had packed his bags and kissed her goodbye, promising to tell her as much as he could and, if possible, let her know his whereabouts and when he would be home. He told her to do whatever it took to make their wedding the best it could be. He promised to come back to her, and his last vision of his future wife was her leaning against the white column on the front porch as he drove away.

He told the guard he was there to see the Vice President. No name was given, and none was requested. After a quick check of the undercarriage of the Jeep, the guard got the okay from the guardhouse and the gate went up. Schiffer drove through, parked, and was quickly ushered through to the residence and into the Vice President's office.

Stubblefield was on the phone, rolling his eyes and shaking his head at whoever was on the other end of the line and at whatever gibberish he was listening to. Pointing at the phone, he mouthed the word "idiot" and then motioned for Schiffer to come forward. He held up a finger that he'd only be a minute longer.

"Yes, thank you, Senator. I'll be sure to pass along your idea to the President. Yes . . . yes, I'll be sure to make it a priority. I know how important this legislation is to you. Thanks . . . thanks for calling." He practically threw the phone back into the cradle and then rubbed his face with his hands. "Man, these people," he snapped. "Don't they know I have more important things to deal with? They're always maneuvering and plotting about some stupid crap. It's all about the money. All of them want more money for their constituents so they can get reelected. The more money they get, the more power they keep. Whether it's actually good for the America people is not their first concern."

Schiffer stopped in front of Stubblefield's desk. "Maybe when you're President you won't have to deal with it."

Stubblefield looked like he wanted to offer a biting comeback to the low blow, but he held his tongue. "Are you all ready?"

"Yes, sir."

"I hope I didn't cause any problems with your fiancée."

Schiffer shrugged. "She's not happy if that's what you mean."

"You should have told her that she needs to focus on the wedding."

"I did, and she's still mad. She was badgering me to take her with me."

"You don't even know where you're going."

Schiffer laughed. "That's what I told her."

"You got any thoughts on a team?"

"Yes, sir."

Stubblefield nodded. He didn't ask who Schiffer had in mind. He stood and walked around the desk. He reached into his suit coat and pulled out a folded document. He unfolded it and showed it to Schiffer, who noticed the words *The White House* at the top.

"This is a national security directive," Stubblefield said. He pointed to the signature. "Signed by the President. I have briefed him on the operation, and he has authorized it. You, me, and the President are the only ones who know about it at this time. As I said before, the fewer number of people who know about this the better."

Schiffer didn't feel the need to put his fingerprints on the paper, but he read it and saw it mentioned targets to apprehend, including, "by any and all means available," Karl Bonhoff, and any associates, who have engaged in the unlawful attempt to influence the policies of the United States Government. He nodded that he had finished it.

"And what if apprehension isn't possible?" *What if he's killed?*

"Well, it would be too bad for him. He shouldn't have been screwing around in U.S. affairs."

"Understood."

Stubblefield folded the document and put it back in his suit coat on the side closest to his pistol. "You'll be based out of Joint Base Andrews, so you'll have quick access to aircraft. If anyone questions why you need it, tell them you're under direct orders from the President. If someone still balks, you call me."

Schiffer nodded.

"I have asked Director Parker to have the CIA continue finding intel on the target and he will forward it to me. Once we find out where the target is located, I will let you know. In the meantime, get a team together and do what you need to do to get ready."

"Yes, sir."

Stubblefield extended a hand. "Good luck and be safe."

CHAPTER 11

Monaco

For all the vast wealth residing in the principality, Monaco, given its size, lacked an airport for the million-dollar jets loved and adored by the rich and famous. Because of that, Senator Lamont was forced to land his chartered Gulfstream at the airport in Nice, France. He had hoped that Karl Bonhoff would have called to say he had a car waiting to take the Senator on the fourteen-mile drive to Bonhoff's yacht docked at the southern edge of Monaco. He had really hoped Bonhoff would send his helicopter to ferry him straight to the helipad on his megayacht. But Bonhoff sent neither, apparently figuring Lamont had enough money to find his own way to the dock.

Lamont descended the airstairs and took in the warm sunshine. A nicely dressed man signaled him that his ride was waiting. The company Lamont hired to drive him was said to be the most elegant in all of Nice, and he decided to go with the dignified black Mercedes sedan over the ostentatious Rolls-Royce Phantom. He was begging for Bonhoff's campaign donations after all.

Once in Monaco, the driver didn't need directions. He simply looked for the biggest yacht there was and headed in that direction. "The Super Stallion," as the yacht was named, dwarfed all those around it. It was Bonhoff's second yacht, the gleaming white beauty with tinted black windows measuring four-hundred feet in length. His old one, "The Stallion," had been thirty feet shorter. But when the fifth richest man in the world had one built at three-hundred-and-eighty feet, Bonhoff had no choice but to go bigger. The fourth richest man in the world would not have anything smaller than those behind him, Bonhoff huffed.

Upon arrival at the dock, Lamont gawked at the size of the seafaring monstrosity, more of a cruise liner than a yacht. Like every good multimillionaire, jealously was a common affliction and Lamont had a serious case of envy going on. Lamont had the wealth to buy a yacht, not a megayacht or a gigayacht as they were being called, but even a model at the high end of what he could afford would look like a dingy next to Bonhoff's beast.

"Senator!" Bonhoff yelled down from what looked like the third deck. He waved him up. "Welcome aboard."

Lamont noticed two men standing next to a Mercedes in front of the gangplank. They looked at him behind their dark sunglasses and motioned him closer.

Once Lamont got within three feet, the man in charge spread his arms, telling Lamont without words to do the same. Lamont complied, and the man frisked him roughly—so roughly that Lamont thought the man was enjoying it. Lamont thought about reminding the man that he was a United States Senator but held his tongue.

Once secure in his belief that Lamont was not hiding a weapon, the man pointed at Lamont's side and said, "The bag stays here."

"Fine," Lamont said, handing over his overnight bag, which the man put in the trunk of the Mercedes.

Bonhoff returned to the railing on the third floor of the yacht and yelled down, "Hurry up! I don't have all day!"

The security guard flicked a hand toward the yacht, telling Lamont he could proceed up the gangplank. Once aboard, he was led to the elevator by a very lovely woman in a very skimpy bikini. She said nothing. The only thing that kept Lamont from staring at the woman's glistening bronzed features was the gold-plated amenities that lined the place. This was what Bonhoff's money could buy, Lamont thought.

The elevator arrived on the top deck of the yacht, and Lamont squinted as the doors opened and he emerged once again into the Mediterranean sun. He looked to the stern and saw the helipad where he could have dropped him off. He wondered where the chopper was. His eyes then took him to the deck, and he noticed four naked women sunning themselves on lounge chairs. *Now that's really what Bonhoff's money can buy.* He tried not to stare, reminding himself why he was there. He knew there would be a time and a place for some fun, but right now he needed to focus on the presidential campaign.

"Senator," Bonhoff said, emerging from what Lamont took for the men's room. "Welcome to Monaco."

They shook hands, and Lamont noticed Bonhoff's hand was still wet. He wore no shirt, his hairy chest a mangled mess of dark and gray. The shorts were white, and the legs were tan. Flip-flops rounded out the ensemble of the fourth richest man in the world.

"I hope your trip went well."

Lamont shrugged and then threw a thumb over his shoulder. "Your man at the dock was a little rough with the pat down."

Bonhoff cursed. "I hate security guards. I never let them step foot on board, and they never step foot in any of my residences. They are nothing but uneducated thugs who would like nothing more than to learn my secrets and steal my money. So they are instructed to stay in the background and let me live my life. I keep them on the perimeter for safety's sake, of course, and to drive me around. As you can imagine, I do have some enemies out there."

"I bet you do."

"Let's have lunch," Bonhoff said, motioning him to follow him across the deck, past the naked women who paid them no attention, and to a table underneath an umbrella.

"This yacht is magnificent, Karl."

"The Super Stallion," Bonhoff bellowed, spreading his arms wide. "Biggest yacht in the whole world."

"I don't doubt that."

"Not even those Russian oligarchs or internet billionaires have one this big. And I know for a fact they're mad as hell that they don't. But that's not surprising since envy and jealousy run deep in the veins of billionaires." He picked up a landline and ordered the captain to shove off. "I thought we could go on a little cruise and talk." He gestured to the yachts nearby and then the sky. "We'll have more privacy out there. You can never be too careful in this day and age."

"Absolutely."

As the yacht motored out into the Mediterranean, a smaller security yacht followed at a distance. The woman in the bikini arrived again and started the men with plates of fruit—melons and berries. Bonhoff ran a hand down the back of the woman's tanned leg before she left to fetch the drinks.

"I hope you like swordfish," Bonhoff said. "We caught it this morning. It's better when it's fresh. We'll have dessert later."

Once the yacht was anchored offshore, Bonhoff looked around at the vast openness of the sea. Lamont could almost see the man's mind dreaming, or most likely plotting, something big.

"Wouldn't it be nice to buy the Mediterranean Sea, Senator?" He took in a deep breath of salt air and gazed out toward the horizon. "I think I could, and then just imagine all the shipping fees I could charge."

Lamont gawked at the man. *Who thinks like that? . . . Insanely rich men like Bonhoff, that's who.* Lamont had no doubt the man had already put a price tag on the body of water and would pay a princely sum to gain control of it.

The woman brought the main dish, and Bonhoff attacked the fish with a knife and fork. He remarked that it was good, "the best," and Lamont hurried to taste it in case Bonhoff wanted to know what his guest thought.

Bonhoff stabbed another piece of fish and shoved it in his mouth. He chewed half of it before saying, "So, you want to run for President of the United States."

Lamont felt a surge of adrenaline coursing through his body. The man across the table was ready to get down to business, and this was what he came halfway across the globe for. Not for the swordfish or the view. He came for the money—money that would help him become the most powerful man in the world. He swallowed and wiped his mouth with a napkin. "That's right, Karl. I think I can win."

"What makes you think that?"

"The Schumacher Administration is on its last legs. The American people want a change at the top. They need hope for a better tomorrow."

Bonhoff rolled his eyes at the canned talking points. "Trotting out the old hope and change again, are you, Senator? You sound like a worthless campaign commercial. Just another run-of-the-mill politician." He shook his head. "I don't give a crap about your message. I want to know why you think you can win. I gave millions to Sanchez and Graham and those losers lost in a landslide. I learned my lesson. I only give money to candidates who want to win at all costs. I like people who can play dirty. People who can lie and cheat and steal. Those are the people who really want it." He threw down his fork, apparently stuffed. "So, do you have any dirt on the President? What about the Vice President?"

Lamont washed down a mouthful of swordfish with an iced tea. Getting Bonhoff's money was going to be harder than he thought.

"I'm working on it. I've started putting together a campaign team. I've got someone who is currently trying to get insider information from the White House. I'm hoping it will give me the scoop so I can be one step ahead of the President . . . or the Vice President . . . whoever is running. I've got a buddy in the administration, too."

Bonhoff frowned. "I was hoping you'd come to me with more than that."

"Karl, I'll get the dirt. But you also have to remember that there is a lot of unrest in the country now. Just the other day we had a riot in Seattle. That was the latest in a string of riots across the country. New York, Chicago, St. Louis. It's been all over the news. There is anarchy in the streets. It has put the Schumacher Administration on the defensive because they can't stop it. It's like a cancer spreading, and I think it's going to be the downfall of the President and the Vice President. I am going to be ready to pounce when it happens."

Bonhoff took a sip of iced tea and set the glass on the table. He sat back in his chair and gave his guest a smile that said he was supremely pleased with himself. "So you think the riots have been productive in hurting the President's chances for reelection?"

"Absolutely. It's really been a tremendous boost to our party. If the country goes down in flames, we get the benefit because the people will give us all the power we want to fix the problems." He used air quotes around "fix."

"Well, who do you think is funding all that?"

Lamont noticed the glint in Bonhoff's eyes. Lamont's jaw almost dropped. He hadn't heard anything. Not even any rumors that Bonhoff was behind it. His eyes widened and he pointed at the man. "You?"

"Hell yes it was me. I'm the only one with the money and the power to do that."

"How?"

"I have a lot of friends throughout the world, Senator. And many of them don't like the United States and especially your boy scout of a President. They consider him to be their greatest enemy, threatening their hold on power. When I have the idea to take down the man, my friends line up to help."

"So . . . San Francisco, Chicago, New York City, that was all you?"

Bonhoff nodded. "St. Louis and Seattle, too."

"And the cop killings?"

"An added bonus. It helps contribute to the chaos. And there is more to come. If the rioting and looting is as productive as you say it is, you'll be happy with what I have planned for the future."

Lamont sat back in his chair, hardly believing the man across the table was the one who had fomented the unrest in the United States. The unrest that could lead to Lamont becoming President. He was still trying to figure out how Bonhoff had done it.

"The politicians in those cities have done little to stop the rioting, and the prosecutors are looking the other way when it comes to charging those people doing all the damage."

Bonhoff pointed at his hairy chest. "All part of my plan, Senator. How do you think those radicals got into office in the first place? I helped put them there. They owe me. Hell, most of them agree with me. They hate the U.S. like I do. This has been a long-term plan to undermine America. If I can't get the laws changed in my favor, I just buy off the prosecutors to look the other way so they don't enforce the laws I don't like. It's worked like a charm. And I target people from top to bottom—from presidential candidates all the way down to school boards. I have put thousands of people in positions of power and, according to you, it's working."

"And you're using Americans to do your dirty work for you."

The man's shoulders shrugged, as if trying to portray some small hint of modesty.

Lamont's admiration for the man was overflowing. That was how you became the fourth richest man in the world—by being ruthless and relentless. It was win at all costs. And it doesn't hurt if you can buy off anyone who can help you accomplish your objective.

Bonhoff leaned forward, ready to get serious. "I'm willing to fund your campaign, Senator. I can provide you with hundreds of millions of dark money. No one in your Federal Election Commission will ever find out where it came from. And no one will trace it back to me either. I've done it too many times to count. Hell, you didn't even know I've been funding candidates for years."

Lamont felt a thrill tingling his entire body. He hadn't known, but with

Bonhoff's money, the presidency would be well within his grasp. It took money, lots of money, and the man across the table was willing to give it to him. The thought hit him that Bonhoff wasn't doing this out of the goodness of his heart or because they were old friends. The man hated President Schumacher, and Lamont knew Bonhoff wasn't doing it for kicks. There had to be other reasons.

"What's in it for you, Karl?"

"I've made billions off of Russia and China. The only one I'm missing is the United States. You give me a country with centralized control in Washington, and I'll make a fortune beyond what I already have." He paused to cherish his next thought. "And I will become the richest man in the world."

"How?"

"Take the green agenda with all those stupid windmills and solar panels. You can say the world's going to end in fifty years if we don't do something and demand an end to fossil fuels. Well, it isn't going to happen overnight. All I need is a President Lamont to cut off the oil spigot in the U.S., and then your countrymen are scrambling to buy two-hundred-dollar barrels of oil to meet their demand for eight-dollar-a-gallon gas." He smiled. "And where are they going to get that oil?" He pointed at himself. "They'll buy it from me and my companies in Russia, Saudi Arabia, Venezuela."

"And Washington will dictate every facet of people's lives."

"Exactly. All of the power will be centralized and run by people like you. Your opponents will never be able to beat you, and the rich will get richer."

Lamont had visions of himself standing in the Oval Office—the leader of the Free World. Or maybe it would be just the "world" because the people would be under the thumb of the elites in D.C. But no matter because he would be running it. His mouth had gone dry, and he hurried to take a gulp of the iced tea.

"What do you say, Senator? I can find someone else to give my money to. There are plenty of people out there who will take my millions and do what I want. That's one of the perks of wealth."

It was all within his reach. Hundreds of millions of dollars were staring him in the face across the table. All he had to do was get into bed with the fourth richest man in the world and be ready to unleash every dirty trick in the book. *I can do this. I can be President of the United States.*

"I'll do it, Karl." He flashed a polished white smile. "I'm going to win."

"We're going to win, Senator," Bonhoff corrected before issuing his orders. "First things first. You show me you can get dirt from the inside and you'll get all the money you need to win. Then you need to start picking off people in the Schumacher Administration. People are willing to jump ship when the going gets tough and now's the time. I want the administration to implode from the inside out. You'll win in a landslide, Senator, and then you'll have the mandate to remake the country and help me become the richest man in the world."

Lamont quickly agreed, the euphoria of the moment washing over him.

Bonhoff raised his glass and offered a toast. "To the next President of the United States."

They clinked glasses, and Lamont enjoyed his remaining iced tea. Bonhoff decided the talk of business was over.

"Senator, have you ever had sex on the deck of a yacht this big?"

Lamont about gagged on his iced tea. *What the hell?* "No, Karl, I can't say that I have."

"Well, today's your lucky day." Bonhoff pushed back his chair and stood. "In more ways than one." He clapped his hands at the naked women sunning themselves, gathering their attention and summoning them for duty. "Pick which one you want, Senator, and let's have some dessert."

CHAPTER 12

The White House – Washington, D.C.

"Mr. President, the FBI Director is here," the President's secretary said over the phone.

"Tell him it'll be a few minutes." Translation: *Make him wait.*

The President sat behind the Resolute Desk. Vice President Stubblefield occupied the seat off to the side. The morning sunshine brightened the Oval Office, but it did little to brighten the spirits of the two men tasked with leading the United States of America.

Both of them had copies of the report on the Seattle riots. Much of it they already knew from watching and reading the news. Some parts of Seattle were still "under control" of the anarchists, Marxists, and assorted rabblerousers who were looking to occupy the areas like had been done in Portland. Snow fencing and plywood barriers had been erected, and the graffiti scribbled on the outside warned all those who entered that they were no longer venturing into the land of the free and home of the brave.

"What a disaster," the President muttered.

Stubblefield agreed. "Those in charge have made a first-class mess of things. The politicians ought to be charged with dereliction of duty."

"It makes you wonder how we've come to this point where law and order are tossed out the window. It's not the America I grew up in."

"No, sir, it's not."

Stubblefield noticed the President pinching his nose and then rubbing his face. He could see the strain the man was under. He thought he'd try to provide some hope.

"Duke called me this morning."

That got the President's attention. He straightened himself in his seat and leaned back in his high-back leather chair. "How's he doing?"

"He's been out at Andrews for the past two days. He thinks he's getting a good feel for this Bonhoff guy. The man isn't easy to track down. Always on the move. Duke likens him to Saddam Hussein. Only stays in one place for a short period of time before he moves to a different residence."

"It helps when you have that kind of wealth. When does he think he can get the operation underway?"

"Within a day or two."

The President started tapping the top of the desk with his finger. "So you're telling me I have to be patient."

Stubblefield smiled. Probably the first smile for either of them that morning. "Yes, sir. We just have to give it a little time."

The President took a deep breath and exhaled. "All right. I guess we should see what the FBI has to say. Hopefully Kurt can give us some good news on the home front while we wait for Schiffer."

Both men stood. The President picked up the phone and pushed the button for his secretary. "Send Director Duncan in."

The door to the Oval Office opened and in walked Director Duncan. He had a smile on his face when he extended a hand. It was the only smile in the room.

"Good morning, Mr. President. Good to see you."

The President shook the man's hand. "Kurt."

Director Duncan turned to the big man next to the President. "Mr. Vice President, always a pleasure."

Stubblefield nodded but said nothing.

"Let's get down to business," the President said, motioning for the Director to take a seat on one of the couches. The President took one of the chairs in front of the fireplace and the Vice President took the other.

"Tell us what you know, Kurt."

Director Duncan situated himself and started rattling off the figures that everyone already knew. Approximately a thousand rioters descended on Seattle two nights before and caused close to $2 million in damage.

"The protest is still ongoing."

The President interrupted. "It's not a protest, Kurt. It's a siege. A violent and unlawful siege of an American city. You need to start treating it as such."

"Yes, sir." Duncan swallowed and continued. "We don't have any leads on who the ringleader is or how it was all coordinated."

The President asked. "How many agents do you have working on this?"

"On what specifically?"

"On the riots, Kurt. And hopefully preventing any future riots."

"I have deployed assets to Seattle, Mr. President. Ten agents from Los Angeles and two from Las Vegas." He made a point to look at Stubblefield as well. "But, as you two both know, it takes time to conduct a thorough investigation."

"What about the rest of the country?"

"In terms of what, sir?"

The President pounded the armrest. "The riots, Kurt! I know you've been out of the country lately, but I shouldn't have to tell you that we've had riots in San Francisco, New York City, Chicago, St. Louis. It's all over the damn country!" He pounded the armrest again. "And I want to know what the hell the FBI is doing about it."

Duncan held out his hand. "I'm sorry, sir. I was just trying narrow down what you were asking about. Yes, I'm well aware of what's going on. I have multiple teams at Headquarters who are sifting through all the evidence and videos taken during the events and—"

"They're not 'events', Kurt," the Vice President said. "They're riots, domestic terrorism, an insurrection. It's not an event. It needs to be stopped. Right now."

The Director looked like he wanted to fire back but he didn't, apparently realizing he was outnumbered. "I can assure you both that the FBI is working night and day to bring to justice those responsible and to prevent future . . ." He looked at the Vice President. "Acts of riots, domestic terrorism, or insurrection."

The President seemed to let the silence that followed hang in the air for dramatic effect, like the thought of firing Director Duncan on the spot was one of the possibilities on how things could go. Stubblefield glanced over at him, himself wondering what he was going to do.

"I've got to tell you, Kurt, I'm not happy with your performance. I haven't seen a press conference out of you or any statements put out by the FBI. Maybe I can chalk it up to you being so busy hunting down these criminals that you don't have time. All I see on TV are burning cities and lawlessness in the streets. I want to start seeing arrests. I want to start seeing the FBI breaking down doors of these pricks before they can burn down another American city." The President shook his head, his voice drifted off. "I'm not happy, Kurt."

"I'll do my best, sir. We'll get 'em."

Stubblefield saw the muscles in the President's neck tense.

The President stood, and Duncan snapped to attention. "Well get after it, Kurt." The President walked behind the couch and exited the Oval Office without another word and without a parting handshake.

Vice President Stubblefield motioned for Director Duncan to exit the door to the hallway. When they made it out into the corridor, Stubblefield noticed a handful of Secret Service agents and staff members.

"Kurt," he said, pointing to the Roosevelt Room. "In here." Once the two were inside and alone, Stubblefield closed the door.

The big man put his hands on his hips. "What the hell is wrong with you?"

Duncan looked shocked. "What?"

"The country's on fire, Kurt, and you act like it's a bunch of punk kids staying out past curfew. Have you gone soft or something?"

Duncan fired back. "I told him I'm working on it, Ty."

Stubblefield noticed the disrespect. "You need to get your head out of your ass, Kurt!"

Duncan took a step closer, not backing down. "Ty, this is my FBI now! I know you think you still run it and maybe you're upset that you've got nothing to do as Vice President, but you need to let me do my job. I know what I'm doing."

The Vice President glared down at the man. He then proceeded to thump his index finger on the Director's FBI lapel pin. "Let me remind you of something, Kurt. It's not your FBI. It's the people's FBI. And right now, it isn't working for the good of the country."

The two men stood in silence, stewing over what had been said.

"Are you done?" Director Duncan asked, his nostrils flaring. He straightened his jacket and prepared to storm out. "Because I have to get to work."

The National Mall – Washington, D.C.

The midday sun was high overhead, and the heat of the approaching summer was giving everyone fair warning of what was in store. Still, the National Mall had no shortage of people.

Staffers on their lunch hours from the various big government bureaucracies ditched their heels and loafers for walking shoes, passing the time with music or podcasts or talk with a colleague. Most could get two miles in with a brisk walk from the Capitol Building to the Washington Monument and back. Those ambitious enough to change into their running clothes could get four miles roundtrip with a quick run from the Capitol steps to the Lincoln Memorial.

Buses lined the streets, dropping off tourists to the various monuments and the Smithsonian. Summer vacation had families visiting the nation's capital, and the scooter rental business looked to be making a profit.

No one seemed to recognize the Chief of Staff to the Vice President, Nate Russo, taking a seat next to a blonde woman on a bench under the shade of an elm tree on the north side of the American History Museum. They sat facing Constitution Avenue, a block east of the Washington Monument. He kept his sunglasses on, so did she.

"I brought you a sandwich," Shannon Swisher said, passing him a turkey and cheese sub.

"Thanks. I was glad to get your call. I was getting famished."

They sat in silence, taking a few moments to eat and watch the parade of sweaty tourists march by. Russo had never officially told Swisher that he was going to work with her. Once they left the bar and went to her suite the other night, Russo had more important things on his mind. She was gone by the time he awoke the next morning with a major hangover. She called two days later and suggested they meet for lunch.

Swisher was the first to finish her sandwich. "Busy morning?"

Russo nodded and downed another bite. "Just the typical meetings and briefings. You know how it goes."

"Was your boss hard at work?"

Russo's eyes widened, his mouth full of turkey and cheese. He had a story to tell. He held up a finger and then swallowed. "The President and Vice President met with the FBI Director today." He winced and blew out a breath, like he was glad he wasn't in on the meeting. "Man, it was tense."

"Was it about the riots?"

"Yeah, the President and Vice President were not happy." Russo looked around. "When the meeting in the Oval Office was finished, the boss took the Director into the Roosevelt Room and chewed him out. A real shouting match."

"Really?"

Russo nodded and leaned closer. "He told the Director he needed to get his head out of his ass."

"Wow. I can't believe that. Were you in the room?"

"No, I was outside, but I could hear it out in the corridor. Everybody could. A couple agents thought they were going to have to barge in. And the Vice President was hot afterwards. I can only imagine what it was like to be Director Duncan. You know how intimidating the Vice President can be. I mean the guy used to play professional football."

The two watched as an ice cream truck headed east, its jingle beckoning anyone wanting to cool down with a frozen treat.

"So would you say the West Wing is in chaos right now?" Swisher asked.

Russo took a drink of the bottled water Swisher brought for him. "It's not chaos. Maybe dysfunction would be a better word. The President wants results and he's not getting them."

The phone in Swisher's purse started pulsing. She fished it out, looked at the screen, and noticed it was Senator Lamont calling.

"I need to take this, Nate. Just give me a second. It could end up involving you." She stood and walked onto the grass behind the bench. "This is Shannon."

Senator Lamont didn't waste any time. "I've got the money, Shannon. I want to go all in."

With the rumble of a city bus passing by, Swisher put a finger in her ear. "Where are you?"

"I'm on my way back, but I wanted to call and tell you that I've got the money."

"How much are we talking about?"

"As much as it takes."

"Can you give me a ballpark of what you're talking about? Hundreds?"

"Yes, hundreds of millions and more if necessary."

Swisher gasped slightly, liking the ideas of what she could do with an open checkbook. "Can you tell me where it's coming from?"

"No, not right now. Not over the phone."

"But it's big?"

"Oh, yeah. It's big. It might take some work to make sure it's coming through the proper channels, but it'll be worth it."

"When do you want me to start?"

"Today. Get the ball rolling."

"When will you announce?"

"Soon. We'll talk about the best time once I get back. You're going to make a ton of money, and I had better be your only client for the foreseeable future, Shannon. We're going to win the presidency."

Swisher looked at the back of Russo's head and smiled. She knew it was big and that meant it was going to make her rich. "Thank you, Senator. I can't wait."

Russo crumpled up the sandwich wrapper. He swallowed his last mouthful and waited for her to rejoin him. "Big news?"

Swisher took a seat next to him. "Yes. It's big, Nate."

"What is it?"

Swisher frowned. "I can't tell you. It's not official yet." She patted him on the leg. "But it is big, and you need to start thinking about the future. Your future."

Russo looked east over Swisher's shoulder toward the Capitol Building. "So you still want me to jump ship?"

Swisher shook her head. "No, not yet. There will be a time for that, but we need you on the inside to keep us abreast on what's going on. Just like today about the FBI Director. It's good to know things like that." When Nate winced, Swisher knew he was struggling with the thoughts of being a leaker. "I'm not asking you to do anything illegal, Nate. You said it yourself that everyone heard the Veep chewing out Director Duncan. All I'm asking you to do is be my eyes and ears so I can shock the world."

"I don't know."

"Nate, it's going to happen, and I want you to be on the right side of history. You need to get out in front of this while you can. When the Schumacher-Stubblefield Administration goes down in flames, your prospects of finding a job in this town will go down the drain with it."

"I gave you information today, Shannon. I think you could at least give me something in return."

Swisher's cheeks rose and, thinking she was going to have to go the extra mile again, reached out and touched Russo's thigh. "Ooh, Nate. Are you feeling frisky again?"

Russo grabbed her wrist and shoved her arm back. "I'm not talking about that, Shannon. I think I deserve to know what you're up to. This is my career you're asking me to put on the line."

With her flirting unsuccessful, Swisher tried to regroup. "Nate, I haven't seen this side of you." She leaned forward and whispered. "I kind of like it. Very manly."

"I'm serious, Shannon. I can go find someone else to work for. The Vice President's Chief of Staff still carries some weight on a resume."

Swisher looked down and flicked a crumb off her pantsuit. Then she turned her eyes toward the Capitol and over her shoulder toward the White House. A glance at the Washington Monument and then over Russo's shoulder to the south and the Jefferson Memorial convinced her no one was in earshot. She motioned for him to come closer and then put her hand in front of her mouth.

"Senator Lamont is going to run for President. That was him on the phone. He's got the money to win, Nate. He's going to be the first one out of the gate and he's going to have so much money behind him he won't have any competition in the primaries." She leaned back and looked at her baby blue fingernail polish. "It'll be a two-horse race in the general election between him and the President. Or the Vice President, whoever it may be."

She let two runners lope by.

"I can set up a meeting if you want. I'll tell him you want the Chief of Staff position and see what he thinks. I know he'll be interested in getting someone of your caliber. He's Harvard, too. First in his class, just like you." When he didn't respond, she stood. He did the same. "Take it or leave it, Nate. I can find someone else if you're not interested." She reached out and touched his arm. "But you're the one I want."

Russo nodded, and Swisher turned to walk away, wanting to force him into making a decision. With all she knew about Russo, his urges, and his innermost desires, she didn't think it would take long.

"Shannon."

Hearing her name, Swisher stopped before entering the crosswalk. Apparently it didn't take but a few seconds. She hid her smile and turned back toward Russo.

"Yeah?"

Russo threw the sandwich paper in a trash receptacle. "I'll do it."

Swisher's smile returned. "You won't regret it, Nate. Let's get together tonight and celebrate."

CHAPTER 13

National Security Agency Headquarters – Fort Meade, Maryland

For the better part of two days, Duke Schiffer had holed himself up in a windowless office at Joint Base Andrews, poring over CIA intelligence reports and anything else he could find on Karl Bonhoff. Much of it was public information driven by the notoriety of being one of the wealthiest men on the planet, but the CIA and other intelligence agencies around the world had been giving him a look just in case.

Once he had a basic understanding of Bonhoff, his potential whereabouts, and how the man operated his personal life and businesses, Schiffer needed something only certain agencies of the United States Government could provide—electronic surveillance.

He drove his Jeep from Joint Base Andrews up to Fort Meade, Maryland, home to the National Security Agency, located halfway between Washington, D.C. and Baltimore. There, with its giant satellite dishes and supercomputers, the NSA can eavesdrop on telephone calls and internet traffic from the farthest corners of the globe. Schiffer was going to need everything the NSA could magically pick out of the air to pull off this mission.

Deputy Director Bruce Mason met him at a private entrance. "Mr. Schiffer?"

"Yes."

"I was told by Vice President Stubblefield to offer any help the NSA can provide."

Schiffer liked the guy's clipped offer. He didn't ask questions. "Good. Thank you."

They walked inside, the building quiet as workers eyed their computer screens. The man stopped Schiffer outside an office and asked for a second before disappearing. He came back out followed by a young man wearing thick, black-rimmed glasses.

"Mr. Schiffer, this is Dustin Borden. He is one of our top technicians, and he is at your disposal for as long as you need him."

Off the record, Deputy Director Mason said Dustin could hack into anywhere at any time and the Agency paid him well to make sure his skills were used for the country's good, and not anyone else's. He was also an expert in electronic surveillance, which only added to his worth. Mason said he would leave the two alone to get acquainted and begin work on whatever it was Schiffer had permission from the Vice President to do.

Just the two of them, Schiffer eyed the man, who acted like making eye contact was painful for him. He had a ponytail, which Schiffer disliked, especially on men. They tended to be pulled, and in his line of work, provided the enemy with an unfair advantage. At least it wasn't a manbun, Schiffer thought. That would have been a whole other matter.

Schiffer stuck out his hand. "I'm Duke, nice to meet you."

Borden looked at the outstretched hand, acting like he wasn't sure whether he was going to get smacked or something. He didn't offer a full handshake, just his fingers.

"How long have you worked here?"

"Five years."

"You know what you're doing?"

"Yes, sir."

When the man turned his head to the side after a coworker passed, Schiffer noticed the ponytail again. If the guy sat behind a computer all day, it wouldn't be a problem. Plus, he liked the man's answers—quick and to the point.

"Well, good. Because I'm going to be asking a lot from you in the coming days. I need you to be ready to take my calls or texts twenty-four-seven. You got that?"

"Yes, sir."

"If I give you someone's phone number, can you tell me where the phone is located?"

"Yes, sir."

"How long will it take?"

Borden adjusted his glasses. "It depends on the phone. Some people have phones that are a lot harder to track than others. Foreign intelligence agencies, for one. Could take me five minutes or thirty."

Schiffer liked that Borden didn't say it was impossible, just that it would take time. "How close can you get me to the phone's location?"

"Within a hundred feet."

That's just what Schiffer wanted to hear. He gave Borden a list of numbers, designating them as Alpha, Bravo, Charlie, and beyond, and said he wanted to know where the phones were at any moment of the day.

"Yes, sir."

"When I call, I'm going to say I want to know where Alpha's phone is located."

Dustin nodded. "Okay. But who's Alpha?"

"You don't need to know who they are. The other thing is I want a phone that won't let anyone do the same to me. Do you have anything like that?"

"Yes, sir. I'll have to call Deputy Director Mason, but he will be able to authorize it."

"Good. Now, go find me the location of the phones for Alpha, Bravo, and Charlie."

Borden scurried back into his office, his ponytail swinging back and forth.

As he waited, Schiffer took out his own phone and went back to studying Bonhoff. The man was elusive, preferring to make his billions in the shadows instead of the corporate boardrooms. The Vice President had told Schiffer that Bonhoff had multiple homes and satellite images revealed they were substantial. The estates in Switzerland and Spain were practically fortresses. There was a megayacht, a custom 757 jet, and five executive helicopters to ferry him to each of his estates. It all provided possibilities.

Borden returned within an hour, a determined look on his face.

"What did you find out about Alpha?"

"London."

"Bravo?"

"Geneva."

"Charlie?"

"Paris."

"Good work. Looks like I'm going to London."

Borden handed Schiffer a phone and said it was the best the NSA had to offer. About the only person who could hack into it or track it would be Borden himself. "Thanks, Dustin. Be ready to take my calls in the next few days."

Schiffer drove back to Joint Base Andrews and grabbed his bags. He called the Vice President from on board one of the CIA's G550 executive jets. He told his boss the cooperation from those involved had been appreciated and proven fruitful. He mentioned some guy named Dustin might be helpful if they ever needed him in the future. There had been no questions asked when Schiffer said he needed a flight to London—"like right now." He was in the air less than an hour later.

"London, huh?" Stubblefield asked, obviously intrigued.

"Yeah. I probably shouldn't say any more over the phone."

"Roger that. Keep me informed when you can."

"I will."

"Good luck."

Schiffer called Alexandra next and told her he was traveling. He deflected so many of her questions that she finally asked why he called.

"I wanted to hear your voice."

He could hear her sniffling in the background. "Please be careful, Duke. Come back to me."

"I will, my love. I forgot to tell you the Vice President said he's looking forward to the wedding at the Cathedral." The comment seemed to buoy her spirits, and they said their "I love yous" before ending the call.

After two hours of sleep, Schiffer awoke and looked at the file he had created. Routine intelligence gathering had indicated Bonhoff had been in Monaco recently, but it was believed he was on the move and heading to London.

Schiffer was glad Bonhoff didn't go to Paris. The gendarmes in the City of Light were still miffed at some of Schiffer's methods, and it was always best to avoid the city if he was intent on doing business. And he was all business now.

Schiffer flipped the file to London. Ten years prior, Bonhoff had purchased the 9,000-square foot house near Knightsbridge and South Kensington on Exhibition Road, a three-block walk from Hyde Park and another six from Kensington Palace. The house had five floors, seven bedrooms, marble flooring, and, at the time of purchase, a $30-million price tag. It was the smallest and cheapest of Bonhoff's homes, but he felt the need to own property in London to keep up with the Joneses and, if the royals ever decided to put one of their palaces up for sale, he would be first in line. Schiffer jotted down the fact that parking was off-street.

Schiffer had discovered the layout of the place from the website of the realtor, a man who bragged about all of the high-end properties he had sold over the years, most of them in the million-dollar range. Satellite views revealed a handful of embassies in the area—Iraq, Bulgaria, Gabon, Oman—none of which would be particularly helpful to his mission. He knew this wasn't going to be easy.

London, England

He landed at Heathrow a little before noon. He showed a fake passport to anyone who asked and was picked up by a man in a van who spoke perfect English—American English, most likely Texas.

"I've been instructed to offer any assistance you need, sir," the man said, looking into the rearview mirror at Schiffer on the bench seat in the back.

"Good to know. Thank you." He figured the man was with the American Embassy, most likely with the CIA or possibly the Defense Department. Schiffer didn't ask, and the man behind the wheel didn't offer.

"The bag you requested is behind your seat."

Schiffer looked behind him and found the bag. As they sped east toward London, he unzipped the bag and found a Glock 43X, a holster, spare magazines, and a silencer. There was also a syringe encased in a tube with red biohazard tape across the upper half, the warnings thereon offering a pretty good indication that its contents were not to be injected without great thought of the resulting consequences. He clipped the holster to his belt at the small of his back. One magazine went into his left pocket and the silencer in the right. The tube containing the syringe he gently placed in the inner pocket of his jacket.

"You want me to take you to the Embassy or your hotel?"

"Hyde Park."

The man's eyes spent a few extra seconds looking in the mirror. "You going sightseeing?"

Schiffer jammed the magazine into the grip and racked the slide, the noise reverberating in the van's interior. "No . . . hunting."

The man nodded and focused his eyes on the road. They continued on in silence until they closed in on the outskirts of London.

"Drop me off outside the Hyde Park Hilton."

"Yes, sir."

Schiffer fished out a flat cap from the bag and put it on his head. The sunglasses were not flashy, but they would hide his eyes from anyone wanting a better look. He sent a text to his new friend Dustin that said, *Be ready. I might need you shortly.*

"Coming up on the Hilton, sir."

Schiffer readied to exit. "Take my bag to the Embassy. Have someone on standby in case I need to get back to the airport."

"Yes, sir." The driver pulled to a stop, and Schiffer opened the door. "Happy hunting," the man said.

Schiffer crossed Bayswater Road and entered Hyde Park. As hoped, the approaching summer had yet to find its way to London, and with the temperature in the mid-sixties, the tan jacket he was wearing would not raise any suspicions but would easily hide his gun. He walked south along the Serpentine until he found the Park's exit toward Exhibition Road.

Schiffer used his thumbs to type out *Location for Alpha* on his phone and sent it.

Dustin responded within sixty seconds. *London.*

Schiffer put the phone in his jacket pocket and felt for the gun at his back. From behind his glasses, he glanced up and noticed the surveillance cameras seemingly on every corner. He checked the map of London on his phone and tapped his breast pocket that contained some cash and a card for the London Underground. The nearest Tube stops were west at High Street Kensington and east at Knightsbridge Underground.

He crossed the street and headed south toward Bonhoff's residence. Just like in D.C., the tourists were out in force, but they dropped off in that part of London. Nobody was looking to take a picture of the High Commission of Jamaica.

Schiffer hitched his belt slightly. Bonhoff's residence, 167 Prince's Gate, was connected with three others, all of them stately. A security fence led to the parking area. Schiffer made note that the fence was easily scalable. The parking lot might provide a nice dark place to put a bullet in someone's skull. He continued past the individual entrances, the white pillars listing an address—164 Prince's Gate, 165, 166. The last set of pillars had no 167.

But the black front door did. He noticed two stone lions guarding the front stoop. There was a mail slot in the door, which was most likely quite heavy. He turned left at the corner and continued alongside the wrought-iron black gate.

Schiffer tapped a message on his phone as he walked. *Where's Alpha?*

Same spot came the quick reply.

Schiffer walked to the next block and made his way back toward Hyde Park. He hailed a cab.

"Good day to you, sir," the driver said.

"Vauxhall Cross."

"Very good, sir."

The driver made quick work of London traffic, crossed the River Thames using the Vauxhall Bridge, and pulled to a stop in an open spot. Schiffer paid the fare and exited. As he crossed the street and headed north, he kept his head down. The new U.S. Embassy in London was just a few minutes of a walk to the south. But he went north.

Schiffer knew the area, had been there before, and knew the capabilities of the people now in between him and the river. He had a good feeling someone inside MI-6, Britain's Secret Intelligence Service, was watching him and everyone else on the sidewalk at that very moment.

What he didn't know was what the target was doing in the area.

Where's Alpha?

Same spot.

Schiffer stopped and brought the phone close to his chest. He loved surveillance cameras when he was looking for bad guys, but right now he didn't want anyone peering into the message on his screen.

Are you sure he's here?

Yes. At least his phone is.

Schiffer pecked out a response. *Where exactly?*

It appears to be a restaurant. Albert Embankment and Glasshouse Walk.

Schiffer pulled the flat cap lower on his forehead and crossed the street. "What is he doing here?" he muttered to himself. The hunt had made him sweat, and he gave a couple tugs of his jacket to get some air.

He slowed when he neared the restaurant, a place with outdoor seating under large umbrellas. Leafy trees provided plenty of shade, and it looked like the eatery was doing a brisk business that afternoon.

The man had to be close, but what was he doing so close to MI-6 Headquarters? Schiffer tapped the letter *Alpha* on the screen.

Still there.

A motorbike roared up the street. There was a darkened SUV across the street out front of an office building. Schiffer couldn't see the driver. A double-decker bus rumbled by and blocked his view, so he focused on the restaurant umbrellas.

And there the man was—sitting by himself at a restaurant. How could that be?

Schiffer almost muttered an expletive. He left the sidewalk next to the road and took the one next to the line of restaurants, delicatessens, and wine bars that ran in a line underneath the train tracks.

The man had his back to Schiffer now. Schiffer could see the black SUV over the man's shoulder. It was still stationary across the street. He got his bearings. He had a clear view of the man now. He was at a table, alone, a knife and fork in his hands.

Schiffer patted the pocket of his jacket, the tube with the syringe still there.

He walked closer. Ten feet now. The SUV across the street was still sitting in the same spot. Schiffer stepped through the opening of a short wall surrounding the outdoor eatery. Five feet and closing. Schiffer wanted it as quiet as possible. Spooking the target could lead to problems. He didn't want to make a scene. The man was using a fork to put a piece of food into his mouth. The doors to the SUV were opening. There was a man stepping out.

Two feet now.

Schiffer put his right hand on the man's back and gripped the man's left arm. The knife in the man's left hand froze.

"Don't move," he whispered in the man's ear. "Drop the knife."

CHAPTER 14

London, England

Knowing the capabilities of the man seated at the table, Schiffer quickly moved to the side, took off his sunglasses, and looked at the man face to face.

"Jeez," the man spat out, making the connection. "You son of a . . ." He lowered his voice when he thought other patrons were taking notice and growled, "Are you insane? What the hell is the matter with you?"

"Nice to see you, too, Noah."

Schiffer took a seat at the table across from Noah Wolfson, the "Wolf," and member of Israel's Mossad, the Kidon to be exact, a group that Mossad claims doesn't exist but includes some of the world's most lethal assassins. He had a long slim face with dark eyes that flashed with a constant intensity. And, at that moment, they were burning with rage.

Wolfson wiped his mouth with a napkin and threw it to the table.

"Funny meeting you here." Schiffer scooted forward. "I wonder what your bosses are going to say when I tell them your spycraft is severely lacking."

Wolfson cursed again and stewed in his seat. "Screw you, old man." He was not known for his manners. "And I'm not a spy," he spat out like he was righteously offended.

"Don't I at least get a handshake?"

Wolfson had grabbed the knife again and had the look of a guy who wanted to take a few swipes at the man across the table. They had met a few years back when the Ambassador to Egypt, Alexandra Julian, was kidnapped along with Ayala Rosenthal, the Israeli Minister of Education. Schiffer, Wolfson, and Rosenthal's husband, Ariel Segel, were tasked with rescuing the two women from behind enemy lines in Cairo. They were all lucky to have made it out alive, especially Wolfson. Whenever he had the chance, Schiffer liked to remind the man across from him that he saved his life when he gunned down five terrorists preparing to throw the captured Wolfson off the roof of the Egyptian Museum of Antiquities. Schiffer was still waiting for the thank you card.

Wolfson gritted his teeth and reached out to offer his hand—the one without the knife.

"Does Britain's Secret Intelligence Service know that you're right down the street from their headquarters?" Schiffer asked.

Wolfson glared at him. His glare was normal, it being his usual countenance considering his cold-hearted nature and hatred for most people in the world. He was a natural-born predator with the personality of a cactus. The hatred that burned inside his heart made him one of the world's best assassins, but he appeared a little more ticked off than usual.

"Do they know that you're here, too?" he shot back.

Schiffer leaned closer. "You know, given your line of work, it's pretty risky for you to be sitting with your back exposed, Noah. I could teach you a few things."

Noah sat forward and whispered, "And I could kill you with this knife, too."

Schiffer chuckled and sat back. "I bet you could." He pointed across the street at the black SUV without looking at it. "Are they here for you?"

"No. It's nobody."

"Are you sure?"

"Yes, I'm sure," Wolfson said, sounding offended. "It's a man and a woman, probably married. He's dropping her off after having lunch most likely."

"Are you working?"

Wolfson shook his head. "I'm on vacation."

"Right."

"I'm entitled to a vacation."

"I don't disagree. I just wouldn't peg you as a sightseeing type of guy." Schiffer looked around. "I could use a friend to talk to."

"Why don't you try the next table."

Schiffer turned serious, wanting to get down to business before they start grabbing someone's attention. It would be best to keep moving. "I could use some help, Noah, and I'd like to talk if you've got a few minutes." He leaned closer again. "Preferably away from MI-Six Headquarters."

"Something tells me your talk might end up putting me in harm's way."

Schiffer offered a mild shrug. "Isn't that what you live for?"

After Schiffer paid for Wolfson's lunch, per Wolfson's suggestion, they hit the sidewalk along the Thames and headed north, putting some distance between them and the British spymasters hard at work inside the walls of Vauxhall Cross. They stopped every so often, pretending to talk but really giving each a chance to see if they were being followed. They kept their heads down and covered—Schiffer's by his flat cap and Wolfson's by a well-worn Wimbledon ballcap. They were doing nothing illegal, but when two men in their profession were prowling around a foreign country, the authorities took notice—if the authorities knew they were even there. They reached Lambeth Bridge, which led directly across the river to the home of the British Security

Service of MI-5. They continued north.

"Are you going to take off that silly hat?" Wolfson said, unable to take it any longer. "You look like you escaped from a nursing home."

"That's the look I was going for, Noah." They both looked at a barge making its way underneath Westminster Bridge.

"I heard you were getting married."

"Yes. To Alexandra."

"Poor woman."

Schiffer grinned, liking the guy's constant sense of agitation. "This is a lot more peaceful than the last time we got together."

Wolfson put both hands in the pockets of his jacket. "Peace is a fleeting thing, especially in the world you and I live in."

"Yeah. It's a never-ending battle." Schiffer reached inside his tan jacket and pulled out his phone. He powered it up, made a few swipes on the screen, and found the picture of Karl Bonhoff. He showed it to Wolfson. "You know this guy?"

Wolfson took a quick glance at the screen and then looked like he was trying to peer through Schiffer's sunglasses. Given how Wolfson stiffened at the sight of Bonhoff, Schiffer knew there was a connection.

"Yes, I know him."

"Do you know him well?"

"He is no friend of the State of Israel."

Schiffer put the phone back in his pocket. "That's what I read. In fact, he's a big supporter of just about every enemy your country has."

"He's been on our radar screen for many years."

"And that's why I came to you. He's no friend of the United States either, although he has been making inroads to many politicians in America. Some of them are fully in bed with him."

"Is he behind the riots?"

Schiffer gave a sideways glance. He wondered what the Israelis knew about Bonhoff's activities. "He's bankrolling them. From what our intelligence has been able to piece together, he's been trying to undermine the United States for years. We finally peeled enough layers of the onion away to determine he's the mastermind behind the plot. And it's a multi-pronged plot. He funds political candidates, bankrolls anarchist groups, anything that can weaken the U.S. until it collapses and can be replaced with a centralized power structure. His money has led directly to the deaths of ten police officers that we know of. Needless to say, the President wants to put him out of commission once and for all."

"And by put out of commission, you mean . . ."

"Whatever it takes." Schiffer looked across the Thames to Parliament and Big Ben. "This guy is causing us real problems, and I intend to do something about him one way or the other. This is a big ask, Noah, but I sure could use your help. You're the best."

Schiffer let the praise sink in. It was not something given lightly, and he meant it. The man next to him was a professional killer.

"And I need the best because this is going to be one of the trickiest missions to pull off. The guy has more wealth than we can dream of, and he'll use every last penny to keep us from getting to him."

Wolfson took his time responding. It was a big ask, but it was also an opportunity to silence Bonhoff forever. "I don't work in big teams. In fact, I prefer working alone. You know that."

"I know, but I was hoping we could get Ariel to sign on. Just the three of us." He flicked Wolfson on the arm. "Maybe we could get the gang back together just like old times."

Wolfson frowned. "If I remember correctly, those old times you're talking about had us being shot at by terrorists."

"Yeah, and I saved your life when those terrorists were going to execute you on top of the Museum of Antiquities."

Wolfson looked like he was going to spit in Schiffer's face at being reminded of that part of the operation.

"It might be a chance to redeem yourself." When Wolfson said nothing, Schiffer continued. "Ariel's in Paris."

"How do you know?"

"The same way I knew you were in London eating at an outdoor café just a block north of MI-Six Headquarters."

"You could have gotten lucky."

"I'd like to think preparation had something to do with it. I've got a plane waiting. I was hoping we could get our intelligence services together to determine the best place to find the target and then come up with a plan. Can I count you in?"

Wolfson looked at his watch, as if he was deciding whether he had the time to hunt down the billionaire recluse and be home before dinner. It would take much longer, and there was a chance none of them would be coming home for dinner.

"I'll consider it. Obviously this has to be approved by my bosses or it's a no-go."

"Understood." Schiffer checked his own watch. "When can you leave?"

"I need to tie up some loose ends. I have a morning flight to Tel Aviv."

"I have a plane. You can ride with me. I'll contact Ariel and see if we can meet tomorrow."

"Fine."

Schiffer pulled out his phone and called his man at the Embassy to pick him up on the east side of Westminster Bridge. The man on the other end said it would be ten minutes. He then handed Wolfson a card with Schiffer's phone number and told him to call him in the morning.

"You need a ride somewhere?"

"No, I'll walk."

"Would you care to divulge why you're here?"

"Not particularly."

"Is it a woman?" When he saw the slight reddening of the man's cheeks, Schiffer couldn't help but feign total shock. The assassin was smitten! "You mean a woman actually wants to spend time with you?"

Wolfson gave it right back. "I could ask you the same question."

CHAPTER 15

Capitol Hill – Washington, D.C.

FBI Director Kurt Duncan could feel the trickles of sweat running down his back underneath his white dress shirt and dark suit coat. He had been under the hot lamps of the Senate Committee on Homeland Security and Governmental Affairs for the better part of the afternoon, and the grilling from both sides had been brutal. He reached forward to grab the carafe of ice water to refill his glass. It was his third refill, and the ice had long since melted under the scrutiny from the senators looking to pounce on the FBI's recent actions—all in an effort to let their constituents know that they were hard at work doing whatever they claimed to do while in Washington. One side complained he wasn't doing enough to stop the violence, while the other side said his investigations into the riots and looting proved he was out to punish minorities for some unstated reason.

He couldn't win, and he knew it.

The only reprieve he received was from the junior senator from Connecticut. Senator Lamont saw an opening, and he had decided that was the time to lay the groundwork for his presidential bid. His colleagues would huff and puff about the criminals and the FBI, but Lamont wanted to direct his ire to his future opponent in the next presidential election. He began his allotted time for questioning by thanking Director Duncan for his dedication to the Bureau and his service to the country during "these most difficult times."

"Director, I have a few questions," Senator Lamont said, sifting through a stack of paperwork. "We all know you have a difficult job. The FBI is known for investigating crimes, but now you are expected to prevent crimes before they even happen. It's not an easy job, is it?"

"It is not, Senator."

"Now, I know many of my fellow committee members are trying to blame you for all the ills this country is facing right now, but I want to focus on the Schumacher Administration. Have you talked to the President about the riots and the looting?"

"I have, Senator."

"Would you say the President has taken this matter seriously by giving you all the tools you need to do your job?"

The hesitation and the slight shake of the head that the FBI Director displayed would be replayed on all the news shows that evening. He could have responded instantly, saying the President had given him everything he needed and was fully supporting the FBI's actions. But with a grimace on his face, he offered an obviously diplomatic response, "The President wants the violence stopped."

"But do you feel like you and the FBI are receiving the support you need?"

"The President wants the violence stopped. I can tell you that."

The photographers seated on the floor in the well of the hearing room snapped their shutters furiously. When the Director turned to the left to answer Senator Lamont, who was seated on the end, the overhead lights provided a nice photo of a single bead of sweat running down the side of the Director's face.

"Do you believe the FBI has the backing of President Schumacher and Vice President Stubblefield?"

"I'll say it again, Senator. The President, and the Vice President, want the violence stopped."

Reporters in the back were hurriedly jotting down notes. Later on before their fixed camera positions, many would report on the apparent tension between Director Duncan and the President. Others would claim the Director acted like he was silently trying to tell the senators that he was being hamstrung by the President and they and the American people should focus any and all blame on the occupant of 1600 Pennsylvania Avenue.

"Thank you, Director," Senator Lamont said. "I only have one more question. Do you have confidence in President Schumacher's leadership abilities during this time of crisis to actually stop the violence?"

The hesitation was back, and Director Duncan looked down at the table to gather his thoughts. It was a long enough pause that the President's enemies would use it as campaign fodder. "I know the President wants the violence stopped."

"Thank you, Director Duncan, for your candid responses," Senator Lamont said. "Mr. Chairman, I yield back the balance of my time."

Once the chairman gaveled the hearing to a close, the reporters rushed out to tell the world that the FBI Director had no confidence in the President and the country was in great peril with the current Chief Executive. To go along with it, a CNN commentator breathlessly announced the latest poll numbers to show the President's support tanking across America. He would gleefully repeat the claim every hour on the hour for the rest of the day.

Director Duncan stood and gathered his materials, the photographers still clicking away. A handful of senators came down from on high to shake the man's hand, no hard feelings after the grilling because that's just the way the world works in the nation's capital.

When the crowd thinned and the photographers were packing up their cameras, Senator Lamont stepped in front of the Director as he was leaving.

"Director," Lamont said, extending a hand. "I was impressed with your performance. It was getting pretty intense there."

Duncan inhaled and then let out a relieved breath. "You can say that again."

Lamont leaned in closer. "You got time to come to my office and talk? Maybe have a drink?"

Duncan glanced at his watch. He had a thousand things to do, and one of those would probably be getting another ass chewing from the President and Vice President. With the look that said he'd love to talk to an old friend, he nodded.

"Yeah, I sure could use a drink."

Hart Senate Office Building – Washington, D.C.

Senator Lamont had a credenza full of the best booze money could buy. Being one of the richest members of the Senate, he could import the good stuff, and that made him a favorite of his colleagues in the Hart Senate Office Building. On nights the Senate was in session late, Sanchez from New York and Watson from Delaware could often be found sitting around Lamont's office waiting for votes to be called and passing the time by drinking his liquor. They never offered to pay for it and never brought their own, firmly believing the rich had a duty to pay their fair share when it came to wealthy colleagues and their alcohol.

Lamont filled a glass and handed it over to Duncan, who didn't ask what it was because he didn't care as long as it had alcohol in it.

"Thanks," Duncan said, half sprawled on Lamont's couch. His coat was off, and his tie was loose. His security detail was in the outer office, and he had the look of a man who wanted to sneak out of the window and run away.

"We've come a long way from our days hanging out in the Yard," Lamont said.

Duncan let the liquor slide down his throat and waited for it to warm his extremities. "Harvard seems like a million years ago."

The two had first met as freshman at Harvard when they both had dreams of scoring with chicks, getting drunk, making big bucks, and changing the world. Lamont had come from Connecticut, the son of a Wall Street banker. Duncan was from New York, his dad once the Attorney General of the Empire State when the electorate still voted for moderates. Lamont went from Harvard to the Big Apple to make his millions, and Duncan headed south to work in the Department of Justice before joining the FBI. The two remained in touch and swapped stories when they needed to be reminded of the good old days in Cambridge.

"We had a lot of fun there, didn't we?"

The smile on Duncan's face indicated they had. "Crazy fun." He held up whatever he was drinking. "But the booze sure is better now."

Lamont gave him a few minutes to take the edge off after a long day on the hot seat. Then it was time for Lamont to get down to business.

"I'm not happy with the way the President is running things, Kurt."

"Join the club." Duncan threw his thumb over his shoulder. "I think there are probably a couple hundred representatives and senators across the street who are already platinum members."

"I'm sure there are. That's why I think I need to do something about it." He paused for dramatic effect. "I'm going to announce my candidacy for President of the United States, Kurt."

Duncan's eyes widened, and he blinked a few times to focus. "Wow."

"Are you surprised?"

Duncan sat up, giving Lamont his full attention. "I guess not. I'm sure it crossed my mind when you decided to run for the Senate. Are you sure now's the right time to run?"

"Yes, now's the time. The people are ready for a change. They're tired of the President, and that includes the people in charge in Washington. Am I right?"

Duncan offered a mild shrug. "Well, you're not wrong."

"The President is an outsider, Kurt. He doesn't know the way Washington works. The way you, I, and everyone across the street know how it works. He doesn't know how to play ball to get things done in this town."

"You haven't been an insider that long, Greg."

Lamont raised a finger. "But the difference is, I am fully content to play within the rules of the system. Washington is built for politicians who want to be rewarded for playing the game according to the established rules. It's the classic—you scratch my back, I'll scratch yours. You vote for my project, I'll vote for yours. You change the law so I can make millions in the stock market and hide those millions from taxes, then I'll be sure to reward you on the back end with whatever scheme you've cooked up."

"You're right on that."

"I can beat him, Kurt. I know I can. And I can beat Stubblefield if he tries to run."

Duncan agreed. "Ty would be a pushover in a campaign. He hates politics. You'd wipe the floor with him."

Lamont noticed a spark in the Director's eyes when he mentioned the Vice President. He kept pushing. "You need to think about your future, Kurt. I don't think it's where you're currently at with the FBI. The President and Vice President aren't going to take the fall for their own actions. They're going to blame you. You're going to be made the scapegoat for anything that goes wrong."

Duncan sat forward, his eyes focused on the empty glass of liquor in his hands. Lamont could see his nostrils flaring. He knew Duncan was unhappy with those in the White House, and he wanted Duncan to let it all hang out.

"I heard the Vice President ripped you a new one the other day."

Duncan's head snapped toward his old friend. "Where did you hear that?"

"People talk, Kurt. This town leaks like a sieve. You know that." He pointed a finger at him. "But if I heard it, then it means other people are hearing it, too. You need to think about making sure you're protected for the long term. Schumacher and Stubblefield will be gone, and you want to have a career after they've been booted out of office. You don't want to go down with the ship. And, more importantly, you don't want to let them throw you overboard. You need to think about what's best for you. Cover your ass now so you still have a future in this town."

Duncan licked his lips, like he needed another drink. "So you think I should resign?"

Lamont held out his hands, stopping any such thought. "No, I don't think so. You can still be of value at the FBI." He left unsaid that he wanted Duncan to be of value to him, not the Bureau.

"What if the reporters say that I met with you after the hearing? Will they make a connection once you announce your running?"

Lamont waved it off like it was nothing. "Just tell them we're old college buddies. And you can say you're going to meet with other senators to get their take on the riots. It'll look like you're on the ball and searching for an answer to the country's problems." Lamont smiled. "Plus, I'll be sure to drop the hint with our friends in the media that they should focus their fire solely on the President and Vice President."

Lamont walked over and took Duncan's empty glass. After refilling it and handing it back, he sat near Duncan on the couch.

"I've got big plans for this country, Kurt. The whole world is going to be run from Washington, and I want you to be a part of it. The rich are going to get richer, and the powerful are going to get more powerful. And that means you and me. Once we get full control, we'll be able to do anything we want."

Duncan took a sip. "You really think you can win?"

"I know I can win. I've already got big money waiting in the wings for me to announce. I'm going to bury the President in spending and there's no way he'll be able to keep up."

Duncan shook his head. "I don't know, Greg. It seems like I'd be sticking my neck out there."

"I've got the money, Kurt. And don't forget, we have the media on our side. Once we get a narrative out there, true or not, they'll run with it. It's happening. I'm going to start a movement, and I want you to be a part of it. Let me introduce you to some people who are going to be helping me. You can feel them out and see what you think. I bet you'll be pleasantly surprised."

Duncan sighed like it had been a long day and now he was having to take in Lamont's dream of becoming President of the United States.

Sensing the hesitation, Lamont leaned in. "If I was President and you could have any job in my administration, what would it be?"

The pause meant Duncan was giving it serious thought. "Secretary of State."

"Ah, the world traveler in you is coming out."

"The job does come with a lot of perks."

"You'd be great on the world stage as America's diplomat." Lamont sat back and rested his arm on the back of the couch. "You want to be Secretary of State in my cabinet—done," he said, snapping his fingers like he already had the power to make it happen. "You'll be my first nomination. Just think about it, Kurt. Two old Harvard grads who go on to become President and Secretary of State. Think of the power we would have."

Duncan raised a glass and chuckled. "And I bet we wouldn't have to pay for drinks up in Cambridge."

Lamont laughed and slapped Duncan on the back. Just two old pals yucking it up and plotting to undermine the President of the United States while they're at it.

"If you've got anything on the Vice President that would help me, I'd appreciate it."

Duncan mouthed an expletive. "That guy," he muttered.

"What?" *Go ahead, you can tell me, old buddy. Get it out of your system.*

"He still thinks he runs the FBI. I know he's not happy with being Vice President because he doesn't have any power. I told him that to his face when we were going at it the other day."

Lamont let the man rant and rave, hoping Duncan would unload all his burdens. "So he's not happy, huh?"

"I think he's bored out of his mind. But he likes to stick his nose where it doesn't belong. Always so gung-ho and acting like he's the only one who can save the world." Duncan looked like he was going to squeeze the glass he was holding into pieces. "He acts like he's such a badass because he carries a pistol. It's like he thinks he's Aaron Burr or something and needs it in case he's ever in a duel. I can't stand the guy."

Lamont sat back and let his friend get it all off his chest. It was exactly what he wanted to hear.

"Well, if I was needing someone to give me dirt on the Vice President, I certainly picked the right guy to talk to."

CHAPTER 16

Tel Aviv, Israel

Duke Schiffer and Noah Wolfson landed at Ben Gurion Airport at 1 p.m. A Mossad car was waiting to pick them up, and they were whisked away to the headquarters of the Israeli spy agency near the shores of the Mediterranean.

Outside a secure entrance, Schiffer took the time to smell the air. Every time he stepped foot in Israel, Schiffer could feel the tension. The Israelis were always on guard, knowing one slip up could cost hundreds, if not thousands, of lives. Enemies across the globe had their crosshairs firmly fixed on the country, and it led to a constant feeling that everyone was on edge.

Once inside, they took the elevator to the fourth floor. As soon as the door opened, the man standing in the hall broke into a smile.

"Duke," Ariel Segel said, his arms opening. "Good to see you, my friend."

The men embraced like brothers who hadn't seen each other in years. They had been comrades in arms. Segel had helped Schiffer save Alexandra, who would someday be his wife, and Schiffer had helped save Ayala Rosenthal, Segel's better half. The connection between the two would last forever.

"Good to see you, too, Ariel."

Segel shook Noah's hand and then ushered the two into his office that looked out toward the tranquil blue waters of the Mediterranean. As the Deputy Director of Mossad's Collections Department, which is responsible for Israeli's vaunted espionage program, Segel had stepped back from the role that younger guys like Wolfson currently occupied.

Schiffer and Wolfson took seats in front of Segel's desk.

"I hope I didn't cut your vacation short in Paris, Ariel."

"How did you know I was in Paris?"

Schiffer laughed. How did spy agencies know anything? They just did.

Segel quickly understood the futility of his question. "No, you didn't cut short my vacation. We were on our way home."

"And how is Ayala?"

"She is good. She has decided to take life easy for now and look after Moira. She just celebrated her ninth birthday a week ago." He turned a picture frame on his desk toward Schiffer. The picture showed mother, father, and daughter smiling on the beach.

"That's a wonderful picture. It looks like a happy family."

"It is." Segel turned the picture back toward him. "A thankful family. Thankful that we're all still together. How is Alexandra doing?"

"She is doing well. She's spending most of her time preparing for the wedding."

Segel smiled like a proud father. "I was glad to receive an invitation. I know Ayala is looking forward to seeing Alexandra."

"You three are always welcome."

Schiffer caught Wolfson glancing at his watch, patience not being one of the man's strong suits. Segel noticed it too and opened the folder in front of him.

"Well, perhaps we should get started." He looked at Schiffer. "So your country is looking at dealing with Karl Bonhoff."

"That's right. Bonhoff has been bankrolling political candidates in the United States for some time, and they have taken it upon themselves to disregard laws throughout the country. The progressives don't have a majority to change the laws, so they put in friendly prosecutors who look the other way. It's led to criminals roaming wild without fear of arrest and prosecution. We have evidence he is funding anarchist groups and movements to defund the police. And he is the money behind the riots that are plaguing U.S. cities right now."

Segel twirled a pen in his hand, not acting surprised at what he was hearing. "What's his endgame?"

"A collapse of the system. Government takeover of the entire economy and justice system. Socialism run amok."

"And, of course, he'd have a hand in the government machinery."

"Yeah, he'll be the one who decides the winners and losers, and he'd make a lot of money doing it."

Segel dropped the pen on the desk. "And now your government wants him stopped."

Schiffer nodded. "That's right."

Segel stepped around his desk and dragged a chair closer to the two men. He passed around photos of Bonhoff that had been taken over the years. There were pictures of Bonhoff in a tailored business suit at a climate change conference in Davos and at an economic forum in Brussels. There were plenty of other pictures of the man, bare chested, on his yacht, his Spanish villa, and on a beach in Nice, France. Beautiful women in various stages of undress were prevalent in many of them.

Schiffer looked at a picture and then passed it to Wolfson.

"So you've had him under watch for a while now."

Segel nodded. "Yes, for several years."

"Why haven't you gone after him before?"

"He has mostly been an American problem."

"But our problems are often your problems."

"True, but the State of Israel must pick its battles, Duke. And it must do so wisely. Bonhoff has powerful friends, friends with nuclear weapons. He buys off some, skims off others. If we were to take him out, people might want to take out their wrath on us. There are even some in your country who would not look favorably upon us if we decided to act. We have to be cautious."

Schiffer held up one of the photos. "But you're obviously curious."

"We're cautious and curious. We have to be ready in case the time comes that we have no other choice but to act." He eyed Schiffer. "Or when the friends that we do have in the United States want to take him out, we want to be prepared to offer any assistance we can give."

"Well, this is your lucky day because that's why I'm here," Schiffer said. "President Schumacher wants him stopped. Whatever it takes. So, if you're interested, we'd like to work together on a plan."

Segel let a grin crease his face, letting Schiffer know he had made Segel's day. "I was hoping you'd say that."

"What have you come to know about him?"

Segel recited Bonhoff's entire file to Schiffer. The ex-German was extremely paranoid and lived as reclusive a life as the fourth richest man in the world could. He had multiple phones, one for incoming calls and hundreds of others for outgoing calls. It was thought that he funneled his illicit activities through certain individuals who passed along orders and set the plans into action. That way Bonhoff's fingerprints wouldn't be found anywhere near the scene of the crime. His company was run by a handful of likeminded henchmen whom he trusted but kept at a distance in case they decided to stab him in the back or rob him blind. Segel said Bonhoff has corporate offices, but he rarely went in, preferring instead to do his day-to-day work via computer. The man also hated Jews, claiming on more than one occasion that they had stolen large sums of money from him.

"Wow, you guys have really done your homework."

"Like I said, we're always curious."

Schiffer knew Bonhoff had been on Israel's radar and it was jumping at the chance to get him. He knew something else about his friend. "You cut your vacation short, didn't you?"

A sly grin crossed Segel's face. "When I heard why you wanted to meet, I knew I needed to get home." Segel took a drink of water and then got down to specifics. "There's more. He hates police officers, security guards, and any type of law enforcement authority with guns," he said. "When Bonhoff was a child, his father was dragged from the family home by the East German Stasi. Bonhoff Senior was believed to have had knowledge of subversive activities and tortured for the identities of those working for the West. The Stasi extracted the information from the man and dumped his then-crippled body on the family's front lawn. Karl Bonhoff learned at a young age to hate the police. He also vowed revenge on Germany and ultimately got it when he manipulated the market and shorted the Deutschmark to a tune of billions of dollars in profits. Germany suffered through a terrible recession, and it is just now getting out of it."

"You started out by saying he doesn't like cops," Schiffer said. "Does that have relevance besides wanting to defund the police?"

Segel nodded. "It does. He doesn't like bodyguards. He won't even let them in his residences. They have to stay on the perimeter. He figures that if no one gets in, there won't be a problem. He doesn't have anything against guard dogs, though, so that would be a concern for anyone looking to pay him a visit."

"What about when he's on the move?"

"He seems willing to have an armed guard drive him, but he also has been known to have some bodyguards in separate cars. He obviously has the money to make that happen."

"So now I know what he doesn't like," Schiffer said. "What does he like? Is there anything that we can exploit?"

Segel sat back in his chair and gave it some thought. "Obviously, the man likes his money. Greed and an unquenchable thirst for power could be his undoing if we could find a way to exploit it. He also likes his women—beautiful women. There are women available at all his residences. He has no trouble recruiting them to satisfy his every needs. He's like Hugh Hefner without the magazine and the smoking jacket."

Schiffer took a second to think about all he had been told. There was a lot to go on, and every little bit could make the difference.

"What do you know about his homes?" Schiffer asked.

Segel reached for a binder on his desk. Mossad's file on Bonhoff was more than a passing interest. He opened it and positioned it on the coffee table in front of Schiffer and Wolfson.

"He has a place in London," Segel began.

"Yeah, I know about that one," Schiffer said, remembering the front façade of the place. "I walked by but didn't figure knocking on the front door would do much good. There was a parking area that had potential."

Segel flipped to the next tab. "He has a place just outside of Paris that looks like something Napoleon would have built for himself."

"Have you seen it for yourself?"

"Yes, it's a fortress. We haven't been inside, but it's rumored to have a large bunker. It's a possibility, but obviously the French might not like it for foreign countries to be conducting operations on their home soil."

"Yeah, and when it comes to the French, I'm still on their naughty list."

The next tab showed Bonhoff's penthouse at the Odéon Tower in Monaco. The Israelis had included two drone photos from above—both of them showing a handful of naked women sunning themselves near the pool below the dance floor.

Segel pointed at the pictures. "Like I said, he likes his women."

"From what I've been able to gather so far," Schiffer said, "the CIA believes he might be in Switzerland right now."

Segel nodded and flipped past the information on Bonhoff's residence in Spain. He stopped at the tab for the mansion near the St. Moritz ski resort. Schiffer sucked in a breath at the pictures, hoping Alexandra wouldn't get any ideas if she ever saw the palatial estate.

"This is his Switzerland home," Segel said. "For most of the year, he goes back and forth between it and Monaco."

He provided the particulars of the place near St. Moritz. Bonhoff had it built five years before at a cost of $195 million. It consisted of seven floors, a private ski lift, walls covered with 24-karat gold, a steam room, a salt chamber, a home theater that cost $2 million, and panoramic views of the Swiss Alps.

"This might be the best place to get him," Segel said. "It's the most isolated. London, Paris, and Monaco would have no shortage of eyewitnesses and security."

Schiffer nodded, still gawking at the photos of what insane wealth can buy. "How did you come across this information?"

"We were able to bribe some of the workers of the construction company. That's how we got the layout. There was also a story in one of those trendy magazines about homes of the rich and famous that paid Bonhoff a million dollars to show off some of the interior." Segel turned the page and pointed at the next picture of what looked like an indoor pool. "This is actually an underground lake. The mansion is built over the top of it. I have to hand it to the guy, it's an amazing place."

"Security?"

"Again, only on the perimeter, but it is formidable. Gates, sensors, armed guards. It's not known whether there are dogs."

"What about the lake that runs up to his property?"

"It has security devices in the water for at least two hundred yards out. A boat wouldn't make it, and a swimmer wouldn't be able to navigate the nets and bars without setting off the alarms."

Segel grabbed the TV remote and turned on the flat screen hanging on the wall. He pressed a couple of buttons and soon the satellite view of St. Moritz came into view. All three men stood and walked closer to the screen. Their minds started calculating what could be done to get inside the seemingly impenetrable fortress.

Schiffer pointed at the screen. "There is plenty of space on the grounds to land a chopper, but I'm sure that would be met with quick resistance."

Segel agreed. "Same with parachuting in or trying to come down the ski lift. You wouldn't make it to the front door. And if you did make it to the front door, it would probably take military-grade explosives to blow it off its hinges."

"What about a sniper?"

"Bullet-resistant windows. If you could even get a decent shot."

"Deliveries?"

"From what we can tell," said Segel, "all deliveries are left at the front gate and then brought in. A box truck wouldn't get beyond the guards."

"Caretakers? Chefs? Maids?"

"Long time members of Bonhoff's staff. They all live nearby and are checked every day before they go to work. And apparently they do their best to stay hidden in the background." Before Schiffer could ask, Segel said, "He doesn't go outside much. He has an indoor pool and enough cover that he can enjoy the views in privacy. He doesn't ski either."

Schiffer started rubbing the back of his neck. He knew the President and Vice President were counting on him. But nothing came easy in his business, and this one was going to be tough. Wolfson was standing next to him. The man hadn't said a word in the entire meeting, but Schiffer could sense the man was looking at all the angles to see if he could find a hole, a weak point, anything to give them an advantage.

"You've been awfully quiet, Wolf. What do you think?"

After a few more seconds of studying the screen, he pointed at the mansion. "What about the underground lake?"

Segel and Schiffer chuckled at the thought. When they noticed Wolfson wasn't joking, they leaned in for a closer look. It seemed out of the realm of imagination. An impossible task. *Wasn't it?* They looked at each other.

"It has to get water from somewhere." Wolfson pointed to the left of the mansion. "It's worth a look to see if there are any caverns around the lake. It might provide some access."

Segel added, "There are caverns and underground lakes in that area. It's a possibility."

"So if we can't go through the front door," Wolfson said, "we'll just come up from underground."

"I can check with our intel team to see if they have anything on the geological makeup of that particular area. It's likely that no one studied infiltrating the house from underground because no one thought it would be possible. And it might be impossible."

Schiffer could feel his heart pulsing. He studied the screen again. He actually thought Wolfson's idea was brilliant—potentially brilliant if there was a path from the main lake to the one inside the mansion. All things were possible until you found out differently. It was worth the chance. He decided to reserve his praise for Wolfson for the time being.

"What would we be looking at once we got inside in terms of surveillance?" Schiffer asked.

Segel said, "There aren't any security cameras on the inside. Bonhoff has a healthy fear of the CIA and Mossad, so he doesn't want our prying eyes spying on him. It's been rumored, however, that he does have cameras in the bedrooms." Segel shrugged. "Apparently the guy likes to watch what's going on."

Schiffer nodded. "And if he's recording, it gives him plenty of ammunition for blackmail if he needs it. If we can get our hands on the videos, it might be of use to us." He directed another thought to Wolfson. "Are you good with scuba diving?"

Wolfson gave him an icy stare and then said, "I'm good at everything."

Schiffer looked at Segel and then at Wolfson. "Are we doing this?"

Wolfson nodded but offered nothing more.

Schiffer turned to Segel. "So long as I can get the okay from the Director and the Prime Minister, we'll do it."

Wolfson spoke up. "We're going to need to train beforehand. To make sure we know all our gear works for a water infiltration."

Segel switched off the TV. "We'll need a good size lake that we can use."

A smile crossed Schiffer's face. "I think I know where I can find a lake that will give us what we need."

"Where?" Wolfson asked.

"How would you guys like to see my house?"

CHAPTER 17

Washington, D.C.

The brand-new conversion bus with shiny chrome wheels took up four parking spots on Constitution Avenue at the corner of 16th Street in the nation's capital. Just south of the Ellipse, those in the bus could peer through the leafy trees and see the southside of the White House. To anyone who walked by and took notice, the cat was out of the bag to those looking at the bus wrapped in green and white with the giant head of Senator Gregory Lamont smiling back at them. The slogan, "A President we can count on," was emblazoned across both sides for all the onlookers to see.

The bus was Lamont's first big campaign expenditure, and the plan was for it to crisscross America to bring Lamont's message to the masses. He, of course, would fly by private jet to the next destination and hop on the bus to look like a man of the people traveling the roads of the U.S. in hopes of learning the concerns of ordinary Americans—although he couldn't care less and only hoped to stay long enough to get the obligatory video of him doing the political grip-and-grin with the truckers, the farmers, the ironworkers, the old folks at the senior center, and the classroom full of wide-eyed kids of every color who have no clue who he is.

Lamont stood in the private area at the back of the bus, straightening his tie in front of a full-length mirror. The big day was upon him, and he believed it would be the first of many. He could have announced his candidacy in Connecticut, but Shannon Swisher worried no one would show up to his hometown of Hartford. When Swisher reached out to her friends in the media, they said they would send a camera crew, but none of the big-name D.C. reporters were willing to trudge up to Hartford on a Saturday afternoon in June for Lamont's big announcement. So D.C. it was.

"How do I look?"

Swisher fronted Lamont and made a slight adjustment to the green tie over the white dress shirt. A dark suit coat covered his shoulders and a U.S. Senate pin glistened on his lapel. Conspicuously absent were any hint of an American flag or anything red, white, and blue.

"Like you're going to be the next President of the United States," she said.

Lamont bent down to get a view north out the windows. "It looks like a good crowd is showing up. You've really done some great work in a short period of time."

Swisher had passed all of her other clients to her underlings so she could focus solely on Lamont's campaign. Along with the bus, she hired a camera crew to film Lamont's every move. The video would be cut, edited, reshot, and perfected before it went out to a streaming service for a weekly show documenting her client's run for President of the United States. It would be a soap opera that no one would want to miss.

To make sure the camera crew had plenty of enthusiastic Lamont supporters on hand to kick off the campaign, Swisher had hired six busloads of welfare recipients, union workers, and college students to fill the space in front of the makeshift stage. They were bought off with cash and pizza with the only requirements being that they clap when told to clap and boo when told to boo. Once campaign staffers started seeing large amounts of green grass on the Ellipse, they hoped to ward off any embarrassment by enticing passing tourists to join the crowd with free gift cards to fast food establishments. Signs promoting *A New America* and *Reimagine Everything* and *A Change for the Common Good* were in the hands of those gathered and ready to be held aloft.

"Just remember," Swisher said with her last-minute instructions, "You're the first candidate to announce. All eyes are going to be on you, and you're going to be the only opposition to the President. Focus all your fire on him. We're going to hit the ground running and there will be no stopping us."

"Is the speech in the teleprompter?"

"Yes, it's all ready. Don't rush. Take in the adulation and milk this for all its worth. The longer you take, the more airtime you'll get. It's like free advertising."

Lamont told Swisher to go out and make sure the campaign cameras were ready to roll. He took out his cell phone and dialed Bonhoff, the man bankrolling the entire operation.

"Karl, it's Greg Lamont."

"Senator," Bonhoff said before launching into his question. "When will I be seeing my money being put to use?"

"Today, Karl. In fact, in about ten minutes, I'm going to make the announcement just across the street from the White House. You should turn on CNN. We've got an enthusiastic crowd. It all begins today. We're going to take back America and rebuild it in our own image."

"Good," Bonhoff said. "I'll start moving some more money around. I want a full-court press. I want the President buried in campaign spending."

"Your wish is my command, Karl. I'm going all in and we're going to win."

Once the call ended, Lamont looked at himself one more time in the mirror. With Bonhoff's money behind him, he didn't think anything could stop him from becoming the Leader of the Free World. He opened the door and stepped into the front of the bus. The camera was rolling and it caught the look of a determined man.

"Let's go take back America," he said dramatically. He had rehearsed his line and it was good enough that he didn't have to do a second take.

The door to the bus opened and Lamont waited long enough to get the camera in position. He stepped out into the heat of midafternoon in the swamp of D.C. His hand shot up in a wave, a huge smile on his face. He pointed in the direction of a tree, as if he had made eye-contact with a long-lost friend who had come to join his crusade. Music started blaring from the speakers and he made his way to the podium, stopping every so often to shake hands with his adoring admirers. He took a few selfies with a blonde college coed and kissed a baby that had been thrust in his face.

To show his vitality, he jogged up the ramp to the makeshift stage and threw his arms wide to the adoring throng. The only thing missing were the balloons falling from the sky. He walked to the east side of the stage, threw in a few thumbs-up for the crowd, and then made his way back to the left, placing his hand over his heart like the paid-for adulation meant the world to him. Staffers off to the sides were furiously throwing their arms in the air to keep the crowd's momentum going.

Finally, Lamont stepped to the microphone. After a few more seconds of cheering, he pleaded with those gathered to quiet down, as if the riotous applause could continue deep into the night.

"Thank you very much!" he yelled into the microphone. "Thank you all!"

He began his speech with his vision for America—a new way of life where every need is taken care of and every dream fulfilled. A place where everyone succeeds, and no one is left behind. As President, he promised to transform the country into a land of government handouts from sea to shining sea. No one would be left wanting, and somehow it wouldn't add a cent to the national debt.

"The President's failed policies have done nothing to put food on your table and money in your pockets. This must change, and I am the one to change it."

The reporters who showed up would dutifully delete any mention of Lamont's anti-capitalist diatribe given that the man saying it had made close to a hundred million bucks on Wall Street. They would also neglect to note his three houses and his love of private jets. He went on to offer a litany of "human entitlements" the Lamont Administration would graciously grant every man, woman, and child, including those who made it across the border in search of hope, change, and a free handout.

He continued the onslaught against the President. "He has made our streets unsafe and he has lost the trust of the American people. Our allies have no respect for the man, and he is a danger to the world order. When you elect me as President, I will bring together the community of nations and we will work together to save our world, our planet, and our future."

While the crowd applauded on cue, Lamont couldn't help but think of Bonhoff. He'd bet good money the man had a smile on his face at that moment given the community of nations comment. When the leaders of the major industrial countries colluded to enrich themselves and their benefactors, Bonhoff would be well on his way to becoming the richest man in the history of the universe.

Lamont was beginning to sweat. He had a thought to tell Swisher that next time he needed a stage with some shade. He decided to run with it. He whipped off his suit coat and threw it to a staffer, acting like he was ready to sprint across the Ellipse, scale the White House fence, and take on the President right then and there.

He thundered into the microphone. "I want you to march over to the gates of the White House and let your voice be heard. Wave those signs to let President Schumacher know that his time in the White House is nearing an end because a new America is on the horizon."

The crowd cheered.

"Thank you very much," he said before pumping his fist into the air. "Now . . . let's go remake America!"

The music started blaring again, and Lamont walked to both sides of the stage to wave to the sweaty hordes who were itching to get back to their air-conditioned buses and head home. Confident that his staff had enough video of him smiling and waving, Lamont hustled back to his bus. He took a step up into the bus before turning back for the camera. He pumped another fist in the air like he was riding the wave of an unstoppable force.

He headed for the private area in the back followed by Swisher. She shut the door behind her.

"Well? How was it?" Lamont asked, taking a swig from a bottle of Perrier and sitting on the couch.

"Beautiful, sir," Swisher gushed. "Just beautiful."

He wiped the sweat off his forehead. "It was getting warm out there. Do you think it was a good start?"

"Senator, I think you might have sealed the election in your favor on your first day."

Lamont was jazzed, buoyed by the energy of the crowd. "That felt awesome. We can do this, Shannon."

Swisher started scrolling through her social media feeds and said the press was gushing over Lamont—the new hope for America.

"We have to keep up the momentum. The money's going to be rolling in, and we have to make sure the President gets so far behind he won't ever be able to catch up."

Lamont felt his phone buzzing in his pocket. He looked at the screen and smiled. Bonhoff had sent a text that he saw the speech and loved every word of it. Bonhoff said he was going make him the next President of the United States.

"I can do this, Shannon," he said softly, still staring at the screen. "I can actually do this. I'm going to be the next President."

The White House – Washington, D.C.

An hour after Senator Lamont's campaign kickoff, the President returned to the White House on Marine One after a trip to Walter Reed to get his annual physical and make the rounds of greeting the wounded warriors of America's military. Lamont's bus was somewhere on the road in Virginia and his rent-a-supporters had trudged on with their lives. A few tourists took notice of the President's helicopter flying past the Washington Monument and touching down on the South Lawn.

After saluting the Marine at the bottom of the stairs to the chopper, he strode across the grass. A handful of lucky tourists waved him over, and he greeted them with a smile, a few selfies, and a handful of autographs. Once complete, he started to walk toward the entrance to the White House and gave a wave to the assembled members of the press, who were straining behind the rope like snarling dogs held back by their chains.

With the twin turboshaft engines of Marine One still idling, one reporter shouted louder than the rest of those around her. "Mr. President! How are you feeling?"

The President gave a thumbs-up. "I feel good." He took another step.

"Are you going to run?"

A grin crossed the President's face. "I hope to get a few miles in later today."

"Mr. President, any comment on Senator Lamont's announcement to run for President?"

The President raised a hand like he was going to wave off the question, but then he added, "Good luck."

"Have you made a decision whether you're going to run for reelection?"

He put his hand to his ear like he didn't hear.

"Have you made a decision to run!?"

He kept walking but turned his head. "No, not yet."

"When will you announce?"

He stopped and cupped his hands around his mouth. "You'll be the first to know," he said with a smile that said they'd be the last ones to know.

A rabid flamethrower from MSNBC spat out one more before he got in the door, "Are you going to resign in disgrace, Mr. President!?"

The cameras behind the press caught the President's left cheek rise slightly, like he was trying not to laugh. He continued through the door without dignifying the question with a response.

Stubblefield was waiting for him.

"I see the jackals are in fine form today," the Vice President said. They turned left down the center hall.

"Yeah, they don't take days off."

"How was your physical?"

"Everything's good. The doctor said my knee looks fully healed, so I'm cleared to run as much as I want."

"That's good to hear."

They walked through the Palm Room and out the doors to the West Colonnade on their way to the Oval Office.

"How's the riot investigation coming along?" the President asked.

"I think we might have a person of interest."

The President stopped to give him his full attention. "Oh?"

"Homeland Security and the CIA are trying to put the pieces of the puzzle together." Stubblefield pulled out a folded piece of paper from his suit coat and handed it to the President. Once the President took a few moments to get a good look at the man in the photo, Stubblefield said, "Viktor Kozlov. Russian. Might be former KGB, not really sure of that yet. He has shown up at several of the riots and appears to be the man in charge. There's some thought that he might be a mercenary offering his services to the highest bidder."

"And Bonhoff can bid pretty high."

"You got that right."

The President lowered his voice. "How are we doing on the operation?"

The President had spoken with Prime Minister Meyr and both agreed to move forward with Operation Eagle Claw. At that time, there were less than ten people who were aware of the plan to put Bonhoff out of business for good.

"I'm going to meet with Duke today. I told him to make a list of things he'll need. There's a plan in place, and I'll fill you in on the specifics once everything is finalized. Duke wants to do some preliminary training before the real thing and he thinks he has a place here in the States that will allow for a dry run."

"Does he have a team?"

"Yes. Two men."

"Just three total? That's it?"

"Yeah. So far."

"You have confidence in them?"

"Absolutely. They worked together in Egypt. The smaller the number, the less likely to set off the alarm bells." Stubblefield looked at his watch. "They're supposed to be arriving within the hour."

The two stepped into the Oval Office, and the President said, "Let me know if there's anything I can do to help."

"Thank you, sir. I will."

CHAPTER 18

Near Mineral, Virginia

While in the air over the Atlantic, Duke Schiffer had phoned Alexandra and told her he was heading back to D.C. to talk with the Vice President. He also told her he was bringing along some friends, who he "just happened to run into" while somewhere overseas. One of those friends was Ariel Segel, and Schiffer said he convinced Segel and his wife and daughter to join them on a quick trip to the States. Schiffer added that it was a low-key visit, but Ayala was looking forward to seeing Alexandra again.

"That's wonderful. I can't wait to see them."

"Sorry about the short notice," Schiffer said.

Alexandra didn't seem to mind, just curious. "Does this have anything to do with this secret mission you won't tell me about?"

"Yeah." He cut off the expected response. "So I would appreciate no more questions. I also need to use the house tonight."

"Tonight?"

"For a while."

"What do you mean 'use the house'?"

"I said I would appreciate no more questions."

This received a loud huff from Alexandra. He could almost see her fuming through the phone.

"What do you want me to do?"

"I'm not sure yet. I'll let you know."

Once he hung up, he had huddled with Segel and Wolfson to discuss their shopping lists. The geologists employed by Mossad had been working overtime, and they came to the hurried conclusion that it was possible that entrance to Bonhoff's underground lake could be found through the main lake. There was no certainty in their conclusion, and Segel said they'd have to play it by ear. The underground lake gave them the best chance of getting Bonhoff in his house undetected. And even though it was risky, it was a chance worth taking.

It was decided that Schiffer and Wolfson would attempt the entry with Segel monitoring the operation from a vehicle. Segel started making calls to intelligence agents to get a van, preferably black, and make it so it wouldn't stick out like a sore thumb in St. Moritz.

When Wolfson mentioned the need for scuba gear, Schiffer said he knew a few people who could hook them up with the best stuff. They would need flashlights, flex cuffs, knives, first aid kits, and enough ammo to ensure getting the job done and getting out of Dodge alive. Schiffer added it all to the list that he would email to the Vice President. The discussion then moved on to weaponry, and both Wolfson and Schiffer agreed they wanted something light, accurate, and capable of spending time under water.

The plane had landed at Joint Base Andrews, and Schiffer, Segel, and Wolfson had a short meeting with the Vice President. Schiffer told him the plan and said he could use some help getting the women out of the house that night. Stubblefield looked at Ayala and Moira, both of whom were waiting patiently near the car to take them to Schiffer's house.

"How old's the girl?" he had asked.

"She's nine."

"The President offered to help in any way he can. Why don't I ask him to have a night at the White House for the women—the First Lady, Second Lady, Alexandra, Ayala, and the girl. Maybe they can watch a movie and use the bowling alley."

"That would be perfect. Just for a few hours so we can get some work done."

After a short rest, Alexandra, Ayala, and Moira were driven up to Washington for an evening at the White House. Alexandra had wondered loudly why Duke and his friends weren't coming, but Schiffer said they were going to have "a guys' night out." She had given up on asking questions, so she told him to be careful and said they'd be back by eleven.

Once they had the house to themselves, Schiffer, Segel, and Wolfson started unloading their gear. The plan was to use Schiffer's boat to take them to the far side of the lake under the cover of darkness. Segel would take the helm, and Schiffer and Wolfson would make a dry run with their wet suits and weaponry for an "assault" on the Schiffer house. As to Bonhoff's mansion, it was estimated that the closest place to insert themselves into the water was a mile and a half away. The Virginia lake offered plenty of distance to get in a good practice.

The special delivery from the U.S. Navy provided Schiffer and Wolfson with the top-of-the-line gear that would get the job done. Along with the wet suits, the Navy SEALs supplied some of their newest "jet boots," a pair of thrusters that attached to divers' legs to help propel them through the water. It would save them time and energy, especially considering the amount of gear they would be carrying. Having never seen them before, Wolfson was impressed, which was a big deal in itself.

At nine o'clock, the June sun had finally given way to the blackness of the night, and the flurry of summer activity on the lake had ended for the day. Perfect time for the team's practice session to begin. Wolfson and Schiffer suited up, checked their air and the lighting equipment, and got into the boat. Segel motored them to the east side of the lake and powered down.

"Stay close," Schiffer said to Wolfson, who grunted like he didn't need to be told.

They got into the water and checked the compass on their wrists. Segel handed a M4A1 assault rifle to each of them that they secured to their chest rigs.

"Ready?" Schiffer asked.

Wolfson had already secured his mask. He gave a thumbs-up.

Schiffer looked up at Segel. "Start the clock."

Schiffer and Wolfson headed down into the depths. Once the battery-powered jet boots kicked in, they moved at a quick pace. All the while, they adjusted their goggles and tested their gear. When the depth gauge on Schiffer's right wrist indicated they were nearing the shore, they stopped to let Schiffer extract the mini periscope attached to his chest. He raised it up and let the glass break the water's surface. The darkened house was off in the distance, and he handed the periscope to Wolfson to let him take a look.

Wolfson gave him a thumbs-up.

Schiffer pointed to the surface.

The two surfaced and found Segel monitoring them from the boat. Segel gave them the elapsed time and said they didn't give off any sign of their presence at that depth. All in all, they were content with the first practice. It had gone well, but one dry run wasn't enough for Schiffer.

"Let's do it again."

Schiffer and Wolfson hauled themselves out of the water and into the boat. Segel fired up the motor and headed east. After a short distance, Schiffer pointed toward the north and said they should try a different route. They chose a cove on the north end of the lake about a mile and a half from the house.

"Let's stick close to those docks," Schiffer said, pointing to the landowners' boat docks lit up for the evening. "It'll give us some obstacles to focus on and get around."

They entered the water again, and Schiffer said, "Start the clock."

Schiffer and Wolfson found the water murkier on the north end, but they were able to maneuver around the dock pilings and underneath the boats in the water. Just before they were to make the turn toward the west, Wolfson grabbed Schiffer's calf to stop him. He pointed to his jet boots. Without words he was saying—batteries are dying.

It was not unexpected. The batteries to the jet boots didn't last long, but they could be changed under water. Once the switch was made, the men were both glad they were able to practice it.

Once back on the move, they stopped at the same spot near the shore. Schiffer extracted the mini periscope and extended it just above the water line.

This time something was different. And given the tingle Schiffer felt up and down his spine, he knew it wasn't right.

There was a light on in the house.

Schiffer blinked his eyes to focus, making sure he wasn't seeing some distortion with the night vision. But it was clear. There was a light coming from the second-floor window. He used that room as an office. The three had gone over the plan in that room earlier that evening. He knew that light wasn't on when they made the first practice run. Was someone there? Only a dozen people knew about the operation.

He passed the periscope to Wolfson, who took a few extra seconds to scan the surroundings.

Wolfson pointed two fingers at his eyes, like he saw the same thing Schiffer did.

So I'm not the only one that noticed something out of place. Schiffer put an index finger to his lips and pointed up. They broke the surface and found Segel, the boat floating silently fifty yards away in the darkness. Schiffer activated his comms unit.

"Eagle, you copy?"

"Loud and clear," Segel whispered back.

"That light wasn't on the first time around, was it?"

"Negative. I was thinking the same thing."

Schiffer looked at the house again, his senses on high alert. The first floor was dark. He checked his watch. Alexandra and their guests wouldn't be back for another hour. If they had returned early, he was sure there would have been lights on in the rest of the house.

"Eagle, you see any movement on the outside?"

Segel scanned the yard with his night-vision goggles. "Negative. I don't see anything out of the ordinary. You think there's a problem?"

When Schiffer looked back at the second-floor window, he saw a person moving behind the see-through curtains.

Someone was in his house, and that was a problem.

Now it was time to find out who.

"Cover us, Eagle. We're going to check it out." He turned to Wolfson, who had his night-vision goggles over his eyes. "I guess our little training session just got a little more real."

Schiffer and Wolfson eased silently through the water until they could touch bottom. Just as the operation called for, once on dry land, they removed their scuba gear and sank it underwater. Wolfson took the north side of the dock and Schiffer the south. They readied their rifles, and Schiffer motioned for them to advance. They crept silently through the grass, and Schiffer caught sight of someone walking in front of the upstairs window. The person looked big, definitely not Alexandra.

Could the operation have been compromised? Was someone rummaging through their plans? Bonhoff had the money to buy people off. A whole host of scenarios ran through Schiffer's mind. None of them good.

They moved forward until they reached the deck on the back of the house. Still no movement on the outside. Someone must be waiting for them. Schiffer thought whoever it was didn't do themselves any favor by turning the light on, but he thought it could be a trap.

Schiffer checked the sliding glass door and found it unlocked, as he had left it. The house had security cameras, but they only captured the view of the outside. The alarm system would have been blaring if tripped, but it hadn't been activated. Schiffer didn't feel it necessary when he was close by. He slid the door back, inch by inch, without a sound.

The only way Schiffer was going to find out who was in his house was to confront the person at gunpoint. He whispered to Wolfson that the stairs were the only way to the second floor.

"Cover me."

They both stepped inside, neither of them hearing a sound other than the hum of the air conditioner. The contrast between the heat and humidity of the outdoors and the coolness of the house chilled their skin, still damp from their time in the water.

Schiffer edged forward, gun raised, finger on the trigger. He stepped up the first set of stairs, his eyes waiting for someone to whip around the corner and let loose a hail of bullets.

He kept going, step by step, the carpet silencing his movements. The only thing he could hear was his heart thumping in his chest. He took a breath, trying to calm himself. Acquire the target and fire. That's all it would take.

Another step closer. If whoever was in there had Alexandra and the others as hostages, he'd kill the person without a second thought.

He made it to the top of the landing. Wolfson came up behind him and covered the bedrooms. Schiffer moved forward a foot, a shadow in the office stopping him. The shadow moved, and Schiffer crept closer. Two feet from the door. He fingered the trigger and readied to unleash a double tap to the head.

One more step and he wheeled into the room ready to fire.

"Son of a . . ."

CHAPTER 19

Near Mineral, Virginia

"Evening, Duke," a seated Vice President Stubblefield said, looking up at the man pointing a gun at him.

"What the hell, man?" Schiffer snapped, lowering his rifle. He hurried to hold out a hand when a charging Wolfson came looking to join the fight. "We're clear, Wolf. We're clear."

"Evening, Mr. Wolfson," Stubblefield said, grinning like he knew he had set the two men on edge.

Schiffer spat out an expletive and raised his voice. "I almost shot the Vice President of the United States." He secured his gun. "Are you crazy?"

The big man leaned back in the chair behind the desk like he owned the place. "I just wanted to see how the training was going."

"You could have called ahead."

"I thought I would throw a little wrinkle into your training. Unexpected things have been known to happen, and you have to be prepared to deal with them."

Wolfson had his usual ticked off looked to him. He grunted and told Schiffer he was going to change.

Once the man left, Stubblefield pointed toward the now vacated space. "You comfortable with him?"

"Yeah, he's top notch. No worries on that end." Schiffer remembered the other member of his team and activated his mic. "Eagle, you copy?"

"I copy," Segel responded over the radio.

"We're clear here. You can tie up the boat and come in."

A still steamed Schiffer started peeling off his equipment. "Where in the world is your security detail?"

"I had most of them stay at the end of the lane. The last time I sent them here you pulled a gun on them." He grinned again. "I didn't want you to start shooting."

"I thought they were supposed to be by your side at all times."

Stubblefield shrugged. "I had them check the house. It was clear. There's a Suburban in your garage with a counter-assault team just in case." He patted the gun hidden under the left side of his suit coat. "Plus, I do know how to protect myself, Duke. In case you've forgotten."

Schiffer left to go change into something more comfortable. He returned with Wolfson and Segel and an armload of beers for the three of them and the Vice President. With all four taking seats around the desk, they discussed the operation. Schiffer reported that their training had been helpful. The equipment worked well, and he and Wolfson agreed that it was up to the task.

Stubblefield stood and hovered over the diagrams of Bonhoff's Swiss mansion sent over by Mossad. He had been studying them for the last half hour. It was an ambitious plan, and a lot could go wrong. He had his doubts. More importantly, he had growing concerns about losing Schiffer. The Vice President needed him. The country needed him.

Stubblefield had the power to call it off. He could tell the President that they were going to have to find another way to expose Bonhoff's subversive activities and end the man's plot to undermine the American way of life. Stubblefield had thought it through, and he had yet to come up with a better option than sending Schiffer and the Israelis.

"You really think you can get in through this underground lake?"

Schiffer gave a half shrug. "Only one way to find out."

They looked over the maps and satellite images of St. Moritz and the surrounding Alps. Stubblefield used his finger to follow the roads that ran to Bonhoff's mansion.

"Are you sure you can't just shoot your way in?"

Segel shook his head. "Although Bonhoff doesn't like security guards, he still has plenty on the perimeter of the property, including the lakefront. Armed and ready. Gunfire might not set off as many alarm bells as it would in an urban setting, but it would tip him off. And he does have safe rooms." Segel pointed at other mansions surrounding the lake. "The area is isolated, but there are still enough rich neighbors with security guards and cameras to worry about drawing attention with large amounts of gunfire in the dark of night."

Stubblefield nodded and rubbed the back of his neck. Segel made valid points, and it was becoming clear that the underground lake might indeed be the best and only way to get into the mansion undetected.

"Is there a plan B?"

Schiffer hesitated for a moment while he looked at Segel and Wolfson. "No. If we have to improvise, then we'll do it on the fly."

Stubblefield considered it and then looked at Schiffer. "You think you have everything you need?"

"Yes, sir."

"Have you had enough time to train?"

Schiffer looked at Segel and Wolfson again and received nods from both of them. "So long as the operation is still a go, we're ready."

Stubblefield looked at the maps, studying them one last time to see if there was something he could add to help make the mission a success. It was his call, and he knew full well he was putting the lives of the three men on the line. He was also putting the President and himself on the hook if something didn't go as planned. If it ended badly it would kill his political career before it even got started.

He knew he could call off the operation or put it on the backburner. But that would be the easy way out. And the Vice President knew tough decisions had to be made for the good of the country. He made his decision and looked at Schiffer.

"We need to get him, Duke. And we need to get him as soon as possible."

The three men looking at him all nodded. Stubblefield's phone lit up, so he checked the message. "Alexandra and friends are ten minutes out. Probably time for me to head back to Washington." He called his lead Secret Service agent and told him to get the limo ready to roll.

He walked around the desk and shook hands with Wolfson and Segel. "Thank you, guys, and good luck to you." He pointed to Schiffer. "And keep an eye on this guy for me. He's the best I have."

* * *

Schiffer asked for a moment alone with the Vice President, so Wolfson and Segel went downstairs to wait for Alexandra, Ayala, and Moira to return.

Stubblefield didn't wait for Schiffer to start whatever he wanted to talk about. "You sure you're ready for this?"

"Yes. We're ready." *It's now or never*, he thought to himself.

Schiffer walked over to his desk and opened the top drawer. He reached in and grabbed a white envelope with the word *Alexandra* written on it. He had written the letter on the plane ride from Tel Aviv and debated whether he should give it to her. He decided he'd give it to her on one condition.

If he didn't make it back.

He and Alexandra had met under intense circumstances. Rescuing her from the clutches of terrorist madmen in Egypt was a heck of a first date. But he knew right away that she was the woman for him. She was smart, gorgeous, and just the right bit of feisty to spice up the relationship. If he could dream up the perfect woman—it would be Alexandra Julian. He couldn't imagine his life without her by his side.

Schiffer loved his job, knowing that he was making a difference in the safety and security of the United States. He loved Alexandra, too. He had never met a woman that made him that happy, and he hoped the letter conveyed his love for her and let her know how much she meant to him.

He handed the letter to Stubblefield. "I want you to give this to Alexandra if something happens to me."

The Vice President stared at the letter, like he knew what it was and why it had been written. "Why don't you give it to her?"

Schiffer shook his head, like it wasn't his style. "I just want her to read it if I don't make it back."

Stubblefield put both hands on his hips. "If this mission is too much for you, Duke, I'll call it off."

"No. It's what I want to do, and it's the right thing to do." He held the letter closer. "Please."

Stubblefield sighed and took the letter. He put it in the pocket of his suit coat nearest his pistol. "Be careful." He stuck out his hand. "And come back safe."

CHAPTER 20

Cambridge, Massachusetts

In the late afternoon, Senator Lamont and FBI Director Duncan walked past the Weld Boat House on the banks of the Charles River. It was like old home week for them. They had spent countless hours on the river back in their days as members of the Harvard rowing team. Now, on the weekend of their thirtieth class reunion, the memories came flooding back.

With the summer in full swing, the students normally traipsing around campus were largely absent. Wearing dark pants and Harvard rowing polos with Harvard baseball caps on their heads and sunglasses shielding their eyes, those who were around had little idea that the man on the right was the Director of the FBI and the one on the left could very well be the next President of the United States.

Senator Lamont had yet to receive Secret Service protection since he was not yet the party's nominee, but this was a personal weekend and the only campaigning he planned on doing was begging his rich former classmates to fork over their hard-earned money to his presidential campaign.

As FBI Director, Duncan usually had a security detail of two men who would ferry him around Washington. Some days he would drive himself, saying he needed the alone time. That weekend, he told the guards his visit to Cambridge was a personal one and they could take a few days off. The security team didn't give it a second thought, since no trouble was expected where he was going and most Americans couldn't pick the FBI Director out of a lineup.

"A lot of good times on this river," Lamont said.

They watched a rowing team glide by before Duncan said, "Some of the best times of my life."

The two men had been stars on Harvard's heavyweight rowing crew, and old timers still talked about how Lamont and Duncan led the charge to defeat "the enemy" in the annual Harvard-Yale Regatta four years in a row. Not only were the two men stars in the classroom, they were studs on the river as well.

"We'd get up early in the morning and do our rowing workouts, go to class, and then search for where the night's party was."

Duncan continued the walk down memory lane. "I don't know how we did it all. We used to chase so much tail. It was like every night. Get drunk and then find some chick to score with."

"Or chicks," Lamont added with a laugh. "I wonder if those women even know that they were hooking up with the future senator from Connecticut and the future Director of the FBI."

"Let's hope not. Stuff like that has been known to come back and bite people."

Despite the ex-wife and child he once had to pay off, Lamont waved off the concern. "Most were too drunk to remember our names anyway."

Duncan chuckled. "Yeah, I guess you're right. I don't remember any of their names. And there were a lot of them."

The two men continued walking past the John W. Weeks Bridge. A couple of aspiring artists were out with their easels and dabbing their brushes in their colors. No one paid them any attention.

With their remembrances of days gone by complete, Lamont hoped to steer the conversation in a different direction. "Have you given any more thought to what we talked about in my office?"

They took a dozen steps before Duncan said, "It was hard not to think about. My old college roommate told me he's running for President of the United States. It's kind of a big deal."

"That's right, and it's happening, Kurt. It's the start of a movement."

Lamont's enormous ego had only expanded to the bursting point after he announced his presidential run. Since he was the first out of the gate, he had shot to the top of his party's list of hopefuls. If there were any others hoping to jump into the race, he had deflated them like a three-day-old balloon. Shannon Swisher and his campaign team spread the word in every TV appearance and in every print interview that Lamont's campaign was the best funded operation in the history of American politics. They gleefully told anyone who would listen that they would swamp the President in campaign spending, that was if the President hadn't already decided to bow out in abject fear of the Lamont juggernaut.

"The polls show me way ahead of the President. Some have me ahead by double digits."

"Those polls are rigged, Greg. You know they are heavily weighted in your party's favor. They do it to start a narrative or to try and dispirit the other side."

"Not all of them are slanted. In some polls, it's neck and neck between me and the President." In the silence, they heard a bird chirping. It gave Lamont a chance to regroup and reload. "I can win this thing, Kurt, and you need to get on board."

They crossed the Charles on Western Avenue and headed toward Harvard's Business School.

"I thought you said you didn't want me to resign."

Lamont held up his left hand to stop any such thought. "I don't. Not right now. When the time comes, you can say that you have lost faith in the President's ability to lead and resign in protest. That would be perfect. Or maybe you can say he's done something illegal and you can't serve an administration that doesn't follow the law."

"I don't know of the President doing anything illegal."

"I'm not saying he has already. Maybe in the future." Lamont leaned closer and lowered his voice. "There are people out there who will make things up if we need it. Put out some fake news, add a whistleblower, doctor some evidence, anything like that and it forces the President to play defense. While he's stuck in the mud trying to get traction, I'll look like the white knight ready to ride to the American people's rescue."

"So if you don't want me to resign now, what do you want me to do?"

Lamont shrugged like he was throwing out an idea off the top of his head, when, in reality, he had been thinking about it for a week. "Maybe the FBI drags its feet on the riot investigations. You can tell the American people that the FBI is doing everything it can . . . but maybe say it takes time to see results. The President can't do anything to you."

"He can fire me."

"He won't fire you, Kurt. Stubblefield was Deputy Director when Schumacher appointed him Director. You were Associate Deputy Director and Stubblefield just moved you up a notch. Neither of them wants the FBI's reputation to be tarnished. If the President fires you, both of them will look bad because you've been there and served under Stubblefield."

"They could still fire me and make me the scapegoat."

"I don't think that's going to happen. The rioting and looting are the President's Achilles heel right now. The country is unhappy with him not being able to stop it."

"Any other ideas?"

"You could always redirect the FBI's focus to some other types of crimes—bank robberies or the mob or white supremacists—something that the President can't fault you for looking into. The American people can't blame you for doing your job."

They turned right on Kresge Way, the trees shading them from the afternoon sun.

"You're asking me to take a huge gamble, Greg." Duncan winced and shook his head, like he was having serious doubts. "If your campaign blows up, I'd be left high and dry. If President Schumacher is reelected for another four years and then if there were eight years of Stubblefield in the White House, I wouldn't be able to set foot in Washington for over a decade."

"My campaign is not going to blow up, Kurt. It's gaining momentum every single day. I already have the endorsements of ten governors and half my caucus in the Senate. I have a hundred-plus members of the House, too. People are clamoring to get on board because they can see that change is in the air and I'm the only one who can make it happen."

Duncan took in a deep breath as he thought it over. "Just drag my feet, huh?"

Lamont nodded. "That's right. Or have the FBI focus on something else. There's nothing wrong with directing the FBI's resources to focus on other crimes. Just not the riots."

The shake of the head indicated Duncan wasn't convinced. They turned left on Harvard Way and headed toward the football stadium. In front of the library, Lamont stopped his friend to try and seal the deal.

"What's holding you back, Kurt?"

"It's a big ask, Greg. I've worked my way up the ladder, and I've got a pretty good gig right now. Director of the FBI can open a lot of doors for me in the future." Lamont could see the man's wide eyes through his sunglasses. "And those doors can be very lucrative. I don't have the fortune to fall back on like you do."

And the older he got, that fact gnawed on him every day. His friends from college who went to work on Wall Street were now enjoying the good life with Fifth Avenue penthouses and second homes in the Hamptons. He was still feeding from the government trough, while his friends were swimming in riches.

"Sometimes I think I chose the wrong profession in terms of making money, Greg."

Lamont reached out and touched Duncan's arm. "Kurt, the opportunities I'm offering will be more lucrative than you can imagine. Not only will you have your current job on your resume, you'll also have Secretary of State to add on top of it." He greased the wheels some more. "And who knows, after my two terms, maybe you can run for President. Then you won't be talking about a million-dollar retirement. It'll be hundreds of millions waiting for you."

Duncan placed his hands on his hips and looked at the sidewalk. After a few seconds of thought, he looked at his old friend. "You really think you can win?"

"Absolutely."

"A presidential campaign will cost hundreds of millions of dollars. You don't have that kind of money."

Slightly offended given that his wealth wasn't chump change, Lamont pointed a finger at Duncan. "I've got the money, Kurt. It's pouring in as we speak."

"It's going to take more than a bunch of union donations and Hollywood handouts to put you over the top."

Lamont was getting perturbed. He thought he had done a good enough job of selling his prospects that he and Duncan should have been sharing a beer by then. "I'm getting the money, Kurt. And it's more money than anyone can ever imagine."

"I'm going to need more than that, Greg. Just like the saying goes, you're going to have to show me the money."

Lamont knew he had a little more work to do, but he wanted Duncan on his side. He needed the insider knowledge. The only thing able to stop the riots and the looting was the FBI thwarting the attacks before they happened. The man at the helm was on the verge of joining his side, and Lamont knew that Duncan jumping ship would be the first domino to fall that would send the President to an early retirement and Lamont to the White House.

Lamont knew how to show Duncan the money, and once he did, Duncan's hesitation would end in a heartbeat. "I can show you the money, Kurt. In fact, I can show you whenever you've got the time."

Duncan appeared satisfied for the time being. He stuck out his hand. "Good."

Lamont shook his friend's hand and smiled. They continued walking down Harvard Way, and Lamont was riding high. He pointed across the street.

"Someday we're going to have our names on one of these buildings, Kurt. Just think about that. The Kurt Duncan School of Foreign Policy."

Even behind his sunglasses, Lamont saw the look of a man who was imagining his name splashed across the façade of one of the buildings. Maybe there would be a dignified statute of himself welcoming all who entered.

"We're going to own this place someday, Kurt. We're going to be the most famous Harvard grads of all time." Lamont slapped his friend's back. "Now, let's go get hammered like the good old days."

CHAPTER 21

Boston, Massachusetts

"I'm ready when you are," Viktor Kozlov said into his phone.

On the other end of the line was Karl Bonhoff, safely ensconced in his massive estate in Switzerland. It was high noon in Boston, and Bonhoff was just sitting down to a six o'clock dinner near St. Moritz.

"What's the weather like, Viktor?"

"It's hotter than hell."

Kozlov was standing under the midday sun in Boston's Public Garden. He was one of the few not scurrying to find shade or staying inside altogether. Some hearty souls were hoping for a breeze with a ride on the swan boats.

The solitude gave him some privacy as he gazed up at a statue of General George Washington. The Father of the Country was depicted in bronze riding a horse, a sword in his right hand, dignified, determined, looking off into the distance as if he spotted a band of British Redcoats on the horizon. Like most things of interest in Boston, it was over a hundred and fifty years old.

Kozlov couldn't help but imagine the horse and Revolutionary War hero lying in the dirt. It would be an awesome visual for his handiwork. Bonhoff's money had helped fund Kozlov's operations from coast to coast. Kozlov had everything he needed—from paying for rioters and materials to keep the fires burning to opening the doors of the jails to let the criminals run free.

"A heat wave came in, and it's baking Boston right now."

The weather forecasters were predicting triple digits to roast Boston and much of the eastern seaboard for the next three days. Perfect weather for what Kozlov had in store. The hotter, the better. People without air conditioning had no choice but to head outside and hope for a cool breeze in the shade. Large quantities of alcohol would be consumed, and soon those on their front stoops would have nothing better to do than start drunken brawls with anyone they could find. It was a way of life.

And that suited Kozlov just fine.

"That's good to hear, Viktor. You think now's a good time?"

"Yes, it's excellent." Kozlov spat on the sidewalk. "High heat and angry people are a perfect match."

"Good. That's what I wanted to hear. You did good work in Seattle. The authorities are still trying to take back the streets."

"Just like you wanted, Boss."

It didn't take long for the Boss to start giving out more orders. "It's time to start ratcheting things up, Viktor. I've been dipping my toes into the presidential waters, and my man needs America to start burning."

Neither of them knew that Bonhoff's "man" had been just across the Charles River the day before talking to the FBI Director. It was probably for the best, otherwise Kozlov might have had second thoughts about targeting Boston.

Kozlov spat on the ground. He had a quick thought to scale the statue in front of him and steal General Washington's sword right out of his hand. "How hot do you want the fire?"

"I want a raging inferno that lasts the entire summer."

"I can do that."

"I want the Boston Tea Party to look like child's play. And I want more than some punks smashing windows and stealing purses. You need to start pitting Americans against Americans. Let them fight each other and we'll watch America descend into chaos."

"Consider it done." Kozlov spat again. "When you wake up in the morning, Boston will be up in flames."

It took Kozlov the better part of the afternoon and early evening to get all the pieces where he needed them. The call on social media had gone out, and Kozlov thought it appropriate to include a picture of a single lantern—letting the few who knew their history that the attack on Boston would be coming by land, not by sea. He wondered if this was how Paul Revere felt during the hours before his famed midnight ride. Revere was trying to warn the colonists. Kozlov was hoping to frighten the hell out of them.

His army of anarchists, rioters, looters, Marxists, and other assorted reprobates would come from the Back Bay, the South End, Charlestown, Kendall Square, and everywhere in between. The plan called for them to split up into groups, some in the North End who would head south and others in Bay Village who would head north. They would converge on Boston Common and lay waste to the heart of Boston.

Those in charge of the city had unknowingly played right into his hands. With the bail reform movement, criminals who were arrested were processed and quickly released with a notice to appear. Jails were routinely emptied, and it provided valuable recruits for Kozlov's planned mayhem. No one feared the justice system any longer.

The crowds started gathering at eight o'clock near Faneuil Hall and Quincy Market, and soon the number swelled to over three thousand and spilled over toward City Hall Plaza. The chants started soon thereafter—the angry mob demanding justice for some jailed comrade and retribution against

President Schumacher for his "reign of terror" on the United States.

Kozlov liked what he was seeing. The people were sticky with sweat and mad as hell. He held a sign that said *The Revolution is Upon Us!* and used it to hide his face from the security cameras. Not that it mattered at that moment because the rebels started smashing windows and setting fires.

A donut shop was the first to be gutted and then a coffee shop.

"This way!" Kozlov yelled. It was like herding cats. The mob unsure of which way to go. "Go to the Common!"

Screams echoed off the buildings along with the car horns of those unfortunate enough to see the wave of rioters heading their way. Some abandoned their cars and ran for their lives. The crowd marched south on Tremont Street, throwing bricks and lighting cars on fire.

Kozlov was happy with the progress—the mob was loud and energized, acting like Boston was their city now. They were in control.

The sirens came north on Tremont to meet the rioters, but the cops were quickly outnumbered. A handful of athletic thugs scaled the wrought iron fence of the Granary Burying Ground. It didn't take long for the two-centuries-old grave markers of the Revolutionary patriots Paul Revere and John Hancock to be toppled in a cloud of dust. The crowd cheered, their first real scalps of the evening.

At Kozlov's prodding, the marchers kept going with Boston Common in their sights. Kozlov grunted when he saw police in riot gear heading from the west.

"Keep going! They can't stop us!"

The rioters from the south had reached the southern end of the Public Garden and soon the fun would really begin. Three of the swan boats were set aflame and shoved away from the dock. The heat of the day and drought-like conditions meant trees went up like kindling.

"Keep going! Take the Common! Take the Common!"

The riot police shot off their tear gas canisters, but it did little more than further agitate the crowd. Kozlov tied a black handkerchief over his face. Others came prepared with gas masks.

The surge continued. Those in the Common enjoying a summer's eve were running in fear. A few drunken Red Sox fans thought they would try standing up for their city but were pummeled and left for dead.

A gunshot rang out and then five more.

The rioters were scattering like cockroaches. The police had fired on two men with guns and both went down.

"They shot them! They shot them!" Kozlov yelled. He grabbed a black man and put a gun in his hand. "They killed a black man! Kill them!"

The enraged man took the gun and started firing wildly. A police officer on a horse went down with a gunshot wound to the head. More shots filled the air. The horse got spooked and took off, further adding to the chaos. Kozlov didn't have time to realize he had just started a race war. He would celebrate that later.

"Get them!" he yelled, pointing at the cops. "Get them!"

The crowd had nowhere to go but charge toward the cops, who were retreating as fast as they could. The air smelled of sweat and smoke, the entire Common lit with burning trees. With the cops on the run, gunfire erupted into the air. The surge continued. The Common's carousel was ransacked, and the *Make Way for Ducklings* sculpture in the Public Gardens was demolished.

Still carrying his sign, Kozlov smiled. He had done it again. Boston was on fire. The city hadn't seen this much turmoil and unrest since the Massacre in 1770. Today would be the Second Boston Massacre. Kozlov had the feeling it would be the beginning of the end of America.

Kozlov kept walking. The cops were nowhere to be found. The mob had overtaken the Common. They were in charge. He found his way back to the George Washington statue. He had to do it. He had to have it.

He threw down his sign. "Somebody give me a boost!"

Two men propelled him high enough that he could get on the pedestal. Then he hauled himself onto the rump of the horse behind General Washington. The crowd erupted in approval. Behind his black handkerchief mask, Kozlov thrust a fist into the sky.

Then he set about getting what he wanted. Old George had had his sword broken and stolen so many times over the years that the bronze one had been replaced with a fiberglass model. It made it much easier for Kozlov. With a couple pulls back and forth, he yanked the sword from Washington's hand and waved it triumphantly in the air. The crowd roared, another scalp, and the roar became louder when Kozlov started whacking the General in the neck.

He slid off the horse and then lowered himself down the pedestal. Others were looking to take his place at toppling the statute. That was fine with Kozlov. It was time for him to vanish. He would keep the sword as a souvenir, one of the spoils of war. He stuck it down inside his pantleg and held the end under his shirt.

Mission accomplished.

CHAPTER 22

The White House – Washington, D.C.

The President had been alerted to the mayhem in Boston shortly after it started. He had been getting ready for bed, but instead found himself leaving the White House Residence on his way to the West Wing. Once there, he summoned Vice President Stubblefield, the Secretaries of Defense and Homeland Security, and the Chairman of the Joint Chiefs of Staff to the White House to meet in the Situation Room.

The Vice President arrived first, and neither of them was in a good mood. It had become an all-too-often occurrence lately. On hold on the phone, the President mumbled an expletive when Stubblefield walked in. He flicked his hand toward the opposite end for Stubblefield to take a look at what was going on.

Stubblefield walked to the wall of TV monitors to take in the destruction. Pictures of flaming cars and trees seemed to play on an endless loop. Most of the views came from news choppers because reporters were too afraid to make a live report from the ground. Live feeds from the Boston Police Department showed thousands of rioters destroying everything they could. Statues were toppled and dumped in the Public Garden. American flags were torn down and torched. Total destruction.

Having ended his call, the President punched a button and waited for the duty officer to come on the line. "Get the FBI Director on the phone."

"Yes, sir." The man's voice came over the speakerphone.

While he waited, the President drummed the fingers of his right hand on the table. "What a mess."

Stubblefield was shaking his head in disgust. He was in full agreement with the President's assessment. Neither of them knew whether the police had been overrun or whether this was another progressive city looking the other way as anarchists "exercised their right to free speech."

Either way, the President was looking to put an end to it. And he was ticked off that it had already taken this long. He looked at his watch. "Where the hell is everybody?"

The duty officer's voice came over the speakerphone. "Sir, Director Duncan is unavailable."

The President wondered if he heard correctly. He picked up the receiver. "I'm sorry?"

"Director Duncan is unavailable to take your call, sir."

"What do you mean he's unavailable?"

"His chief of staff said he's away from the phone and the Director had given him instructions not to be bothered."

"Did you tell him who was calling?"

"Yes, sir. I said the White House was calling."

"Get me the Deputy Director then." The President kept the phone to his ear, waiting. He looked like he was going to throw the phone through one of the TVs on the wall. "I ought to fire Duncan right now."

"Mr. President, Deputy Director Lynch is on line one."

"Thank you." The President stabbed the button for line one and didn't wait to find out who was listening on the other end. "Where the hell is your boss?"

Caught off guard, Deputy Director Lynch coughed trying to catch the breath that had just been knocked out of him by the force of the President's verbal blow. "I'm sorry, Mr. President, say again."

"Where is Director Duncan? I've been told he's unavailable to take my call."

"He told me he was attending his college reunion this weekend, sir. He also said he was going on an overseas vacation. I'm not sure when he's getting back exactly."

"Well, find out where he is and tell him to get back to Washington right now. And that's an order."

"Yes, sir."

"And until that time, get your ass to the White House."

The Vice President had been looking at the TV but gave a sideways glance to the President. His boss didn't curse often, but he was letting it fly that night.

Defense Secretary Javits hurried in and apologized for the delay. He set down his materials and made himself ready to execute any of the President orders.

"Get me the Governor of Massachusetts," the President said into the phone.

Joint Chiefs Chairman Cummins and Homeland Security Director Michaelson marched in. Michaelson had been on the phone with the Mayor of Boston and he said the city was in need of immediate help. Michaelson also said he put Homeland Security on alert in New York City and Philadelphia just in case.

Three minutes later, an exasperated Governor Laurie Williams came on the line. A far-left progressive, she had been a fierce critic of the President over the last several weeks and said the rioters across the country were simply exercising their rights and demanding what was just. Now her commonwealth's capital city was on fire.

Sounding like she was out of breath, she babbled on a mile a minute and not much of it was coherent.

The President rolled his eyes and stopped her. "What's going on, Governor?"

"I . . . I . . . I don't know, Mr. President. Things have gotten out of hand."

"You don't say." The President's voice rose. "You're the elected leader of your state, Governor, what the hell are you doing to end the violence?"

"We've sent out messages on social media calling for people to protest in peace."

"These people are not protesting, Governor!" the President yelled into the phone. "They're destroying your city! Call out your national guard!"

"But . . . but . . . we want peace, Mr. President. People don't like it when there are cops carrying guns around."

The President laid down an ultimatum. "If you don't send in your national guard in the next five minutes, I'm going to order them to go in myself."

Javits started nodding his head like he was on it.

It sounded like the Governor was listening to someone give her instructions. "I don't know whether you have the authority to do that, Mr. President."

"I absolutely have the authority, Governor! It's called the Insurrection Act and right now there is an insurrection in your state!"

Someone said something to her, and the Governor finally said, "Mr. President, I'll have to meet with my Attorney General to see what powers I have."

"Don't bother, Governor. I'm sending in the national guard." He snapped his fingers to Javits, and the Defense Secretary picked up another phone. "If you get in the way, I'll have you arrested, too."

The President hung up and started throwing out orders. "Do whatever it takes to save Boston." He asked that the press secretary be summoned and start working on a statement. He also wanted all the news networks to be notified that he had called out the national guard.

The Situation Room was a flurry of action, people trying not to talk over others at the table as they barked out orders.

The President walked to the wall of TVs and joined Stubblefield. "We've got to prevent this from happening again, Ty."

"I know, sir. We're about ready to roll. The assets are on the ground getting everything set." He leaned in. "I'll text Duke to greenlight it."

"Good."

Javits spoke up. "Excuse me, Mr. President, I've just talked with General Thompson. He says the Massachusetts National Guard is on the move as we speak."

"Good. Give him whatever support he needs. Let's start moving federal personnel that way. And be ready for an influx of arrests. We'll need a place to corral 'em. Get the Navy involved in case you need some ships to house these idiots."

United States Embassy – Bern, Switzerland
At 4 a.m., Duke Schiffer received a coded message from Vice President Stubblefield that read: *Look at the news. 11th Officer Down. No More. Greenlight.*

Schiffer scanned the news articles about the "Siege in Boston," as the headliners had started calling the riots. Stubblefield didn't need to say any more. A twenty-year veteran of the Boston Police Department had been killed, raising the number of police deaths to eleven since the countrywide riots began. Three others were seriously wounded along with a police horse. Schiffer could feel his blood starting to boil. It was time to put Bonhoff out of business before the next attack could be carried out.

It was time to exact some American justice.

Schiffer, Segel, and Wolfson had landed in Bern late the night before. They had hoped for a day of scouting the target near St. Moritz, almost four hours from Bern, but the attack in Boston put the operation on the fast track. Given the sensitivity and size of the equipment that they needed, it was determined that the CIA would discreetly deliver the large box of materials to the Embassy in Bern for Schiffer and his men to pick up. That way the American and two Israelis wouldn't have to answer any questions if the authorities checked their plane.

The plan had been to pick it up once the sun came up, but the Vice President's text told Schiffer that they couldn't wait any longer. They needed to get on the move. He called the assistant to the Ambassador and woke him from an apparent deep sleep.

"I need to pick up a package," Schiffer said to the half-awake man.

"What?"

"There is a box of materials for me at the Embassy. I need it sooner than expected."

Still groggy, the man said, "Who is this?"

"I'm someone who needs the box of materials."

"Can't it wait until morning?"

"No, it can't."

They went around and around like that for three minutes before the man cursed and grunted, saying he would be there in fifteen minutes. Schiffer was waiting in the man's office when he barreled in with a full head of steam and proceeded to vent his frustrations in person.

"Who the hell are you? What's your name?"

"I don't have a name."

"Well, what the hell is this about?" the man spat out, now fully awake and ready to make whoever roused him out of bed pay for it. "What's so important that you have to drag me out of bed in the dark of night?"

"It's classified."

The man grunted and fell into his seat behind his desk. He cursed some more as he rummaged through his paperwork. He thought there was something about a large box being delivered. Unable to find it, he decided to direct his ire at Schiffer.

"You think you're some hotshot who can waltz in here and boss me around?" He shook his head. "You people are all alike. You think I ought to drop everything and grant your every wish. What I should really do is go back to bed and make you come back at nine like every other person who wants to do business with the Embassy. We need to start teaching people a lesson in manners."

Schiffer gritted his teeth. He wanted to yank out the Glock he had on his hip and jam the barrel into the man's eye socket for wasting his time. He noticed the official photo of President Schumacher, in a suit and red tie with the American flag behind him, hanging on the wall. He made the calculation in his head and figured it was 10:30 p.m. in Washington.

"In fact, I think that's what I'm going to do, Mr. No-Name. I can't find the paperwork so you're just going to have to wait because I have a thousand other things to do before I act as your delivery boy."

Schiffer sighed. "I could call my boss and have him get ahold of you if you'd like to talk to him."

"You think you're such hot stuff, don't you? Who do you work for? The CIA? Diplomatic Security Service? You're not pretty enough to be one of those FBI types. Got to be CIA or DSS. They both think they can do whatever they want and everyone else is just supposed to drop everything and genuflect in their presence."

With the guy denigrating every federal law enforcement agency he could think of and then lecturing him on etiquette and the ways of the world, Schiffer texted a message to Vice President Stubblefield that he could use the President's help with the Embassy officer in Bern. He gave the man's name and, with a tap of the screen, he sent the message halfway across the world. He gave it a few seconds for the message to reach the satellites and make its way to D.C. for the recipient to register the request.

Then he looked up at the man. When the man didn't speak, Schiffer crossed his left leg over his right knee and glanced at his watch. "Should be about thirty seconds."

"What? What are you talking about?"

They sat silently eyeing each other before Schiffer said, "Ten seconds."

Having enough of Schiffer, the man rolled his eyes and closed his folder. He mumbled that he was going back to bed. He was about ready to stand up when the phone rang. The man looked at the red light blinking on his direct line. Regular people didn't have his direct line. And no one unimportant would be calling his direct line at that hour. Each ring of the phone sounded more ominous.

"You might want to get that. I don't think the President is in a good mood and you don't want to make him wait."

The man gulped. His shaking left hand reached for the receiver, clutching it like a stick of dynamite. He punched the red button. "Hello."

In the silence, Schiffer could hear the President's voice. The man behind the desk jumped out of his seat to full attention. In doing so, he tipped over a glass of water on his desk, some of it splashing his pants and the rest soaking his paperwork. Schiffer offered to help by looking for dirt under his own fingernails.

"Yes, Mr. President!" the man croaked, his voice an octave higher than Schiffer remembered. "It is an honor to speak with you, sir. How can I help you?"

Schiffer heard his name being mentioned, and the man's eyes widened when he looked at the man still seated in his office. He gulped again, really needing that water that he had spilled. "Yes, sir. I'll make sure he gets what he needs right now." The President said something, and the man responded, "Thank you, sir. Thank you."

Thinking the end was near, Schiffer stood. The man trembling before him said goodbye and then managed to return the phone to its cradle. He suddenly had a look of fear in his eyes. "I'm sorry, sir. I think your delivery is in the storage garage. I can take you there now."

Once in the elevator to the ground floor, Schiffer noticed the man eyeing him like he was afraid Schiffer was going to shoot him. The crotch of his pants was wet, but Schiffer didn't know whether it was the spilled water or whether he peed himself. Once the elevator doors opened, the man hurried forward and showed Schiffer where the box was located.

Schiffer called Wolfson and Segel and told them to bring the van to the back gate. The three then loaded the large duffel bags and suitcases.

"You need me to sign anything?"

The man shook his head. "No, sir, you're good to go."

Schiffer invaded the man's space, the man shrinking like he knew he was going to get kneed in the nuts. Schiffer stuck out a hand. "Thanks for the help." After he offered a limp shake, Schiffer reached up and patted him on the cheek. "Now you can go back to bed."

CHAPTER 23

Near St. Moritz, Switzerland

Schiffer, Wolfson, and Segel were out of Bern before the sun came up. Segel drove so he could get a feel for the van's capabilities. Mossad had provided them with a loaded Volkswagen passenger van with two bench seats and plenty of storage space for their gear. The black van with tinted windows had *Five-Star Limousine* stenciled in gold on the side. It looked legit, and anyone in St. Moritz calling the number would get a friendly customer assistant, actually a Mossad agent, who would dutifully schedule the ride for a future time.

But there would be no rides given in the future. There were no openings for that particular day either. And, if everything went as planned, *Five-Star Limousine* would be out of business within the next twenty-four hours.

Upon arriving in St. Moritz shortly before noon, they took a drive through the alpine resort town that had twice hosted the Winter Olympics. It was a beautiful place, even in June, and Schiffer thought it would be spectacular for a winter vacation with Alexandra. The trip down Via Serlas revealed this was not a place for people without money. On both sides of the streets, the brick-lined sidewalks led the way to high-end stores like Omega, Cartier, Stefano Ricci, Valentino, Ralph Lauren, Gucci, and Michael Kors. Louis Vuitton was hurriedly working to remodel his space so he could start peddling his wares again.

With Segel and Wolfson up front, Schiffer scanned the surroundings from the first-row bench seat.

"The looters in my country would be salivating right now if they could see all the wealth of possibilities."

Nearby, the Palace Hotel had a room available for a thousand bucks a night. Others in the price range highlighted their posh, stately, and lavish accommodations. Free parking and breakfast included. A sign on a restaurant window was already advertising for the upcoming Oktoberfest in late September. And like every glamorous playground where the high rollers were known to flock, a casino beckoned one and all to part with their money. Drinks were on the house.

"These streets are narrow," Segel said, maneuvering the van between the sidewalks and bollards. "Let's hope we don't have to make a mad dash through this part of town."

Schiffer and Wolfson agreed.

"Not a lot of cameras, though. That's surprising."

"Maybe they're just well hidden," Schiffer said, looking for the usual black globes watching people's every move.

The three men noticed the usual summer tourists, backpacks looped over their shoulders and cameras in their hands. The three made their way out of the southern part of St. Moritz, the buildings giving way to impressive vistas of snow-capped mountains.

"There it is," Segel said, pointing across the lake.

Off to the left in the distance, the three could make out a portion of Bonhoff's $195-million estate. Given the satellite footage, some parts looked familiar—the abundance of fir trees, the huge windows, and the private ski lift. The place looked like it had grown up out of the lake and the mountain. The one thing the footage couldn't accurately portray was the enormity of the mansion. If getting inside wasn't hard enough, finding Bonhoff could take a while.

They made two passes before finding a campground to park the van within sight of the lake. Once they stopped, Wolfson hurried out and placed magnetic black signs over the company name on the side of the van. People might wonder why a limousine was parked in a campground, but with the signs and darkened windows, it looked like a small motor home.

The three men took in the geography, noting the mountains in the distance with the blanket of trees on the bottom half. If necessary, it could provide a hiding place or an escape route. As to the lake, there had been talk of procuring a boat—from a rigid hull inflatable boat favored by Navy SEALs to an aluminum jon boat used by the average fisherman—but they ultimately decided it was unnecessary. It might draw attention to themselves, and it was best to take the hidden route under the water.

What they couldn't see was the underground lake inside Bonhoff's house. One of the hidden wonders of Switzerland was its underground lakes. The largest such lake in Europe was located in St. Léonard, about a five-hour drive from St. Moritz. It was over 800 feet long and almost 100 feet wide. The average depth was 13 feet, and it offered a year-round water temperature of 52 degrees. Anything similar would work well for Schiffer and Wolfson—if they could find their way in.

With their scouting session over, they headed south. Along with their operatives, Mossad utilizes the work of its *sayanim*, a collection of people scattered around the world who help and assist Mossad agents with logistical issues. No questions are asked, and no reasons are given. If an agent needed a rental car, a friendly *sayan* can provide the car and the forged paperwork that no investigation would uncover. If a hotel room needed to be rented, *sayanim* may pose as a couple in love and in need of a room. They would then pass off the key to the agent and check out when the time was right.

Joe was one such *sayan*. He owned a hotel south of St. Moritz and did a brisk business during the ski season. His parents were living in Germany when the Nazis started rounding up the Jews. His father was sent to a concentration camp and never seen again. His wife, pregnant with Joe, escaped and fled to Switzerland, where, once the war was over and it was clear her husband was dead, she married a man who owned the Royal Swiss hotel. Joe was raised in the hotel, lived in the town his whole life, and followed his eternal vow to help his Jewish comrades in any way he could.

Today was one of those days. Through discreet channels, word was spread that "Mary and Joseph" would be traveling in the area and wondered if there was any room at the inn. He said there was, as the summer season saw a drop off in tourists. A room was available. It didn't have a view of the Alps, but it was on the backside on the corner with plenty of privacy.

Segel backed up the van to the ground level room. There was a key in the door, and Schiffer went inside to check it out. Once it was clear, the men grabbed a duffel bag each and brought them inside. For the next several hours, they went over the plan again. Once darkness descended on St. Moritz, they would suit up and begin the operation.

Segel would take the two men to the drop-off point and make sure they were underway. He would then drive the van to the rendezvous point.

"If you can find a way in through a cavern, try to contact me. It probably won't work, but you never know. And again, if you don't think it's possible to get to the underground lake, then call it off and meet me at the pickup point. We'll regroup and figure something else out."

Schiffer and Wolfson nodded, but neither of them was thinking about anything other than succeeding. If they were able to access the mansion through the underground lake, they were to notify Segel and proceed to take out the target. Once complete, they were to hightail it out of there and meet up with Segel.

Once the plan was reviewed, the men checked their gear. Swim fins and jet boots. Cameras and periscope. Both Wolfson and Schiffer had M4A1 assault rifles with quick-attach suppressors, a flashlight fitted to the rail interface system with an on/off pressure pad, a M68 Close Combat Optic red-dot sight, and two spare thirty-round magazines.

With the gear ready, Segel took a nap and Wolfson decided on a shower. Schiffer perused the internet, checking the stories about the riots in Boston. One story showed President Schumacher surveying the destruction under heavy guard—first via air and Marine One and then with a walk through Boston Common and the surrounding area. The lasting image in Schiffer's mind was the President standing with his hands on his hips as he looked down at the desecrated grave of John Hancock, the stele tombstone of the signer of the Declaration of Independence lying on the ground. Workers at the Granary Burying Ground were readying to hoist it back into place, but the President wanted to see it with his own eyes to remind himself what America was up against.

The three men shared a meal, but little was said. A check of the weather forecast revealed calm winds, clear skies, and cool temperatures were expected for the evening. Wolfson checked his gear again, and Schiffer could almost see the man visualizing how the mission was going to be executed, all the way to the point of putting a bullet in Bonhoff's brain. Schiffer admired the guy—he was a professional to the core.

Schiffer contacted ponytail Dustin and asked him where Bravo's phone was located. Schiffer knew it was possible that Bonoff had multiple phones, but if nothing came up as Switzerland, the team might have to rethink going forward with the operation. Within five minutes, Dustin reported back that Bravo's phone was near St. Moritz in Switzerland.

Schiffer offered a final text. *Thanks, Dustin. Good work.*

With an hour before the planned departure, Schiffer had a thought to call Alexandra. He wanted to hear her voice again, maybe ask her how the wedding was shaping up. He'd tell her he'd be home soon and then he'd suggest they get away for a while. He smiled to himself when he figured she would start asking a thousand questions that he couldn't answer. He didn't make the call.

The three men started suiting up. Wolfson and Schiffer donned their scuba suits and covered them with running pants and hooded sweatshirts. If they were stopped, they'd look like they were out for an evening run. Segel put on a white dress shirt, black tie, and black suit coat to look every bit the part of a limousine driver—with the exception of the radio earpiece in his ear and the handguns holstered at his waist and on his ankle.

Segel carried the bags to the van, like a good limo driver would. He surveyed the hotel surroundings. The parking lot was full, but the hotel occupants appeared to have called it a night. All was clear.

Schiffer and Wolfson went about wiping down the room, taking their trash and making sure none of their gear was left behind. When Segel started the van, Schiffer and Wolfson, their hoods up, left the key in the room, locked it, walked the ten steps to the van, and took a seat in the back. Segel maneuvered the van out of the parking lot and made the fifteen-minute drive north toward St. Moritz.

Stubblefield had not contacted Schiffer. He could have sent him a message calling off or postponing the mission. With no word, the greenlight was still on. Schiffer had never seen Stubblefield as concerned as the last time they met. He wasn't sure if it was Stubblefield's uncertainty at being able to stop the riots or the dangerousness of Schiffer's mission.

"ETA five minutes," Segel said.

Wolfson cracked his knuckles and rolled his neck. He said nothing, his steely eyes focused. Schiffer focused on his breathing, exhaling to blow out anything that might distract him.

"Coming up to the drop-off point."

Schiffer and Wolfson removed their hooded sweatshirts and athletic pants. They strapped the jet boots to their thighs and readied to grab their scuba gear.

Segel checked his mirrors. There was no traffic, and no one would be stopping at the scenic lookout at night.

Schiffer looked out the back window. "It looks like we're clear from the rear."

Segel pulled into the lookout point and killed the headlights. The three of them looked in every direction, scanning for any movement.

"It's clear," Segel said.

Wolfson opened the sliding door and exited. Schiffer followed and immediately helped Wolfson put on his breathing apparatus. Once complete, Wolfson did the same for Schiffer. They grabbed their weapons and headed for the water.

There was no backup. No contingent of Navy SEALs on standby ready to swoop in to rescue them. Schiffer and his two-man team were it. If they failed, their home countries would probably deny their existence and they would be lost to history as long-forgotten soldiers in the cause for justice.

After putting on their swim fins, Wolfson was the first in the water followed by Schiffer. The water was cool, cooler than the lake in Virginia. They switched on their headlamps and lights attached to their chests.

Segel stood above them, keeping an eye on the surroundings. "Good luck," he said.

Schiffer checked his compass to get his bearings. He took a breath and readied his breathing mask. "You ready?"

Wolfson didn't hesitate. "Yes."

"All right," Schiffer said, securing his mask. "Let's go."

CHAPTER 24

Near St. Moritz, Switzerland

In the depths of the lake, the headlamps helped Schiffer and Wolfson stay close together. With the jet boots powered up, they made good time. Every so often, Schiffer checked the underwater compass on his wrist and, with a tap on Wolfson's arm, they redirected.

Within twenty minutes, the headlamps started reflecting off the bottom of the lake. The two men slowed, checked the compass, and angled away from Bonhoff's house to bypass the obstructions that were supposed to be in place. Once closer to shore, they started looking for cave entrances, anything that would lead to a cavern and potentially into the underground lake.

They headed south of the property, searching every dark space for an entrance. Schiffer was the first to find the opening, tapping Wolfson twice with importance. They swam in and surfaced, only to find a cave with no way forward.

They swam back out and continued south. Schiffer could feel his heart rate increasing. The farther they got away from Bonhoff's property, the less likely they would find their way back underground. He tapped Wolfson. They looked at each other, and Schiffer held out his hands palms up.

Wolfson pointed up for them to surface. After switching off their headlamps, they broke the water line and then listened to the eerie silence. The darkness enveloped them, and on that moonless overcast night and in the blackness of the lake, they felt strangely like the last two men on the planet.

"We're going to run out of air in ten minutes," Wolfson whispered.

With the outcrop of trees, they couldn't see Bonhoff's mansion, just the lights of St. Moritz off in the distance.

"Let's try the north side," Schiffer said. "If we can't find a way in, we'll have to improvise."

The two swam out from the shoreline in front of Bonhoff's mansion, close enough to discover that there were indeed security measures in place—mainly obstructions that would impede even the best of swimmers.

They continued to the north side of the property and swam inward. The cool water was beginning to take its toll, and both men felt like their skin was shrinking. Schiffer used his headlamp to look at the regulator's display. They'd be out of air soon and, if they had to abandon the search for the entrance to the underground lake, they'd either have to ditch much of their gear to make the long trip back across the lake or hike through the forest to confront any unknown security measures.

Wolfson was in the lead when his headlamp turned back toward Schiffer, who caught up with him. They had already changed batteries in their jet boots once, and the second set was dwindling fast. Wolfson's appeared to be on empty. He pointed to his thigh.

Schiffer motioned him forward. They had to keep going.

A red light began flashing on Schiffer's regulator. He was in the danger zone for running out of air. They kept moving forward. They were going to have to surface, but at that point, they may be in view of any of Bonhoff's security guards patrolling the shore.

Their strokes became more urgent. The solid rock of the shore was upon them. They were a long way from where they started, and their frigid skin wouldn't last a return trip. They kept moving, their hands grasping at the rock to propel them forward.

Then the rock went away.

Now beyond the shoreline, Schiffer and Wolfson swam in, the realization that they had at least made it to a cave where they could surface and regroup. Schiffer hurried to raise the mini periscope. Seeing nothing, he tapped Wolfson and pointed up.

When they surfaced, their headlamps illuminated the cave. They swam forward and found higher ground out of the water.

"I have two minutes left," Wolfson said, looking at his regulator. "The jet boot batteries are gone."

Schiffer took a breath. "They did the job, though." He didn't think it would work, but he activated his comms unit. "Eagle, you copy?"

There was no response.

He turned to Wolfson. "You good to go?"

Wolfson made sure his equipment was in order and said, "Yeah."

They walked around the cave and found an opening, big enough to crawl through. They wound up in a cavern.

"Where do you think we are?" Wolfson asked. Their headlamps reflected off the rock, both of them wondering how many people had actually been in that exact spot on earth.

"We're still north of the mansion, but we're closer than when we came in."

Another hundred feet of walking led them to a drop-off and a pool of water. They couldn't see the bottom with their handlamps.

Wolfson asked the question that both of them were thinking. "You think it goes anywhere?"

"Only one way to find out."

"I don't have much air left."

Schiffer looked at the hole again. He wondered what he was doing. What was he doing in Switzerland in the bowels of a mountain trying to sneak into the mansion of the fourth richest man in the world? He knew the answer.

Because America needed Duke Schiffer.

"I still have about four minutes left. I'll go in and take a look."

Schiffer climbed over the rock formation and down into the pool. Before he put his mask on, he looked up at Wolfson and said, "If I'm not back in ten minutes, get yourself back out to the lake and make contact with Segel." He was about to secure the mask, but he wanted to add one more thing. "And tell Alexandra that I love her."

He didn't wait for Wolfson to respond. He waded in and went below the water line. Wolfson clicked the timer on his digital watch. Schiffer swam into the hole and found a tunnel that would lead people who were claustrophobic to panic. He kept on, wondering how he was going to back out of the tunnel if there was no exit.

He checked his watch, it was getting close to sixty seconds. He reminded himself to keep enough air to get back. He tried not to overreact, focusing on moving forward, but as hard as he tried, he couldn't stop the image of Alexandra popping into his head.

Come on, come on.

Schiffer started using the walls to help propel him forward, but then he thrust his hands against the rock to stop his forward progress. He switched off his headlamp.

There was light in the distance. Artificial light. Man made.

He maneuvered to a point where the tunnel ended and a space opened above him. He pulled the periscope out and tried to keep it steady and not disturb the water surface.

Bingo.

After one quick scan, he found a spot to turn around and then hauled ass as fast as he could back through the tunnel. He made good time because the regulator said he hadn't used a full two minutes roundtrip.

Once he reached the starting point, Schiffer broke the surface and immediately put his finger to his lips. The chances of anyone hearing him were minute, but he wasn't about to risk it. He gave a thumbs-up to Wolfson, pointed back from where he came, and held up five fingers of his left hand and made a zero with his right. He pointed to his eyes and then shook his head, indicating that he had not seen anyone. He motioned for Wolfson to join him.

Wolfson climbed over the rock formation and lowered himself into the pool. "Fifty feet or fifty yards?" he whispered.

"Yards. It's a straight shot in. I only used up two minutes of air. I've got a little power left in my jet boots. Grab my legs and hold on. It's tight quarters, but the boots will help a little. Once I stopped, I used the periscope to check things out. I didn't see anyone. Turn your light off when I stop."

Schiffer took the lead with Wolfson holding on to a leg. At times, both used their hands to help propel themselves along. The trip seemed shorter this time around, and Schiffer's only thoughts were focused on the mission at hand. He came to a halt when he saw the lights in front of him. Both switched off their headlamps.

Schiffer put the periscope up and saw no one. They swam forward and out of the tunnel. Ten feet below the surface, both men saw the Swarovski crystal lights on the bottom of the lake floor that looked like stars on a dark night. They detached their rifles from their chest rigs and readied them, just in case.

Schiffer pointed up, and both of them rose, breaking the surface with barely a ripple. Their guns came up next and, after dumping the water from the barrels, were ready to fire. Schiffer pointed off to the side to a collection of red velvet lounge chairs along the rock wall.

"Let's get out and take cover behind that pillar."

Wolfson provided Schiffer with a boost and gave him a chance to survey the scene from dry ground. Schiffer then helped Wolfson haul himself out of the water.

"This is unbelievable," Wolfson whispered, finally getting a look at Bonhoff's underground lake and the Venetian artwork on the ceiling.

They stripped off their scuba gear and secured everything they no longer needed in black pouches. Wolfson then tied them together and sunk both to the bottom of the lake. Schiffer grabbed a towel from one of the lounge chairs and did his best to dry off, especially his shoes—standard all-black Chuck Taylors favored by Navy SEALs. The last thing he wanted was to give himself away with shoes squeaking on the marble floors. He passed the towel to Wolfson.

Schiffer unzipped a waterproof black case and took out a small body camera that he attached to the front of his vest. Wolfson unzipped his and took out a flash drive and a magnetic transmitter. He then secured them in a pouch and wrapped it around his thigh with Velcro. They each attached the suppressors to their rifles, tested the lights, and jammed in a dry magazine. Almost ready, they kept their black swim hoods up, exposing as little flesh as possible.

"Sound check," Schiffer whispered into his mic.

"Loud and clear," Wolfson responded.

"Eagle, you copy?" Schiffer whispered. When thirty seconds elapsed, he gave it one more try. "Eagle, do you read?"

"I read you, Duke. You're breaking up a little."

"We're in." He waited before saying, "Repeat, we are in."

"Roger that."

Schiffer looked at Wolfson. "You ready?"

Wolfson nodded.

"Five floors up. Let's go."

Their steps were light and silent. Their weapons up and ready. They crept along, checking the spa, the sauna, and the Himalayan salt chamber. It took them five minutes to clear the first floor. They headed up the six-sided floating staircase, hugging the walls. The next floor contained the mansion's wine cellar and exercise rooms. They kept going up.

They discovered the movie theater on the next level. The screen rivaled any of those at a real theater. But nothing was playing, and no one was waiting in the seats for the next show. The level also contained a separate TV room.

Schiffer pointed to Wolfson to check it out. In the darkened room, Wolfson gave a quick blast from the flashlight. Wolfson whispered the room was clear.

The screens on the wall showed live feeds of the bedrooms, and Schiffer and Wolfson saw the first signs of life in the place. Schiffer counted fifteen women, all of them in various stages of undress, in the five bedrooms. Some of them looked young, too young to be there. Those naked were not lacking for anything. They seemed to be sitting around, like they were waiting for someone looking to partake of why they were there. He wondered if they were there willingly, and he had every desire to keep them out of the line of fire.

"See if you can find a computer terminal," Schiffer whispered. "Let's document this."

Wolfson found the computer array behind the wall of TVs, all of the electronics hidden from view. He grabbed the pouch secured to his leg. He inserted the flash drive to the terminal on the back side and saw the light blink green. He raised the WinSys 3020 transmitter's antenna and flipped the switch. Whether it would transmit, they would have to wait and see. He came back and flashed a thumbs-up to Schiffer.

When they were on the second to last floor before the main level, Schiffer heard the first male voice. He thrust up a hand. He held up two fingers and then one more. Three men total conversing within earshot.

Both Schiffer and Wolfson steadied their breathing. The moment of truth had come, and it was time to execute the plan to take out the fourth richest man in the world and end his financial reign of terror on the United States.

They blended in nicely in the darkened staircase, the lights of the main level brightening the area above them.

One step at a time. They kept their focus upward, ready to put a bullet in the brain of anyone who spotted them and alerted Bonhoff. If that was the case, Schiffer and Wolfson would have no choice but to go in with guns blazing.

Schiffer was in the lead. It was his mission. He told himself to breathe. Calm and steady.

The voices were getting louder now. Three men. Some laughing. Some bragging. Talk of money.

Schiffer was five stairs below the main level. Three more steps and he could raise his gun above the lip of the staircase. If he had a shot, he could take out the target.

Wolfson sidled up next to him. They made eye contact, both of them ready to take the shot. Schiffer motioned that he wanted to go up to the lip and look over. He wished he had brought the periscope. Wolfson nodded.

They crawled a step up, both of them releasing any pent-up breaths. Steady hands, eyes ready to lock onto the target and pull the trigger.

Another stair closer. One more to go. Wolfson was right-handed, Schiffer a lefty. Their weapons were nearly touching as they leaned into the staircase.

The voices were louder now. English was being spoken. One man dominated, bragging about all his money. "I can do anything I want, whenever I want," he said. It had to be Bonhoff.

With Bonhoff running his mouth, Schiffer figured the man wouldn't know what hit him.

Schiffer turned his head to the left and received the nod from Wolfson. It was go time. This was why they traveled halfway around the world to get the man behind the violence and mayhem in America. Another inhale before a slow and silent exhale.

Their heads rose slightly above the main level, the barrels of their rifles coming to a halt just over the lip. Wolfson and Schiffer both saw the back of the target's head. It would be an easy shot.

Bonhoff was sitting facing the thirty-five-foot floor-to-ceiling windows that looked out toward the darkened Alps. The walls of the reception room were covered in mink fur, and the bright lights reflected off the fur and kept Schiffer and Wolfson hidden in the darkness.

"I am going to take down America once and for all," Bonhoff bellowed. "And you boys are going to help me do it."

Schiffer could feel Wolfson releasing the tension inside of him. He was ready to put a bullet in the back of the man's skull. That's all it would take—one pull of the trigger and it would be mission accomplished.

Schiffer moved the red-dot optic to the left and flinched. He felt his lungs gasp at what he saw.

His movement caught Wolfson off guard, but Schiffer moved the red dot to the man on the right of Bonhoff just to make sure. Schiffer could feel his heart racing. This wasn't supposed to be happening.

Wolfson regrouped. He feathered the trigger and released the breath that steadied the sniper for the shot. He was about to fire when Schiffer's hand crossed in front of the sight before grabbing the barrel.

Schiffer was shaking his head. Without saying a word, Wolfson said in no uncertain terms that he had a shot and it was time to take it.

Schiffer mouthed the word "No." He pointed emphatically behind him.

Wolfson had the look about him that said he was about ready to shoot

Schiffer and then carry out the mission. His face twisted with fury before he relented.

Before leaving, Schiffer raised his mini camera over the lip of the staircase and snapped a picture of the three men. He took another to make sure. Then the two men crept backwards, keeping their eyes and ears open. Bonhoff was still ranting, his voice echoing throughout the place.

Schiffer and Wolfson made it to the home theater level before Wolfson grabbed him roughly.

"I had the shot," Wolfson hissed. "I didn't risk my life to have you chicken out."

"This is my operation, Wolf. I make the call. We have to abort."

"What? Are you crazy? We have the shot. We can get him."

"No!" Schiffer whispered loudly. "We can't."

"Why the hell not?" Wolfson had the look in his eye that said Schiffer had better have a good answer.

Schiffer stifled an expletive from escaping his lips. There were so many problems right then that he had trouble thinking straight. "We can't because the guy on the left is currently running for President of the United States."

"What?"

Schiffer nodded his head. Too many problems, and that wasn't even the worst of it. "And the guy on the right is the Director of the FBI."

CHAPTER 25

Near St. Moritz, Switzerland

"Are you sure?" Wolfson asked.

"Yes."

"What the hell is he doing here?"

"I don't know. But what I do know is that he's not here on behalf of the administration."

Schiffer could feel the sweat running down his back. *What the hell is the FBI Director doing meeting with the man who is bankrolling the violence and destruction in the U.S.?* He needed to contact the Vice President, but he couldn't do it from there.

"We're going to have to get out of here."

Wolfson had to restrain himself from yelling. "Do I have to remind you that we sank our gear? And there's no way we can make it back through the tunnel to the cavern and then beyond that. No way."

Schiffer knew the man was right. Swimming out from the underground lake was not a possibility. "We're going to have to go with Plan B."

"We don't have a Plan B," Wolfson snapped.

"Well we're going to have to figure one out," Schiffer shot back.

"Why don't we just shoot our way out?"

"Because until I know what's going on, I don't want anyone knowing we were here."

Schiffer pulled back his swim hood and wiped the sweat off his face. Walking out the front door was out of the question. Even going out the back door was fraught with danger. They could probably fight their way out toward the lake, but then they'd have to swim to the rendezvous point, with no guarantee that they'd make it.

"What about the ski lift?" Wolfson asked, his mind refocused on the matter at hand.

"We'd be sitting ducks up there. It would be like a shooting gallery."

"What about setting fire to the place? The fire department will be a distraction."

Schiffer thought it over. It was a possibility. The two men walked by the room with all the TV monitors. The scantily clad women were still waiting in the bedrooms. The only way to get to them would be to ascend the staircase to the ground level. Even if they could be directed to cause a distraction, two men with guns walking out the front door would catch the guards' attention.

"Well, what are we going to do?" Wolfson asked.

Schiffer looked at the monitors again. One of Bonhoff's greatest weaknesses was women, and that would be widely known by his security. It was worth a shot.

"Eagle, you copy?"

"Copy, Duke. I was getting worried."

"There's been a problem," Schiffer said quietly. "We have to abort."

"Is the Wolf still with you?"

"Yes. I can't give you a reason for the decision right now, but we have to abort. We need a way out of here."

Segel took a few seconds before responding, "What do you want me to do?"

Schiffer told Segel his idea. It sounded crazy when he actually said it, but it was the only thing he could come up with. There were a couple questions asked, and a few answers given. No one knew if it would work.

"Give me thirty minutes," Segel said.

* * *

"I thought Greg was pulling my leg when he said he was going to bring the Director of the FBI to my house," Bonhoff bellowed.

Bonhoff had welcomed the two men to his mansion under the cover of darkness. Neither Lamont nor Duncan came with security. It was just two old college buddies taking a European vacation to meet secretly with the fourth richest man in the world.

"Who would have thought that?" Bonhoff said.

He was wearing white pants and a white shirt, the top three buttons of the shirt undone and showing his hairy chest. Lamont and Duncan had ditched the usual suit and tie and gone with khakis and sweaters. All three of them had a glass of liquor at their sides.

"I never would have dreamed of it, Karl," Lamont said. "But it is an honor to be here. This is the most spectacular home I think I've ever seen."

Before the beaming Bonhoff could respond, Duncan added, "It really is impressive. Hard to believe actually."

"It better be impressive for the amount of money I paid for it." He finished his scotch and refilled his glass.

Lamont leaned forward, wanting to get down to business. "The reason I brought Director Duncan here is I wanted to show him that I'm serious about winning the presidency. He knows full well that it takes a lot of money to win, and I wanted him to know that the man behind the funding of my campaign is serious about winning, too."

Bonhoff sipped his scotch and nodded. "I'm dead serious. I want that Schumacher out of the White House."

Director Duncan gulped before asking, "Can I ask what's in it for you, Mr. Bonhoff?"

"Oh, please, Kurt, we're on a first name basis here. You can call me Karl." He took another sip and set the glass down on the table next to him. He looked Duncan directly in the eye. "I want to be the wealthiest man on the face of the earth. With money comes power, and I will become the most powerful man in the world, too."

Lamont silently bristled, wanting to remind him that, as President, he would technically be the most powerful man in the world because he could unleash nuclear war and obliterate every country on the face of the earth. Instead, he held his tongue.

"And if Greg becomes President, I will have someone with the power to make it all happen." Bonhoff leaned back and put his hands behind his head. "I already have the leaders of Russia, China, Iran, and half the rest of the world in my back pocket. It has proven very lucrative."

Lamont asked the question that Duncan was afraid to. "The Director and I are old friends. He wants to be on the winning team. Obviously, he works for the Schumacher Administration right now, so he would be taking a huge risk by joining forces with the opposing team. He'd like to know if there's something in it for him."

Bonhoff smiled, like he knew the men were putty in his hands. They both wanted something, and they'd be willing to do whatever it took to get it. He thought for a second, his eyes drifting up to the fur-covered walls.

"I can put you in charge of security, Kurt. It will prove very lucrative for you in the long run. I'll give you a salary of one-million dollars per year."

Duncan's face flushed. He looked like he was reluctant to complain before the billionaire. "No offense, Karl, but that's not much. As a former Director of the FBI, I could make that in a security job in the U.S. Even more if I'm on the board of directors of any company I want."

Bonhoff countered. "I'll start you off with a hundred million dollars in a bank account. It'll all be yours. You'll be my head security man and, when it comes time to collect the money owed to me from around the world, you can keep one percent for yourself."

Lamont could tell the hundred million figure caught Duncan's attention. Duncan could make good money in the private sector, but not a hundred million.

"I'm serious about getting Greg into the White House, Kurt. I want him to be President. I'm willing to bankroll the campaign to make it happen." Bonhoff leaned forward, a serious look on his face. "But if you can help us now, it will be much appreciated."

Duncan winced. "Help? What kind of help are you talking about?"

Bonhoff shrugged. "Maybe the FBI looks the other way when it comes to the riots. The President's poll numbers are plummeting. If they keep going, he might not even make it to the end of his term. He might resign in disgrace."

Lamont looked at Duncan. He had essentially told him the same thing about the FBI dragging its feet. But it meant more coming from the man promising Duncan a hundred million bucks.

"He's not asking you to do anything illegal, Kurt," Lamont said, teaming up with Bonhoff and trying to push Duncan past the finish line.

Duncan looked down at his hands. After a few moments of reflection, he smiled and looked at Bonhoff. "I can do that."

Bonhoff clapped his hands and stood. Duncan and Lamont stood as well. They all shook hands. The reflection in the giant windows showed three men, slapping each other on the back. From anyone on the outside, they looked happy.

Happy with the knowledge that they were going to destroy America and remake it in their own image.

"How about some dessert, Kurt?" Bonhoff offered.

Lamont caught the look from Duncan and waggled his eyebrows in reply. It was time to celebrate. He had told Duncan on the way over that the "dessert" would be some of the best he ever had—and you could have your pick! This was what being on Bonhoff's side would bring. And now they could celebrate all night long.

A big old grin widened across Duncan's face. "Yeah, I'd love some dessert."

* * *

After hearing from Schiffer, Ariel Segel drove the *Five-Star Limousine* straight to the place where he knew he'd find what he was looking for—the Casino St. Moritz. With a pocket full of euros, he asked six women if they'd like to go to a party at the Bonhoff residence. The women, all local, had just enough clothing on to leave something to the imagination. They all were well aware of Bonhoff and the man's money, and most of them would have gone for free but Segel insisted paying them up front.

Once the women were ready in the van, Segel stashed his guns in the glove box and then hustled the van south of St. Moritz.

"Mr. Bonhoff wants you to have a good time, ladies," Segel said, his eyes looking in the rearview mirror. "He likes excited women."

Segel didn't have to say any more. The women squealed and fawned like they had done it a thousand times before.

"Feel free to flirt with the security, too."

Segel rolled up to the security gate and five men with guns appeared out of the two guard shacks. The leader held out a hand for Segel to stop. Segel hit the button to lower the window.

"Special delivery for Mr. Bonhoff," Segel said. He threw a thumb over his shoulder and winked.

"We aren't expecting any deliveries tonight," the man said.

Just then the doors on both sides of the van opened.

"Hey, baby, are you going to come party with us?" the youngest blonde cooed to the man with the gun.

On the other side, a redhead in a red-sequined dress reached out and rubbed the arm of another guard. "Oh, my, such big muscles you have."

Segel raised his hands. "I don't know who requested them, but I was told to bring them here."

"Won't you please come party with us?" the blonde begged. "Pretty please."

Segel could tell the man was doing his best to contain his urges. The man licked his lips and said, "We'll have to frisk them."

"Of course," Segel said, opening his own door. He leaned his head back in. "Ladies, if you could step out for a second so these men can take a look."

The women were happy to do so, and the security guards decided to take their own sweet time running their hands over the women's bodies. One man hurriedly patted down Segel, wanting to get back on checking the blonde one more time.

Once the fondling and groping had ended, the women got back in and Segel put the limo into gear.

Before closing the door, the blonde tickled the chin of the lead guard. She winked and said, "I'll come back for you later."

The limo cleared the gates and Segel activated the mic hidden in his suit coat. "Schiffer, you copy?"

"Roger, I copy."

"I'm in with the limo," Segel said. He drove slowly up the drive. "I'm almost at full occupancy, but I think I can fit you two into the back. Can you get to the front of the house?"

"Affirmative. We're on our way."

Schiffer and Wolfson hurried to the ground level and found a sliding glass door to exit. They were on the north side of the mansion when Segel pulled to a stop in the circle drive. In the darkness, they hurried to the van.

Segel opened his door and got out. He locked the side doors and said, "Stay here, ladies. Just one second." He hurried to the back and opened the rear doors.

Both still armed, Schiffer was in first followed by Wolfson. Segel threw a blanket over the top of them.

The redhead caught a quick glimpse of the two men in wet suits. She was the only one to notice. "Hey, what's going on?"

Segel hurried around and got in. He threw the van into gear and slowly pulled away.

"What's going on? You said we were going to party."

Segel slowed and turned in his seat. "Ladies, there's been a change of plans." He handed over a fistful of euros. "I'm taking you back to the casino. You got that?" The look he gave them must have done the trick because they all nodded. "When we get back, I'll give you each another hundred euros. Just keep doing what you were doing when we came in."

Women nodded, none of them sure of what they had gotten themselves into. Now all they had to do was get out the front gate.

Segel activated his mic. "We're coming up to the guard shacks. Five men, heavily armed."

"Roger," Schiffer radioed from the back. "Let us know if they're going to open the rear doors."

The van crept forward. If they opened the gates, Segel could floor it and take his chances.

When he got closer, the five guards reappeared. This time on the interior of the gates. They looked confused. Segel cursed. "Three guards on my left, two on my right," he whispered into his mic. "Standby."

The lead guard held out his hand. Segel hit the button to lower the window.

The guard looked at Segel and then the women in the back. "Is there a problem?"

Segel used a finger to motion the man closer, like he had a secret to tell. He whispered in the man's ear. "Mr. Bonhoff said they're not young enough." He added a wince that said he was afraid to offend the women.

The guard grunted like he wasn't surprised. He nodded to the women. "You ladies have a good evening."

The blonde earned herself a tip from Segel. "Come to the casino later, baby. We'll be partying all night long. I'll show you a good time."

Segel waggled his eyebrows and put the shifter into gear. The guard motioned to someone in the shack to open the gates. "Have a good night," Segel said before letting out a breath when they exited through the gates.

"We're clear," Segel said into his mic.

After Segel dropped the women off at the casino, he drove south of St. Moritz to the campground they had stopped at the day before. Once he stopped, he hurried to open the rear doors. Wolfson was the first out.

"What the hell happened?" Segel asked.

Wolfson cursed in Hebrew and decided to unleash the violence that he had been deprived of. He started back for Schiffer to take a swing at him.

Schiffer had thrown his legs out of the van and saw the blow coming. He threw his arms out in defense. They grappled for a bit before Schiffer said, "Get off me!"

Segel grabbed Wolfson and dragged him off. He told his comrade to take a walk to calm down. With peace restored, Segel walked back to the van.

"What happened?"

"I had to call it off."

"What for?"

"A United States Senator and the Director of the FBI were in there talking to Bonhoff."

Segel used the same Hebrew expletive that Wolfson had. Schiffer stood and threw his weapon into the van.

"I need to make a call."

* * *

Schiffer walked off into the darkness and powered up his phone. He kept his distance from Wolfson. Both of the men were so pissed off right then that who knows what they would do to each other. He punched in the number and waited.

Vice President Stubblefield came on the line. "Yes."

"It's me. We've got a problem."

Five seconds of silence passed before Stubblefield said, "What kind of problem?"

"A big one."

"Is your team still intact?"

"Yes, sir, we're all safe."

"Well, then, what's the problem?"

Schiffer kicked at a pebble. "I'd rather not tell you over the phone."

"These are secure lines."

Schiffer looked east, back to where he had spent the last two hours. The adrenalin from the operation was starting to wear off. It was replaced with soreness from all the exertion and the weight of what he had learned pressing down on his mind.

"With what I have to tell you, they might not be secure enough."

Schiffer heard the big man blow out a breath.

"Well get back here as soon as you can then."

CHAPTER 26

Number One Observatory Circle – Washington, D.C.

Duke Schiffer called shortly after midnight Switzerland time. Stubblefield had been in his office at the Vice President's Residence since 5:30 a.m. He hadn't slept much, wondering if he would hear word from his man on the ground. He had been worrying about Schiffer ever since he last saw him—when Schiffer handed him the letter addressed to Alexandra. Stubblefield worried that he made the wrong decision in sending him. He was the man Stubblefield sent into harm's way, the man who he could trust implicitly. He didn't know what he'd do if he lost him.

He had thought it might be time to let Schiffer retire. To let him enjoy life. Get married to Alexandra and have a houseful of kids. He wondered if he wanted Schiffer to hurry and complete this mission before the wedding because he knew Schiffer would want it to be his last.

When the call finally came, it didn't sound good. Schiffer would have told him if the target had been killed or if foreign authorities were ticked off that Schiffer and his team were conducting operations on their home turf. But there was none of that. Just that the mission had failed.

And now he had to wait to find out why.

Nate Russo knocked on the half open door to the Vice President's office and stuck his head in. "Good morning, sir."

Stubblefield raised his head and offered a gruff, "Morning." There was nothing good about it.

"I was wondering if now is a good time to go over the day's schedule."

Stubblefield didn't wait for Russo to rattle off the day's itinerary. "Cancel everything after two o'clock."

Russo looked at the schedule for clarification. "But sir, you have a meeting with the Swedish foreign minister."

Stubblefield discarded any notion of meeting with the man with a flick of the hand. "Reschedule it."

Russo readied his pen to jot down a note. "What should I tell him?"

"Something came up."

"Anything I need to know about?"

"No." Stubblefield flicked his hand again toward the door to end the meeting.

"Yes, sir. I'll get right on it."

Stubblefield busied himself as best he could for the rest of the morning. He called the President and told him an issue had arisen with regard to "the operation." When the President asked for specifics, Stubblefield said he couldn't give any because he didn't know what they were other than Schiffer and his team were safe. He said Schiffer was due in Washington by mid-afternoon. Stubblefield told the President he would contact him as soon as he knew what was going on.

Schiffer arrived shortly after 3 p.m. He cleared the front gate and parked his Jeep outside the Residence. Russo ushered him into Stubblefield's office.

"Can I get you anything?" Russo asked Schiffer.

"Coffee, please."

Russo exited to get the coffee, and Stubblefield and Schiffer waited until he came back with the cup and shut the door.

In the silence, Stubblefield looked at Schiffer and tried to figure out what he was about to be told. He didn't know whether he should ask the questions or let Schiffer provide the details.

"So your team is safe?"

"Yes, there was no issue on those grounds. Although there's one guy who isn't too happy with me right now."

"What about Bonhoff?"

"Yes. I saw him."

There was a knock on the door.

Stubblefield looked across the office. "Yes?"

Russo opened the door and stuck his head in. "Sir, did I leave my phone in here?" He looked around and saw he had left it on the credenza when he went to fetch Schiffer's coffee. He picked it up and said, "Sorry for interrupting, sir."

Stubblefield nodded like it wasn't a problem. "Close the door." He then returned his focus to Schiffer.

"You saw Bonhoff?"

"Yes, we got into his mansion. We had to go through the underground lake to get there."

The Vice President's cheeks rose at hearing that. *That's why Schiffer's the best.*

Schiffer gave a report of what he and Wolfson had seen in Bonhoff's mansion. He mentioned the women in the bedrooms and the transmitter that was placed in the computer terminal inside the house. They would have to contact the Israelis to see if any video had been captured and sent to Mossad. Schiffer moved on, noting how they crept up the staircase, the voice of Bonhoff echoing off the cathedral ceilings. They made it to the top, the target was detected, and pictures were taken.

Stubblefield sat transfixed at the story—Schiffer replaying it like a movie. The Vice President could feel the tension rising and he waited for the climactic scene.

"I had him in my sights, sir," Schiffer said, looking dead straight into Stubblefield's eyes. "The red dot was on the back of his head and I had a finger on the trigger. I know Wolfson had the same view. I was a split second away from completing the mission."

Stubblefield's eyes were wide, wondering why Schiffer hadn't done it. It wasn't like him to not execute the plan. It had to be big. "What happened?"

"He wasn't alone, sir."

Stubblefield sat back, the fingers on his left hand tapping the desk. There were a million possibilities—a foreign leader, a wanted terrorist, some buxom-blonde that people would recognize from TV.

"Well, who was with him?"

Schiffer reached inside his windbreaker and pulled out a couple of folded pieces of paper. He got up and walked around the Vice President's desk. He laid the first piece of paper in front him.

The paper looked like it had been spat out of a color printer, but the picture was good quality. Stubblefield picked it up and studied it.

Schiffer pointed to the man seated in the middle with the back of his head to the camera. "Bonhoff."

Stubblefield looked closer at the man on the left of the picture. "Is that who I think it is?"

"Senator Lamont."

Stubblefield leaned forward and rested his chin in his hand. He wasn't totally surprised that Lamont would try to tap into the billions that Bonhoff had already been pumping into the coffers of U.S. political candidates. Still, it was a risky move to go over to Switzerland to meet with Bonhoff considering all that was going on in America. If word got out that Lamont was taking money from the man who was funding the riots, it could be the end of Lamont's campaign.

The Vice President shook his head like he was disgusted with the politics of Washington. "Sometimes I wonder whose side these people are on."

"It gets worse," Schiffer said, handing over the second piece of paper. He stepped back to gauge Stubblefield's reaction.

Stubblefield's eyes widened. Then the nostrils flared slightly followed by a tightening of the neck muscles and gritting of his teeth. The tension in the big man's body was so high it looked like a balloon ready to pop, or maybe a volcano ready to explode. The only things moving were his head shaking back and forth and his chest rising and falling.

"Like I said—a big problem."

Stubblefield took the picture and brought it closer to his face. There was no mistaking who the third member of the cabal was. And even from the profile picture, Duncan had a particularly smug grin on his face at the time the photo was taken.

"The FBI is working against us, sir. The Director is coordinating with the administration's political enemy and a sworn enemy of this country."

Stubblefield spat out an expletive. He balled his fists and pounded his right one down on his desk. "Who knows about this?" he growled.

"Just you, me, Wolfson, and Segel."

The two made eye contact. "You confident that they'll keep it to themselves?"

Schiffer nodded. "Yes, absolutely. But Wolfson's not happy that we didn't take the shot. He looked like he was about ready to slug me once we got out of there. But it was my call, sir, and I'm the one to blame."

Stubblefield quickly shook his head. "No, you did the right thing. It was the correct call." He pounded the desk with his fist again.

Schiffer sat down in the chair in front of Stubblefield's desk. "Why would Director Duncan do this?"

Stubblefield ran his hand down his face. His expression was one that said Schiffer's bombshell was about as bad as it could get. It didn't take him long to come up with a reason.

"You hear it all the time on CNN, Duke. People are mad that I have so much say as Vice President. Some people think I'm still running the FBI, and I know Duncan doesn't like it that the President and I are constantly looking over his shoulder. Now we have a pretty good idea who the reporters are talking about when they mention their sources inside the administration."

"Do you think the Director's been looking the other way when it comes to the riots?"

"I wouldn't doubt it. I don't know how long he's been in bed with Bonhoff, but he and Lamont go way back. I think they were college roommates."

"So we know how high up it goes in the Bureau, but we don't know how far down the chain of command it goes. It would be a disaster if a bunch of HBOs are involved."

Stubblefield nodded and grimaced. He had worked hard to make the FBI the foremost law enforcement agency in the world and, if a number of High Bureau Officials were in on it, Duncan's possibly treasonous activity could destroy the Bureau's credibility forever.

"Most of the higher-ups are ones that I put in place. Duncan was moving up the ladder the same time I was. I think he thought he was next in line to become Director when I got the nod from the President. I kept him on for continuity purposes, but he and I didn't gel very well. Now it looks like he's trying to join forces with his old buddy to take down the President."

"What's in it for him?"

"What's in it for everyone in this town—power and money."

Thirty seconds of silence went by before Schiffer asked, "What do you want me to do?"

The big man got out of his chair and walked slowly toward the window, his mind trying to think of the next move. He could confront Director Duncan that evening and demand an answer for his actions. Or he could wait and see how far Duncan had sold out his country.

Stubblefield walked back to his desk and punched a button on his phone. The call went to the President's Deputy Chief of Staff. "Tim, I need to meet with the President. It's urgent." The man said something, and Stubblefield responded, "Thank you."

He ended the call and then punched another button. "Get the cars ready. We're going to the White House."

Once Stubblefield put the phone back in its cradle, Schiffer stood. "Anything from me?"

"I need you to go with me."

"Yes, sir."

Before leaving the office, the Vice President took the two sheets of paper on his desk and folded them. He put them inside the pocket of his suit coat nearest his pistol. After he did so, he pulled out an envelope with *Alexandra* written on the front.

"I guess I should give this back to you."

Schiffer took the letter and looked at it. "Thank you."

Stubblefield buttoned his coat and headed for the door. "I guess now that you're back, you have a wedding to get ready for."

"Yeah," Schiffer said with little emotion. "The big day. Only a couple days away."

The Vice President offered a tired smile, like a proud father who would soon send off his son into the married world. In the back of his mind, he wondered if this was the last mission he sent Schiffer on. Maybe it was for the best—at least the best for Schiffer and Alexandra. Maybe not so much for the country. There was so much more to do.

And try as he might, Stubblefield couldn't imagine giving up Schiffer just yet.

CHAPTER 27

The White House – Washington, D.C.

The Vice President was the first to arrive in the Situation Room. The President had suggested meeting in the Oval Office, but Stubblefield wanted maximum privacy.

"That bad, huh?" the President asked over the phone.

"Yes, sir, it is."

"I'll be down there in twenty minutes."

Schiffer had driven separately and, after he cleared the gates, he parked his Jeep on West Executive Drive. He secured his Glock in the glove box and headed into the front entrance of the West Wing. He walked through the lobby, took a right, and down the stairs to the ground floor and the Situation Room in the southwest corner of the West Wing complex.

The President walked in and found both men seated. "This it?"

"Yes, Mr. President, just us."

The President didn't like the looks he was getting. Serious looks, like bad things had happened or were about to happen. "Sorry I'm late. I was meeting with the Swedish Prime Minister and she likes to talk." He took a seat at the head of the conference table under the Presidential Seal hanging on the wall. "She says you weren't able to meet with the Swedish foreign minister today."

"Yeah," Stubblefield said, gesturing toward Schiffer across the table. "Something came up."

The President eyed Schiffer and nodded. He knew this wasn't going to be good. "All right, let's hear it."

The Vice President took the lead. "Duke and a Mossad agent, Mr. Wolfson, were able to infiltrate the Bonhoff mansion near St. Moritz." Stubblefield couldn't resist telling the President that they had actually entered via the underground lake.

"Wow," the President said. "Well done."

Stubblefield then hurried through the report of Schiffer and Wolfson's movements throughout the mansion.

"Duke and Wolfson had eyes on the target and a shot to take him out."

The President looked at Schiffer and then over at Stubblefield. "But . . ."

"But Bonhoff was with some people that caused Duke to rethink the plan."

Stubblefield reached into his suit coat and pulled out the two sheets of paper. He slid the first sheet toward the President.

The President picked it up and squinted at the picture.

"The man with his back to the camera is Bonhoff," Stubblefield said.

The President squinted harder at the man on the left. "Is that Senator Lamont?"

Both Schiffer and Stubblefield nodded.

The President's mind swirled with intrigue. The man on the left of the picture had recently promised to defeat President Schumacher in the next election and rumors had been circling that Lamont had the money to go toe-to-toe with the incumbent President. Now the President knew there was some truth to those rumors.

But intelligence sources had linked Bonhoff to the riots in the U.S., not to mention the funding of progressive candidates across the country who were hell-bent on defunding the police and creating a socialist government with D.C. in charge.

"Well, I guess if this got out, it could certainly do damage to his campaign. I was hoping we could put a stop to Bonhoff's funding, but now it looks like we're going to see plenty more of it with the Lamont campaign." He slid the paper back toward Stubblefield before looking at Schiffer. "Is Lamont the reason you didn't take out Bonhoff?"

"Part of the reason, sir."

The President's eyes moved back across the table to Stubblefield looking for clarification.

"I'm sorry to have to show you this, Mr. President," Stubblefield said, readying to slide the second page across the table. "I feel like I have some responsibility."

The President nodded that he was ready to take a look, but his response indicated he wasn't ready for what he saw.

His eyes widened, and he sucked in the breath that had escaped him. "When did you take this?"

"Last night, sir."

The fury released from the President was immediate. "That son of a bitch!" He pounded the table with his fist. "I ought to call him into the Oval Office and fire his ass right now!" He let out a flurry of profanities that he would spit out only in the confines of the secure Situation Room. "Then I'll have the Secret Service handcuff him and march him out of the White House and into the nearest jail cell."

"I felt the same way, Mr. President," Stubblefield said. "I know Kurt and I don't get along, but I didn't think he'd risk tarnishing the Bureau's reputation by getting into bed with the likes of Bonhoff, not to mention the candidate who's looking to defeat you in the next election."

The President cursed again. He pushed back his chair and set about pacing the length of the room toward the TV monitors on the opposite wall. "I can't believe this."

"I know, sir," Stubblefield said. "It's hard to take in."

The President stopped behind a high-back leather chair and looked at Schiffer. "Now I know why you didn't take the shot."

"Yes, sir. But there was a part of me that wanted to put a bullet in all three of their brains."

The President nodded. He acted like he could do that same thing himself right then and there. "You did the right thing."

"He's dragging his feet with the FBI," Stubblefield said. "If he's signed on with Lamont and Bonhoff, all he has to do is have the FBI look the other way until your poll numbers are so low that no one will want to vote for you."

The President shook his head, still in disbelief. "He took an oath to support and defend the Constitution against all enemies, foreign and domestic."

"Yes he did," Stubblefield said.

"Well, I think it's pretty clear now that he has failed to faithfully discharge the duties of his office."

"I agree."

The President walked back to his chair and sat down. He put his hand on the phone. "I'm going to fire him tonight. I'm going to bring him in here, show him the picture, and then I'm going to fire his sorry ass."

Stubblefield held out his hand to stop the President from punching the number. "Mr. President, maybe it would be best if we wait."

"Wait? I don't know if the country can take much more of what's going on, Ty. We need to get to the bottom of all this and put a stop to it."

"I totally agree, Mr. President, but right now, we don't know how far down the chain of command this goes. It could be that Duncan has gone rogue and it's just him making the calls based on what he thinks is best for Lamont and Bonhoff."

"You think Bonhoff has bought him off?"

"I don't know. It's possible."

The President looked at Schiffer. "Did you hear anything last night?"

Schiffer shook his head. "No, sir. I didn't. We were in and out pretty quick. And to be honest, I was dealing with the shock of seeing Lamont and the Director there. I wanted to get out of there before it turned ugly."

The President rested his elbows on the table and folded his hands. "What do you want to do, Ty?"

"I think we need to tap the Director's phone."

The President closed his eyes and sighed. After he opened them, he said, "You want to put a trace on the FBI Director's phone."

"Yes, sir. And it needs to be done as quietly as possible."

"You mean not going through all the legal hoops to get the tap."

"Yes, sir."

The President muttered a curse word under his breath. *That son of a . . .* He rubbed his right hand against his now aching head.

"I can take the fall for it, Mr. President. I can be the one to order it."

The President leaned back in his chair and looked at the ceiling of the Situation Room. *How had it come to this?* It was nights like these that made him wonder why he still wanted the job. His mind had a quick thought of retiring to west-central Indiana, where he could spend his evenings sitting on the back porch with the First Lady watching the moonlight on the Wabash. It was nights like these that made him long for his Indiana home.

But he was President of the United States. The American people had elected him, and he raised his right hand and swore to preserve, protect, and defend the Constitution of the United States. And right now the country was under assault. The rights and liberties of free men and women were at stake if he didn't act.

It was time to act.

He looked at his Vice President. "Do you have the number?"

"Yes, sir."

The President picked up the phone and the Situation Room's duty officer responded. "I need the Director of the National Security Agency on the phone immediately." He hung up, knowing the demand would be met in short order.

He gestured toward the Vice President. "Give me the number."

Stubblefield scrolled through his phone and found the number of the FBI Director's cellphone. He scribbled it down on a notepad and passed it down the table.

The phone rang, and the President put it on speaker. "Director Ackerman is on the line, sir."

"Thank you. Put it through." After three seconds of silence, the President said, "Director, are you there?"

"I'm here, Mr. President. Is there a problem?"

"Yes, but I don't want to go into it too deeply right now."

"What can I do for you?"

"I need to put a trace on a phone." When the silence lasted longer than expected, the President said, "I know this is out of the ordinary, Ryan, but I need it done."

Director Ryan Ackerman cleared his throat. "Mr. President, I mean no disrespect, but isn't that a call that should be directed to the FBI?"

"I'm calling you, Ryan, and I need it done immediately. You can do it, can't you?"

"Yes, sir, I can have it done, it's just a little unorthodox way of going about it. There's a lot of paperwork involved and then we have to get a federal judge to sign off on it."

"I know how the process works, Ryan. But there's not going to be any paperwork or federal judges on this one."

"Okay . . . but would you like for me to contact the Attorney General to run it by him?"

"No, Ryan, I don't want you to contact anybody. It's my decision and I'm responsible. This is a matter of national security and I need it done now."

That seemed to appease Director Ackerman, who said, "I'm at my desk, Mr. President. If you have the number, I can run it through the computer and send it along to those who can get it done. They'll contact the cell carrier and get it up and running within a couple hours."

The President read off the ten-digit number and waited. Those in the Situation Room could hear Director Ackerman clicking away on his computer. They all knew what was coming.

"Um, sir," the Director said, pausing like he knew he could be in for an ass chewing for all the questions. "That number is flagged. It's . . . um . . . it belongs to Director Duncan."

"I know who it belongs to, Ryan."

"Are you sure you want to do this?"

"Yes," the President said without hesitation. He thought he had better lay down the law while he was at it. "Director, I shouldn't have to tell you that this is being done under the utmost secrecy. There are two other people with me right now in the Situation Room. I trust them with my life. The only other person who knows about this request is you." He waited to let that little tidbit sink in. "It had better stay between us, too. You understand?"

"Yes, sir. Once it's up and running, I will personally handle it and report to you. I'll have the name associated with the number redacted. So it'll just be me knowing who we're talking about."

"That's good. Thank you, Ryan."

Director Ackerman sounded like he was having trouble coming up with the final words to say. "Are you a hundred percent sure you want me to do this, Mr. President?"

"Yes . . . Do it."

CHAPTER 28

Philadelphia, Pennsylvania

With a new Phillies hat covering his bald head, Viktor Kozlov was sitting on a low brick wall just east of the corner of South 6th and Chestnut Streets in Philadelphia. The sun was high overhead, but he had some shade from the tree on the other side of the sidewalk.

Facing the south, he had a perfect view of Independence Hall. Being Russian, he had no special feelings about the place where America's Declaration of Independence and Constitution were debated and signed. He couldn't care less about George Washington, Thomas Jefferson, Ben Franklin or any of the other Founding Fathers. They were all dead and buried.

Just like the United States would be once he was done implementing Bonhoff's plan.

If he turned around and faced north, he could peer into the building housing the Liberty Bell. Beyond that, the National Constitution Center had a steady stream of tourists walking in and out. He started envisioning how his latest operation would unfold.

Philadelphia had no shortage of residents mad at the world and angry at government. Poverty was plentiful, unemployment was the highest in the nation, and a record number of people, three hundred so far, had been shot and killed by the middle of June. If the trend continued, six hundred homicides were not out of the question.

And if Kozlov could move that number higher in the next day or two, he was happy to oblige.

When his phone buzzed, he took it out of his pocket and looked at the screen. It was Bonhoff. He made the calculation and figured it was six o'clock in Switzerland, noon in Philly. He rose from his seat on the brick wall and walked into the grassy area north of Independence Hall so he could avoid the tourists using the sidewalks.

He tapped the screen. "Yes."

"Viktor. Where are you?"

"The City of Brotherly Love."

Bonhoff chuckled, knowing there would be no brotherly love on the horizon. In fact, if Kozlov worked it right, American "brothers" and "sisters" would be going at it to help make a mess of the entire city. "How are things looking?"

Kozlov spat on the grass, still wet from the sprinklers that had watered it a half hour before. "It's hot out, and it's not supposed to cool off for days. Perfect weather for people to get out and rampage through the streets."

"When do you think you can get started?"

Kozlov waited for a family of three to pass by on the sidewalk. "I can do it tonight if you want. Everything is in place. The social media call to action will go out as soon as I say the word." He smiled, almost not wanting to divulge what he had in store. "I think you'll be very pleased with what I have planned."

Kozlov had been wanting to up his game with every city. Chicago was good. The fancy stores on Michigan Avenue were still boarded up. St. Louis was okay. Seattle was still a mess, the progressives in the city's government too dumbstruck to know what to do. Kozlov loved that the fires were still burning. Boston had been a huge success. The rioters had laid waste to the Common, and the cop killing had been icing on the cake. He still had General Washington's sword.

But he wanted to go bigger this time. Maybe pick off another cop or two. He had already handed out three hundred illegal handguns like they were candy. The only payment he demanded was that the guns be used when the riots started. He didn't care who was shot, just that the bodies start piling up. He made sure to cross the Delaware into New Jersey to arm those in Camden looking for a fight.

Once the destruction was complete, Kozlov planned to jump on Interstate 95 and head south to Baltimore. There were plenty of opportunities down there. Crime was just as bad, and the political leaders had pretty much relinquished control of the streets to the thugs and the gangbangers. No one was safe. He had already been salivating at the thought of taking down that giant American flag at Fort McHenry. Maybe he'd just set it on fire and hoist it up the pole for all the world to see America going down in flames. From there, he'd hop back on Interstate 95 and head south to Washington, where he dreamed the American government would soon be in ruins.

But first things first—Philadelphia. The Cradle of Liberty. The Birthplace of America. The Philly police were short staffed, many of them taking early retirement because the elected officials had turned their backs on them. It would make Kozlov's job much easier.

"When do you want me to light the fire?" Kozlov asked.

"Tonight."

Kozlov looked at his watch. A little past noon. Plenty of time to get the word out to his underlings on the ground. He waited to respond until an overweight National Park Ranger waddled by on the sidewalk. "I can do that."

"You won't be having any trouble with the FBI," Bonhoff said.

"Oh? How did you make that happen?"

"Let's just say I have friends in powerful places, Viktor. Money can buy a lot of things."

"That's good to hear."

"I've made some deals recently, and nothing is going to stop us now. I've got the right people in the right places, and we're going to wreck that country and rebuild it just like we want it."

Viktor waited for Bonhoff to say it. He knew it would come.

"And I'll be the richest man in the world."

Viktor grinned. There it was. Right on cue. Viktor spat on the grass again, itching to light the fire. "I guess I had better get started then."

"Yes, you do that. Like I said, you won't be having any trouble with the FBI so make it big."

"Oh, it'll be big, sir."

"Good." Before ending the call, Bonhoff offered one last morsel to sweeten the pot. "I'll pay you double, Viktor, if I see that piece of crap Liberty Bell being dragged through the streets."

Viktor smiled. He had already thought of that one. What a glorious sight it would be.

FBI Headquarters – Washington, D.C.

Six blocks east of the White House, Director Duncan entered his seventh-floor office at the J. Edgar Hoover FBI Building. Having returned from his "vacation" in Switzerland, he was ready to get back to work. Jet lag was not a problem. Even though he had barely slept, the meeting with Bonhoff had invigorated him.

He was going to team up with his old college buddy and they were going to be in charge of the United States. They'd remake it the way they dreamed of—the intellectual elites telling the riffraff how to live their pathetic lives. The government would take their money, spread it around, and watch their power and authority increase with every passing year. In the process, he would become an insanely rich man.

He smiled to himself. *To the victors go the spoils.*

Duncan and Lamont had discussed their plans for the upcoming weeks. Lamont was going to hammer the President for being ineffective, for lacking the will to end the violence. He would claim the President didn't care about the poor minorities in the inner cities and was probably glad the cities were burning. Lamont's friends in the media would pile on the President, calling him every derogatory term they could think of while they replayed videos of the fires and destruction night and day.

For his part, Duncan decided his first day back would be the perfect time to announce the FBI's latest initiative. The higher-ups at the Bureau were caught off guard when he passed around a two-page memo outlining the FBI's focus for the upcoming months. His morning staff meeting made no mention of the aftermath in Boston or how the Bureau's investigation was going.

"I'm going to have a press conference this afternoon to announce the initiative," Duncan told the men and women seated around the conference table. He didn't ask if there were any objections. There were none, mainly because those gathered were too stunned to offer any suggestions.

Shortly before 1 p.m., Director Duncan looked himself in the mirror and straightened his green tie. He buttoned his suit coat and made sure his hair was in place. He offered a quick swipe of the FBI pin on his lapel. A keen observer would notice his usual American flag pin was missing that day.

He made his way to the press briefing room and strode to the podium. There were a fair number of media in attendance, but Duncan wasn't disappointed. His statement would be passed around and the nightly news commentators would make reference to it. It wouldn't be a bombshell, but Duncan wasn't looking to throw bombs that day. He was just going about his job as Director of the FBI.

"Thank you all for being here," he said, spreading out the two sheets on the podium. "I wanted to address the FBI's latest initiative in the war on violence in this country. It is a long time in coming, but an important one that needs to be confronted. I have sent out a directive to the fifty-six FBI field offices in the country to ratchet up their investigations of militia groups that are plaguing the United States. These groups harbor some of the worst that America has to offer, and many of them have the violent intent to overthrow the government. They will not do so on my watch."

The reporters were scratching out their notes. Most of them thought they would be hearing about the latest riots, but Duncan had gone a different direction.

It was a brilliant move on the Director's part. The President could not publicly complain that the Director was not doing his job because no one was in favor of violent militia groups intent on overthrowing the government. The President would have to keep his mouth shut.

Sure the President might yell at Duncan in private that the FBI's focus should be on those who were actually rioting, looting, and burning down American cities, but Duncan could take those blows. He was the Director of the FBI after all, and he would tell the President and Vice President that he could run the Bureau the way he wanted. And if the President decided to fire him, he could walk out the door and tell the American people that the President was no longer an effective leader and a change at the top needed to be made.

For the next several days, the media would question the President's judgment, claiming he was taking his eye off the ball while cities across the country burned. It would be perfect for the Lamont campaign to latch onto and hammer the President on the campaign trail.

Duncan noted that the FBI would put extra agents and resources into rooting out violent militia groups and making the country a safer place to live.

"Thank you all very much," he said in concluding his remarks. He grabbed his paperwork and stepped away from the podium.

One reporter held up a hand and asked, "Do you have any comment as to the investigation of the Boston riots?"

Director Duncan nodded his head as he stepped toward the door. "The investigation is ongoing. We're on top of it."

He threw a thumbs-up to let everyone know that there was nothing to worry about. The FBI had it covered. Then he left the room without taking any more questions.

On his way back to his office, he received a text message from Senator Lamont. *Watched your presser. Brilliant! Loved the green tie, too!*

Duncan smiled and responded. *I thought you'd like that.*

Lamont texted a quick reply. *It was just what we need to win! Keep it up!*

Duncan fired off one more. *More to come.*

CHAPTER 29

Near Mineral, Virginia

After spending the previous night in Washington, Schiffer returned home and hit the top step of the second floor just in time to hear Alexandra yell at him not to come into the bedroom. She said it with a purpose, too, like he had better comply or else. It wasn't exactly what the future husband wanted to hear from his fiancée a day before the wedding after he had been out of town for nearly a week. A thousand thoughts raced through his mind, and most of them ended with a single gunshot to the forehead of any man hurrying to try and pull his pants up on the other side of the wall. He put his hand on his Glock. If the man tried to make a jump for it out of the second-floor window, Schiffer decided he'd grab his sniper rifle and engage in a little target practice.

He leaned closer to the door, listening for any whispers or rustling or clanging of another man's belt.

"Why not?"

"Because I'm trying on my wedding dress," she yelled back through the closed door. "It's bad luck to see the bride in her wedding dress before the big day. I want you to be surprised when you see me walking down the aisle."

Schiffer stood down for the time being. He had a thought about going outside to check the window just in case but, in the end, he trusted Alexandra.

"What time do we have to be at the Cathedral to check it out?"

"Four!" she shouted back. "I told you that on the phone earlier."

Schiffer frowned. He didn't think she had told him, but he decided to let it slide. No sense getting involved in that no-win situation. He had at least learned that much when it came to relationships.

He went back downstairs and grabbed a bottle of water from the fridge. Walking out to the back deck, he stopped and looked out over the lake. While the calm water usually brought him a sense of peace, it failed on that day. Too much on his mind. He remembered when he, Wolfson, and Segel had trained to infiltrate Bonhoff's mansion. Then his mind replayed the lake in Switzerland and coming up into the mansion. It was a heck of a success in that regard.

Until he didn't take the shot. If he had put a bullet in the back of Bonhoff's brain, he would have been over it by now and moved on with his life. But he felt like he let people down—the President, the Vice President, the country. Not pulling the trigger would gnaw at him until the day he could make up for it.

But it didn't look like that would be happening any time soon, if ever.

He took a sip of water, wondering if he made the right call. The President and Vice President said he did, but he wasn't so sure. If he had killed Bonhoff, Duncan and Lamont would have a lot of explaining to do. Maybe he should have killed all three.

The sliding glass door opened behind him. "Hey there," Alexandra said.

The wedding dress was off, replaced by a red tank top and cut-off jean shorts frayed at the edges. He knew she'd look good in a bridal gown, but he'd take what she was then wearing over just about anything.

"Hey."

She sidled up to him and put her arms around his waist. He breathed in her strawberry-scented shampoo and ran his hands down her back. He could get used to that.

She looked up at him with her brown eyes. "Everything okay?"

"Yeah."

"You sure?"

"I'm fine."

"You're not getting cold feet, are you?"

"No, of course not."

"Well what is it then?"

"I just have a lot on my mind."

Alexandra sighed the sigh of a woman who thought the only thing on her man's mind should be their wedding day. "You want to talk about what went on when you were somewhere you couldn't tell me about?"

"No."

She laid her head on his chest, apparently thinking it was no use drawing out whatever demon was plaguing his mind.

"What time is Ayala going to be here?"

"Any minute now. She's bringing Moira with her. She said Ariel had to meet with some friends at the Israeli Embassy so they decided to drive down."

Schiffer glanced at his watch. "I have to pick Noah up at Reagan National at three."

"So we'll just meet at the church?"

"That sounds good to me."

She looked up at him again. "I love you."

He lowered his head and pressed his lips against hers, remembering what was in store for him for the rest of his life. Thank God for her. "I love you, too."

Hart Senate Office Building – Washington, D.C.

Nate Russo had taken the day off from his duties as Stubblefield's Chief of Staff. Summers were the best opportunity to use vacation time, since most members of Congress fled town. Plus, it wasn't like the Vice President had much for him to do anyway.

As he entered the waiting area of Senator Lamont's Senate office with Shannon Swisher by his side in that early afternoon, he could hardly contain the smile on his face. And it wasn't just because he had slept with Swisher the night before. He was getting used to it, although he'd be lying if he said he didn't wonder how long the sex would last. Probably until he had provided every last bit of information he could on what was happening inside the Vice President's office.

On the ride up to Capitol Hill, he had rubbed Swisher's inner thigh the whole way in the back seat of the Town Car. She didn't tell him to stop. He knew she wanted him to continue what he was doing—at least the spying operation inside the West Wing—and he was happy with the fringe benefits of their arrangement.

But there were more reasons to smile than having nightly rolls in the hay with the sexy Shannon Swisher. He was going to get a job offer today—one that he had been waiting for and one that would lead to him becoming the Chief of Staff to the next President of the United States—Gregory Lamont. The job was still well off into the future, but he was going to seal the deal that morning.

And if necessary, he brought a few extra gifts to sweeten the pot. It was going to be a good day. And if he could convince Swisher that there was more to discuss, it would be a good night as well.

* * *

Senator Lamont had just finished texting Director Duncan when his secretary buzzed him that Swisher and Russo had arrived for their meeting. He set the newspapers on his desk off the side. Bonhoff had called him the night before and cryptically told him to keep an eye on things going on up in Philadelphia. Lamont woke up excited, expecting bad news for President Schumacher and good news for the Lamont for President campaign.

But Lamont thought the news was disappointing. The riots in Philly had fizzled. Although the FBI had not been intimately involved in looking to thwart the attack, the Department of Homeland Security had. According to news reports, the Mayor of Philadelphia and the Governor of Pennsylvania wanted no part of what they had seen in Boston, and the National Guard was quickly called out to protect the statues, monuments, and historic buildings. President Schumacher's offer of assistance was immediately accepted. The expected riots and looting never materialized. Sporadic gunfire was reported throughout the city, which was not out of the ordinary, but it did not appear that anyone had been killed.

Lamont knew you can't win them all, so he told himself to focus on the good news. Director Duncan had begun his plot to slow walk the FBI through the riot investigations, and now Lamont was going to meet with a White House insider who could provide him with dirt on the President and the Vice President. Yes, life was good.

There was a knock on the door, and Swisher entered with Russo behind her.

"Good afternoon, Shannon."

"Good afternoon, Senator." She gestured toward the man next to her. "I want to introduce you to Nate Russo, Vice President Stubblefield's Chief of Staff."

Lamont walked out from behind his desk, a smile on his face. "Nate! Good to finally meet you. I've heard a lot about you." They shook hands. "Shannon has spoken wonders about your career here in Washington. She says you're top notch."

"Thank you, Senator. Shannon and I go way back. She speaks wonders of you, too. But that's not surprising given our common Harvard pedigree."

Lamont laughed. "That's right. We need to stick together in this town. Otherwise nothing would get done." He motioned for Russo and Swisher to take seats in front of his desk.

They started with small talk. The weather. How the summer was going. What Russo thought of Lamont's campaign kickoff speech. Russo said it set just the right tone.

"How are things in the White House?"

Russo glanced at Swisher, who nodded like he should feel free to let loose. "If I had a word to describe it, Senator, it would be disarray."

It brought another smile to Lamont's face. "Music to my ears, Nate." Lamont leaned back in his chair, feeling the need to get comfortable for a good long talk on taking down the White House. "Shannon tells me you've provided some valuable information we can use in the campaign."

Nate nodded.

"I can't tell you how much I appreciate having someone of your caliber on the inside. Someone who gets what I'm trying to accomplish as President."

"Yes, sir. I agree wholeheartedly." Nate leaned forward, appearing ready to get down to the nitty-gritty. "The White House doesn't know what it's doing. They're ticked off at the FBI Director for dragging his feet. I can only imagine what they're thinking after Director Duncan's little speech this morning. The Vice President's probably on the warpath."

Lamont rocked slightly in his chair, looking like life was too good to be true. He let Russo talk, letting the man vent the frustrations of an underappreciated employee. *Let it all out, Nate. I'm here for you. You'll feel better if you get it off your chest.*

When Russo was done, Lamont said, "Shannon tells me you're wanting a job in my administration." There was no qualification "if I win." It was a foregone conclusion in Lamont's mind. He had not only measured the drapes in the Oval Office, he had already bought the replacements. He was that confident.

Lamont was ready to promise Russo anything he wanted. It would still be a long time before a President Lamont stepped foot in the Oval Office, and things could change in a heartbeat in D.C. If he found someone better than Russo, he'd discard him like yesterday's trash. And he could do it without a second thought because he could always let word leak that Russo had a history of not being the most loyal of employees.

"Yes, sir. I want to be Chief of Staff to the President of the United States. Your Chief of Staff."

Lamont liked Russo's style—direct, confident, almost cocky. Harvard types had that swagger that the lesser folk—namely those from Yale—didn't have.

Lamont decided he was going to make the man's day. He snapped his fingers and said, "Done. If everything Shannon says about you is true, I'm glad to bring you on board."

Russo smiled. Swisher smiled. Lamont smiled. It was practically a love fest in Senator Lamont's office.

Swisher piped up. "Can you believe we're already filling positions in the Lamont Administration?"

Lamont rocked back and forth, practically giddy that they were actually doing it. "I feel like we should open a bottle of champagne to celebrate."

Russo sat back in his chair, the cocky look still on his face. He held up a hand to put the party on hold for a second because he had something else to get excited about. "You might want to wait because I have some more information that could be of use to you."

Lamont had a thought as to why Russo hadn't said something earlier. Obviously because he was saving it in case he needed another card to play. *Man, I like this guy*, Lamont thought to himself. He sat forward and rubbed his hands together in anticipation of an expected juicy tidbit. "Excellent. Whattya got?"

Russo pulled out his phone. Before he powered it up, he said, "The Vice President has been seeing someone on the side."

Lamont's eyes widened. He looked at Swisher. Scandal! His eyes shot back to Russo. "You mean he's been fooling around with a woman?"

Russo shook his head. "No, it's a guy."

Lamont gasped. So did Swisher. She had no clue.

"You mean the Vice President is gay!?" Lamont said, shocked to the core.

"No, he's not gay," Russo shot back, looking like he couldn't believe the others had even gone that route. "He's happily married . . . but there has been a guy coming in recently. Very hush-hush. He doesn't sign in on the visitor logs. He's not listed on the schedule. It's all off the books."

Lamont took a second to try and figure out where this was going. "Do you know the man's name?" he asked—curious but not concerned. At least not yet.

"Schiffer. Duke Schiffer."

Lamont mouthed the words Duke Schiffer. The name sounded vaguely familiar, like he might have heard it bandied about in Washington. "Do you know him?"

"I know he used to work for the FBI."

Lamont wasn't sure he liked where this was going. "What's he doing for the Vice President?"

"I haven't been able to find out yet. Like I said, very hush-hush. The Vice President doesn't tell me what they're talking about."

"Shouldn't the Vice President tell his Chief of Staff what he's up to?"

"You would think," Russo said. He sneered and spat out, "He doesn't like Harvard grads."

Lamont made a face. The fingers of his left hand started drumming the desk.

Russo held up his phone. "But I think I might have an idea of what they were talking about." He made a few swipes on the screen and tapped a couple icons. Then he waited for the surprise to come. In the quiet of Lamont's Senate office, the unmistakable deep voice of Vice President Stubblefield echoed off the walls. Most of it was small talk and light banter.

Lamont leaned forward, straining to hear every word. When Stubblefield said the word "Bonhoff," Lamont gasped like someone had reached down his throat and ripped out his lungs.

"How did you get that?" Lamont asked, a noticeable tremor in his voice.

"I pretended to leave my phone in the Vice President's office. He didn't know I was taping their conversation."

Lamont could feel his heart racing. He balled his fists so the others couldn't see him shaking with fright.

"Senator, are you feeling okay?" Swisher asked, obviously noticing the blood draining from Lamont's face. "You look a little pale."

Lamont tried to get it together. "When did you record that?"

"Just yesterday. Schiffer has come in a few times over the last several weeks, but I haven't seen him since I recorded this."

Son of a . . . If the Vice President knew that he and Director Duncan met with the man funding the riots, it could be the end of both of them. Lamont pushed the newspapers on his desk off to the side. He looked at his desk calendar looking for an excuse to end the meeting. "I have another appointment. You'll have to go. It was nice to meet you, Nate. Shannon, I'll talk to you later."

"Is something wrong?" Swisher asked.

Hell yes, there was something wrong. He lied. "No, I just forgot I have to take care of something. It totally slipped my mind. We'll talk more in the coming days." He hurriedly walked them to the door. As soon as it closed, he was on the phone.

On the second ring, Director Duncan picked up. "Greg, how are—"

"We've got a problem!"

"What's wrong?"

Lamont paced the office, his right hand massaging his aching forehead. "I think he might know."

"Who?"

"The Vice President. I think he knows about Bonhoff."

There was silence on Duncan's end until he said, "How do you know?"

"I heard a recording of the Vice President talking about Bonhoff."

"A recording? Where did you get a recording?"

"It's not important where I got it," Lamont snapped.

Apparently trying to be the voice of reason, Duncan said, "Greg, Karl Bonhoff is a known figure. He's believed to be the money funding progressive groups in the United States. Some of it consists of legal donations to left-wing causes. There's no definitive evidence that Bonhoff has been funding the riots. I'm sure the Vice President was just talking politics. Maybe he was discussing strategy with his campaign advisers. Maybe he's going to run."

Lamont then dropped the bomb, although he had no clue how explosive it would be. "He was talking to a guy named Schiffer."

Duncan went dead silent before he cursed.

The profanity didn't help Lamont's anxiety. "You know him?"

"Yes, I know him. He's ex-FBI, and he's trouble. Big trouble."

"Kurt, the tape was made yesterday! Who knows how long they've been looking at Bonhoff. They could have been watching us!"

Duncan cursed again, louder this time.

"What if they know we met with Karl? The man has been funding the riots! If the American people find out, it will ruin us. You need to do something!"

"Me? What do you want me to do?"

"You need to take care of this. Get rid of that Schiffer guy. He may know things."

"I can't get rid of him. That's crazy."

"You're already in this deep, Kurt. You've got to do something to get us out of this mess."

"I can't do it myself, Greg. I'm the Director of the FBI!"

Lamont let out an expletive. He thought his friend should have manned up and told him he'd take care of it. Now Lamont only had one place to turn—that ruthless SOB funding his campaign. Bonhoff had minions all over the country, all of them ready and willing to do his bidding.

"I might be able to get someone. But you have to find Schiffer."

Duncan grunted his displeasure, but said, "I'll find him, Greg. You just get someone to take him out. And do it fast."

Lamont hung up and then hit the speed dial for the fourth richest man in the world. He waited through three rings and prayed he wouldn't get a voice mail. Bonhoff finally picked up.

"Greg! How are—"

"Karl, I'm sorry to interrupt, but it's an emergency. I've got a real problem."

Lamont ran through the facts as fast as he could give them. Bonhoff quickly agreed it was a problem that needed to be taken care of. They didn't need the Vice President or Schiffer snooping around where they didn't belong. He acted ticked, like having to save Lamont's ass was going to cost him in the future. Lamont was practically begging for help.

"I can send someone to you, Greg. He'll take care of it. You'll just need to tell me where to send him."

Lamont finally took a breath for what seemed like the first time in hours. "Thank you, Karl. I'll let you know as soon as I can. But please tell your man to hurry!"

CHAPTER 30

FBI Headquarters – Washington, D.C.

If Senator Lamont was in a panic over the revelation that the Schumacher Administration was looking into the dealings of Karl Bonhoff, Director Duncan was in a full-blown meltdown. Lamont might have been able to brush off the meeting with Bonhoff as one involving multimillionaires who were acquaintances in Lamont's former days on Wall Street. Or maybe one involving a candidate seeking donations from Bonhoff-funded groups.

Duncan, however, was a different story. He was the Director of the foremost law enforcement agency in the world. And being seen with the man secretly funding the riots infesting America's streets and the movement to defund the police would not be able to be explained away. It would look bad and, even worse, some people might say he was conspiring with the enemy.

Because that was exactly what he was doing.

Duncan didn't know what the Vice President knew about his dealings with Bonhoff and Lamont. Perhaps he knew nothing. But it was Schiffer's presence that scared the hell out of him. Schiffer was not a political strategist or a campaign adviser. He would not have been discussing how Bonhoff's dark money could impact an election.

No, it was much worse than that. Duke Schiffer was a covert operative. Someone off the books who was known to make bad people go away in the dark of night. Only a handful of people had any knowledge that Stubblefield regularly called on Schiffer to "check things out." And if Stubblefield had sent Schiffer to snoop around Bonhoff's business, Duncan knew he could be in some trouble. He cursed the thought that he had been careless. He never should have gone to Switzerland.

Duncan paced back and forth in his spacious seventh-floor office. With paranoia rattling his bones, he told himself to calm down. He was the Director of the FBI, for goodness sakes. He had been trained to deal with complex situations that would cause regular Americans to want to hide under their beds and never come out.

He took a deep breath and then let it out. "Focus," he said. "I can handle this."

He had a thought that he might be able to take care of the problem himself.

As a career FBI agent and now Director of the FBI, he had met his fair share of unsavory types in his work—some of them were in prison and some of them were still working the streets. He could call in a favor or two, make Schiffer go away, and move on. It could be done and no one would know.

But it would take time. And he didn't have time.

Lamont said he could get someone, and Duncan knew that could only mean he was going to call Bonhoff and beg for one of the man's henchmen to do the deed. Duncan was fine with that. Let Lamont and Bonhoff get their hands dirty. If Bonhoff's man took out Schiffer, Duncan thought he could have the FBI take out the assassin. He would look like the lawman riding in on his white horse to hunt down the hunter. The American people would praise his leadership. Schiffer would be gone, Bonhoff's assassin would be gone, and Duncan would come out smelling like a rose—as if nothing happened.

That was the way to go.

But he had his part to do. He needed to find Schiffer, and he needed to find him quick. He didn't want to come out and call Schiffer out of the blue. That would raise red flags. He could have one of his Deputy Directors find Schiffer, but that would leave a trail. The less people in the know, the better. He needed a legitimate reason.

And if by magic, he found it.

When he walked behind his desk, he had glanced at his calendar. There was a note written on his calendar for the next day—all it said was *Schiffer/Julian wedding at National Cathedral*. He had received an invitation months earlier, probably as a courtesy to all the bigwigs in D.C. and because Schiffer had once been a valued FBI employee. Duncan had sent his RSVP, although he hadn't planned on attending. But now it would give him a reason to call.

Duncan picked up his office phone. "Get me the number for Alexandra Julian," he said to his secretary on the other end of the line. "I want to call her and congratulate her on her wedding. I'm not sure I'm going to be able to make it tomorrow." He added the last sentence in case his secretary was ever called to testify before a grand jury.

"I have the number, Director. Would you like me to initiate the call?"

Duncan thought about it but decided he didn't want the FBI phone logs being the subject of a Freedom of Information Act request. It was "personal" business anyway. "No, thank you, Irene. I'll call her on my cell phone."

He steadied himself before dialing the numbers. Inhale, then exhale. *Just ask where Duke is. There's nothing wrong with that.* He wiped his moist hand on his white dress shirt. *It has to be done. There's no other way.* Inhale, then exhale.

Eyeing the number he had written, he tapped it out with his thumbs and then hit the call button. Inhale, then exhale. He was about to inhale again when a female answered.

"Hello."

The breath had been snatched from him leaving him speechless.

"Hello."

Get it together! He cleared his throat. "Yes, excuse me. Is this Alexandra?"

"Yes, this is Alexandra."

Duncan thought he could hear an engine running, like she was in a vehicle going somewhere. "Hi, Alexandra, this is Kurt Duncan over at the FBI. I don't mean to bother you, but I just wanted to call and offer my best wishes on your upcoming nuptials. It's tomorrow, isn't it?"

"Yes, it is. I'm really excited that the day is finally here."

She sounded so pleasant to Duncan. So happy. *It's a shame what's going to happen to your fiancé.* "I'm sure you are."

"Did you need to talk to Duke?"

"Is he there with you?"

"No, I'm on my way now to meet him at the National Cathedral to make sure everything's in place for the ceremony. We're supposed to be there at four."

Bingo. The National Cathedral. Four o'clock. It would be an easy spot for Bonhoff's man to make the hit and then melt away into the Friday Beltway traffic. *Get her off the line and make the call.*

"Well, that's wonderful, Alexandra. I'm sure the Cathedral will be a memorable place for your wedding." *Or a funeral*, Duncan thought. "I'll try to give Duke a call as soon as I can. It's no big deal. If I can't reach him, I hope to see both of you tomorrow. Of course, you know how the job is, you never know what's going to come up."

"I understand, Director. Thanks for calling."

Duncan tapped the screen to end the call. *Damn, I'm good. She'll never know the reason for the call. Hell, she might even be caught in the crossfire. And the good thing about that is, dead people don't talk.*

The thought of having a decorated former FBI agent killed crossed his mind for a second, but his conscience quickly discarded the concern with the very real fear that Duncan's own livelihood was on the line. Schiffer needed to go. He didn't work for the FBI now anyway. He was nothing more than the Vice President's personal hit man. He needed to be taken out. Duncan took a breath. He had talked himself into believing what he was doing was actually good for the country. Feeling confident now, he hit the speed dial for Lamont.

"Yes," Lamont said hurriedly.

"I know where the target is heading. He's going to be at the National Cathedral at four. Get him there."

"I'll pass it along." Lamont thought of one other thing. "They're going to want to know what he looks like."

"I'll send you a picture from the target's personnel file. He'll be easy to spot. He looks like an FBI agent."

"Good."

"Make sure you tell them that the target is most likely armed." Knowing Schiffer, Duncan thought he should emphasize the last point. "And he knows how to use it."

Baltimore, Maryland

Viktor Kozlov spat on the red brick of the pier jutting out into Baltimore's Inner Harbor. He sat alone on a bench overlooking the water. A homeless man looked to be sleeping on a bench on the opposite side of the pier. The USS Constellation was moored behind Kozlov's right. The U.S. Navy had built her in the 1850s, the last of the warships powered solely by sails, and she saw action in the Civil War. The ship was now a National Historic Landmark and a magnet for sightseers. Kozlov found those facts interesting.

There were a handful of tourists milling around the Inner Harbor in the middle of the day. The progressive leaders of Baltimore had stood by and done nothing to stop the violence plaguing the city, so those outsiders wanting to see Fort McHenry and shop near the Inner Harbor did so in the light of day and hightailed it out of there before dark when the criminals ran free.

That was fine with Kozlov. Although he liked seeing tourists fleeing in terror when the riots and looting started, he could still get the job done with the criminal element roaming the streets at night. The call had gone out on social media that tonight was the night to burn down Baltimore.

Kozlov had big plans. He wanted the fire to be so big that people would write poems about it and eventually use it as the country's new national anthem—an anthem not celebrating the land of the free and the home of the brave but allegiance to the big government masters who controlled the everyday lives of their peasant subjects.

He got up from his bench and walked back to the sidewalk to get the lay of the land. He turned right, noticing the three park benches. There was a white construction worker on his phone seated on the first one, a mom and young daughter with a Teddy bear in her arms in the middle, and a homeless black man on the end. *What a collection of people*, Kozlov thought.

He looked toward the water. There were two dozen paddle boats shaped like dragons bobbing up and down in the water, all of them waiting for occupants. He had plans for the boats that night. Filled with gasoline, lit, and set adrift, they would look like a Chinse New Year celebration gone wrong. He could already see the pictures of the destruction and ruin in his mind.

With his mind full of dreams, the phone buzzed in his pocket. He looked at the screen and saw it was Bonhoff.

"Yes?"

"Viktor, where are you?"

"Baltimore."

"Forget about Baltimore. I need you to get down to Washington."

Kozlov sensed a change in Bonhoff's tone. It was one that he hadn't heard before. Gone was the braggart who promised to soon be the richest man in the world. It was replaced with a tone laden with worry. "What's the problem?"

"I need you to take care of something. Right now."

Kozlov spat on the bricks. "Where?"

"Washington National Cathedral." Bonhoff proceeded to give a short version of what was going on. He said Lamont and Duncan had slipped up and Kozlov needed to get rid of a guy named Schiffer, who had been poking his nose in the wrong places. Bonhoff said that if Schiffer was eliminated, Lamont and Duncan would owe him big time, and he intended to bleed them both dry to pay him back.

"I know where the Cathedral is."

"The target is supposed to be there at four this afternoon. Can you get there?"

"Yes, I'm only an hour away."

"This has to be taken care of, Viktor." Bonhoff paused before stressing, "Today."

Kozlov's steps picked up before he broke into a jog. He had to get back to his car. He checked his watch. It would take an hour to get down to D.C. More if the traffic was bad. He needed to get a move on.

"Viktor, are you still there?"

"I'm heading to the car right now, Karl. I'll take care of it." Kozlov was running now, and he didn't notice the people looking at him as he ran with a phone to his ear. He didn't care. The burning of Baltimore was off for the time being. He had a new mission. "I expect to be compensated."

"I'll double it, Viktor. Just do it as quietly as you can."

Kozlov rolled his eyes, like an operation of this nature could be done quietly. It would be as loud as it took to get the job done. "I'm going to need a picture of who I'm looking for."

"I'll have it by the time you get to D.C."

Kozlov slowed as he found his car parked at a meter.

"One more thing, Viktor."

Kozlov hit the fob to unlock the door. "Yes?"

"The target is most likely armed and dangerous."

Kozlov smirked and spat again. "Yeah, well . . . So am I."

CHAPTER 31

Washington, D.C.

Duke Schiffer drove toward the pickup and dropoff zone at Reagan National Airport and saw a tall, thin man in a baseball cap and sunglasses eyeing his Jeep from a distance. Like a wolf eyeing his prey, the man had obviously zeroed in on the target, and Schiffer knew the eyes behind the shades were probably scanning left and right for anything out of the ordinary.

Schiffer pulled the Jeep to the sidewalk, slowed to a stop, and lowered the window. The man said nothing. He opened the back door and placed his suitcase on the seat. Then he got in the passenger seat and stared straight ahead.

"Afternoon to you, too, Noah."

Wolfson glanced at Schiffer behind the sunglasses and then nodded.

Schiffer smiled and put the Jeep into gear. "Good flight?"

"It was fine."

Schiffer was glad to get that much out of him. The man was as stoic as they come, but it contributed to his success.

"Like I told you earlier, we're just going to head straight to the National Cathedral to meet with Alexandra and Ayala. We'll do a quick walk through regarding the ceremony and then I'll get you to your hotel. Dinner will be at six."

"Fine."

They hit Interstate 395 without another word being said. When they got on Washington Boulevard on the west side of the Pentagon, Schiffer noticed the Israeli assassin giving the building a good look, like he might find something of value. They crossed the Potomac using the Arlington Memorial Bridge, made the loop near the Lincoln Memorial, and headed toward Foggy Bottom.

"Sweet ride," Wolfson said, looking around. "I like the magnetic mounts." He grabbed the Glock 19 under the glove box.

Schiffer thought that might have been the first compliment he had ever heard out of Wolfson's mouth. "Glock here, too," he said, patting the butt of one of the pistols mounted to the left of the steering wheel. "I've got a go-bag behind the seats—Sig Sauer MPX submachine gun, five thirty-round magazines, spare pistol magazines, tourniquets, flash bang grenades." He pointed behind him. "I had them put in ammo drawers under the back seats, too. Way in the back, there's a lockbox with a couple M4s."

"Nice." Wolfson appeared genuinely impressed.

"I just got the red-and-blue lights installed yesterday."

Schiffer veered the Jeep onto Waterside Drive and stopped at the light at Massachusetts Avenue. After cranking up the air conditioning, he said, "Have you been to Washington much?"

"A few times."

"Care to tell me about them?"

"Not really."

"Any place else in the country?"

Wolfson was looking out the window when he said, "Las Vegas."

"Did you win?"

Wolfson turned and gave Schiffer a look that said he was disappointed he even asked. "I always win."

A smile crossed Schiffer's face. Wolfson never changed. As they waited for the light to turn green, Schiffer said, "I know you're not my best friend and all, especially after what happened the other day, but I really appreciate you being here. It means a lot that you'd come all this way."

Wolfson looked at the passing scenery and shrugged. "You saved my life once. I guess I owe it to you to be here."

Schiffer almost gasped at the statement. This was a big moment for Wolfson. "So you admit that I saved your life."

Wolfson emitted a sound like an angry dog's growl. "Don't push it."

When they neared the Naval Observatory, Schiffer pointed out the window. "Vice President Stubblefield's residence is behind those trees."

Schiffer told Wolfson some of what had been discussed with the President and Vice President when he returned from Switzerland. Neither of them was happy, and a plan was in place to figure out what all Lamont and Duncan were up to.

Up the road, Schiffer turned on Wisconsin Avenue, and off to the right they could see the pinnacles on the north and south towers of the National Cathedral.

"Nice place for wedding, huh?" Schiffer asked.

"I guess if you're into that thing."

They went to the intersection at Woodley Road, turned right heading east, and entered the Cathedral grounds on the north side. The Jeep slowed as Schiffer searched for a spot. Seeing Alexandra's car down the way, he pulled in.

"They're probably already inside," Schiffer said, turning off the engine. "You're welcome to come inside and look around. Like I said, we won't be too long. Half hour at the most. Just a quick walk through."

Wolfson shook his head. "I'll sit out here. Or maybe I'll take a walk and stretch my legs. It was a long flight."

"All right. I'll leave the keys."

Schiffer had changed into his nicest black tactical pants, his "dress tactical" as he called them, and an untucked white dress shirt that concealed the Glock 43X on his left hip. He walked in and found Alexandra, Ayala, and Moira all gawking at the ornate surroundings of the Cathedral. Ayala gave him a hug, and Moira told him she was excited to be the flower girl. He thanked them for coming and said Noah was waiting out in the Jeep. As Alexandra looped her arm through Schiffer's, Reverend Harrison acted as their guide, going through the steps for the ceremony and what they should expect. Alexandra said the florist had promised to have the flowers in place in plenty of time before the guests were set to arrive. She also said they decided to have the pictures taken after the ceremony.

"It really is spectacular, isn't it?" Alexandra whispered to Schiffer, her eyes gazing up to the vaulted ceiling of the nave and the sea of colors brought about by the two rows of flags from the fifty states.

Schiffer nodded. "Yeah."

She pulled away slightly. "Yeah? That's all you have to say?"

"It's nice."

Alexandra sighed, like he should be gushing with awe and wonder. They stepped away from the group to have a moment of privacy. "What's wrong?"

"Nothing."

"You're lying, Duke." She unhooked her arm from his. "Something's wrong."

Schiffer shook his head. It wasn't the right time. As much as he looked forward to marrying Alexandra, he couldn't get the failed mission in Switzerland out of his head. And with what he learned about the FBI Director, it weighed on his mind even more.

"I just have a lot to think about, Alexandra."

"About the wedding?"

He smiled. "No. Not about the wedding."

"What is it then?"

"Just work."

"Maybe talking about it will help."

Schiffer smiled and kissed her on the cheek. He knew she was going to be badgering him until the day he retired. He tried to focus on her and the journey in life that they were about to embark on. Maybe it would take his mind off the fact that his last mission was a failure.

"We'll talk after the wedding," he said, hoping it would placate her for the time being. "Let's get everyone to the hotel so we can get ready for dinner."

* * *

Viktor Kozlov stepped out of his car and spat on the pavement. After leaving Baltimore, he had taken Interstates 95 and 495 through Maryland until he exited near Chevy Chase. He entered the District of Columbia on Connecticut Avenue and made his way to Wisconsin Avenue, which ran on the west side of the Cathedral.

The quick trip gave him plenty of time to scout out the area. There were several roads leading into and out of the nearly sixty acres comprising the Cathedral grounds, any one of them giving him the opportunity to kill the target and hightail it out of there. From the Cathedral grounds, Massachusetts Avenue on the south side would lead toward Washington, where he would have greater time blending in with the tourists and bureaucrats on their way home. To the west were various parks and residential areas before reaching the Potomac River. A short distance farther down Wisconsin housed the Embassy of the Russia Federation. There were plenty of possibilities for escape.

Now he just had to find his prey.

He pulled the hat down lower on his head, his eyes darting left and right behind his sunglasses. As he pretended to search for something in the trunk of his car, he glanced at the front doors to the Cathedral. He recognized it from various funerals of Presidents shown on TV. He remembered where the family would gather and the hearse would drive off with the flag-draped casket. He planned on doing the same, except he intended to leave the dead body on the front steps.

A lone member of the Cathedral's police force sat in a white SUV at the entrance. Kozlov wasn't worried about him. The man looked bored out of his mind, maybe even napping. He was probably old and retired from the police department and likely a step too slow to prevent anything major from happening.

Kozlov lit a cigarette and checked his watch. It was four o'clock. He had two pistols ready to go—one in the car and one hidden on his hip underneath his jacket. A sniper rifle was in the trunk, but Kozlov didn't think he needed it.

His phone buzzed. He hoped this was what he had been waiting for. He stabbed the screen with his finger and then read the message. He tapped the link, and it took him to the FBI's personnel photo of Duke Schiffer. The message said the photo was dated but still provided a good likeness. When Kozlov spread his fingers across the screen to enlarge the picture, he felt a twinge in his gut. It was the look in Schiffer's eyes. It was a look of a guy not to be messed with. Kozlov knew the look. He gave that look to others.

Kozlov took the cigarette out of his mouth and blew out a cloud of smoke. He spat on the pavement again and focused on the picture of the man he was sent to kill. He envisioned Schiffer being armed, as Bonhoff said he would be, so Kozlov knew he had to be quick and decisive to keep the element of surprise. No funny business. Just pull the trigger and get out of there.

The phone buzzed again with another message. *Get it done now.* He grunted, not needing to be told. That was why he was there. He thought about firing off a response but held back. His boss would see his success on the news that evening.

He got back in the car and started it up. Flicking the cigarette into the street, he drove through the intersection, the sleepy Cathedral cop at the main entrance paying him no attention. Kozlov went a hundred yards and turned left off Wisconsin Avenue onto South Road and the southern grounds of the Cathedral. He found a nice place to park under a shade tree with a clear view of the front doors. He was a quick right turn away from the exit road heading south, where he could turn west and head back to Wisconsin Avenue or continue south until he reached Massachusetts Avenue. Whichever way he picked, he would vanish into the late afternoon traffic.

He studied Schiffer's picture one last time and then erased it. He grabbed the pistol off his hip, ejected the magazine, and then put it back in. He chambered a round and returned it to the holster under his jacket. He kept his phone on him in case he needed to pretend to be taking pictures of the Cathedral. Leaving the engine running, he stepped out and closed the door.

He took the sidewalk winding its way to the Cathedral. There were two dozen tourists walking around and taking pictures. He wasn't worried. Once he shot the target, the tourists would dive for cover or run for their lives. None of them would be able to identify him. He stopped in front of the Cathedral and looked up at the twin towers. A smile crossed his face.

It was time to go hunting.

CHAPTER 32

Washington, D.C.

While Ayala took Moira outside to find the Cathedral's Darth Vader gargoyle, Duke and Alexandra paused to look up at the west rose window with its kaleidoscope of colors radiating in the afternoon sunlight.

"It's beautiful, isn't it?" Alexandra asked.

Duke nudged her. "Just like you."

"I can't wait for tomorrow," she said, reaching for his hand.

"Me either."

At the front doors, they shook hands with Reverend Harrison who was waiting to answer any last-minute questions. Hearing none, he said he looked forward to seeing them tomorrow. Once Duke and Alexandra stepped across the threshold, Duke pulled down his sunglasses to try and shield his eyes from the glare of the sun reflecting brightly off the wide-open front drive of the Cathedral.

Before they took the steps down to the sidewalk, Alexandra reached out to touch his arm. "Oh, I forgot to tell you, Director Duncan called."

Schiffer's head snapped to his left, wondering if he heard correctly. "Director Duncan? When?"

"About an hour ago when we were driving up here. My brother called right after that, so I forgot about it."

"What did he want?"

"He wanted to wish us well on the wedding. He said he was going to try and call you sometime."

He turned and faced her. "What did you tell him?"

Alexandra shrugged. "What do you mean? I made small talk. Thanked him for calling."

"What else?" When she paused, he pressed on. "Think, Alexandra, what else did you tell him?" He could tell he shocked her with his forcefulness, but he needed to know.

"I don't know, Duke. I told him we were about to check out the Cathedral and he said he might try to stop by on his way home. What's the big deal?"

Schiffer's antennae went up. He scanned the area out front of the Cathedral. Tourists, some walking, some taking pictures. He saw the man in the hat immediately. The man was looking right at them. He had a laser-like focus on his target. The man's hand started to rise. Schiffer didn't go for his gun. He went for Alexandra.

"Get down!"

The first bullet hit the Cathedral's Indiana limestone. With no pillar to dive behind, Schiffer had pushed Alexandra back through the opened front door and landed on top of her. The second, third, and fourth shots hit the door. Having rolled to his right side to shield her, Schiffer grabbed the gun from his left hip and fired a shot toward in the man's direction.

"Stay down!"

With the shots ended, Schiffer hurried to his feet. The tourists were screaming and running in every direction. Schiffer saw the man in the hat running toward the south. When Reverend Harrison raced to a stop, Schiffer yelled, "Get her to a secure room!"

Then he took off running down the steps and across the sidewalk. The man in the hat was behind the wheel and heading south. Schiffer fired a shot that hit the rear of Kozlov's car, shattering its left brake light. He was almost to the brick drive in front of the Cathedral when a black blur almost ran over him.

It was Wolfson. He had heard shots and jumped in the driver's seat. Scattering frightened tourists, he slammed on the brakes and came to a stop. Schiffer yanked open the back door and dove in.

"Go! Go! He's in the car!"

Kozlov turned west on Massachusetts Avenue and sped through the first red light he came to. In the back of the Jeep, Schiffer grabbed the Sig-Sauer MPX from his go-bag and jammed in a thirty-round magazine. Wolfson found the switch for the flashing lights and floored the Jeep through the intersection.

Schiffer lowered both passenger windows. He flicked the selector switch on his MPX from full to semi-automatic and leaned out the right side first. "Let's go!"

Kozlov was weaving in and out of traffic, at times veering into the eastbound lanes.

"You're going to have to get closer, Wolf! There are too many cars in the way!"

With traffic in front of him, Wolfson yanked the Jeep over the curb and onto the sidewalk. Once clear, he veered left back onto the road and hit the gas.

Schiffer leaned out the window and lined up the shot. "Hold it steady!" He pulled the trigger, and the shot hit the right rear bumper of Kozlov's car. Kozlov made a hard left in front of traffic, cars skidding to a stop. He headed south on Idaho Avenue, and Wolfson lost sight of him for a second. Wolfson made the left turn and gunned the throttle. It was a one-way street with cars parked on both sides.

"Be ready! I might have to shoot through the windshield!"

The brake lights on Kozlov's car blinked on.

"He's going to have to turn!" Wolfson yelled, seeing the stopped cars ahead of him at the T-intersection. "He's going to have to turn!"

Schiffer thought the man would head back to Washington, hoping to get lost in the sea of people. He shifted over to the driver's side and leaned out the window.

"He's going left!"

Schiffer readied his weapon. He was a natural lefty so the left side shot was best. "Steady, Wolf. Keep it steady."

Kozlov slammed on the brakes and made the corner. Schiffer let out a breath and feathered the trigger. The man's head was centered in the red dot. A car door opened, and Wolfson's hands flinched on the wheel. Schiffer pulled the trigger, but the slight movement sent the bullet wide left into Kozlov's left-front quarter panel.

Schiffer cursed and then yelled, "Come on! Come on! Push it!"

Now speeding east on Cathedral Avenue, Schiffer knew Kozlov had three choices once he hit Massachusetts Avenue. Head straight for D.C. or make the quick left or right turn on Wisconsin Avenue. Cathedral Avenue would end only fifty yards from Wisconsin, so Schiffer figured Kozlov wouldn't want to make another turn. He would want to put some distance on his pursuers. Schiffer thought Massachusetts would be the way to go.

Schiffer grabbed his phone and speed-dialed Vice President Stubblefield. The big man picked up immediately. "We've had shots fired at the Cathedral. Shots fired. White male subject is on the move. Four-door sedan."

Kozlov veered right onto Massachusetts, and Wolfson was only forty yards behind now. Kozlov had the green light at Wisconsin Avenue and he barreled through without making the turn.

"He's on Massachusetts Avenue!" Duke yelled into the phone. "He's heading toward the Observatory. Four-door brown sedan."

"I'm on it!" Stubblefield responded.

With Observatory Circle approaching, Schiffer knew Kozlov would have to curve around to the right. He slid over to the right side of the Jeep and leaned out the window.

Kozlov passed the main entrance to the Naval Observatory and started the curve.

Wolfson mashed the gas and gained ground. They rounded the bend, the Jeep's engine humming at full song, the trees flashing by. Schiffer eyed Kozlov's right rear tire and fired. The rubber exploded, and Kozlov struggled to keep control. He came to a screeching halt when he saw what was in front of him. Stubblefield had sent out the alarm, and Secret Service vehicles had roared out of the gates to block the road. Agents had their weapons ready.

"He's going to run!" Wolfson yelled slamming on the brakes, throwing

Schiffer into the back of the front seats.

With the ten-foot-tall wrought iron fence surrounding the Naval Observatory, Schiffer knew Kozlov was going to head for the woods to the east. Schiffer threw open the door and ran behind the Jeep. Kozlov was on the move, firing wild shots toward the Secret Service agents to the south.

Schiffer sprinted toward Kozlov, waiting for the shot. He didn't want the man to get into the forest of trees and gain an advantage. Schiffer was closing, fifty yards now. Kozlov dropped one gun and pulled another out of its holster. More shots rang out. Agents were yelling. Sirens wailing.

Kozlov turned for the trees, his last avenue of escape. Schiffer came to an abrupt halt. The man who tried to kill him and his fiancée locked eyes with him. The red dot in his optics was centered on Kozlov's forehead. Schiffer didn't need to let out a breath. He didn't need to get any closer. He didn't need to think about it. He pulled the trigger, the shot echoing off the trees. The dead man dropped to the pavement.

Schiffer inched forward and motioned for Wolfson to check the man's car. Upon reaching the man, Schiffer raised his gun in the air to signal to the agents approaching that the target was down for good. Before anyone could get close, Schiffer knelt beside the body. Seeing the phone in the man's pocket, he fished it out and slipped it into the leg pocket of his tactical pants.

"It's clear!" Wolfson yelled from the car.

The air was filled with sounds of sirens from both ends of Massachusetts Avenue.

"Wolf," Schiffer said over the din of noise. "Get back in the Jeep. Let's get out of here."

Schiffer told the approaching Secret Service agents to radio the front gate that he was coming. He got behind the wheel with Wolfson in the front passenger seat. They went to the Naval Observatory's main entrance, which was on a hard lockdown along with every other inch of the grounds. He pulled onto the sidewalk, knowing the Secret Service wouldn't be too keen on letting any vehicles in right then.

The normally quiet guard shack was buzzing with energy, and heavily armed men stood ready to repel any invasion. Schiffer and Wolfson were allowed to walk in and then were escorted to the Vice President's Residence. On the way, Schiffer phoned Alexandra. She said she, Ayala, and Moira were safe inside the Cathedral. Schiffer said he'd have the Secret Service pick them up and bring them to the Observatory.

Vice President Stubblefield met Schiffer and Wolfson as soon as they entered. He shook Wolfson's hand and then Schiffer's.

"You all right?" Stubblefield asked Schiffer.

"Yeah, we're fine."

"What about Alexandra?"

"She's fine. I just talked to her. She's still at the Cathedral."

"What the hell happened?"

"We should probably talk somewhere private."

Stubblefield led the way to his office and closed the door. Seated near each other and with their voices low, Schiffer ran through the facts since the beginning when the first shots were fired outside the Cathedral, followed by the car chase through the streets of Northwest D.C. and ending outside the gates of the Naval Observatory.

"Did you recognize the man?" Stubblefield asked.

"No. I didn't get a good look at him with the hat and sunglasses, and his face was a little messed up when I last saw him lying on the ground."

"Could it have been the Russian we've been looking for?"

Schiffer nodded. "It's very possible." He cleared his throat. "There's something else I didn't tell you. Right before the shooting started, Alexandra and I were about to exit the Cathedral. She said Director Duncan had called her."

Stubblefield's eyes narrowed. "Called her?"

"Yeah. She said he called to offer his best wishes on the wedding."

"Anything else?"

"She told him we were on the way to check out the Cathedral."

Schiffer didn't have to tell Stubblefield what he was thinking because the big man was thinking the same thing. Stubblefield folded his hands in front of him, his mind deciding what the next step was. He knew it wasn't going to be good.

"We need to talk to the President," he said.

Schiffer undid the Velcro closure on his pant leg and pulled out the dead man's phone. "I took this off him. I figured you could make sure the right people get their hands on it, just in case we can't trust someone."

Stubblefield nodded. "I'll have them get right on it."

CHAPTER 33

The White House – Washington, D.C.
　Once he heard what happened, President Schumacher invited Duke, Alexandra, her brother, the Segels, and Wolfson to the White House for dinner, the pre-wedding get-together having been cancelled out of an abundance of caution. Since the National Cathedral was a crime scene and given that no one was for certain who all was in on the shooting, the President also offered to let Alexandra and Duke have the wedding ceremony in the East Room of the White House the next day.
　"You would do that for us?" Alexandra had asked.
　The President motioned to Schiffer. "For this guy? Hell yes I would."
　Despite the attack, Alexandra was determined to not let it interfere with her wedding day. The plan was quickly cobbled together. The ceremony would be held in the East Room, the dinner would be in the State Dining Room, and the reception and dancing would take place back in the East Room. Alexandra was thankful, as was Schiffer. They accepted the President's offer, and Alexandra went about ensuring the flowers, the photographer, and every other thing was redirected to the new venue.
　But there were other important matters to take care of.
　While Alexandra was preoccupied with the wedding, Schiffer went to the Situation Room to meet with the President and Vice President. Director Parker from the CIA, was also on hand. No one from the FBI was present. No one was talking about the weather either. It was all business, and those seated around the table looked like they were ready to drop the hammer on the people behind the attack.
　The President was sitting at the table, listening intently. Stubblefield was providing most of the answers.
　The evidence was pouring in like a firehose. Fingerprint records indicated the man Schiffer killed outside the Naval Observatory was a Russian named Viktor Kozlov. Facial recognition software determined the man had been at each of the major riots throughout the country.
　"I think this is the guy behind the violence," Stubblefield said.
　He had passed Kozlov's phone off to the Secret Service, who passed it

along to the CIA. Calls and text messages to Kozlov were suspected to have come from Bonhoff.

"The last messages came shortly before four o'clock and directed Kozlov to make it happen today. It was definitely a hit on you," Director Parker said, motioning to Schiffer.

"They knew you were looking at Bonhoff," Stubblefield said to Schiffer. "I don't know how much they knew, but they wanted you out of the picture."

"How would they have known I was looking at Bonhoff?"

Stubblefield leaned back in his chair and looked at the ceiling. There were a handful of people around him that would have known he had been meeting with Schiffer.

Schiffer added, "I don't think there's any way that Lamont or Duncan could have known I had eyes on them in Switzerland. We would have heard something by now."

Stubblefield didn't know the answer, but he was determined to get to the bottom of it. There were discussions on what to do with Bonhoff—whether they should connect him with Kozlov and the riots or wait and see if they could connect all the dots, including with Duncan and Lamont. It didn't take long before the connections were made.

The Situation Room's duty officer entered and looked at the President. "Excuse me, sir."

"Yes?"

"The Israeli Ambassador is here. He would like a word."

"The Israeli Ambassador is here?"

"Yes, with Mr. Segel and Mr. Wolfson. They were admitted in, and they're waiting in the West Wing lobby."

The President looked at Stubblefield, who nodded. "Bring 'em down here." When the duty officer left, the President said, "This ought to be good."

The three Israelis were welcomed into the Situation Room and all of them took seats around the table.

Ambassador Caleb Friedman said he came at the direction of Prime Minister Meyr, who wanted to provide information that the President might find useful.

"All right. Let's hear it."

Ambassador Friedman opened a manila folder and pulled out a DVD. The President called in one of the duty officers and had him ready the DVD for playback. When it was ready, the duty officer handed the remote to the Ambassador.

"Mr. President, the video you are about to see was obtained through the efforts of Mr. Wolfson and Mr. Schiffer. As part of their operation, they were provided with devices that Mossad has had in secret development for over a year." The Ambassador passed a picture of the two pieces. "The flash drive is inserted to a computer hard drive, and the WinSys 3020 transmitter and antenna is attached to a wall or desk. Once up and running, they essentially take over the system, record all data, including video, that comes through the computer and then uploads the data to Mossad servers." He stopped and looked at Wolfson and Schiffer. "Their actions have provided a gold mine of data."

The President motioned for him to play the videos.

Ambassador Friedman pointed the remote at the screen and pressed the button. The first video, in full color, showed a bedroom with white carpet and a bed with red satin sheets. The camera appeared to have been mounted in the ceiling as it looked down directly over the bed.

It took a few seconds before a blonde female appeared on the screen. She wore an ivory chemise with spaghetti straps that hung over her tanned shoulders. She appeared to be looking at someone off camera. As if doing what she was told, she climbed into bed and knelt. She used her right hand to flick the strap off her left shoulder. She used her left to do the same on the right. The chemise fell to her waist, exposing her large breasts.

A man appeared on the screen. From high above, he was shirtless and with only his boxers remaining. He told her to lie down. Once he removed her chemise and panties, he climbed on top of her.

"Is that Senator Lamont?" the President asked.

Ambassador Friedman nodded. "Yes."

Those seated at the table watched as Senator Lamont had his way with the female, and she acted like she had done it before. The President got up from his seat on the opposite end of the room and walked closer to the screen. His two daughters, both blondes, were in their twenties and thirties. He wondered how this young woman had gotten to that point in her life.

"How old do you think she is?" he asked, trying to make his own determination.

"Our guess is sixteen or seventeen," Ambassador Friedman said. "Bonhoff has multiple women available to him at all times. They vary in age ranges."

The President walked back to his chair and said he had seen enough.

Ambassador Friedman used the remote to move to the next video. The screen showed another bedroom with blue carpet and white sheets on the king-sized bed. A man was the first to show up on screen, and it looked like he was pushed backward onto the bed. The President didn't even have to ask because it was readily apparent that it was Director Duncan.

A blonde woman, probably late twenties, appeared on the screen and straddled Duncan. She threw off her bra and then smacked Duncan in the face, the slap of skin echoing off the bedroom walls. She was in control, and Duncan was fine with it. She yanked off his pants, and they went at it like dogs. Another woman, also blonde, arrived and joined in. Duncan enjoyed them both. The second woman brought the whip, and the domination of the FBI

Director began. Despite the pain the woman inflicted on him, he appeared to be loving every minute of it.

The President shook his head. "This is what the Director of the FBI was doing when the country burned."

Ambassador Friedman stopped the video, those around the table having seen all they needed to know. "Mr. President, on behalf of Mossad, the DVD is yours to keep. All we ask is that you not divulge where you got it."

"Of course, Mr. Ambassador. Thank you. We'll figure out what we're going to do with it."

Ambassador Friedman, Segel, and Wolfson then left the Situation Room. The duty officer came back in.

"Sir, the NSA Director is here to see you."

The President smiled. "Well, let's see if Director Ackerman is bringing gifts, too."

Director Ackerman arrived carrying a silver briefcase. "Good evening, sir. I trust this is a good time to discuss the investigation with what you asked of me a few days ago."

"It is. Have a seat."

Director Ackerman put the briefcase on the table, undid the claps, and pulled out a computer tablet. He made a couple swipes and taps on the screen. He started by saying that the investigation was ongoing, and the NSA was trying to see how far the conspiracy went. When he looked at the President, he frowned. "I regret that I have to bring these to your attention, sir."

The President motioned for him to continue. "Let's see what you've got."

Before he tapped the play button, Director Ackerman said the tap of Director Duncan's phone included text messages and audio recordings. The first text message of importance came after Duncan's press conference where he said the FBI was going to investigate violent militia groups.

"Who did he text?" the President asked.

"Senator Lamont. They texted about the speech, and Lamont said he was happy with it. He thought it was what he needed to help him win. I think it's pretty obvious from the start that Director Duncan and Senator Lamont were working together for Lamont's gain."

The President nodded for him to continue.

Director Ackerman said the first audio recording after the trace began took place when Lamont called Duncan to say there was problem. He added some background. "Sir, when Senator Lamont mentions 'he,' he is talking about the Vice President."

Lamont: *"He was talking to a guy named Schiffer."*

Those in the Situation Room could hear agitation in Lamont's voice—agitation tinged with a good dose of fear. They heard Duncan respond with an expletive.

Lamont: *"You know him?"*

Duncan: *"Yes, I know him. He's ex-FBI, and he's trouble. Big trouble."*

Everyone looked at Schiffer, who had a stone-cold look on his face.

Lamont: *"Kurt, the tape was made yesterday! Who knows how long they've been looking at Bonhoff. They could have been watching us!"*

The voice of Duncan cursed again, louder this time.

Lamont: *"What if they know we met with Karl? The man has been funding the riots! If the American people find out, it will ruin us. You need to do something!"*

Duncan: *"Me? What do you want me to do?"*

Lamont: *"You need to take care of this. Get rid of that Schiffer guy. He may know things."*

Duncan: *"I can't get rid of him. That's crazy."*

Lamont: *"You're already in this deep, Kurt. You've got to do something to get us out of this mess."*

Duncan: *"I can't do it myself, Greg. I'm the Director of the FBI!"*

Senator Lamont's expletive echoed off the walls of the Situation Room.

Lamont: *"I might be able to get someone. But you have to find Schiffer."*

The President was shaking his head when Director Ackerman tapped the screen to stop the recording.

"Sir, the phone that Mr. Schiffer took off the assassin this afternoon had a picture from his FBI personnel file. The man couldn't have gotten it from too many places. Unless there is someone else in the FBI leaking information, it had to come from Duncan—either through Lamont or Bonhoff."

Schiffer spoke up. "Alexandra said Duncan called her this afternoon. She said he wanted to wish us well on the wedding. She told him when we were going to be at the Cathedral."

Director Ackerman sighed. "Mr. President, I think it's pretty clear that Director Duncan participated in the assassination attempt of Mr. Schiffer."

The President pounded his fist on the table. He pushed back his chair and started pacing the room. He let loose a string of profanities.

"I ought to fire him right now." The President looked at his watch. It was almost eleven. He looked like he was ready to strangle the man. "What I'd really like to do is fire him on national TV. Or have the cameras rolling when he tries to enter the White House gates. I'd like to see him handcuffed and hauled off to jail."

"Where's Director Duncan right now?" Vice President Stubblefield asked.

"I believe he's still at FBI Headquarters overseeing the Cathedral shooting investigation," Director Ackerman said.

Stubblefield stood and buttoned his suit coat. "Mr. President, maybe you could let me talk to him first."

CHAPTER 34

Alexandria, Virginia

Director Duncan told his security detail that they could take the night off. He had been hunkered down at FBI Headquarters for the entire evening and wanted to drive home alone. The shooting at the Cathedral and outside the Vice President's Residence had sent the Bureau into a flurry of activity. Roads were closed, crime scene tape was put up, and evidence technicians had worked well into the evening taking pictures and collecting shell casings.

The White House had been strangely quiet, Duncan thought. A Secret Service spokesman had gone before the cameras to document that Vice President Stubblefield had been made aware of the shooting at the Cathedral and was, at no time, in any danger when the shooting stopped outside the Naval Observatory. There would be no further comment.

Duncan had his top deputy give the FBI's press conference, making sure the world knew that the Director was monitoring the investigation and giving it his full priority. The FBI had yet to interview the two men who eyewitnesses said had engaged in a high-speed chase and gun battle with the assailant. Duncan had a pretty good idea who one of the men was.

And the thought that Kozlov had failed to kill Schiffer sent shivers down Duncan's spine.

Behind the wheel of his black Suburban with tinted windows, Duncan exited the interstate at the Alexandria exit. For an instant, Duncan had thought about running. Get out of the country and head for the hills. He could demand Bonhoff protect him or else.

But Duncan told himself he wasn't a coward. He was the Director of the FBI. Plus, he hadn't done anything wrong. At least nothing that could be traced back to him. He winced at remembering the phone call to Alexandra, but he quickly discarded any concern because the call was perfectly legit. It was about the wedding, totally innocent. Alexandra probably received a hundred calls that day, so his wouldn't raise any red flags.

He needed to be careful, though. He decided to put some distance between himself and Lamont. Just for the time being. No sense drawing unneeded attention to himself on that front.

The other thing he needed to do was focus on the riot investigations.

Although not yet publicly disclosed, the preliminary reports indicated the man killed had been the front man for the riots in multiple cities. Given his call to Lamont earlier that day, Duncan figured Kozlov had connections to Bonhoff. He decided he needed to play up the fact that the FBI had finally hunted the man down, and the American people could sleep well knowing that the person behind the violence and destruction had been disposed of.

Duncan rolled to a stop at the light. He smiled to himself. *That's what I'm going to do. I'm going to have a press conference tomorrow and tell the American people that they can rest easy because the FBI has saved the day. The President and Vice President won't dare disagree.* He smiled to himself. *This can work.*

Nearing his driveway, he turned on his signal and hit the button for the garage door opener. He pulled to a stop in the garage and shut off the engine. He knew he could sleep soundly that night because he had a way out of this mess. And that's all he needed–a way out.

* * *

After lowering the garage door, Director Duncan used the key to open the door from the garage to the kitchen. Once inside, he locked the door and deactivated the alarm. He yanked off his tie and threw it on the counter. Grabbing a bottle of scotch, he poured himself half a glass and took a good long sip. The liquid rolled down his throat and soothed his soul. He thought about grabbing the bottle, but he didn't want to have a hangover. He needed to be on his game for the press conference tomorrow.

He took his glass and headed for the living room. When he flicked on the light, the glass fell from hand and shattered on the stone-tile floor.

"What the hell!?"

Vice President Stubblefield was sitting in a leather recliner. "Good evening, Kurt."

"What the hell is this!?" Duncan spat out. He reached inside his suit coat but froze.

"Don't even think about it," Schiffer growled. He had come from somewhere behind Duncan, and the gun in his left hand was pointing straight at Duncan's head. "Put your hands where I can see them."

Duncan didn't know who to look at—the menacing Stubblefield or the downright scary Schiffer. He apparently didn't want any part of Schiffer, so he slowly put his arms out.

"Why don't you have a seat, Kurt."

Duncan scowled. "I am the Director of the F—"

Schiffer used the back of his right hand to slap Duncan hard across the back of his head. The man grunted in pain. "He said sit down." Schiffer forced Duncan into a recliner and started rummaging through his pocket.

"Hey! Hey! I'm the Director of the FBI!"

Schiffer pulled out the man's phone and threw it onto the couch.

Stubblefield sat in silence, the look on his face as hard as a rock. He had worn the dark suit he had been wearing earlier, although the tie was gone and the top button of his shirt undone. He could tell Duncan noticed the black leather gloves covering his hands.

"You want to explain yourself?" Stubblefield said in his deep voice.

"How did you get in here?"

"How I got in here is the least of your worries, Kurt."

"Screw you, Ty! You think you're such a badass with your pistol and everything." Duncan acted as if he was regaining some of his composure, like he thought he could talk his way out of whatever was going on. "This is breaking and entering. Do you think you can walk in here without being seen? I am going to take down the sitting Vice President of the United States for breaking and entering into my house!"

Stubblefield waited for Duncan to go quiet. "How do you think you're going to do that?"

Duncan smirked like the man across from him was an idiot. "You think I don't have security cameras in this day and age? I've got 'em all over the place, and they record everyone going in and out of this house. You're going down, Ty."

"Is that so?"

"That's right. And I'm going to enjoy watching your fall from grace."

Stubblefield smiled, almost amused at the man's bravado. "You also have a security system, Kurt. One that you thought you disabled when you walked in the door." He raised his palms. "Yet here we are in your living room having a conversation. I don't hear the cavalry coming to your rescue."

Apparently, realizing the man had a point, Duncan muttered an expletive then swallowed and licked his dry lips.

Stubblefield tapped the armrest with his finger, his patience wearing thin. "So, I'll ask again. You want to explain yourself?"

"I don't know what you're talking about." Duncan acted like he was going to plead the Fifth, as if that would save him.

"Why don't you start by telling us how you tried to have me killed," Schiffer said.

"I didn't try to have—"

Schiffer inflicted another blow to the man's head.

Duncan grabbed his ear in pain before yelling, "You need to control your man, Ty! He's going to go down too! What do you think the American people are going to say when word gets out that Schiffer is your personal assassin? Or that you send him all around the world to do your dirty work. I'm going to have both of you arrested! You're both going to jail!"

The tapping of Stubblefield's finger quickened. He let the man rant before reaching to the side of his hip and grabbing a computer tablet. With his gloved finger, he tapped in a code and the screen lit up. He set the tablet on the end table next to him and hit the play button. The pictures and sounds of Duncan's wild night in Bonhoff's bedroom came to life—first one naked woman and then another before the sound of a whip started crackling in the air.

His eyes wide in disbelief, Duncan's red face drained of color. "Where did you get that?"

Stubblefield didn't respond right away. He was watching the screen when the blonde whipped Duncan across his bare buttocks. Stubblefield winced. "Oof, I didn't know you liked it rough, Kurt. I guess you really don't know a guy until you see the camera footage from his night of bondage."

Duncan swallowed before spitting out, "Go to hell, Ty." He flicked a hand in the Vice President's direction. "There's nothing illegal about it."

Stubblefield hit the pause button so they wouldn't have to listen to Duncan's grunts and groans. "It might not be illegal, Kurt, but it does open the FBI Director up to blackmail, and that's never a good thing. I would have thought you would have had better sense that that."

"I'm not going to be blackmailed, Ty. It was a one-time deal."

"Well, that's refreshing to hear." Stubblefield paused long enough to let Duncan think his wild night of kinky sex was the reason for the interrogation. "But, of course, that's not the real reason we're here, Kurt. Why don't you tell us why you and Senator Lamont were in Switzerland meeting with Karl Bonhoff."

Duncan quickly tried to regain the upper hand. "Greg and Bonhoff are old friends from Wall Street. They made a lot of money together. Greg invited me to meet him. There's nothing illegal about that either."

"What did you three talk about?"

"None of your damn business."

"Did you talk about joining forces with Senator Lamont in his presidential campaign funded by Bonhoff's dark money?"

"Nope."

"Did you talk with Senator Lamont today?"

"No."

"What about Alexandra Julian?"

Duncan flinched, having no quick answer for that one. He couldn't lie about it because everyone in the room already knew the answer. He shifted uncomfortably in his seat, as if preparing for another blow to the head from Schiffer. He hurried to come up with a believable response.

"Yes, I did. I wanted to wish her well on her upcoming wedding."

"That's nice of you. Did you contact Senator Lamont after that?"

"No!" Duncan snapped.

Stubblefield reached quickly into the pocket of his suit coat closest to his pistol. It was so quick that a flash of fear crossed Duncan's face, like he thought he was about to get a bullet between the eyes. Stubblefield instead pulled out his phone, tapped the screen, and held it up.

Duncan's voice was heard. *"Yes, I know him. He's ex-FBI, and he's trouble. Big trouble."*

Once the incriminating evidence ended, Duncan licked his lips. "So you're tapping my phones, Ty. I bet that's without authorization, too. You're just racking up the impeachable offenses tonight. The President is going down, too. You'll both be thrown out on your asses when I'm—" He flinched when Schiffer raised his hand to smack him.

"You tried to have him killed, Kurt," Stubblefield said, pointing toward Schiffer.

"I did no such thing."

"You let someone know where Duke was going to be and then you sent a picture of him so the assassin would know who he was gunning for."

"You can't prove that."

"We already have, Kurt."

Duncan cursed. "This is nothing but a setup. You and the President have been trying to run me out of the FBI for months now."

The Vice President stared at Duncan, the man he had recommended to head the Bureau. He wondered how it had come to this. He reached inside his suit coat again and kept his hand there. Duncan prepared himself for the worst.

"What? Are you going to shoot me, Ty? You think you're Aaron Burr or something? Are you going to murder the Director of the FBI in his own house?" His shouting grew louder, the panic of what was to come causing him to lash out. "Is the Vice President of the United States going to have blood on his hands tonight!?"

Stubblefield gritted his teeth. He wanted to. He wanted to whip his Glock out of its holster and put a bullet between Duncan's eyes. He reached deeper into the pocket and grabbed a pill bottle. He stood towering over the seated Duncan and threw the bottle in the man's lap.

"I wouldn't want to waste a bullet on you, Kurt." The Vice President straightened his suit coat and grabbed the tablet off the end table. "Tomorrow afternoon Duke here is going to get married. I have the honor of walking the bride down the aisle." He pointed his finger at Duncan. "You won't be there."

Duncan glanced at the pill bottle laying near his crotch before daring to look up at Stubblefield.

"You have a way out of this, Kurt. You can save what dignity you have left and leave this world with some semblance of honor. You might even save the reputation of the Bureau—if that means anything to you."

Stubblefield took two steps toward Duncan and glowered down at him.

"But if you're still around tomorrow morning, you will be arrested at eleven a.m. and charged with conspiracy to commit murder, seditious conspiracy, and advocating the overthrow of the government. There might be more charges to follow. Once convicted, you'll spend the rest of your life in prison. And I guarantee the men in prison will love to get their hands on the former Director of the FBI."

Duncan broke eye contact with Stubblefield, his face ashen and his shoulders heavy.

"I trusted you, Kurt. I recommended the President make you Director." Stubblefield walked closer. "I guess you really don't know a guy until the truth comes out."

He reached out and smacked Duncan's face hard with the back of his hand. Duncan barely moved, like he knew he deserved it.

Stubblefield and Schiffer walked out.

CHAPTER 35

The White House – Washington, D.C.

The President was up early the next morning, entering the Oval Office before the sun rose over the nation's capital. The First Lady said she and the Second Lady, Tina Stubblefield, were going to help Alexandra Julian get ready for the wedding and make the day special for the happy couple. The President said he had a few things to do before the ceremony but told her to call if she needed anything.

He spent the morning with various advisers, the CIA Director, the NSA Director, and the Director of Homeland Security. Dots were being connected at a furious pace, and the President wanted the American people to know what was going on.

At 11 a.m., the President left the Oval Office and walked with a purpose down the hall to the press briefing room. It was times like those that he wished his dearly departed Chief of Staff William "Wiley" Cogdon was still around. The man would have been so hyped up on Red Bull and adrenaline that he would be convinced that President Schumacher could take on the world.

With a full house of reporters in attendance and photographers clicking away, the President took his place behind the podium and said he wanted to update the public on the shooting in D.C. the previous afternoon as well as the violence plaguing the country.

"As you know, a shootout took place yesterday at the National Cathedral and the surrounding area before ending outside the U.S. Naval Observatory. The evidence has indicated that a lone gunman was involved in an attempted assassination attempt on a government employee. While I cannot divulge the name of that employee at this time, I can tell you that no bystanders were injured in the shooting. Despite some damage to the exterior, the National Cathedral has already reopened for services."

The President turned a page in his folder. "I can also tell the American people that the assailant who was shot and killed outside the Vice President's Residence was a foreign operative named Viktor Kozlov."

No mention was made of the man's Russian heritage, but it wouldn't take long for the Russians to start distancing themselves from ever even knowing the man.

"There is strong evidence to indicate Kozlov was involved in the looting and riots, acting as the point man in multiple U.S. cities, including Chicago, St. Louis, Seattle, and Boston. We know that this man did not work alone, and the investigation will continue until we root out all those involved in the violence."

The President was on a roll. He turned to the next page. "On a related front, it is believed that the rioters and anarchists have received funding from multiple outside groups, including foreign entities. I have instructed the FBI, the CIA, the Secret Service, and the Attorney General to determine who is receiving this illegal money and where it is coming from. Any group, any politician, and any government official receiving illegal contributions from these foreign entities will be held to account. In the coming weeks, we will let the American people know who is taking this dark money, how much is being taken, and whether or not that money has been used in any subversive activities."

The President couldn't wait for the progressive politicians and their cronies to start running for the hills and putting as much distance as possible between them and Bonhoff's dark money groups. He imagined them already being on the phone to their campaign treasurers to pay back the illicit donations. He closed his folder, energized that steps were being taken to combat the violence and those who perpetrated it.

"I can assure the American people that justice will be served. Thank you very much. And may God bless America."

The President took two steps from the podium before the questions started. One reporter shouted something about the investigation.

"We'll have more to say on Monday."

"Are you going to run for re-election, Mr. President?"

The President stopped, a smile crossing his face. It was a smile that said it was time to let everyone know. "As long as the American people will have me, I'm not going anywhere." He tapped his watch. "Now if you'll excuse me, I have a wedding to attend."

Number One Observatory Circle – Washington, D.C.

Vice President Stubblefield was straightening the tie of his tuxedo in a mirror when the President concluded his press conference. With the TV on, he chuckled when he heard the President say he planned on sticking around. Stubblefield knew he would, and he was glad for it. The country needed the steady hand of President Schumacher at the helm.

He liked the President's statement about cracking down on the illegal money and those using it to the detriment of all that was good about America. Stubblefield was all for holding people to account and bringing them to justice.

And that was what he intended to do. Right now.

He picked up the phone and pressed the button for his Chief of Staff.

"Come into my office."

A few seconds later, Nate Russo hurried in. "Yes, Mr. Vice President."

"Grab your jacket. We're going to the White House."

Russo's eyebrows scrunched. "Sir?"

"We're going to the White House."

"Is there a problem? I just watched the President's news conference."

"There's a wedding."

Russo nodded. He knew that much. It was on the day's schedule. "Sir, I really don't know the bride and groom well. I wasn't invited."

Stubblefield waved it off. "That's no problem. How often do you get to see a wedding at the White House? It'll be a good time. Good food. Dancing. You might even find a woman you like."

Russo had no choice but to relent. He grabbed his suit coat from his office and headed outside where the Vice President's motorcade was idling in the driveway.

"Get in," Stubblefield said.

The sirens on the Secret Service vehicles started echoing off the trees, the flashing red-and-blue lights reflecting off the Residence's windows.

The Vice President took the seat facing the front and Russo sat across him facing the rear. Once the head of Stubblefield's Secret Service detail made one last check and got in the front passenger seat, the motorcade was on its way.

"It looks like the President is going to run again," Stubblefield said, making small talk.

"Yes, sir, it sure sounds that way." Russo unbuttoned his coat, looking uncomfortable.

Once the motorcade left the Naval Observatory grounds and hit Massachusetts Avenue, the pace picked up and the American and Vice-Presidential flags on the front of the limo flapped straight out in the wind.

"What are your plans, Nate?"

Russo squinted his eyes at his boss, as if he hadn't heard any concerns about his future before then. "Sir?"

"What are your plans for the future? Once your days as my chief of staff are done."

Russo looked out the window as the motorcade rounded Dupont Circle and took Connecticut Avenue toward the White House.

"I don't know, sir." He swallowed. "I haven't thought much about it. I guess I was waiting to see if the President decided to run for re-election."

Stubblefield nodded. His phone buzzed, and he reached inside his jacket on the side closest to his pistol to retrieve it.

"Yes?" Stubblefield listened to what the caller said before responding, "We're almost there."

The motorcade veered off Connecticut Avenue onto 17th Street. Only three more blocks to Pennsylvania Avenue and the north side of the White House.

"You should think about what you want to do in the future, Nate. It's good to have dreams to shoot for."

Russo licked his lips. "I'll do that, sir."

The limo made the left-hand turn onto Pennsylvania Avenue and beyond the barricades preventing any non-official vehicular traffic from going forward. The motorcade slowed and pulled to a stop in front of Blair House, just west of Lafayette Square.

Stubblefield's phone buzzed again. He tapped the screen and put the phone to his ear. "Yes?"

Something important must have been said because the Vice President put his hand over the phone and said to Russo, "Would you give me a minute while I take this?" He nodded toward the door that Russo should exit to give him some privacy.

Agent Simpson opened the door for him. Once Russo exited, Agent Simpson shut the door and got back into the limo. Looking out the window, Stubblefield's face hardened, his eyes glaring at his Chief of Staff. Russo caught the look and peered in. He never saw the Secret Service agents approaching from behind him.

"Mr. Russo," the lead agent said.

Russo turned around.

The lead agent didn't have his gun drawn, but the four agents with him did. "You're under arrest. Put your hands behind your back please."

Russo was smart enough to comply. There was nowhere to run. "What am I under arrest for?"

"Conspiracy to commit treason," the agent said, placing the cold steel around his wrists. "Your girlfriend is being arrested as we speak."

"I don't have a girlfriend."

"That's good." The handcuffs clicked shut. "Because where you're going, you won't be having any girlfriends for a long time."

Russo was turned around to be marched off into a waiting Secret Service vehicle.

Stubblefield made eye contact with him one last time. Then he looked ahead at the two agents in front. "Let's go."

The White House – Washington, D.C.

Vice President Stubblefield took the elevator up to the second floor of the Residence. In the West Sitting Hall, he found the President in his suit.

"Looking good, Mr. President."

"Thank you, Ty. You look pretty good yourself." He mentioned that the First Lady, the Second Lady, and the bride were in the west bedroom putting on the finishing touches. He motioned to the White House photographer to take their picture. "You know we make a pretty good team."

"Yes, sir, I think we do."

"I hope I didn't catch you off guard with that remark about me staying on the job for a little while longer."

Stubblefield grinned. "No, I was glad to hear it."

"That's good." The President leaned closer. "I don't know if you heard, but someone leaked the video of Senator Lamont to Governor Hinton."

Stubblefield chuckled. Governor Christine Hinton had had her sights on the White House for years, some even saying she believed the presidency was her birthright. Rumors had swirled that she was none too happy that Lamont got the jump on her in his campaign. But the video of Lamont engaging in sex with underage women would soon be making the rounds of CNN and MSNBC. Lamont's campaign would be over before it started.

"Let those progressives eat their own," Stubblefield said.

"That's right."

Stubblefield looked down the Center Hall. "Have you seen Duke?"

The President pointed down the way. "Lincoln Bedroom."

Stubblefield walked down the hall and knocked on the door jamb. Schiffer was putting on his jacket.

"Nice tux," Stubblefield said.

"Thanks."

"You kind of look like a secret agent."

Schiffer straightened his bow tie and gave his best Bond impression. "Schiffer... Duke Schiffer."

"You nervous?"

"No. I'm ready."

Stubblefield grinned like a proud father. They had been through a lot over the years, and America had been better off for it. A part of him wondered if this was the end. He could feel the water starting to pool in his eyes.

"You know I'm proud of you, don't you?"

Schiffer nodded.

"And I appreciate all that you've done for me and this country." He stuck out his hand.

Schiffer shook it and said, "Thank you, sir."

Stubblefield checked his watch. "You had better get down there. It's almost time."

The Vice President took the elevator down to the first floor and found Alexandra in the Red Room. He gave her a light hug, not wanting to mess up the bride's dress or makeup. The First Lady and Second Lady left to take their seats.

"You look beautiful."

"Thank you, sir."

"I just saw the groom. He's looking handsome in his tux. I told him he was a lucky man."

Alexandra laughed so she wouldn't tear up.

Down the Cross Hall, they could hear ruffles and flourishes performed by the Marine Band followed by an announcement. "Ladies and Gentlemen, the President of the United States accompanied by the First Lady."

The Marine Band's rendition of *Hail to the Chief* echoed through the first floor, and Stubblefield knew he was up next.

"Ready?" the Vice President asked, holding out his arm.

"Yes, sir, I'm ready."

They entered the Cross Hall and waited. When the Marine Band began to play Jeremiah Clarke's *The Prince of Denmark's March*, those in attendance in the East Room turned their attention to the Vice President and the bride on the red carpet in the Hall. Stubblefield took his time, wanting the crowd to look at the bride's beauty and his pride. He could see the smile on Schiffer's face. They entered the East Room with the camera flashes brightening the place.

When they met the groom, Stubblefield reached out to shake Schiffer's hand one more time. He then turned, gave the bride a hug, and said loud enough that only she could hear. "Take good care of him for me."

Stubblefield took his seat next to the Second Lady and across the aisle from the President. With the Marine Band nearing the end of the music, a Secret Service agent approached the President, whispered in his ear, and handed him a note.

The President read the note, gave it a moment's thought, and then stood. He walked across the aisle, handed the note to the Vice President, and returned to his seat.

Stubblefield unfolded the piece of paper and read the words written on it.

The FBI Director has been found dead in his house of an apparent suicide.

Stubblefield looked to his right at the President, who had focused his attention on the bride and the groom. The Vice President folded the note and put it in the pocket of his suit coat closest to his pistol. He then looked in the direction of the happy couple.

"Dearly beloved."

CHAPTER 36

Venice, Italy

After the wedding, Duke and Alexandra Schiffer flew to Rome and spent a few days taking in the sights—the Colosseum, the Pantheon, Trevi Fountain, the Vatican—before taking the train north to Venice. They took the vaporetto to their hotel and spent two days touring the city as a newly married couple. They didn't think much about anything other than themselves and the future that awaited them.

"It really is a fantastic place," Alexandra said, her arm locked around the crook of Duke's elbow, as they strolled past the restaurants, churches, and gelato shops. She looked at him when he didn't respond. "Don't you think?"

Duke shrugged. "It's okay."

"Just okay? I think it's one of the most beautiful cities in the world. Would you ever want to live here?"

Duke was quick with the response. "No. We already have a house on the water. And there's not enough space." He balled his fists and tightened his shoulders. "It's too cramped, and I haven't seen any green grass since we've been here."

They walked in silence for a good distance before Alexandra asked, "Are you still mad about that guy last night?"

Duke frowned, upset that she brought it up. There had been "an incident" the night before when the two lovebirds were enjoying the sights of the Grand Canal by way of a gondola, of which Duke initially protested as a tourist trap and grossly overpriced. He told her he could sing to her in their boat on the lake back home for free.

He relented, of course, because of the "happy wife, happy life" thing. But it wasn't the money that bothered him. It was the gondolier, the Venetian crooner who spent the entire ride ogling Alexandra and singing love songs to her in Italian. Once Duke had enough of the man's amorous advances, voices were raised, fingers were pointed, and profanity flew in multiple languages.

"Are you jealous?"

"He was hitting on you. It was like your husband wasn't even there."

"Duke, I think he was just doing his job."

"He's lucky I didn't throw him into the canal."

They stopped at a café and gelateria near the Piazza San Marco and the Basilica. Each of them ordered chocolate and then they took a seat at one of the iron tables with wire chairs. While they ate, Alexandra used the time to check her phone and catch up on American politics. They had been off the grid for several days, and she didn't like being out of the loop as to what was going on. Her eyes widened when she looked at the first story on the screen.

"Oh my gosh, Senator Lamont is withdrawing from the presidential campaign." She read off how a sex tape had surfaced showing Lamont with an underage female. Calls for him to drop out of the race came quick from all sides. "Apparently he's gone into hiding."

"He got off easy if you ask me."

"I wonder how someone got the video."

Duke bit the inside of his lip, giving nothing away. "I don't know. Maybe he has some enemies. You know how ruthless politics can be."

Alexandra swiped the screen to scroll to the next story. "I still can't believe Director Duncan had a heart attack. He wasn't that old."

Schiffer had already read that news. It was discussed in back channels that a drug overdose would not look good for the FBI, so a heart attack was inserted as the cause of death. Duke thought Duncan got off easy, too.

"You just don't know when it's your time to go."

Alexandra's eyes widened again. "Did you see that the Vice President's Chief of Staff was arrested?"

Duke nodded. "I heard some rumblings that he was taping the Vice President's conversations and leaking them. That's a big no-no." He left unsaid that he was involved in those conversations.

"So much going on."

While Alexandra kept scrolling through the news, it gave Duke a chance to think about the future. Everything she had just read off to him, he was involved with in some way or another. He had been serving his country for close to twenty years, most of them with the FBI but the last few with the "special projects" from Vice President Stubblefield.

With her eyes still on the screen, he smiled at her. One of those special projects had been to rescue her from the clutches of terrorists in Egypt hell-bent on killing her. If that hadn't happened, if he hadn't been sent into the lion's den, he never would have met her, never would have fallen in love with her, and never would have gotten married to the most beautiful, intelligent, and fun woman he had ever met. Plus, he had met some friends along the way. The Segels had mentioned getting together on a yearly basis, and Wolfson said he'd be up to meeting—"maybe."

And the most important thing was that he felt like he was doing good for the people of the United States. He had helped save the President's life on at least two occasions, and the Vice President once in New York. He had also silenced a sniper menacing the U.S., rescued an Ambassador, and helped thwart a terrorist attack on the Big Apple that would have knocked out the electrical grid for at least a year. All in all, it was a good life, a productive life.

But there was something gnawing at him. Like there was still more to be done. And one thing in particular. Alexandra's news report told him what he already knew. Justice had been or was being done—in one form or another. Lamont, Duncan, Russo, Swisher. They were all being held to account for their actions or, in Duncan's case, justice had already been served.

But there was still one person out there that had yet to get what he had coming to him.

Bonhoff was still out there, still spending his billions with the intent of undermining the United States. As the fourth richest man in the world, he could continue to do it for the rest of his life. He could continue to send his dark money to the U.S. to help defund the police and put in place the progressive candidates who want to transform the American way of life and put all the power and authority in big government bureaucrats.

And Duke had a clear shot to get him . . . but he let him go.

Alexandra looked up from her phone. "So what do you want to do for the rest of the day? We could take a boat to Murano and see the glass factories."

Duke dropped his spoon in the empty cup of gelato and pushed it away. Maybe he was just going to have to come to grips with the fact that getting Bonhoff was the one mission that failed. He had his chance and that was it.

"Duke?"

He was startled for a second. Not because of Alexandra but from the phone buzzing in his pocket. He looked at the screen and smiled. "It's the Vice President. He probably wants to know how the honeymoon is going." He tapped the screen. "Hello."

"Duke?"

"Yes."

Eyeing him, she whispered, "Tell him I said hello."

"Alexandra says hello."

"I hope you two are having a good time." Stubblefield lowered his voice so that only Duke could hear. "You got a minute?"

Duke looked at Alexandra. He winked and held up a finger. He got up and walked closer to the water for some privacy.

"What's up?"

The Vice President told Duke that he had received a call from Ariel Segel with an interesting proposition. He laid out the details and waited for a response.

"Do you think it's a possibility?"

"It might take a little planning and some ingenuity, but the Israelis appear to be on board. They think it's worth a shot."

Could I get another shot at it?

Duke looked down at the pavement, pacing three feet one way and three feet the other. He was being given a second chance, and in his line of work, you rarely got a second chance.

Stubblefield said it was totally up to Duke. He wasn't trying to influence him one way or the other. He was just passing on what the Israelis had told him.

Duke rubbed the back of his neck. Thoughts were racing through his head, thoughts that he had never had before. He was a married man now—a man with new responsibilities in life. He knew he couldn't pass up the opportunity, but what about Alexandra? They had been married less than a week. They had their whole lives to enjoy together. What would she think if he told her he had to go away for a while? What if he didn't come back?

He grabbed the railing with his free hand, his eyes looking out over the water to the Church of San Giorgio Maggiore. He felt a hand start rubbing his back.

Alexandra stood close to him, concern etched on her face. "Is everything okay?" she asked.

Duke looked into her eyes—those beautiful brown eyes that he couldn't get enough of. He had a thought, an idea. Maybe he shouldn't have had them, but he couldn't help it.

"Mr. Vice President, can I call you right back?"

Stubblefield said that was fine, and Duke tapped to end the call. He put the phone in his back pocket and reached out to rub Alexandra's arms. She was so beautiful—the most gorgeous woman he had ever met. To him, she was irresistible. No man would ever turn her down. No man would want to spend a second away from her. But he was being given a second chance—a chance he couldn't pass up.

And that's why he had to ask.

"How would you like to go to Monaco?"

CHAPTER 37

Monaco

Duke Schiffer had several options to consider before leaving Venice for Monaco—the main one being how he and Alexandra would get there. A trip by train from Venice to Monaco ran a little over seven hours and driving would take six. A flight from Venice to Nice, France, would get them there in under ninety minutes. All of the options had their benefits and pitfalls. Train and air travel would get them to their destination with little hassle. But there would be plenty of surveillance cameras and ID checks. It would also put them in contact with other passengers, flight attendants, train conductors, and ticket takers, all of whom might recall seeing the couple when asked by the authorities.

And with what Duke Schiffer had in mind, the authorities would definitely be involved.

In the end, Duke decided they would rent a car and drive the three-hundred miles.

It would give him and Alexandra time to talk about things that would be inappropriate for the ears of prying passengers. She had asked him why the Vice President had called, apparently sensing that something was up. He told her Stubblefield thought they might enjoy visiting Monaco. There was plenty of shopping and a casino to keep them busy. There was the Mediterranean, too. It would be a nice little vacation spot before they headed back home.

"He called about an operation, didn't he?" she had asked as if she could read him like a book.

When Duke didn't respond, she said she was entitled to know what he was up to. She was his wife in case he had already forgotten.

He had tried to deflect with some humor. "There's always that gondolier."

That only got him a quick smack on the arm by the back of her hand. In the end, he decided he would lay it all out for her—the President and Vice President's plan, the covert mission into Bonhoff's mansion that led to the discovery of Lamont and Duncan, and the resulting aftermath. He told her he had unfinished business and it would gnaw at him if he didn't take the chance.

America was counting on him.

Prior to renting the car, he fished out one of the three fake passports that he had hidden in the liner of his suitcase. He had used his real one to get into Italy, but now it was time for someone else to be the one traveling. He went with the American one under the name of Lucas Conrad. He handed a fake one to Alexandra.

She stared at it, gawking at her picture and the name Wendy Sheridan from Toronto, Canada, attached to it. "How did you . . . ? Why did you . . . ?"

"You always have to be prepared in my line of work, Alexandra."

She nodded and then hurried to close the passport and shove it in her purse like it was going to burst into flames.

After leaving the island, they stopped in Marghera and found the car rental agency. Wearing a New York Yankees ball cap, Duke rented a Fiat compact and paid in cash. He picked up Alexandra two blocks away, and they took off across northern Italy.

Before they had any further discussions, Duke pulled out his phone and hit the speed dial for ponytail Dustin back at Fort Meade. He looked at his watch, wondering if the man would even be at work yet. He wanted to see if Stubblefield was really on to something.

"Dustin," Schiffer said. "You remember me?"

It took a few seconds before the man said, "Yes, sir. How can I help you?"

"Are you at your computer?"

"Yes, sir."

"Where's Bravo?"

"Just a second, sir." There was more silence before Duke could hear some tapping on a keyboard followed by a mouse click.

"It appears his phone is in Monaco."

"Thanks, Dustin. Good work. I might be calling you again in the next day or two."

Duke ended the call and looked at Alexandra. "So far, so good. It looks like the target is still in Monaco."

They rode in silence for at least fifty miles, although Duke could tell Alexandra was itching to discuss the operation's details. He hadn't seen her this apprehensive since their time together in Cairo. She finally succumbed to the need to know.

"What are you going to have me do?"

Duke looked at her and laughed. "You? What makes you think I'm going to have anything for you to do?"

"Because you asked me whether I wanted to go to Monaco." She reached out and touched his arm. "I want to help, Duke."

"No. No way." He had thought about it but ultimately decided against it. "Maybe you can get some sun or something."

"Duke!"

"Alexandra, I'm not going to put your life at risk."

"But it's okay to put your life at risk?"

He eyed her with a look that it was obvious. "Yes." He hurried to get her off the subject of her taking part. "We'll meet with Noah and Ariel and come up with a plan. Bonhoff lives on the top five floors of the Odéon Tower. Obviously taking the elevator up to the top is probably not going to get us in. So we have to figure out a way."

Alexandra used her left hand to twirl her hair, something she did when she was deep in thought. "Could you use a drone to take him out?" She was just throwing out ideas, trying to offer any assistance she could think of.

"Of course, we could. But I doubt the Prince or the Prime Minister would like it if drone missiles were flying through their airspace. Too much risk for collateral damage."

"So you want it to look like an accident?"

He smiled, liking her way of thinking. "That would be nice. And accidents do happen."

"What happens if it doesn't look like an accident? Will the authorities demand accountability if they knew the U.S. and Israel were conducting operations on their home turf?"

Schiffer drummed the steering wheel. It was a good question. He usually let the politicians in the U.S. figure out how to deal with diplomatic disagreements. There was no reason to make enemies out of friends. "That's why we need to make it look like an unfortunate accident."

"How are we going to get out of Monaco when we get it done?"

Duke didn't like her use of the term "we," but he did like her optimism. She was already thinking the operation would go well, even though they didn't even have a plan, just the knowledge that Bonhoff was there.

"Haul ass to France or Italy. There's the Mediterranean, too."

"I thought you said you're persona non grata in France."

Duke shrugged. "I am, but it's a possibility. Maybe a last resort, and I might have to call in some favors pretty quick but still a possibility."

Alexandra watched the Italian countryside go by. "The United States doesn't have a diplomatic mission in Monaco."

"Okay."

"But there is the embassy in Paris and a consulate general in Marseille. It would take over two hours to drive to Marseille."

"You know anyone there?"

"I might know a few."

"Good. We'll keep that in mind."

Having exhausted her growing list of questions, Alexandra actually fell asleep on the way. Duke wondered what she was dreaming about. She ended her honeymoon early so she could join him on a mission to take out the fourth richest man in the world—the man who had bankrolled the killing of American cops and servicemembers and fomented chaos and discord across the United States.

He glanced over toward her. She was leaning against the window in a peaceful sleep. He noticed her tanned legs all the way down to her pink painted toenails. In that moment, he had a thought to find the nearest airport and send her home. She would be safe there. He wondered if he should go with her. Maybe let the Israelis take care of Bonhoff. She started stirring before finally opening her eyes and turning toward him.

"Are we there yet?"

"We're almost to the border."

The inviting blue waters of the Mediterranean Sea were off to the left. They'd leave Italy, pass through a quick stretch of France, and enter Monaco with the sun still up. The plan was to meet with Wolfson and Segel that evening to come up with a plan.

Once in Monaco, they travelled on the Avenue Princesse Grace, the street some say is the most expensive in the world. From what Duke and Alexandra could tell, they were right. And it wasn't just fancy handbags and jewelry. One after the other, there were dealerships for Mercedes-Benz, Maybach, Ferrari, Rolls-Royce, Lamborghini, Maserati, Bugatti, Bentley.

"Don't get any ideas," Duke said. "We can't afford to live here."

Their compact Fiat fit in fine with the Volkswagens and Mini Coopers, but the preferred mode of transportation for the lesser folks in Monaco appeared to be moped. There were hundreds of them parked along the street.

"There it is," Duke said, pointing up at the Odéon Tower. "On the other side of it is France. Keep that in mind."

The Israelis had contacted a local *sayan* who procured lodging at a small hotel on the southwestern end of Monaco. After finding an underground parking garage, Duke and Alexandra found the hotel and the pizzeria next door. Segel was seated at a table with Wolfson. He gave them the nod that the coast was clear, and they took seats under the shade of a tree.

"The streets are narrow," Schiffer said, the first words out of his mouth.

Segel nodded. "Especially when you don't know where you're going."

When the waiter stopped by, Duke spoke in passing Italian and said he and Alexandra would have a sausage pizza and soft drinks. Nothing out of the ordinary, nothing that that would lead the waiter to remember them. Wolfson and Segel had ordered sandwiches and water. The waiter left, and the conversation continued.

"I'm glad you two could make it," Segel said to Duke.

"I wouldn't want to miss out on the fun."

As usual, Segel did most of the talking as Wolfson's eyes scanned the surroundings behind his sunglasses. He said he and Wolfson had been in Monaco for two days, along with two other two-person teams from Mossad.

They had been scouting and plotting, watching the police and getting the lay of the land. Segel went through what the teams have discovered.

At their current location, they were within walking distance of the dock where Bonhoff's megayacht was moored. Segel said Bonhoff had gone aboard and headed out to the Mediterranean on both days—mid-morning until mid-afternoon. A second yacht followed it out to sea.

"Security?"

"Most likely," Segel said.

"Does it give us any chance?" Schiffer asked.

"An insertion by sea in the light of day?" Segel shook his head. "It would be difficult with the security yacht." He answered Schiffer's next question before it was even asked. "Blowing a hole in the hull might sink it, but Bonhoff would most likely be rescued by his security. Risky with little chance for success."

"What about when he comes back?"

"He's driven back to his penthouse at the Odéon Tower."

Schiffer nodded. "We drove by it."

"He usually has two security cars. One in front and one following behind. From the looks of it, the windows of his Bentley are bulletproof."

The pizza arrived, and Duke and Alexandra each took a piece. They ate in silence, giving them time to think. They were running out of options, and Schiffer began to wonder if Stubblefield had sent them to Monaco without fully thinking through what they would be looking at.

Or maybe the Vice President knew Schiffer would figure out a way.

Schiffer finished his slice and wiped his hands on a napkin. "What about the Odéon Tower where he lives?"

"Forty-nine floors," Segel said. "Bonhoff owns the top five floors. We had a drone up yesterday. He was on the rooftop deck near the pool in the early evening last night. It looked like there was a party going on. At least thirty people present, half of them women in various stages of undress. Some of them acted like waitresses—serving drinks and food. The others looked like they were there to entertain the men. Loud music and strobe lights from the dance floor. By the end of the evening, some were using the water slide from the dance floor into the pool."

Duke looked at Alexandra. She had nibbled on her slice of pizza. He didn't know whether she wasn't hungry or whether it was nerves for listening in on what her husband and the Israelis had in store for Bonhoff. The waiter returned and asked if everything was good. Schiffer answered in Italian that it was.

When the man left, Wolfson spoke up. "We have to get up to the rooftop deck with the other partygoers. It's the only way we can do this quietly."

Schiffer knew the man was right. He unscrewed the cap of his bottled water and took a sip. "What about security inside the building?"

"Residents have an identification card that allows them to bypass security," Segel said. "Everyone else has to pass through magnetometers like at the airport. Access is restricted to the penthouse. You have to be buzzed up."

"How do you know this?" Alexandra asked, the first time she had spoken. She looked and sounded like she was having a hard time comprehending it all.

Segel gave her a smile. "We have our ways." He added. "There is a separate service elevator for caterers and hotel staff."

When the waiter came back and left again, Schiffer and Segel agreed they had spent enough time eating and it was time for them to leave. They paid their bills and took a walk toward the Mediterranean. In the early evening, they found a stretch of beach with only a handful of people catching the last rays of the day.

When they were sure they had some privacy, Segel pulled out his phone and showed Schiffer pictures of the Odéon Tower, actually two towers of blue glass that stretched toward the sky. He pointed out the pool on the top of the easternmost tower. The top of the western one looked like it had air conditioning units. The towers were the tallest buildings in the immediate area, and the French hills off in the distance wouldn't provide a clear shot.

Schiffer shook his head at the lack of available options. "Wolf is right. The only way is for one of us to get up to the penthouse."

The three men stared in different directions, their brains working overtime to figure out a way. There was always a way. Sometimes it came with little planning, others with a good deal of ingenuity. They just had to figure it out.

But the clock was ticking.

"Maybe I could get up there," Alexandra said out of the blue.

The three men each broke their trance and turned their eyes toward Alexandra. They all looked like they couldn't believe what she had just said.

"What?" Schiffer asked.

Alexandra shrugged. "Maybe I could get up there."

Schiffer held out his hand, trying to put an end to any such nonsense. "No, you're not going anywhere near it."

"And why not?" Alexandra shot back.

"Because it's too dangerous," Duke shot back.

The two Israelis glanced at their surroundings, somewhat uncomfortable at being in the middle of the husband-and-wife spat that was taking place. They didn't see anyone nearby and were smart enough to stay out of the squabble.

"I want to help, Duke."

"No." He said it with enough force that he hoped that would be the end of it. He was wrong.

"Well then, you're not going either. I'm not going to let you risk your life if you won't let me help you."

"Alexandra."

They went at it for another minute before Segel finally had to act as referee and separate the two. He walked Schiffer twenty yards down the beach to give him a chance to cool down. Schiffer was shaking his head, muttering something about Alexandra being out of her mind.

Segel positioned himself so that Schiffer was facing away from his wife. He waited until Schiffer looked at him. "You know she might be able to do it, Duke."

Schiffer's eyes widened, having a hard time believing what his friend had said. "You cannot be serious. You want me to use my wife to kill Bonhoff? My wife of less than a week. Are you crazy?"

"She doesn't have to kill him." He raised his hand to stop Duke from responding. He calmly repeated what he said, "She doesn't have to kill him, Duke."

"But who knows what he would do to her. What were you thinking?"

Segel got closer and lowered his voice. "Well, what the hell did you bring her here for?" he growled.

Schiffer didn't have a good answer. He wanted to get Bonhoff more than anything and he guessed he thought Alexandra could come along for the ride. Now he knew he should have sent her on the first plane back to the States. "It's too dangerous, Ariel. I can't ask her to do this. It's not her way of life. She could end up getting killed."

Segel put a hand on Schiffer's shoulder. "I know it's dangerous, Duke, but she doesn't have to kill him. She doesn't have to do anything except get one of us up to the penthouse, and then we can take Bonhoff out."

Schiffer went back to shaking his head, not liking the idea one bit.

After a few seconds of silence, Segel softened his voice. "Can I be totally honest with you? I mean, brutally honest?"

Schiffer looked at him, wondering why he would even ask such a thing. "Of course."

"I don't want you to get ticked off at me or take a swing at me for what I'm about to say."

"What?"

Segel turned Schiffer around. Wolfson and Alexandra were still standing twenty yards away. Alexandra had her hands on her hips, her brown eyes staring daggers at her husband.

"She's a beautiful woman, Duke. You're a lucky man. Given the type of women that I've seen around Bonhoff, she'd fit right in. With the right dress, she'd get up to the penthouse without a problem. Plus, she doesn't have to carry a weapon with her. The security will think she's just one of the other women who are there to party and have a good time."

Schiffer shook his head back and forth. "I can't believe we're even talking about this . . . You want me to use my wife as bait?"

"It's our best shot, Duke." Segel then walked in front of Schiffer and looked him square in the eyes. "And right now . . . it's our only shot."

CHAPTER 38

Monaco

The meeting with Segel and Wolfson ended with Schiffer saying he'd think about using Alexandra. He needed time to clear his mind. The operation was risky enough, but bringing his wife into it added another layer of risk that he still wasn't sure he was ready and willing to take. He wondered if he could ask Segel if the Israelis had any women who could do it—someone fitting the mold of Bonhoff's beauties but trained in dealing with tense situations and knowing how to protect themselves if things got out of hand. Alexandra was highly educated, but not in the ways of a covert operative. One slip up could prove fatal.

In the end, he decided to go ahead with Alexandra taking part. If the planning revealed something he didn't like or she didn't feel comfortable doing, he'd call her part off and send her home.

The plan was to take another day to work out the finer points of the mission. He would have liked a couple months to train her, but they didn't have time to practice and work out the kinks. Getting Alexandra up to the penthouse was probably the easiest part. Security guards would take one look at her body and wave her through, unless they wanted a cheap feel and frisked her. The hard part would be getting Schiffer up there. He had made the decision that the only way he would let Alexandra take part was if he was the one to go up to the penthouse to get Bonhoff. Segel and Wolfson agreed and set about getting the extraction points set up with the rest of the Mossad agents.

The next morning, Segel showed up at the Schiffers' hotel room with a woman named Arianna. She was a Mossad operative, approximately thirty-five years old, and had the look of someone who could walk the streets of Monaco and fit right in. She had two jobs that morning—take Alexandra to the beach to get a nice suntan and then take her shopping for the perfect dress for later on that evening.

While the women were sunning themselves at the beach, Schiffer, Segel, and Wolfson watched as Bonhoff's megayacht set off into the Mediterranean for his daily ride on the water. From the dock, they took a car with Wolfson at the wheel northeast to the Odéon Tower. With the high-rise buildings packed together in such a small space, it was hard for them to get their bearings. And with the narrow roads, even the three-and-four story residences made it difficult to know where they were. The sun helped to give them an idea of the direction to the Mediterranean. But at night, it would be more difficult. Construction was prevalent—cranes, fencing, shipping containers—the powers that be wanting to use every bit of space to entice the world's wealthiest to make their way to Monaco.

They made multiple passes around the two towers, Wolfson gaining a better understanding of the roads curving in and around the area. Still he was anxious.

"I can't believe they drive one-thousand-horsepower race cars through these streets," he said, dodging a man on a moped.

They found a high spot to park to scout out the towers with the sea in the distance. Even from their vantage point, they could look through the glass of the top two floors of Bonhoff's penthouse and the see-through slide that led to the pool. Each floor below had a blue glass façade to the terrace and then more blue glass to the inside. The glass seemed to melt into the blue Mediterranean sky.

"It's tall enough that you could almost parachute off the top floors," Segel said, thinking out loud.

"Yeah, but who knows where I'd end up or where the wind currents would take me. Probably into the high rise next door."

"What about rappelling?" Segel asked. "It would give you an alternate way of getting out of there if you can't use the front door to the penthouse. Those terraces are open."

Schiffer used his hand to shade his eyes from the sun. "It looks like there's a railing above the terrace glass. All I'd have to do is secure the rope and rappel down a few floors. I bet nobody locks their terrace doors because all of them are private. I hop on the terrace, run through the unit, and get to the exit. Like you said, it might be a second option."

Wolfson wasn't ready to agree just yet. "How are you going to get a rope up there? It's going to need to be at least fifty feet long, so you're not going to be able to carry it up there with you unless you act like you're an electrician carrying a spool of wire."

Schiffer nodded. "Yeah, we probably ought to figure out the way to get me up there first."

"We'll work on the rope just in case," Segel said. The phone holstered on his hip started buzzing. He looked at the number and said he might have an answer to Schiffer's need. "Yes?"

Two days earlier, intelligence specialists at Mossad had hacked into the Odéon Tower's computer system and found a treasure trove of information—from the names of residents and their apartment numbers to the names of the staff and their addresses in and around Monaco. The previous evening, a two-man team had followed one of the members of the café crew to his apartment. The man fit the description of what Segel was looking for—white male, late thirties, medium build, clean cut. According to the café staff's work schedule, the man was set to work that evening from 8 p.m. until 4 a.m.

"Hold on."

Segel muted the call and told Schiffer and Wolfson what he had learned. After a quick vote, Segel told the man on the phone to go ahead with the plan.

"Do it by six," Segel said, ending the call. He holstered his phone and then looked at Schiffer. "Okay, if all goes as planned, that should get you in the building."

"It might get me in, but I need to get upstairs."

"We'll work on it. You might have to improvise."

The three men drove around some more, all of them coming to the conclusion that there needed to be two getaway cars that evening. It would be too easy to get boxed in with the narrow streets and switchbacks. They picked out landmarks and gave them names. The hilly nature of Monaco led to the construction of multiple stairways between buildings leading down the hill to the next road. The trick was finding one. They stopped at Larvotto Beach, the sandy area packed with tourists under restaurant umbrellas. Segel said it was a lively spot at night, and it would provide a place for Schiffer to get lost in the crowd if need be.

"Where's the extraction point if we need it?" Schiffer asked. "Once word gets out, the authorities are going to put the whole country on lockdown—borders, too."

Segel pointed toward the sea. "We have special forces on standby. Rigid inflatables. They'll be anywhere up and down the coast wherever we need them to get us out of here."

"You've really thought this through."

Segel nodded. "We want to get Bonhoff as bad as you do."

The three got back in the car and ran through the whole plan again before returning to the hotel in the late afternoon. With Alexandra and Arianna still out shopping, Schiffer studied satellite maps of Monaco, tracing roads away from the Odéon Tower and down toward Larvotto Beach.

He also looked at the website for the Odéon Tower, which promised elegance and luxury to all its occupants. The website even included a timeline of pictures documenting the construction of the tallest building in Monaco, and Schiffer noted both towers had three elevator shafts—two for passengers and one for service staff—and a stairwell. The apartments started on the twentieth floor, and each one offered floor-to-ceiling windows and a private terrace. The Odéon had a café with a bar and seating area, and Schiffer familiarized himself with the menu which was heavy on Italian.

In the early evening, Segel arrived carrying a bag. He unzipped it and pulled out a pen. He showed it to Schiffer. "Fully functional pen," he said, before unscrewing it to reveal the syringe hidden inside. "But this part has enough juice behind it to kill a horse. So make sure Bonhoff is the only one to get it." He pulled out a second one. "I thought Alexandra could put one in her clutch."

Schiffer looked at it, wondering if he should put that burden on Alexandra. She wasn't trained in stabbing someone with a poisoned syringe. Was it worth the risk? What if she screwed up? "I'll think about it."

Segel reached into his bag again and started laying out the electronics—earpieces, microphones, and hidden cameras.

"We'll hide a camera in Alexandra's clutch. That will give us an idea of what's going on inside before you get up there."

The women returned, but they said little to the serious men seated at the table. Neither Alexandra nor Arianna was giddy with what they found, and they didn't show off what Alexandra would be wearing. Both of them knew what was going down that evening. Arianna left to take the dress for "alterations."

Schiffer walked Alexandra to their room and did his best to talk her out of going through with the operation. He thought Segel had a way to get him up to the penthouse. Schiffer said he could take care of it. There was no reason for Alexandra to take the risk.

"No," she said firmly. "I want to do it. This is how I want to serve my country."

He knew she could be stubborn, so he didn't try to dissuade her any more. He went about showing her the equipment they would be using. The earpiece, the microphone.

Segel arrived with her newly purchased clutch and handed it over. Schiffer showed her the camera in the clasp and told her to make sure she kept the clasp facing away from her.

Schiffer unzipped the bag and pulled out the pen. He decided he'd let her take it, but he would stress how dangerous it was. "Only use it as a last resort. If you jab it anywhere on him, depress the plunger and then get the heck away from him in case he takes it out and tries to stab you with it."

Alexandra nodded and watched him screw the pen back together.

He showed her several pictures of Bonhoff on his phone. He told her he would be easy to spot because every woman would be looking at him.

"And I've heard him in person. He's full of himself. He'll be the one doing all the talking." He smiled and added, "He'll be the guy acting like he owns the place."

Segel took a call and, after thirty seconds, said, "Good, bring it to the hotel." He looked at his watch and then Schiffer. "Your uniform is on the way."

"How'd they get it?"

"They went to his apartment and knocked on the door. Once he answered, they shoved a needle in his neck. He'll be asleep until tomorrow afternoon and it's a good bet he won't remember anything that happened in the last twenty-four hours."

Schiffer nodded and looked at Alexandra. His beautiful wife that he was sending into the lion's den that night. He reached out and caressed her cheek. "It's probably time for you to get dressed."

Schiffer stepped across the hall to put on his café staff uniform—a maroon jacket with gold trim and dark trousers with a gold stripe down the legs. It fit perfectly and included a microphone hidden in the left collar. On his phone screen, Segel tested the image from the camera hidden in the second to top button on the front of the black dress shirt. He gave it a thumbs-up.

"Put the jacket on so I can see if it blocks the view."

It didn't, and Schiffer looked at himself in the mirror. The nametag read "Stefan," and Schiffer made the mental note to respond to someone calling for Stefan.

"The guy wears glasses," Segel said. "We got an identical pair with fake lenses so someone from a distance will think it's him. If someone asks, tell them Marco is sick and you're filling in for him."

Schiffer was fine with it. The glasses would distract people from looking too intently at his face. He put the syringe pen in the front pocket of his jacket.

"As soon as we get there," Segel said, "there's going to be a catering cart waiting for you near the Dumpsters. There's a fifty-foot rope hidden underneath the bottom shelf. The rope has a loop on one end so you can secure it over the railing quickly. There's a stopper knot on the opposite end in case you need it. The carabiner will be attached to the underside by a magnet."

Wolfson handed over a lanyard. "Here's your work identification. The computer techs at Mossad made you the newest employee at the café. Use it to clock in. It also will get you access to the elevator up to the forty-fourth floor. You'll have to get buzzed up to go any higher. Hopefully Alexandra will be able to do it." He handed over a cell phone. "This is similar to Marco's phone. The six-digit code is all ones. Use it for a distraction if you need it. Press the button on the side to switch channels between the four of us."

Schiffer put the lanyard around his neck and inserted his earpiece. Segel made a sound check from the bathroom. "I hear you, Ariel. Can you hear me?"

"Yes, loud and clear."

Segel looked Schiffer up and down one more time. "I think you're ready."

"I'll go check on Alexandra."

Schiffer stepped across the hall and entered his room. He closed the door behind him and walked into the bedroom. He almost gasped at what he saw—his wife wearing a caramel-colored mini cocktail dress by Versace that glittered like gold. It also exposed half her tanned thighs and a good portion of her breasts.

"How do I look?"

She walked toward him in her gold stiletto heels that gave her four more inches in height. He could feel his heart pounding in his chest—his beautiful hot wife smiling at him. *What are we doing?* He was about to call it off.

"I'm ready, Duke. I want to do this."

She stepped closer, close enough that he wrapped his arms around her. His hands ran up and down her back.

"You look so beautiful," he said softly, looking into her brown eyes. He blinked and shook his head. "I can't believe I'm letting you do this."

She kissed his lips. "I'm going to be fine, Duke. Like you said, all I have to do is get up to the penthouse and let you up. I'm the one who should be worried about you."

There was a knock at the door. It was time to go to work.

He handed over her earpiece and had her test the microphone in one of the straps that was straining mightily to contain her breasts from falling out.

He went into the bathroom, switched the channel, and then whispered, "Can you hear me?"

She turned her head toward the left strap. "Yes, I can hear you."

He couldn't believe he was doing this. "I love you," he whispered.

"I love you, too."

CHAPTER 39

Monaco

From their hotel on the southwestern end of Monaco, Wolfson drove with Segel in the front passenger seat. Duke and Alexandra held hands in the back. Little was said, Duke not wanting to fill Alexandra's mind with even more information. She didn't appear nervous, but her silence indicated she was focused. He decided to go over the plan one more time.

"The women show up after eight. Just walk in with them. It's okay to be overly flirtatious with the security guards if they take notice. Get up to the sky penthouse and keep your eyes peeled for buttons near the doors to buzz people up."

She nodded like she understood.

But Duke could see concern in her eyes. "You don't have to do this, Alexandra. With my uniform, there's a good chance that I'll make it up to the penthouse without needing your help."

She shook her head. "No, I'm ready. I'll be okay."

"Whisper into your microphone whenever you get a chance. I want to know what's going on, where you are and what you're doing. Ariel's going to be in a car somewhere near the front entrance. Wolf will be driving around on the back side. If you need help, get out of there and use the mic to contact them."

"We're almost there," Wolfson said. He looked at Duke in the rearview mirror. "I'm going to drop you off behind those trees up ahead and then we'll drive Alexandra around to the main entrance."

Duke squeezed Alexandra's hand and looked his beautiful wife over one last time. "Just get me up to the penthouse. That's all you have to do."

"Be careful," she said softly.

Wolfson pulled to a stop, and Schiffer was quickly out the door. He didn't look back, his mind focused on getting inside the service entrance. He didn't rush, walking like he was supposed to be there. The darkness helped, and he stayed in the shadows. Upon approach, he saw two men dressed like him smoking cigarettes near the loading dock. He could hear them speaking in English with some Italian thrown in.

He waited until they flicked their cigarettes to the ground and headed toward the entrance marked *Employees Only*. He noticed they scanned their ID cards to open the door. He checked his surroundings and looked for the Dumpsters. There, just like Segel said, was a four-wheel serving cart that looked like it had been discarded. Schiffer walked over to it, used the folded white cloth to drape over the top shelf, and started pushing it to the back door. With the fifty-foot rope coiled underneath the bottom shelf, it took a little extra effort to push it up the ramp.

He checked his surroundings and then spoke into his left collar.

"I've got the cart and I'm going in. Copy?"

Through his earpiece, he could hear Segel say, "Loud and clear. We're almost to the front entrance."

Schiffer held out his ID card to the reader and the door lock clicked. He pulled it open and rolled the cart inside. The café kitchen was bustling with activity, and Schiffer blended in with hardly a second glance. He used his ID to clock in and then looked for the way out. The chefs were barking out commands, and service staff were checking plates with their customer orders. With the heavy aroma of Italian and Mediterranean food and steam filling the air, Schiffer found a cart with a stainless-steel buffet serving station and hurried to place it on his own.

"You!" someone yelled behind him.

Schiffer froze. He could tell the word was directed at him. He knew where the back exit was in case he needed to make a run for it. He had no weapon on him, other than his pen and his bare hands.

"You!"

Coolly, Schiffer turned toward the voice and pointed a finger at his own chest. He said nothing.

"Yes, you!" the man in the white chef's hat yelled. "Put these trays in there!" he ordered pointing toward the service station. "Get them to the penthouse! Now!"

Schiffer nodded and quickly went to work. He placed the three trays of hot appetizers—fried calamari and scampi with tartar sauce, grilled octopus with roasted artichokes, and grilled squid—into the buffet station and placed lids on top of all three. With a glance out of the corner of his eye, he followed one of his coworkers out of the kitchen.

"Alexandra is out of the car," Segel reported.

Schiffer rolled the cart through the swinging doors, keeping his head down as best he could. The staff members started lining up near the service elevator. Some pushed carts, some held buckets of champagne and ice. All of them were being frisked.

Schiffer muttered an expletive under his breath. He lowered his head and whispered into his collar. "Standby. I'm at the elevator."

He watched the security guard frisk the workers, most of those in front of him being men. The guard was rough, and he didn't appear to be in a good mood. He ran his hands down the arms, the torso, the pants pockets, all the way to lifting the legs of the trousers to look for weapons. The staff members crowded into the elevator and up it went.

The security guard grunted and motioned Schiffer forward.

Schiffer rolled the cart to a stop and presented himself like the guy did before him. The man did the pat-down, roughly running his hands over Schiffer's body. Once completed, the guard eyed him suspiciously, as if he didn't recognize him.

Schiffer knew this could make or break the mission, and he worried the man would grab his walkie-talkie and ask for a café supervisor. He took a chance at speaking.

"I'm new here. I just clocked in and they told me to take this up to the penthouse."

The guard frowned like he hadn't been notified that someone new had been hired. Seeing the lanyard around Schiffer's neck and the ID card tucked in his shirt pocket, the guard yanked it out and looked at the name and the face.

"I was supposed to start work tomorrow afternoon, but my buddy Marco is sick so they called me in early."

The man looked like he was about to tear the lanyard off Schiffer's neck. "You're supposed to have your ID card where we can see it."

"Oh, I'm sorry. I'll be sure to do that." When the man started to go for his walkie-talkie, Schiffer saw movement at the front entrance. "Wow . . . look at those women . . . They're beautiful. I bet you don't mind frisking them."

The guard turned in time to see a dozen scantily clad women walking through the front doors. With their stilettos and glittering dresses, they strutted toward the elevators like they were on a fashion show runway. Alexandra was on the left, talking to a blonde with long legs and big breasts like they were old friends from high school. Smiles abounded and eyes sparkled—they were all about to party with the fourth richest man in the world. The guard suddenly lost interest in the lowly staff member with the trays full of appetizers.

He smirked at Schiffer and put him in his place. "You just worry about the food. Don't look at the women. And don't talk to them. They're not for you. They're for Mr. Bonhoff." He tossed the ID card back to him and then flicked his hand toward the service elevator.

The elevator returned to the ground floor, and Schiffer used his ID card to open the doors. He rolled the cart inside and pushed the button for the forty-fourth floor. Before the doors closed, he looked out in time to see the security guard groping Alexandra as he frisked her.

Once the doors closed, and knowing there would be cameras everywhere, including the elevators, Schiffer lowered his head to his collar and whispered. "I'm in."

"Roger that," Segal said. "Alexandra's on her way up, too. Wolf is dropping me off at the second vehicle. We'll have eyes on the penthouse in a couple of minutes."

* * *

Alexandra was surprised how calm she felt when she walked through the front door of the Odéon Tower. When Wolfson saw a van full of women pull to a stop, he hurried to pull in behind. Segel made a show of opening her door like she was a VIP, and she glided out like a Hollywood starlet. Then, she simply followed the women inside and acted like she belonged.

She latched on to a blonde wearing a shiny silver cocktail dress and made small talk. The woman's name was Gisella, fresh in from Milan, and she seemed very excited to party in Bonhoff's penthouse. It was her first time.

When they approached the elevators, Alexandra caught sight of her husband rolling a cart into the elevator. They briefly made eye contact before a guard started running his hands slowly up and down her legs before squeezing her buttocks. She bit the inside of her lip and waited for the groping to end. The man waved her through and set his sights on fondling Gisella.

The elevator closed with all twelve women squeezed inside. The conversation was lively, and Alexandra thought some of the women might have started the party earlier. Given their height and their measurements, she definitely fit in with the crowd. There was some talk between a handful of them, like they had been there before. One said she hoped to ride the slide naked this time around. They all giggled.

Alexandra glanced at her clutch and moved her hand off the clasp to expose the camera lens. The ride to the forty-eighth floor was quick, and she told herself to be calm. She needed to find a button to buzz up the service elevator from four floors below. That's all she had to do.

The doors opened, and the women spilled out into the elegant foyer full of marble columns and polished floors. Alexandra and Gisella followed those who knew where they were going.

"Oh my," Gisella gushed, taking it all in. Her eyes were wide with wonder at what Bonhoff's money could buy. "It is so very beautiful."

The foyer quickly ended and opened into the night sky that made the penthouse the envy of all in Monaco. The salty air of the Mediterranean hit their noses, and the darkened sky made the lights on the pool deck pop.

"I'm at the pool level," she whispered toward her spaghetti strap.

"Roger that, Alexandra," Segel said calmly. "You're breaking up a little on the audio. The video is working."

Alexandra looked around the pool deck. Her friends were not the first batch of women to have arrived, and she guessed there were thirty in attendance. Some of them were topless, others in dresses like hers that showed off a lot of tanned legs. She saw a handful of men milling about. None of them looked familiar. She wondered who they were—billionaires, politicians, maybe horny royals with money to buy access to that type of party.

"Ladies! Welcome!"

Startled by the man's booming voice, Alexandra spun around and gasped.

Her heart rate had already been sky high, but now it felt like it was about to beat out of her chest. She knew who it was. She was face to face with the fourth richest man in the world—the man who had paid money to have American police officers and service members killed, the man who had a hand in trying to kill her and her husband the night before their wedding.

"Beautiful," Bonhoff said, looking her up and down. He smiled at what he saw. She thought there might have been a hint of recognition when they made eye contact, but the moment ended in an instant. He said something about sharing dessert with Alexandra later. He was quickly distracted by Gisella's breasts and moved on to her. He told her maybe the three of them could have dessert together, and the starstruck Gisella beamed with delight. Bonhoff made his way through the group, eyeing each woman and fondling a few he liked.

"Enjoy yourselves, ladies. We have food, music, dancing, and feel free to strip down and enjoy the pool. You'll never see anything like it in all the world."

Bonhoff made his way to a group of men and bragged loudly about something.

Alexandra stood staring at him, but she shook when she heard Segel's voice in her earpiece. "If you can hear me, Alexandra, you need to find the button for the service elevator."

As best as she could deduce, once the women made it up to the penthouse, they had the freedom to walk around, get in the pool, eat the food, flirt with the guests, and dance the night away. She made a point to fan herself and then asked one woman where the powder room was. The woman pointed back toward the foyer where they had come.

There were four women in the restroom. Some were tidying up their mascara, others checking themselves in the mirror. They said nothing to her, their minds too focused on having a good time or bedding one of the billionaires in attendance. Alexandra fished out her lipstick from her clutch and ran it over her lips. She put it back in and noticed the syringe pen.

She exited the restroom and headed back toward the elevators. Her eyes drifted up to a security camera in the corner before she saw the control panel with the buttons. Not wanting to overtly push the button for fear someone was watching, she pretended to have trouble with her stilettos. She placed her right hand over the button for the service elevator and used her left to adjust her heel. Once fixed, she wobbled slightly to add to the effect. She righted herself and made sure the camera was facing out on her clutch.

Then she walked back to the party in search of the man her husband was going to kill that night.

CHAPTER 40

Monaco

Duke Schiffer was starting to think he was going to have to come up with a Plan B. He had spent the last fifteen minutes in the reception area of the forty-fourth floor waiting for the penthouse elevator to be sent down. There had been no more café staff members making the trip up the elevator. He worried someone would notice him on the security cameras. The last thing he wanted to do was go back downstairs and have to confront the guard again.

"Where is she?" he whispered into his jacket collar.

"She's in the restroom, Duke," Segel said. "Give it another minute." While they waited, Segel added, "The target is there, Duke. You're going to be looking at a crowd of about fifty, mostly women."

Schiffer lowered his head. "Any guards?"

"None that we can see . . . Standby, Duke . . . She's heading back to the party."

A split second later, the main elevator dinged its arrival. Schiffer grinned, knowing his wife had come through when it counted. That was all she had to do. Now all he had to do was complete the mission and get them both out of there.

He rolled the cart into the elevator and hit the button for the forty-eighth floor. When the doors closed, he straightened his jacket and pretended to brush a piece of lint off the shoulder. Then he tapped the pen in his pocket. The elevator dinged, and the doors opened.

Schiffer pushed the cart through the ornate foyer before seeing the dark sky above and breathing in the Mediterranean air at the pool level.

"I'm in," he said.

"Roger, Duke. The video is working." Segel hurried to add, "I'm having trouble hearing Alexandra's audio."

A wince crossed Schiffer's face. He thought it was just him. "Roger that. I can't hear her either."

He saw a woman carrying a tray of drinks. He pointed at his cart and the trays of appetizers. She pointed off into the distance at an area beneath the dance floor above. He nodded and wheeled his cart in that direction. His eyes scanned everyone, looking for Alexandra's gold dress or Bonhoff himself.

There were a dozen women in the pool, twenty others in various groups.

A female's scream rang out behind him. He flinched and turned, just in time to see a naked woman flying off the end of the slide into the water.

In the darkened corner underneath the dance floor, he set the trays of appetizers on the table next to the plates and utensils. Behind the table, one had a panoramic view of the bright lights of Monaco before they ended into the blackness of the Mediterranean Sea. He pushed the cart behind the table and stood between it and the railing. He checked the buffet area. It was empty at the moment, most of those in attendance too busy gawking at each other to be hungry.

He bent down and grabbed the black rope hidden under the bottom shelf. He looped an end over the railing. After a glance behind him, he made sure the entire rope was through the loop and then let it fall over the side of the tower into the dark night. With the knot on the railing snug, he secured a carabiner to his belt. With his second option ready to go, he returned to checking the appetizers.

"The rope's in place on the sea side," he reported to Segel. "Where is she?"

"She's not responding, Duke," Segel said. "I've tried contacting her five times in the last two minutes."

"What about the video?"

Segel's voice was laden with worry. "I don't know. She's got the camera facing the wrong way."

Schiffer could feel the hair standing up on the back of his neck. He cursed and said, "I'm going to find her. Keep trying to contact her."

* * *

Alexandra returned to the pool area and looked for the friendly face of Gisella. She needed someone to talk to so she didn't appear out of place. The earpiece had been crackling in her ear for the better part of the last ten minutes, and she wondered if anyone noticed her tapping her ear like she was having hearing problems.

Twice, she had excused herself from Gisella to whisper "I can't hear you" into the hidden microphone. The only response she got from Segel was static. The nerves were starting to get to her. She looked around the entire pool deck but didn't see Duke, and that worried her even more. She and Gisella went up to the dance floor, and they gyrated to the thumping music with a handful of other ladies for a couple minutes. There was no sign of Duke up there either.

She worried Duke might not have made it up to the penthouse. Maybe he was waiting for her to push the button again. Maybe he had been hauled off by security. Without a phone, she had no way of contacting him.

She had to make a decision. She could abort the mission and leave, hoping she could find Duke or make contact with Ariel or Noah.

Or she could complete the mission herself.

She opened her clutch and reached in for the syringe pen. She unscrewed it but didn't pull it apart. It was ready. All she had to do was pull apart the pen, take the protective cap off the syringe, plunge it into Bonhoff's flesh, and run like hell. That's all it would take.

She tried to control her breathing. *I can do this*, she thought to herself.

After fanning her face, she told Gisella she was going to take a break from the dancing and get some air down near the pool.

As she walked down the stairs to the pool level, she still saw no sign of Duke. She whispered into her microphone, "Can you hear me?"

The response was static.

"Did Duke make it up?"

More static.

She tried one more question, but got nothing but static that wouldn't go away. Any further questions would be useless. She used a fingernail to fish out the worthless earpiece and dropped it in her clutch. Frustrated, she hit the bottom step, putting the clasp of the clutch against her body. She started looking for Bonhoff.

She didn't see him around the pool area or talking with the group of men congregated near the bar. She walked back toward the foyer. Instead of taking the elevators, she turned left and rounded the corner. She tried the door, and it was unlocked. She peered in, her heart beating hard. It was now or never.

Once inside, a spiral staircase led to the floors below, to the unknown. *I can do this*. She took a deep breath and stepped a stiletto down on the first marble step.

The floor below opened into a massive living space with white leather couches facing out toward the floor-to-ceiling windows. The lights were on, but she saw and heard no one. She took the stairs down another floor.

Her heart was pounding, and she wondered what she would say if a security guard found her snooping around. Her breathing was almost out of control. *Calm down*, she whispered. She opened her clutch and found the earpiece. She decided to try it again and inserted it back into her ear.

"Can you hear me?" she whispered.

She heard nothing, but at least it wasn't static. Before closing her clutch, she saw the syringe pen, all she needed to do was find Bonhoff.

She walked down the hall and tried a door. It was locked. Another few steps, trying to keep her stilettos from clicking off the marble floor. She found another door and tried the handle. It clicked, and she pushed the door open.

It was a bedroom with windows looking out toward the Mediterranean. She stepped inside, the lights on but dim. The sliding glass door was open to the terrace, and she could feel the warm breeze coming in from the sea.

She stepped forward, one step at a time, listening for any sounds. There was nothing but the faint thumping of the techno music from two floors above. The thumping of her heart was louder. Another step toward the terrace. She thought she could go out and see if she could make contact with Ariel. Maybe she would be able to hear him out there.

She remembered the camera in her clutch and realized it was pointed the wrong direction. She turned it around so the lens faced out. She stepped around the massive bed, the silky red sheets in disarray like someone left them that way since the morning. A serving tray still had remnants of breakfast, a plate of half-eaten steak and eggs, a knife and fork, and a half mug of coffee.

The breeze was blowing stronger now, the curtains swaying back and forth. She made it to the terrace and licked her dry lips.

"Can you hear me?" she said into the microphone. She thought she heard Segel say "say again," so she said louder, "Can you hear me?"

"Yes, I can hear you."

Alexandra nearly jumped out of her stilettos at the voice coming from behind her. It wasn't Ariel's voice in her ear.

It was Karl Bonhoff standing right behind her.

"Looking for someone?" Bonhoff said, joining her on the terrace.

Alexandra was backed up against the railing. She hurried to respond. "No, Mr. Bonhoff, I was just talking to myself."

Bonhoff eyed her up and down before stepping closer. He reached up and ran a finger down her cheek. "What are you doing in my bedroom?"

She licked her lips and gulped. "I'm so sorry. I didn't know this was your bedroom. I was looking for the restroom."

He got closer, leaving her nowhere to go. "You're very beautiful. What's your name?"

Alexandra didn't like the look in his eyes, like a lion readying to devour his prey. She wondered if he could see her heart thumping through her cleavage. "Wendy."

"Wendy . . . Hmm, that's an interesting name. But you don't look like a Wendy."

"I'm Wendy . . . Wendy Sheridan."

"Where are you from, Wendy?"

"Canada."

Bonhoff chuckled, amused at her answer. "You're not from Canada." His look quickly hardened. He invaded her space and roughly grabbed her right breast with his hand. "You're from America."

With nowhere to move, she could only shake her head. "No, I'm from Canada. You can check my passport."

Bonhoff put his left forearm against her throat and pushed her hard against the rail. He groped her breast roughly. "Do you think I'm stupid?" he hissed.

His eyes ablaze with anger, he said, "I got to be the fourth richest man in the world because I am smarter than everyone else. And after everything that has gone on in your country, you don't think I'm on high alert for Americans looking to screw me over like they did to Senator Lamont and Director Duncan?"

"I don't know what you're talking about. My passport is in my clutch."

Bonhoff looked down at her hand. He yanked the clutch out of her hand and threw it off the terrace. "I knew you looked familiar. And I don't need to look at your passport. I've got something just as good. It's called facial recognition software. I helped finance its creation. I've made billions selling it, and now every face gets scanned when someone walks into this building." He pulled a phone out of his back pocket and showed her the screen.

Her eyes widened at the picture of herself—her official portrait when she was U.S. Ambassador to Egypt. She wanted to scream, but Bonhoff pushed his forearm harder into her neck.

"It's nice to meet you, Alexandra." He looked like he enjoyed seeing the fear in her eyes. "You're going to die tonight. And then I'm going to tell the world that the United States sent an assassin to kill me. I will make your country pay for this." He slapped her across the face and then started to pull up her dress. "But before I do that . . . I'm going to enjoy some dessert first."

CHAPTER 41

Monaco

"Duke!" Segel yelled. "He threw the clutch off the terrace!"

Segel had been giving Duke the play-by-play for the last two minutes, his voice growing with greater intensity every second. Schiffer had hurried out to the foyer and around the elevators only to find the doors locked.

"Duke, you got to get down there!"

"Where is she?"

With no elevator or stairwell access to the penthouse floors below, Schiffer had no other choice. He ran back to the pool level.

"Where is she, Ariel?"

"They're on the seaside terrace, two floors below." He hesitated but added, "Duke, he knows who she is. He knows who she is!"

The sight of the café staff member running across the pool deck caught the attention of those around—women and men wondering what was going on.

"She's in trouble, Duke. You got to get her out of there!"

Schiffer's mind worked in overdrive. He cursed himself for putting Alexandra in this position. He should have sent her home.

"I'm at the rope, Ariel. Where is she in relation to the dance floor?"

"Right underneath, two floors down."

Schiffer secured the rope in the carabiner and went over the edge, the only sound being the screams from above. He rappelled down one floor, and when he pushed off the terrace, he caught sight of Alexandra struggling against the forearm of Bonhoff.

He came in hot and missed Bonhoff's head by two feet before crashing hard into the glass, breaking it into a thousand pieces. The commotion stunned Bonhoff, but only for a moment. He threw Alexandra to the ground and went after Duke, kicking him in the ribs. With his side aching and the rope still through the carabiner, Schiffer struggled to right himself.

"I'm going to enjoy killing you, too," Bonhoff growled. He reared back for a kick to Duke's head, but Duke blocked it, sending Bonhoff off balance and back against the railing.

"Get out of here, Alexandra! Go!"

Duke saw Alexandra rush inside. He was on a knee when Bonhoff grabbed a chair and swung it wildly toward Duke. The chair shattered another window, and Duke lost his balance on the broken pieces of glass. Bonhoff rushed forward and kicked Duke hard in the ribs, forcing Duke back. He was going for another strike when Duke blocked it and threw a right upper cut into Bonhoff's crotch.

Bonhoff howled in pain. "You mother—" Bonhoff then grabbed a piece of broken glass and took a swipe at Duke's biceps, slicing through his jacket.

Duke winced and grabbed the cut in his arms. He deflected a second swipe, but Bonhoff barrel rushed him hard against the railing. Bonhoff had the weight advantage, and the rope hindered Schiffer's movements.

Duke headbutted Bonhoff, and the billionaire cursed with rage. He raised the broken piece of glass in the air looking to jam it into Duke's neck.

Schiffer's eyes widened. Not at the glass, but at the sight of Alexandra coming back through the open doors. "Get out of here!" he yelled at her.

She hurried forward and jammed a steak knife into Bonhoff's side.

Bonhoff spun around and growled like a wounded grizzly bear. When he saw who did it, he roared, "I'm going to kill you, bitch!"

Before he could go after her, Duke put the rope to good use. He grabbed Bonhoff from behind and used his left hand to wrap the rope around the man's neck. Duke tightened the squeeze.

Bonhoff struggled for a breath, but the fight was still on. He backed Duke up hard against the railing, the blow to his back knocking the wind out of him. Sensing the opportunity, Bonhoff used his elbows to swing body blows on him. Then he stomped on Duke's foot and grabbed for his crotch.

Duke tightened the rope even more, but Bonhoff had the height and the weight advantage. He could feel himself being pushed back, farther and farther over the railing. If Bonhoff could get any leverage, he could send Duke over the edge. And Duke knew that Bonhoff would go after Alexandra and kill her.

Duke only had one move left.

He used both arms to grab Bonhoff by the neck and yanked him off his feet. When he did that, there was no turning back.

They both went up and over the railing into the darkness.

"Duke!" Alexandra screamed, running to the edge of the terrace.

Slowly suffocating, Bonhoff was still struggling with the rope around his neck. The stopper knot at the end of the rope had halted Duke's fall ten feet below him, the carabiner straining under the weight. Duke was two feet from the terrace in front of him. He was either going to have to climb up and over Bonhoff or swing the rope toward the terrace.

"Duke!" Alexandra screamed. "Watch out!"

Duke looked up in time to see that Bonhoff had pulled the steak knife out of his side and was using his last breaths to cut the rope above him. If he could hold on above the cut, he'd send Duke plummeting to the earth.

Duke started swinging his legs, trying anything to get his body weight moving. He could see Bonhoff still taking swipes at the rope with the knife. He stopped kicking his legs and let the momentum get him closer to the terrace. He reached out but grabbed nothing but air. He swung back out and then back in. His sweaty left hand reached the railing but slid off.

"Hurry, Duke!"

Bonhoff's red face was focused on the rope. Duke could hear him gurgling for breath, but he made another cut. If nothing else, the man was going to send them both to their deaths.

The rope swung out and back in with greater speed. Schiffer lunged for the railing with both hands when he felt the rope give away above him.

"Duke!"

Duke grabbed the railing with both hands and felt Bonhoff's body whoosh by him. The rope around Bonhoff's neck jerked Duke down before uncoiling and sending the body of the fourth richest man in the world plummeting forty-four stories to the earth.

Duke struggled with his grip on the steel railing. He tried his right hand and then his left. There was no other way. He finally looped an arm around the railing and hauled himself onto the terrace. He heard Alexandra scream.

"Duke!"

He leaned over the railing out of breath and caught the eyes of his wife. "Go, Alexandra! Go!"

The sliding door to the terrace was unlocked, and Duke rushed in. "Eagle, you copy?"

"I copy, Duke."

"We're going to try and get out of here."

"Roger, Duke. Be advised there are police on the way."

Schiffer ran through the empty apartment and into a foyer. "Tell Alexandra to take the stairs!"

Sprinting around the elevators toward the stairwell, he stopped to pull the fire alarm. He entered the stairwell, the emergency siren wailing and lights flashing. He didn't know whether to go down or go up.

He just knew he had to find his wife.

* * *

Alexandra hurried through Bonhoff's bedroom and out into the hallway leading to the elevators.

Segel's voice crackled in her ear. "If you can hear me, Alexandra. Take the stairs down. Take the stairs down."

By the time she reached the stairwell, the fire alarm was blaring so loud in her ears that she couldn't hear Segel. Some of the women from the penthouse party were on their way down, Gisella included. Alexandra could tell the women knew something had happened. There had been a man that used a rope to go over the railing and then they saw a body sprawled out on the pavement below. Some said it was Bonhoff, and panic ensued.

On the thirty-sixth floor landing, Alexandra caught up with Gisella, who looked at her with fear in her eyes and gasped, "You're bleeding!"

Alexandra glanced down to see bloodstains on her dress, but she knew it was someone else's. "It's not me. I'm fine." She grabbed Gisella's hand. "Come on. Don't worry. We're going to make it."

They took one step at a time, the stairwell becoming more crowded as the apartment occupants started pouring through the exit doors to make the long trek down. Alexandra searched for Duke, turning around at each landing to see if he was coming.

She didn't know whether Segel could hear her, but she said "I'm coming down" into her microphone. She wondered what would happen if she was stopped by security.

They were four flights from the ground floor when a man grabbed her from behind. She screamed at the top of her lungs, the man tightening his grip and not letting go. She kicked her legs, but she couldn't break free. She screamed for him to let her go.

"Honey! It's me! It's me!"

With Duke carrying her, Alexandra only felt a handful of steps on the way down. Her heart was pumping fast, but they came to an abrupt halt on the second floor. She heard Duke curse.

"What's wrong?"

"Ariel said the police are headed upstairs." He looked around and then spoke into his microphone. "We're going to take the skywalk over to the other tower. Wolf, we need you at the loading dock."

"Here they come!" Alexandra yelled, seeing the police and security guards coming up the stairwell.

Duke hurried to the cabinet on the wall and yanked it open. He pulled out the fire hose and secured it in between the rungs of the staircase railings. He cranked the wheel to the pipe, and the hose ballooned with water before gushing out the nozzle sending a torrent down the stairs. It would stop the police charge up the stairs for the time being.

He grabbed Alexandra's hand. "Come on!"

They hurried through the skywalk toward the other tower.

"We're heading for the loading dock, Wolf!"

Duke opened the door to the other tower, and they came face to face with the elevator security guard who had groped Alexandra earlier that evening. He was reaching for his handcuffs, a look of smug satisfaction on his face. The look changed in an instant when Alexandra thrust her stiletto into his groin. The man grabbed his aching crotch, and with his face undefended, Duke gave a left hook to his chin. The man went down in a heap.

"Come on!" Duke said, grabbing Alexandra.

They hurried to the other tower, took the stairs to the ground level, and ran through the kitchen. When they barreled through the door to the loading dock, they saw a car idling with Wolfson behind the wheel.

Duke yanked open the back door, pushed Alexandra inside across the back seat, and dove in on top of her. "Go, Wolf!"

Wolfson floored the car out of the loading area and radioed Segel that they were on the move. He took the street south and weaved his way through traffic. Police sirens were growing louder, and blue lights were flashing up ahead.

"Take these things off," Schiffer said, yanking Alexandra's stilettos off and throwing them out the window. "We might be running here pretty quick."

She saw the blood on Duke's arm. "You're bleeding!"

Duke shook it off, focusing on the police cars gaining ground. "It's nothing."

Wolfson yanked the wheel to the left down a side street. Segel kept relaying his location, saying he was parallel to them down the hill.

"We're going to get boxed in if we don't do something," Schiffer said.

Wolfson was thinking the same thing. "We're going to have to ditch! Get ready to run!"

Nearing the switchback, Wolfson slammed on the brakes and brought the car to a halt in a vacant carport. The doors flew open.

"Down the stairs! Down the stairs!" Wolfson yelled. "Eagle, we're coming down to you."

Without her heels, Alexandra kept pace with Duke, and Wolfson pulled up the rear. There were shouts from above, the police on the hunt.

"Stop, Eagle! Stop!" Schiffer yelled as they hit the bottom steps.

Segel slammed on the brakes and brought the car to a halt. Duke pushed Alexandra into the back seat and Wolfson took the front. Segel sped off, heading south. He told Wolfson that Larvotto Beach was out and for him to radio the extraction team to meet them at the Monaco Yacht Club.

The car raced through the streets. The hilly nature of Monaco told them they still needed to get down closer to the water. Segel looked ahead and cursed. They were headed straight for a park. He made a hard left on Avenue de la Madone and then another left on the Avenue des Spelugues. They were getting closer now.

If only the police didn't get in their way.

Segel slowed the car to make the right-hand curve and then down the hill through the Fairmont Hairpin, the tires thumping over the red-and-white Formula One curbs. The air was filled with hot rubber and roaring engines They made it down the hill, and Segel floored it through the tunnel on Louis II Boulevard.

When they emerged from the tunnel, Wolfson yelled into his radio. "Monaco Yacht Club!"

"Tell them to hustle," Segel said. He looked in the rearview mirror at Schiffer. "It's going to be close. Get ready to run!"

The sirens were getting louder, and the blue lights reflecting brighter off the buildings.

"The first pier on the north end," Wolfson radioed. "No, the first one on the north end!" He pointed it out to Segel. "Right there!"

Segel jumped the curb and drove onto the sidewalk. They could see the lights on the yachts in the marina. With the bollards in front of him, Segel slammed on the brakes.

The doors to the car flew open, and they all took off toward the sea.

"Down that pier!" Wolfson yelled.

They were running as fast as they could. Schiffer pointed to his left at the rigid inflatable skimming fast through the water. There were shouts behind them, then gunshots. Nearing the end of the pier, it was either in the Israelis' boat or in the water. There was no turning back.

Duke reached for his wife. "Take my hand!"

Alexandra reached out and took it in hers. After two more steps, they leapt off the pier and into the darkness.

They landed with a thud in the boat, followed by Wolfson and Segel. The engine roared to life, and the boat headed out into the blackness of the sea.

CHAPTER 42

Near Mineral, Virginia

The setting sun had dipped below the trees off to the west, the sky turning a mixture of pink, yellow, and red before darkness would settle on rural Virginia. Duke Schiffer and his lovely bride were watching nature's beauty from the back bench seat of their boat. He had his arm around her, and she leaned close to him. After everything they had been through in the last few weeks, the moments of peaceful solitude on the lake were most welcome.

Duke and Alexandra, along with Segel and Wolfson, had vanished into the Mediterranean night with the help of the Israeli commandos and returned to Italy. After taking off from the airport in Rome, Duke had held Alexandra the whole plane ride home, and he was perfectly content with doing that, and only that, for the rest of their lives. It had taken her two days to stop shaking, but he had been impressed with how she handled herself. With her actions in Monaco and what happened in Egypt, he was wondering if she was a natural at that type of work.

His arm was healing nicely, a large bandage wrapped around his biceps was the only outward sign at the moment. The doctor said he'd make a full recovery, but there would most likely be a gnarly scar to remind him of his late-night visit to the Odéon Tower.

When they were lying awake in bed one evening, she had asked him if he had been scared—scared when he was fighting Bonhoff or when they both went over the railing. He said he would have been lying if he claimed he wasn't scared, but there was a difference between being scared and being paralyzed by fear. The former can focus your mind, while the latter can be lethal.

For the last several days, news out of Monaco had reported the stunning death of the fourth richest man in the world—the billionaire having met his end after being stabbed and strangled before falling to his death from his sky penthouse. Details were sketchy and an investigation was underway, but some tabloids suggested it looked like a mob hit, while others claimed it was a sex act gone horribly wrong. Witnesses were still in the process of being interviewed, but some refused to talk for fear their illicit activities over the years in Bonhoff's penthouse would come to light.

Behind the scenes, the government of Monaco was incensed, fingering the United States and Israel for the "hit job" on Bonhoff, the country's richest resident. The Prime Minister, Felipe Bertrand, was said to have berated President Schumacher over the phone, demanding the U.S. be held to account for conducting operations in the principality and apologize for its illegal actions.

The President calmly replied that there would be no such thing. He then proceeded to rattle off the evidence that had been uncovered indicating the political leaders in Monaco had known about Bonhoff's money laundering and shady dealings with terrorist groups and communist dictators for the better part of the past decade. Some might say Bonhoff was using Monaco as a tax haven to orchestrate his plot to undermine the United States Government, something the President was sure Prime Minister Bertrand did not want to be associated with.

The President then dropped the hammer when he mentioned to Bertrand that there just happened to be an explicit video of the man with a woman, who was definitely not Bertrand's wife, in Bonhoff's mansion in Switzerland. The President noted the woman looked "awfully young" and said it would be a shame if the video somehow found its way into the hands of the media—or, even worse, the local authorities. Bertrand quickly decided he had more pressing problems and dropped the subject.

Duke and Alexandra met privately with President Schumacher on their return. He thanked them for their work and their service to their country, saying it would go a long way to bringing peace to the streets of the United States. Operation Roundup was well underway, and politicians across the country were being outed for taking Bonhoff's dark money. With the Federal Election Commission and the IRS hard at work, the U.S. Government coffers were expected to swell with the millions in fines from the crooked pols.

He did give the couple a hard time for undertaking such a risky operation, saying both of them were too valuable to lose. He offered to let them use Camp David for a week of relaxation whenever they wanted it. For the time being, they were happy being home in Virginia.

As the boat bobbed gently in the water, Duke kissed Alexandra on the forehead. "You want me to sing a love song to you?"

Her body shook when she giggled.

"I bet I'd be better than that gondolier loser that you got the hots for."

She jabbed him in the ribs with her elbow. "Will you stop."

They heard children yelling in the distance, sounding like the kids were having fun in the dwindling hours of the summer evening. Duke and Alexandra had talked about having children and watching them grow up around the lake. Both were looking forward to it.

Duke was about to suggest they head back to the dock when his phone started buzzing. He reached for it and looked at the screen.

"It's the Vice President," he told Alexandra. He hit the button with his thumb. "Hello."

The deep voice of Vice President Stubblefield could be heard through the phone, although Alexandra couldn't hear what the big man was saying.

"We're just enjoying the evening," Duke said to him. "It's been a nice few days of rest and relaxation."

Duke listened for a couple minutes while running his hand down his wife's arm. The Vice President said he was just checking in. He had told Duke how proud he was of him, and he reminded Duke on a couple of occasions that he was America's greatest secret weapon.

It made Duke chuckle. He didn't think of himself that way. He was just glad the operation was over. He was happy with the work that he had done and the mission they had accomplished. America was better off for it. With his beautiful wife by his side, he couldn't think of anything that would make life better.

He ended the call and put the phone on the bench next to him. Then he inhaled the warm Virginia air and the strawberry scent of Alexandra's shampoo.

She turned to look up at him, her eyes asking what the call was about. He took in another breath and exhaled. Then he looked in those brown eyes that he could get lost in forever.

But first things first.

"The Vice President wants to talk to us."

THE END

For Those Who Might Be Interested

Washington National Cathedral's official name is the Cathedral Church of St. Peter and St. Paul.

Formula 1's Monaco Grand Prix first raced through the streets of Monaco in 1929. William Grover-Williams won the inaugural race. Ayrton Senna won the famed race a record six times in his career.

Monaco is divided into four traditional quarters, the most famous being Monte Carlo.

Of the 18 documented couples who have had weddings in the White House, Grover Cleveland was the first President to do so when he married Frances Folsom in 1886.

Rob Shumaker is an attorney living in Illinois. *Justice in the Capital* is his tenth political thriller. He is the author of the Capital Series, which includes *Thunder in the Capital, Showdown in the Capital, Chaos in the Capital, D-Day in the Capital, Manhunt in the Capital, Fallout in the Capital, Phantom in the Capital,* and *Blackout in the Capital.* A standalone thriller, *The Way Out,* was published in 2019.

Did you enjoy *Justice in the Capital*? Readers like you can make a big difference. Reviews are powerful tools to attract more readers so I can continue to write engaging stories that people enjoy. If you enjoyed the book, I would be grateful if you could write an honest review (as short or as long as you like) on your favorite book retailer.

Thank you and happy reading.

Rob Shumaker

To read more about the Capital Series novels, go to

www.USAnovels.com

… ….. ..—

Made in the USA
Middletown, DE
03 July 2022